The Wintermaker

The Dreamcatcher Chronicles

Jason Lee Willis

Lura Publications, LLC.

Mapleton, Minnesota

Lura Publications, LLC
803 Silver Street E
Mapleton, MN 56065

Publisher's Note: This is a work of fiction. Names, characters, places, and incidents are a product of the author's imagination. Locales and public names are sometimes used for atmospheric purposes. Any resemblance to actual people, living or dead, or to businesses, companies, events, institutions, or locales is completely coincidental.

Author's Note: Although set in a fictional Minnesota, this story reflects the terms used in 1962 (Sioux, Chippewa) for the Oceti Sakowin and Anishinaabe peoples.

Book Layout © 2017 BookDesignTemplates.com

The Wintermaker/ Jason Lee Willis. -- 1st ed.
ISBN 979-8-9891198-0-6

Dedicated to Julie,
For helping me chase my dreams.

Special thanks to my "alpha" team of Ron Willis, John Pfeffer, and Christie Jones for early guidance; my editorial team of Raven Eckman and Caryl Bunkowske for creative guidance; and my "spider" team of Sandra Garlow and Alicia Barrott for series guidance.

ACKNOWLEDGEMENTS:
Edward Benton-Benai's *The Mishomis Book: The Voice of the Ojibway*
William Warren's *History of the Ojibwe People*
Aleck Paul's "Origin of Constellation Fisher" as recorded by Frank Speck in 1913
Thomas Hughes' *History of Blue Earth County*, featuring "The Legend of No Soul."
Frederick Baraga's *A Dictionary of the Ojibway Language*
and
Warren Upham's *Minnesota Geographic Names*

Contents

<u>Important People from 1961-62</u>

 Red Dobie—The Face of Death

 Brian "Biff" Forsberg—The Guardian

 Jimmy Nielson—The Warrior

 Christopher Luning—A Leader

 Lily Guerin—The Spider

 Nicole "Nicki" Guerin—A Spiritual Guide

 Migisi—A Spiritual Guide

 Earl "Wally" Crain—A Leader

 Albert Fisher—The Intellectual

 Leonard White Elk—The Poet

For the rest of Hiawatha County, check out the back of the Dream Journal

—Robin Berg

Robin's Photoshop Maps to Help Picture Where Stuff Happens in 1961-62

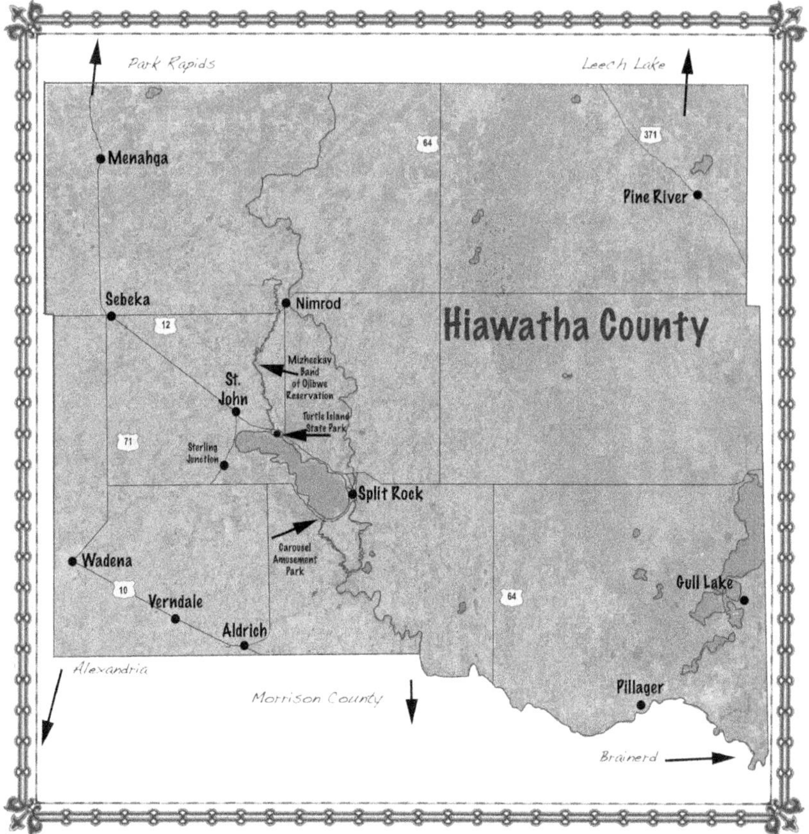

Robin's Photoshop Maps to Help Picture Where
Stuff Happens in 1961-62

Blue Knife River
Crow Wing River
T.I.J.S.
The Nicollet Dam State Park
St. John
Haggard Quarry
Turtle Island
Chippewa Beach
Berg Farm
Split Rock
Carousel Rock Park
Forsbergs
Nielson Farm
Lake Manitou
Old Copper Road
Larson Farm
Guerins
MacPhersons

The Wintermaker

Knob Hill Campground
Wadena County, MN
June 2029

THE DEAD GIRL waited patiently for a bus that wasn't coming. Even in the darkness of her tent, Robin Berg could still see her standing atop the hill. It didn't matter if the ghost was a dream or some hallucination or even real—Robin needed to confront it. She needed answers.

Her hand searched for items of comfort, passing over her pepper spray and flashlight before finding her open backpack. Inside, she found her dream journal and a pen.

Here goes nothing.

As soon as Robin stepped outside the tent, she feared she'd messed up. Reality swallowed up the lucid moment, bringing a dying fire, snoring Rottweilers, and a picnic table covered in half-empty beer bottles. Across the Crow Wing River, slivers of light came from the covered windows and doors of the old camper where her step-father cooked meth with his buddies. Four kayaks on the eastern shore meant Robin was all alone with the dogs on the opposite shore of the river. Robin squeezed her eyes tight and turned to the hill.

Please stay there.

Robin kept her eyes on her bare toes as she walked from the campsite to the stairs that led to the upper level of the campground. The staircase terrified her in either daylight or nighttime since they reminded her of the scene in *The Exorcism* where the demon-possessed Father Karras threw himself in his fight with Captain Howdy. Her hand held the red wooden railing for each of the thirty-nine steps, and even at the top, she refused to look up.

Having walked the stairs dozens of times in the past few weeks, she knew it was another fifteen yards before she reached the parking lot where her father's truck was kept, but instead of using her eyes, she followed her mental image that included Old Copper Road, Bleeding Rock, the Forsberg farm, the MacPherson farm, and the Guerin farm.

The accident must've happened just past the Guerin house, Robin decided, comparing what she knew to the vision of the dead girl that'd woken her a few minutes ago.

Robin sat down on the pine straw. It was a cool night, which is why she dressed in sweatpants and a Brainerd Warriors hoodie. When she opened her eyes, the dead girl stood five feet in front of her.

At least she's not holding a red balloon, Robin mocked her own fears. "What's your name, Sweetie?"

"Danika Knutson." Danika appeared to be a first or second grader, and aside from a lack of a balloon, she looked like the female version of the kid from *It,* dressed in a raincoat, galoshes, and a backpack. She wasn't maimed or rotting—just cold and wet.

She sees me? Do I look real to her, or am I the apparition?

Even the eyes of a dead eight-year-old brought judgment, but Danika didn't say anything cruel. "Do you know when the bus is coming?"

Don't confuse her or she'll slip away. "Honey, I don't even know what year it is."

Danika giggled. "It's 1962."

"What time does the bus usually pick you up?"

"When the bell rings, but…"

"What's wrong?"

"There are no bells because…"

"Why are there no bells today?"

"Because of the storm and the flood."

Damn, this is what they wanted me to learn. Lily and the others tried to explain the disaster that happened, but from the way they told it, it was supposed to happen decades into the future, not a century earlier. *Is this why everything is wrong for me?* Robin found the pen sticking out of the spine of the notebook she held. "I love getting out of school early."

Danika responded, still unaware she'd been dead for more than sixty years. "I'm supposed to take the bus to my grandparents house, but I don't know where my sister went."

Oh, honey, you're dead, trapped in the waters of Lake Manitou. Robin's heart pounded in her chest, not from her ghostly encounter—that was her norm—but because Lily had been right.

Robin looked up to the stars, but the constellation of Orion was nowhere to be seen during the summer. *The Wintermaker—our mortal enemy.* She did find the seven stars of the Big Dipper and the bright North Star reminded her of the grim tales told to her under the willow.

How can I be the one who saves the world?

I'm a freak, a weirdo that everybody hates.

I'm hallucinating about a dead girl that's probably just a figment of my imagination.

For all I know, my step-dad slipped something in my burger and I'm just tripping.

"Did they make an announcement? My teacher didn't say anything to us," Robin pressed.

Danika nodded. "The storm's going to make it flood really bad."

How big of a flood are we talking? "Can I wait here with you?"

Danika nodded.

"I'm just going to work on my homework while we wait," Robin explained why she'd opened up her dream journal. She quickly added a new page for Danika Knutson and jotted down all the incidental details that she'd learned, finishing with a few questions that would guide the remaining minutes of her conversation.

Storm?

Flood?

What's special about 1962?

How did Danika Knutson die?

Robin looked around Knob Hill Campground and overlaid the image of Old Copper Road.

She jotted down a final question: *What the hell happened to Lake Manitou?*

The Roots of Lærad

Mount Hermon, Israel
April 30, 1961

THE SWEET TOBACCO smoke surrounded the Lincoln Continental, where it was parked away from the tour buses and passenger vehicles.

What the hell is taking so long?

Behind the Lincoln, the last of the crowds emerged from the ancient ruins of Caesarea Philippi, found at the base of the towering Mount Hermon. Just past the parking lot, in a crease at the base of the mountain, the legendary Cave of Pan lurked. Its magical spring not only formed the headwaters of Lake Galilee and the Jordan River, but it was rumored to be the Gates of Hell.

Stupid tourists. Red Dobie looked toward the woods in front of the Lincoln. Although nothing prohibited anyone from entering the dense area surrounding the cold stream, he still kept watch while the others scouted out the location.

Charani Bessant, dressed in a white suit, came out of the thicket holding a stack of books to his chest. He looked toward the Cave of Pan, the emptying parking lot, and at the Lincoln before continuing back. *What kind of man wears a white suit?*

The two men were genetic opposites. Red was pale, red haired, squatty, and middle-aged; Bessant was mahogany, black haired, lean, and fresh out of Yale.

"Is everything secure?"

If I had my way, you wouldn't be here, Red thought. "We're at a public 'ancient wonder of the world.' Of course we're not secure." He took a long drag from his cigar. "Everyone's been paid to keep the place shut down for the night. Did you find what you were looking for?"

The Nepalese scholar nodded. "We're going to perform the ritual this evening, for here in Israel, a new day begins at dusk. Are you ready?"

I was born for this.

Red felt the weight of his pistol strapped inside of his jacket and the cool of the metal hilt tucked against his calf. "I'm ready for anything. Lead on." He took a few last puffs from his cigar and tossed the rest onto the parking lot.

A hundred yards from the parking lot, the geography of Israel transformed from rocky mountains to a dense, humid wood. Near the bubbling brook, he saw two figures standing in front of a massive willow tree. The aging gentlemen he knew well: Aleister Sinclair.

"She says there is powerful magic lingering in the air, and that waiting another night would be a mistake," Sinclair confirmed.

The witch has him under her spell. Standing beside the sixty-year-old Sinclair was Aamu Huuhtanen, the twenty-something religious scholar and seductress who'd found her way onto the arm of one of the world's most powerful men.

She didn't even glance at Red, instead focusing her attention on Bessant. "Thank you for finding this place," she said. "I could have searched my whole life and never found it."

Bessant beamed. "The old legends speak of three places upon the earth where the roots connect. Here, in the middle of the world of men; far to the east in the land of giants; and in the roaring kettle known as Lake Manitou, where our new friend Red comes from."

Now the witch, draped in a red shawl, studied him closely. "Come, we must go under the willow."

Red followed, passing through the willow fronds like an emerald curtain. Under the tree, it was already night. The four stood for a moment until Aleister Sinclair sat down. "First, let's find out what happened. Are you ready?"

Aamu's wide eyes were already focused on the branches of the tree, a wry smile on her face.

"Do you mind if I take notes on the ritual?" Charani Bessant asked. "For my studies."

Aamu did not break her gaze. "If my jarl allows it."

Her jarl? Red tried to hide his reaction to her use of the old Norse word for king. Sinclair nodded, and Bessant joined him on the ground.

Without even looking, the young witch reached out her hand for Red's hand. When he stepped back, she frowned. "I will need your help to begin."

It's just a ritual. Red found his switchblade, and with a flick of his thumb, the silver steel glistened in the low light.

She turned to Sinclair. "Let your blood be an introduction, my jarl, the roots will remember."

"Thumb or palm, sir?"

Sinclair presented his thumb. Red steadied the old man's hand, and quickly rolled the blade across the thumb.

In an instant, Aamu's cupped hands collected the drops. She then turned to Red. "The roots will remember your blood as well."

Holding the switchblade in his right, he quickly flicked an open incision onto his left thumb, letting the blood join in Aamu's cupped hand.

With the accumulated blood, she began to wring her hands, as if washing under a sink, creating sleeves of crimson. She collected a low reaching frond and walked it back like a tether as she sat at the base of the tree.

"It is so beautiful," she said, her eyes closed. "I can see … beyond."

"We need you to use your gifts to help us," Sinclair said. "Look past this place. Look to the west."

A slight gasp came from her mouth. "I can see the other root. I can hear the roaring waters. I can hear Nidhogg sleeping in the depths … We're not alone."

"What is it?" Sinclair asked.

"I see others. In the present. The third root has three roots. I see an old man, on a metal folding chair, waiting. I see a woman leaning against a trunk, writing down what she sees in the branches. And there is an old woman of native blood, gathering branches."

I know her, Red thought. *My father told me about her—Lily Guerin.*

Aamu's smile vanished, and she opened her eyes to look at Sinclair. "I can see the present, but there is only one way to travel up the branches or into the roots."

"You're doing this on your own accord," Sinclair began. "No one is pressuring you to do it."

"I'm willing to pay the price," she said, extending her free arm to Red.

"Are you certain?" Red asked aloud.

"When I leave my body, my spirit will spend eternity wandering within Lærad. Where will your spirit dwell?"

I guess she's thought about this. Red took hold of her slender forearm, and with a quick pass from his blade, cut open the vein ascending from her thumb. "May your journey be swift."

Alarm filled her eyes as her mortality pulsed in the air, but she quickly pulled her hand free, placing it on the trunk of the tree, letting the bark catch the blood. "Deep in the roots, I can see the past. High in the branches, I can see the future."

"Look ahead. Tell me what you see in the future," Sinclair instructed.

"I see other faces connecting to Lærad."

"Describe them to us," Sinclair commanded.

"I think I'm seeing the past, present, and future simultaneously. It's all a bit much," she explained. For a moment, her eyes filled with doubt as she glanced down at her blood draining from her body. Then she closed her eyes. "I see someone waiting in the future. A woman."

"Describe her to me," Sinclair said.

Aamu gasped. "It is the goddess Hela. She's real, and she's waiting at the end of the world to bring death to all."

"How do you know it is Hel herself?"

"It's just as she's described in the tales. Half of her face is alive and the other half is the face of death."

"Don't worry." Charani Bessant reached forward to touch the dying witch. "We will prevent this future from coming true. Tell us what you see deep in the roots. Tell us about the past."

With her life fading, Aamu told a familiar tale about a young woman who accidentally woke a sleeping god, who along with Hel would bring about the destruction of the world. The Finnish witch, however, stayed strong until the end, and with the frenzied pen of Bessant writing descriptions, she described generations of faces who also stood under the willow.

"I see him."

For a moment, Red thought the witch had uttered her last words, but she found strength for another breath. "I see him at the beginning as well as the end. They … they … trick him. They … no … no…"

"Who do you see, Aamu?" Sinclair leaned forward.

"The Wintermaker."

"Before the world can end," Sinclair spoke softly, "the triple winter known as Fimbulvetr will arrive."

"The future she sees can be changed," Charani Bessant whispered softly. "We can't let them bring destruction to the world. But there is another way."

"Focus on the past," Sinclair pressed. "Seek a moment of vulnerability. Reach back, let your life save the lives of many."

Aamu grew silent for several moments.

Sinclair is willing to let her die to get his answers, Red observed. *Perhaps he is indeed the descendant of the earliest Vikings.*

The witch took a deep breath. "The roots are weakest around the moment the Wintermaker was woken by the young witch. She unleashed raw magic into the world without any control. If we…" Her breathing grew labored.

"They create a bridge, no, a loop that connects the present to the past. If we attack them in the present, we can use this bridge to the past to destroy what they've done. But it will require more than one death."

"Tell me about this nexus," Sinclair said.

Secrets from the past came forth until her last breath.

When her fingers released the willow frond and her other arm slipped from the bark, Red turned away. *I'm glad I'm not the one who has to sort all of this out. All I need to know is who to kill back at Lake Manitou.*

Snap, Crackle, Pop

Split Rock High School
June 1, 1961

BRIAN "BIFF" FORSBERG plotted his revenge. While his right hand held the pencil, scribbling out words he didn't mean, his left hand found the fourth and final screw under the desk's surface. His thumbnail, toughened by life on a dairy farm, caught the screw head groove, and with the pressure of his index finger, the screw began to turn.

He looked up, first at Mr. Cottingham and then at the clock.

"The sooner you're done with it, the sooner we can both start our summer break, Brian."

Instead of giving a cold glare like he wanted, Biff looked down at his essay, adding more graphite to the lined paper. Below the desk, the screw wobbled and fell into his palm.

His writing pace doubled.

And now to collect the others.

One by one, the other loose screws fell into his palm. He added a period and carefully stood up. "I'm finished."

"Are you?"

Doesn't he think I can write? Asshole.

"Well then, bring it here." Cottingham didn't budge from his throne, and Biff presented himself, a repentant subject.

Outside the window, the buses from the field trip had already unloaded, and children flowed in all directions.

"You're going to be in seventh grade next fall, and the choices you make are no longer those of a foolish boy. Your actions kept you from the field trip today. Do you understand?"

"I'd like to apologize, Mr. Cottingham," Biff began, and then performed the monologue he'd practiced for the past hour. As he spit out insincere words, he set the four screws on the edge of the desk, right behind the stack of math books.

Long after he was out the door, the top of the desk would either fall right off in front of Mr. Cottingham or there would be a sudden clank of screws upon the floor to make him ponder: *Where did those screws come from?*

Either discovery would deliver Biff's message: *Screw you, Mr. Cottingham.*

Biff exited the school doors to find his buddies waiting outside, leaning against the practice field fence. His cousin Jimmy Nielson wore a cheap pirate hat over his blonde hair and an eye patch over one of his blue eyes. Beside him, dark haired Chris Luning held a plastic sword with a fake red jewel in its hilt and had mustard stains down the front of his white t-shirt.

"What's up, losers? How was the circus?"

"It was fun," Chris answered enthusiastically, only to have his smile stolen as Biff snatched the sword from him.

"It was pretty lame," Jimmy said, giving him the right answer.

Biff tossed the plastic sword back to Chris. "Asshole. Because of you, I spent all day in detention with Mr. Cottingham."

Chris looked to his toes in shame.

Jimmy was his cousin by blood, but Chris was his brother through blood. Before kindergarten, he never knew Chris, but during their elementary years, they discovered they lived on opposite banks of the Crow Wing River. Even though they were now official blood brothers with scars to prove it, Chris had told on him. As much as Biff wanted to beat the tar out of him, he knew Chris always—*always*—did the right thing.

Biff shrugged it off. "It was stupid. I honestly thought I was going to throw up for most of the morning. If I hadn't been caught, I probably would have upchucked all over the bus."

"Did you really have to eat all the rice crispy bars meant for the entire first grade class?" Chris asked.

"The bagged lunches were just sitting out on a bench with no note."

Jimmy cleared his throat. "Our bus already left. Do you want a ride? My sister is still cleaning out her locker."

"If the school called home, I'm in no hurry to get back. I'll walk."

Chris offered an alternative. "Hey, my folks are gone for the weekend, so I have to stay with my grandparents. You want to come with me?"

I guess that's his way of apologizing for being a rat. "The grandpa with the car collection?"

"Yeah, Grandpa Albert. The rich one."

Hell yes. Apology accepted. "Sure, I've got time to kill."

"Plus a walk will help you work off those rice crispy bars," Jimmy teased.

"Get bent," Biff snapped. But then he sighed. "We still good for fishing tomorrow?"

"Yeah, the crappies should be in the channel of Turtle Island."

"Can I come?" Chris asked.

Chris was a sweet kid, but he was a coddled city kid. Biff hated it when he came fishing with them. "Thought you were staying with your grandparents for the weekend?" Biff reminded, getting a bit of cruel revenge. He started walking before calling out, "See you tomorrow, Jimmy."

SPLIT ROCK COMMUNITY school was situated on the north side of town. The town was built along the Crow Wing River Valley, which meant everything angled downhill. Along the ridge, however, the newest homes in town were built, and beyond the homes, Albert Fisher's mansion.

A former convent had fallen into financial and physical ruin, and the wealthiest man in the community not only purchased the property but also repurposed the brick into a new home. A brick post gate and wall greeted the boys at the street, and up a long driveway, the brick mansion waited.

Biff didn't give the house much thought, for two buildings past it was the meticulous garage with the classic cars. On a previous tour, the accumulated wealth took his breath away, and his private studies switched from classic mythology to everything Detroit built. The price for visiting the cars was enduring Grandma Eunice's baking.

A shadow caught Biff's eye.

In a blink, a dark figure emerged from under the willow tree. A teenage boy the size of a junior or senior stepped out from the shadows of the tree, took two steps toward the long driveway—and disintegrated into thin air.

Din djävul!

Chris turned when Biff stopped walking. "What's wrong?"

He didn't see it. "Nothing." Biff continued walking, replaying what he'd just seen: a black hat, tattered blue jeans, a long jacket like the old cowboys wore. The teenager even had long hair like a girl.

Biff kept his eyes on his feet, feeling the fool. When he looked up, the willow tree was there; it held no secrets or mysteries. The house, a sprawling brick mansion with windows larger than most walls in Biff's house, also seemed normal.

Then he saw a white image—a teenage girl in a nightgown—climb out of solid brick and down onto the lawn, walking towards the willow.

This time, Biff not only paused but also stepped back. "Did you see that?" His finger pointed toward the willow.

"That's just my Grandpa Albert."

Almost as sudden as the two apparitions appeared, an old man stood holding a folding chair and a book between a part in the willow curtains. Equally startled, he stared right at Biff.

"He likes to relax under the tree in the afternoons. He can be a little strange sometimes, but he's really nice. Let's go say hello."

Strange indeed.

Like most old men, Albert Fisher had his white hair combed to one side and suspenders keeping his thick cotton pants up to his navel. He was using the metal chair as a crutch to help straighten his back.

"Well, what do we have here?"

"Hey, Grandpa," Chris said, wrapping his arms around him for a quick hug.

Mr. Fisher kept his eyes on Biff while reciprocating the hug. "If you're not the spitting image of your grandfather Bjorn, God rest his soul. How is your brother Paul doing?"

"He's stationed in Germany, I guess, but he's not … fighting or anything. He just drives his tank around to remind the Krauts who won the war."

Mr. Fisher chuckled. "Putting on a good show for a defeated enemy. Yes, I understand completely." He turned toward the house. "Let's get you boys some after school snacks. I think Eunice made some rice crispy bars."

The Quarrymen

Old Copper Road
June 5, 1961

BIFF REFUSED TO look at his father as he ate his oatmeal on Monday morning. The kitchen window reflected the darkness of the morning back at him, as if showing a television episode of himself, his father, and his mother. His younger sister Julia still slept, blissfully ignorant of the tense breakfast.

His mother Edna stood at the counter with condemnation in her eyes as his father finished shoveling oatmeal into his mouth, gulped down the rest of his hot coffee, and declared, "Time to go."

Biff followed his father out into the darkness. The dairy cows were strangely silent. The truck doors and engines seemed twice as loud as normal, and with a flick of his father's wrist, the radio was turned off before it played three chords of Hank Williams' "Your Cheatin' Heart."

Biff leaned against the glass of the passenger window. He didn't need any light to know where the truck was going—Old Copper Road.

They drove past the MacPherson farm, the Guerin farm, the Larson farm, past Carousel Amusement Park, through the oaks that reminded Biff of the scene from Wizard of Oz, and up the hill to Jimmy Nielson's farm.

Instead of taking the paved road to the highway, his father stayed on the gravel road. He drove down into the marshy swamp and the old wooden bridge that shook as vehicles passed, and past the Berg farm, the rattiest farm in the county. The shortcut ended in a hundred yards of rutted gravel before it came out at Chippewa Beach Resort, a place where fishermen could buy bait in the morning and a steak in the evening.

From here, the roads continued to improve until Biff could see the western shore of Lake Manitou out his window. The short drive ended at the glow of lampposts—not the city lights of St. John but at the security lights of Haggard Quarry.

Under one of the security lights, a closed gate and shack no bigger than an icehouse stood in the darkness. His father drove right up to the shack and parked.

"Your Uncle Ewan will collect you here. Save some strength for the evening milking."

All this because of a few rice crispy bars.

Biff leaned against the shed waiting for an uncle he barely knew as his father drove off. He'd been told his father's decision had been forming even before Biff had taken a bite of the first bar, but the incident had been the last straw. Soft—that's how his father described him. *He all but called me fat.*

There simply weren't enough chores to do around the farm to serve as punishment, which is when Biff's mother suggested he needed a summer job. Uncle Ewan Haggard was called, and Biff's fate was decided while he was happily eating ice cream at the Fisher Mansion. He was told what was going to happen when he got home that evening.

The set of headlights almost blinded him, but what startled him more was that there was a silent sentry inside of the shack, who opened the gate to let the old truck pass. Biff realized how visible he'd been and gave thought to moving but stayed so that Uncle Ewan would see him upon arrival.

In the next hour, a dozen vehicles arrived, along with the dawn, before his uncle came.

"Hop in," a voice finally called to him, and Biff slid onto the bench seat of the truck.

Uncle Ewan wore an old baseball cap, a short-sleeved plaid shirt, and suspenders to keep his jeans from slipping off his narrow hips and protruding gut.

Apparently guts run in the family.

"So, I'm tasked with making you a quarryman," Uncle Ewan said as the truck drove past the gate.

"I guess."

"Well, I've got a job for you. We'll sweat the sass right out of you. Stay in the truck, I've got a few things to take care of in the office."

Does he think I'm soft too?

The office was a mobile home, parked without any skirting around the bottom but with a simple wooden deck built in front of the middle door. Uncle Ewan stayed inside for almost half an hour. By the time he came out, the sun was shining over Lake Manitou.

Uncle Ewan hopped into the driver's seat and spun gravel as he departed. Instead of returning back to the gate, he turned the other direction, and after a hundred yards of driving along, the truck turned sharply, and Biff almost catapulted out of his seat.

From the highway leading into St. John, he'd always seen the sign for the quarry and pictured a hole in the ground, but his imagination hadn't prepared him for what he saw.

A massive pink hole, large enough to fit the entire MacPherson farm site, appeared out his window. It was deep enough to stack three barns on top of each other.

"Scoot back over, you're going to hit my gear shift."

Biff's heart pounded as he slid back over to the window, where he looked over the rail-less road to the quarry floor below. He'd ridden on all the rides at Carousel Island Amusement Park and had never been so scared. One wrong move by Uncle Ewan meant certain death.

The road crisscrossed the northern wall of the pit four times before finally opening up to the floor, where monsters of mechanism came to life like the dinosaurs of old. Cranes, dump trucks, bulldozers, and machines he'd never seen before lined the quarry floor.

"Your first job: don't get run over," Uncle Ewan commanded. "These machines are big and loud, so you shouldn't have an excuse, but five seconds of daydreaming could cost you your life. Understand?"

Biff nodded.

"Do you see all the machines on the west end? That's where the active blasting is happening. Now, you won't be around when we blast, but afterwards, we end up with debris all over the floor of the quarry. Do you see that building up ahead, along the eastern wall?"

It was another metal building on wheels.

"That's the supply office, and we need to keep the road free of debris so that fuel trucks and the like don't puncture tires on their way in and out of the facility."

They drove straight for the supply building, and the center door opened. A man in a red stocking cap stepped out onto the deck.

"Your second job: sweep the floor. It's that simple. Any big rocks you can pick up by hand and toss in the wheelbarrow. If you can't pick it up by hand, we've got a guy that drives a bucket who can push it out of the way. Any smaller rocks, especially those sharp little suckers that get between the groove in a tire tread, you'll need to scoop up with a shovel. Do you see that pile beside the shop? Dump it there."

They parked, and the man in the red cap stood patiently for Uncle Ewan. "I'm working on a plan to get you home each afternoon. I'm certainly not going to have you walk home like your pa suggested. Did my sister pack you a hearty lunch?"

Biff nodded, grabbing the sack lunch. He opened it, just for confirmation, and saw a rice crispy bar on the top.

You gotta be kidding me.

Uncle Ewan smirked. "Okay then, let's go meet Red Dobie."

CHAPTER FOUR

Rock Around the Clock

Haggard Quarry
June 9, 1961

B Y THE END of the week, the blisters had grown hard, just as promised. Biff studied his hands, knowing that soon he'd be able to shovel without gloves.

The swarm of mechanical ants were all being parked in the southeastern corner, where the steep wall would protect them from the coming blasts. Although the first summer storm was building in South Dakota, the men of Haggard Quarry prepared for their own storm. The men in charge of blasting had been sizing up a new area all afternoon, and once the quarry was emptied, they'd "unleash hell on earth," as Red described it.

A cigar signaled the end of the workday. Red Dobie worked most of the day inside the supply building, and when he stepped out on the wooden deck, Biff knew things would end soon.

Biff set his hard hat and thick leather gloves on the deck, and then flipped his wheelbarrow upside down to cover them.

One week down, eleven more to go.

His punishment had backfired. By Wednesday, Biff loved working at the quarry, and his shoulders already felt stronger. He also got to talk shit with the men, which was even better. Although

Dobie was caustically aloof, like an old cowboy in a western, the men who visited him all day were living comic book heroes.

Biff's favorite hero descended the quarry wall in an oil truck.

Earl "Wally" Crain had forearms like Popeye and was, in fact, also a former sailor, having served during World War II. His oil truck fueled the quarry operation on a daily basis, and because of his regularity, he became the obvious way for Biff to avoid walking home each day. The brash veteran drove his truck as if it were a motorcycle, with sudden stops and starts and unnecessary growls from the big engine.

Biff had known him already as his Boy Scouts leader and the husband of Mrs. Crain, the high school English teacher, but he seemed like a different person the first time he appeared in Haggard Quarry.

As soon as the truck parked, Biff walked to the rear to offer a hand with the fueling hose. He got a nod from Wally, who silently went about his job. Even when he finished filling the big fuel drums, Wally remained quiet as he had Dobie sign the paperwork.

"All right kid, let's go."

Biff climbed up into the passenger seat and left the quarry behind.

"So, how was your day?" Wally asked, handing him a stick of gum.

"Same as yesterday, I suppose. Are you going out fishing tomorrow?"

"Bright and early. I've got to spend a few hours in the blacksmith shop before I can call it a week. What about you? Going fishing?"

"Yeah, we're going fishing for crappies in the shallows of Turtle Island."

"Thinking they're moving into their spawning beds? Who are you going with?"

"Chris Luning and Jimmy Nielson." Biff already missed his friends. Sixth grade felt a lifetime ago.

"Marlin Luning is the foreman at the lumber mill, and Jimmy is Ed Nielson's boy."

"Do you know everybody?"

Wally laughed. "If you stay in Hiawatha County, one day you'll be the same way. I've spent all but four of my thirty-four years here, so yeah, I know folks."

The truck turned north, toward St. John, so that Wally could take the highway east to Split Rock. In the west, Biff saw the thunderheads building on the horizon.

Hope it comes sooner than later. I only get one day a week for myself.

Unlike the winding gravel roads on the south side of the lake, the north side of the lake was a high bluff that allowed vehicles to travel between the two towns in just a few minutes. Biff's favorite part was the Blue Knife River valley, where the view from the passenger seat overlooked the concrete railing to the river and delta beyond.

"Do you ever fish the Blue Knife?" Biff asked.

"Sure, it's chock full of walleyes, but with so many rocks, you're more likely to get snagged than get a bite. Above the dam, by the reservation, the fishing is a lot better."

Biking all the way to the Blue Knife was too ambitious, but in a few years, when he got a car or truck, Biff planned to make the trip.

"Your grandfather Bjorn took me fishing just north of the Jesuit school once. It was tribal land, but he was a 'friend of the Chippewa,' so to speak. We caught a bunch of catfish that day."

His parents didn't talk much about his grandfather Bjorn. "What was my grandpa like? I don't really remember him."

"I suppose not, you must've been a baby and still living in St. John when he had his heart attack. I really looked up to him. He was a mentor to me, especially after the war. He was a quiet fellow, but he read all the time. It always surprised me the tidbits of information that would come out of his mouth." Wally adjusted his rear-view mirror. "It's nice that your pa took over the dairy farm after his passing. You have any thoughts about being a dairy farmer, too?"

"Me? I can't seem to do anything the right way. I was thinking about being a heavy equipment operator or joining the army and driving a tank like Paul."

"Is he still stationed in Germany?"

"Yeah, but he wrote that they might be redeployed somewhere in the fall."

"This Vietnam I've been hearing about?"

Biff shrugged. "I think so."

"Your brother was the first Eagle Scout that Pack 48 ever had. If ever there's someone destined to be a leader of men, it's your brother."

Paul was ten years older than Biff, meaning Paul was closer to Wally in age. *Wally knows my family better than I do.*

"Big shoes to fill, huh? I feel the same way trying to fill the shoes of Bjorn Forsberg."

"My grandpa was in a war?"

"Oh, well, not World War I, if that's what you're thinking. A different kind of war." Wally fiddled with the seam in the steering wheel. "Anyway, when the Japs bombed Pearl Harbor, I enlisted even though I was only a sophomore in high school. I forged the documents, went through basic training, and before anyone found out, I was halfway across the Pacific on the U.S.S. South Dakota. Battleship X, they it called back home."

"Why'd they call it that?"

"The Big Wigs kept the identity of the ship hidden in the press in order to keep Japan in the dark. We saw a ton of action, and one day, when you're a bit older, I'll tell you a few stories."

Wally might be the coolest cat in Hiawatha County. "Did you get your tattoos while in the navy?"

"Truth be told, I got these after the war was over. I ran wild for the first year or two. It took a while for me to readjust to life in Hiawatha County."

The oil truck came into Split Rock from the north, passing over the big bridge where the creek met the Crow Wing River, down busy Market Street, and onto Old Copper Road. The town of Split Rock would not have been able to fill a battleship, and its limited industrialization was a creamery and lumber mill, both of which needed a regular supply of fuel.

At the Fisher Lumber Mill, Biff lent a hand once the truck backed up to the fuel tanks. "Are the rumors about the family true?"

Wally recoiled. "What rumors?"

"Chris said he's not going to date girls until after college because…you know, he's worried if he sneezes on a girl she's get knocked up."

Wally looked around and whispered, "The rumors are true. Marlin wasn't much older than you when he took a fancy to Albert Fisher's only child, so when she got pregnant—underage and out of wedlock—you can imagine the scandal it created. Similar thing happened to Chris's brother with that girl from Georgia. I'm telling this to you so you don't put your foot in your mouth when you're around that family. The town needs those two families."

The topic quickly changed as they got out of the truck to fill the fuel oil tank in the rear of the creamery.

"They say the ghost of the Van Slyke boy haunts this place," Wally offered, raising an eyebrow as they held the fuel line in place. "He died in an explosion, and during big storms or rainy days, they say he wanders these woods looking for his brother."

Biff turned away, looking up the hill toward his farmstead and the growing clouds in the western sky. "Baloney. There's no such thing as ghosts. You're just trying to scare me."

"You've never seen a ghost?"

Is that what I saw a few days ago with Chris? A ghost? "No, have you?"

Wally hesitated, but Biff suspected it was all for play. "Naw, but my father swore he'd seen ghosts and more. If the storm wakes you up tonight, keep your eyes on the woods and tell me if you see anything."

Biff shook his head. "Sure, Wally, sure."

The long workweek finally ended when the oil truck pulled into the lot of the Forsberg farm, where his sister Julia bounced out the front door to greet him. His father, wiping grease from his forearms, stood at the garage. He gave a nod of acknowledgement to Wally before turning away.

"Thanks again, Wally, I'll see you on Monday."

"Hope you find the crappies."

"Yeah, me too."

INSTEAD OF COUNTING sheep that night, Biff imagined reeling in crappie after crappie. It wasn't the storm that woke him from his dream—it was Julia.

The flicker of lightning illuminated his bedroom. With a blanket wrapped around her, she looked like a cartoon ghost. Biff brushed her hand away from his shoulder. "What do you want?"

"I'm scared."

"Go bother Mom and Dad."

Julia shook her head. "They won't believe me."

Again? "Believe you about what?"

She hesitated. "I had another dream just now."

"About Two-Face?" Biff asked in reference to another nightmare during another storm.

Julia nodded. "When I woke up, I could still hear her."

Two Face—the nightmare about the girl who was half alive and half dead.

"It's just the storm," Biff said, glancing at the open window. The wind, rain, and lightning still raged in the darkness. Biff had two choices, and he damn sure wasn't about to stand at the window like a fool looking for ghosts in the woods. So he patted the bed and slid over to make room for his sister.

He put an arm over her little body and felt her shaking slowly begin to cease. He watched the window for a few more minutes before closing his eyes and tried to imagine slip bobbers and knots instead of things that go bump in the night.

Bait for Predators

Old Copper Road
June 10, 1961

JIMMY NIELSON, FILLED with dread, stood at his bedroom window. A thick blanket of fog had been left behind by the big storm, hiding Lake Manitou from sight. Even the barn was almost swallowed by the heavy mist, with the light from the big electrical pole diffused by the moisture in the air.

They won't come now. Not if it's this foggy.

Jimmy looked at his clock. The sun wouldn't rise until 5:30, and even then, it'd take hours to burn off such a heavy fog bank.

Something moved in the darkness, and Jimmy's heart stopped for just a moment until he realized it was his father going to do chores.

He grabbed a fresh t-shirt and slipped into the same jeans he wore yesterday and his leather work boots. He didn't bother tying the laces, and as he left his room, he made no effort to soften his step as he passed by his older sisters' bedrooms.

In the kitchen, his mother was preparing breakfast. To him, she was an old lady, at least in her forties, but when she didn't keep her hair in a bun, she looked years younger. The daughter of Bjorn Forsberg and Emily MacPherson, his mother Bonnie had strawberry blonde hair, now lightened by age. Finally turning her attention away from the stove and to the table, she asked, "Why are you up so early?"

"I'm meeting Biff and Chris to go fishing."

"Do you want me to pack a lunch?"

"Could you?" Jimmy looked out the kitchen window at the wall of fog. *They won't come until the fog lifts, and that might be noon.*

While Jimmy ate his bacon and eggs, his mother quickly switched from breakfast preparation to the construction of sandwiches, including an extra set for Chris and his cousin Biff. With the lunches bagged, Jimmy shoveled in the last bit of food, stood, and kissed his mother on the cheek. "I'm going to see if Pa needs help with chores."

"Don't get lost in that fog," she teased as he walked out the door.

Is she serious?

Unlike his cousin's dairy farm, the Nielson farm had a little bit of everything, from chickens, sheep, pigs, cattle, and a few horses in a barn on their 160 acres. He found his father leaning against a wooden pen with a solitary calf inside the skirt of the barn. "I think this one might have pink eye. We'll keep an eye on him for a couple days. You got plans?"

"I'm going fishing with the boys, remember?"

"Ah, crappies in the shallows. You're going down to Turtle Island?"

Jimmy nodded.

Ed Nielson, the grandson of settlers Martin Nielson and Dolly Larson, had short blonde hair that he covered with a blue and white DeKalb Seeds cap. He wore denim overalls over a flannel shirt and all-season, all-terrain rubber boots that made his stride sound like a giant instead of the small-framed man he was. Despite his size, Jimmy's father was a giant to all the local farmers, who held him in high esteem.

Jimmy also held him in high esteem and almost matched his father in size already.

"Then the price to go fishing is that your friends help haul the rowboat down to the shore for the summer."

His father knew all the rock formations hidden by the lake and could drop the anchor right on top of walleyes. "I just hope they show up."

"At least it's not windy. The fish won't know it's foggy. I'm sure you'll do fine."

JIMMY STOOD ON the hill overlooking Lake Manitou. Even though the fog had not lifted, he knew where he stood from the rocks collected in the corners of each field. Unlike the other farms in Hiawatha County, the Nielson farm bordered almost a mile of lakeshore, giving it a beautiful view but terrible land for crops. The land closest to the lake was the worst, fit for only grazing.

Jimmy's feet followed the sloping hill, but he made sure not to stray too far west, where Jiibay Hollow lurked. The swampy land between the Nielson and Berg farms was overgrown with brush, and after reading Hawthorne's *The Legend of Sleepy Hollow,* terrible dreams of headless ghosts haunted his nightmares. Entering Jiibay Hollow in the fog terrified him, so he purposely walked a longer route just to avoid an imagined fate.

The rising sun made the fog even denser, with only a few yards of visible ground at any time. Nevertheless, Jimmy found the rocky shore of Lake Manitou and the isthmus pointing toward the unseen Turtle Island.

Years earlier, his great-granddad Martin had cleared the boulders away from the shore near the neck, leaving twenty yards of beach. There, Jimmy spotted the posts and chains for the bait traps. He set down his fishing pole, tackle box, and bucket of snacks but proceeded no further.

Entering Lake Manitou alone will get you killed: his great-granddad had told him that, and he'd never forgotten the sinister warning.

So, he waited.

His eyes were drawn to an oddity near the shoreline. At first, he thought it might be just a fragment of a broken muskrat nest, but the intricacy of the twisted twigs drew him closer. A few feet from the object, Jimmy stopped, straightened his back, and then looked all around.

It was a tiny man.

Not a real man, of course, but something fashioned to look like a man. The legs, arms, and head were made of wild sage, bent and twisted and tied together. He'd heard plenty of stories about the lake being haunted, and seeing the relic from the past brought goose bumps to his forearms.

After a thirty-minute wait, the sound of bicycles broke the silence, followed by the sound of bickering. Jimmy stood and whistled.

The bicycles squeaked to a halt.

"Down here, guys." Jimmy began gathering bait from the minnow traps, and by the time Biff and Chris dropped their bikes, he was ready for fishing. "How's life at the quarry?"

As Biff complained, they walked the rest of the way up to the narrows. Even though there was no sign of the sun yet, the fog bank had grown whiter, brighter. Across the channel, the green hump of Turtle Island appeared.

"Hey, Jimmy, can you check my knot?" Chris asked.

With a tug, the line slipped free. "How many times have I shown this to you?" Jimmy chastised as he began retying the knot. Chris was good with the books, but anything out of the classroom took him three times as long to learn.

With the crappies sitting on spawning beds, an accurate cast meant a certain bite, and by the time the fog evaporated, they'd eaten the food and replaced it with fresh fish.

At this rate, they won't even stay until lunch, Jimmy realized. He just wanted company, so he offered a suggestion. "Hey, you know what we should do this afternoon? We should work on the hunting cabin out on Cedar Point."

Biff released a puff of steam. "And spend all day hauling lumber through the woods? I've got better things to do."

"Oh, I forgot, you're a working man now."

"If anything, we should be working on my deer stand."

"Deer don't ever go up the hill to Bleeding Rock; it's haunted!" Jimmy shot back.

It was worth a shot, Jimmy thought when Biff didn't respond. The fishing suddenly went cold, leaving their unfinished conversation lingering.

Chris broke the silence. "Do you guys believe in, you know, ghosts and such?"

Jimmy glanced west to Jiibay Hollow. *Hell yes.*

While his father insisted ravens could mimic human voices, he'd heard too many strange things coming from the wooded ravine. Cedar Point, on the far eastern side of his property, was covered with tall pines and a golden carpet of pine needles; Jiibay Hollow was filled with shadows and tangled branches.

"I think it's all bullshit," Biff weighed in. "I think the adults are just trying to scare us to keep us under their thumbs. Do you see any of the high school kids afraid of ghosts? Don't be a sucker, Chris."

Chris deflated a bit.

"Have you seen ghosts, Chris?" Jimmy asked.

"Probably not. Most likely it's just my mind imagining things in the fog, right? That's probably when people first invented the idea of a ghost. During a foggy morning like this."

Biff chuckled. "Is that why you raced through the woods on Old Copper Road?"

Chris ignored him and turned to Jimmy. "There's got to be a reason the Indians named this place Lake Manitou … Do you believe in the Manitou?"

"My granddad Martin used to tell me stories of the Horned Serpent that lived in the depths of Lake Manitou, but it sounded a lot like the story of the Loch Ness Monster."

"My grandpa Bjorn used to tell me stories about the Tak-Pei, the little monsters who live in holes along the lake shore, but my dad says he just made it all up to frighten me. If there was a monster living under Lake Manitou, then how can Haggard Quarry be deeper than Lake Manitou, huh?"

"My dad told me all the stories were just exaggerations," Chris continued, "but I still have bad dreams about it, especially when it storms. Do you guys ever have bad dreams like that?"

Jimmy looked down, wishing the conversation would end. "Did I tell you that I got a new Playboy with Stella Stevens in it?"

Biff didn't respond and instead stepped over and thumped Chris with a punch to his shoulder.

"Ouch! What was that for?"

"Even if it was real, a spirit can't muster that much force. Without arms or legs, what do you have to worry about?"

Jimmy rolled his eyes and gestured toward Cedar Point.

Biff took the hint. "We should go clean these fish, and then we can help with the hunting shack for a while. Do you still have the issue with Marilyn Monroe?"

"Yeah," Jimmy answered, sensing another kind of fish on the line.

"I think we've caught enough crappies. We should go hang out at your cabin."

"Good idea." *Once again, the bait works.*

A Map of Hiawatha County

Old Copper Road
June 10, 1961

CHRIS LUNING KNEW nothing bad would happen to him with Biff at his side, so he ignored the ghosts lingering in the trees and focused on pedaling. With his fishing pole in one hand, and a bag full of iced crappie filets in the other, control of the bike handlebars came down to a few pressure points with his knuckles, making steering in the gravel precarious.

Biff, by comparison, could let go of his handlebars entirely, finding a mystical source of balance to guide him as they pedaled back home.

Although it was still afternoon, the oak forest surrounding Old Copper Road hid the sky, holding onto the last fragments of the storm. Mud puddles and traces of fog allowed the ghouls to linger in the deeper shadows behind the gnarled oak trunks.

Why doesn't Biff see them?

Or does he just ignore them?

Chris wished Jimmy was with them since he was open-minded enough to acknowledge such things. Even though he felt safe with

Biff, he tried to focus on guiding his bike tire along the most compacted lane.

For safe measure, he recited the Lord's prayer.

Two miles from the Nielson farm, the limbs of the oaks nearly reached down to the road, and even bold Biff stopped talking about sports.

Finally, a billboard, stop sign, and intersection signaled the end of the harrowing journey. Carousel Park was ghoul-proof, Chris reckoned. *Modern places can't be haunted.*

"Did you go to the grand opening?" Chris asked once they came to an unnecessary stop at the eastbound stop sign.

"Carousel Park is for babies," Biff said.

So, no. "Chuck, Helen, and Karson visited over Memorial Day; otherwise, I might have gone. If you want, I could get my mom or dad to bring us tonight."

Biff took a quick breath as if excited but then exhaled in defeat. "Naw, now that I'm working, I don't have time to play all the time." Biff pushed off and glided across the smooth asphalt.

He's still mad at me for telling on him.

Chris followed, and as he did, he saw a slow-moving car approaching Old Copper Road from the south. Instead of continuing on to Carousel Park, it paused at the gravel road for a few moments—and then followed them.

Biff heard it and steered from the middle of the road to the edge. When Chris followed, he almost lost control of his bike. Gravel roads were wide enough for two vehicles to pass, but the main tracks were right down the middle, leaving a narrow path along the edge before turning to loose gravel.

The car approached, and Chris felt the hairs on his neck stand on end. *This is just like an abduction scene in a movie.*

Biff shifted his bag of filets to his pole hand and waved the car past them.

A shiny, brand new red Thunderbird crept past, and seeing the beautiful car, Chris understood why the owner didn't want rocks and dust ruining the finish. It was the kind of car seen in parades, not on Old Copper Road.

Where in the world is it heading?

"Sweet car," Biff said as the sound of the car faded. "That was a brand-new Ford. It still had the dealer plates."

Red, circular brake lights lit up the chrome tail like the eyes of a monster up ahead.

Modern yet still wicked.

Chris looked around for witnesses, but not even the ghouls in the trees were there. The boys were alone.

Biff stomped on his pedal to bring his bike to a skidding halt ten yards from the rear of the car.

A man's arm appeared out the driver window, waving them closer.

Chris followed Biff's lead, who took his feet off the pedals to walk the bike closer. *We could toss the bikes and run.*

"You lost, mister?" Biff asked as he neared the window. Chris could see a second person in the center of the backseat.

Lord, deliver us from evil.

"Is this Old Copper Road?" the driver asked.

"It sure is. If you're looking for Carousel Park, you just missed it back there at the corner."

"No, we're not looking for Carousel Park. We're looking for Dutch Boy Creamery. Are we close?"

A British accent and a fancy car? Who are these guys?

"It's straight down this road. You can't miss it."

"You see, that's the problem. We have missed it half a dozen times, it seems. We tried to find it from Split Rock, and then got ourselves a bit lost out here. Could you show me on this map of Hiawatha County?"

The paper map came into view, but Biff didn't take so much as a step. "Honest, mister, you can't miss it now. It'll be on your left before you get to the Doc Jenkins Bridge. It's straight ahead."

The driver wore a tweed jacket with felt patches on the elbow, and even though the map stayed at the open window, he turned to his passenger to exchange a few words that Chris couldn't hear.

Biff turned and rolled his eyes. The expression meant one thing—idiots.

Chris felt himself calm a bit and walked up to where Biff stood. As he did, he caught a glimpse of the passenger.

A real life Indian!

Chris knew the difference between the local Ojibwe and the passenger. Indeed, the man in the back seat was from the subcontinent of India, or so Chris guessed, dressed in white slacks and a vest over his black dress shirt.

"Do you boys live around here?" the driver asked.

Biff stiffened while Chris nodded.

"Good. Truth be told, we're not really looking for the Dutch Boy Creamery, which has proven to be an elusive landmark. We're looking for a private residence. The directions we have describe it from the perspective of an eastward approach: a bridge, a creamery, a dairy farm at the curve of the road, and a purple house with a big red barn. The third farm on the right, our directions say."

He's just lost, and as a scout, I have a duty to other people. "The Guerin farm?" Chris asked aloud, figuring the directions were now flipped.

"Yes. We're looking for the Guerin farm. Could you show us the way, if it's not too much trouble?"

"It's no trouble at all. It's right over there," Chris said. "Come on, we'll show you."

Biff didn't look pleased.

A cheery smile and a helping hand make life easier for others. Chris remembered the Boy Scout Code and hopped onto his pedals. After an awkward pause where Biff refused to move, he took the lead. A few moments later, Biff flew past him with the red Thunderbird following behind.

His legs jelly, Chris struggled to keep up.

I must keep myself physically strong. Both Jimmy and Biff were farm boys, which made them naturally stronger than Chris, who could only eat the right foods. Biking was his best chance for getting stronger.

The gravel road was fairly narrow, with steep shoulders that led into marsh grass. Hidden under the shadow of the tree was a simple mailbox, where Chris stopped beside Biff and pointed.

The driveway sloped down and away from Old Copper Road, which is why the visitors had probably missed it.

The passenger rolled down his window. "Thank you kindly for the escort. When I tell the others about the hospitality of the folks in Hiawatha County, who shall I say provided me with aid?"

I've done my good deed today. "Oh, um, I'm Chris Luning. And this is my friend Biff."

Biff didn't move a muscle except to ask, "Are you an Indian?"

Reverence, Biff. Show cheer and reverence.

The man extended an arm. "Charani Bessant, and no, I'm not from India. I'm Nepalese, if you must know." The pleasant smile vanished for a moment and then returned. "Thank you, boys. Have a pleasant day."

"You, too, mister," Chris called out.

The red Thunderbird, leaving them behind, turned down the narrow driveway.

"What'd ya do that for?" Biff snarled.

"What? It was the courteous thing to do."

"Guerins are our neighbors; you have no idea who those people were."

Chris didn't linger for a scolding—he'd done the right thing by helping.

Old Bones

Old Copper Road
June 10, 1961

DESPITE ITS BLUSTER, the storm only left behind a thick blanket of fog. Lily Guerin sat down at the end of her dock and wept. Tied to the wooden post, the empty dreamcatcher remained aloof, oblivious to her pain.

Why won't you answer me?

She wiped her tears and looked up. Even in the fog, she could see the channel cut through the field of wild rice. Just beneath her dangling, bare feet, the water was shallow, but past the channel, the cold waters of Lake Manitou held the souls of those she loved, those who refused to speak with her.

I thought for certain …

Her nightmare had been familiar: First, she heard the screams of children. Then she spotted the bodies flailing in the water. They were children, like always, with familiar faces. Piercing the cold water, the horns of the water serpent—the Manitou, the dreaded Wintermaker—moved toward the children like an apex predator. Lily knew she couldn't save all of them, but if she saved the right one …

Now at seventy-eight, Lily's dream ended differently than it had when she was young. Instead of her childhood heroes—her brother Migisi and the gallant Jean Guerin—a pack of white teenagers answered the call for help, pushing her aside to slide down the icy slope and into the mouth of danger.

I can't change the past. I must live with the choices I made.

Lily glanced at the silent dreamcatcher again.

"Bah," she said, clutching the opposite post to help climb back to her feet. She straightened her back, hands on her hips, as she fearlessly looked out at the lake that she'd tamed.

If I feel like this at seventy-eight, how will I endure life at 100?

Routine.

Decades earlier, Lily adopted the habits of a marathon runner, employing physical, spiritual, and mental exercise all centered around pace. Her morning walk, for example, took her from the front porch of her old house, down to the dock, and over to the barn where she greeted all of the animals.

After greeting the animals, she followed the path that led to the oaks. Once, she'd been afraid of the ghosts that haunted Old Copper Trail, mournful mothers seeking their children between Turtle Island and Bleeding Rock, but those mothers had only lost a single child—Lily had enough grief to out-haunt any of them.

She walked the path until she came to Kanaranzi Creek, where the owners of Carousel Park built a decorative concrete bridge that identified the route for gondola rides. Following the narrow outlet to the culvert, Lily turned before crossing onto Carousel Park property.

Two boys on bicycles raced down the road, heading west, holding fishing poles.

Generations have grown up around this lake without fear.

The thought did not bring much comfort though.

She climbed the bank from the ditch to the gravel road and collected the newspapers. In addition to the *North Star News*, the deliveryman from St. John dropped off nearly a dozen other papers that filled the gray, domed mailbox. With the news stacked like firewood in her arms, Lily followed her driveway back down the hill, through the remaining farm field, and to her son's house.

Unlike the simple four-room box she inhabited, the house belonging to Louis, once a five-bedroom beacon of optimism, had fallen into disrepair the deeper into the whiskey bottle her son hid. Shutters held on by single nails, gutters drooped and sagged, clutter gathered around the cracked foundation, and the stairs acted as a barrier she refused to cross.

Between the two houses, her small gardens were framed by spring flowers that waited for the vegetables to appear. A little picket fence wrapped around the small wooden house that was older than any other building on the property. On the outside wall, a rock chimney rose along the side wall to the high, pitched roof. Windows adorned both sides of the central doorway, which had a flimsy screen door.

Unlike the large house, which had red asphalt shingles, the small house had dark wooden shingles, with clumps of moss growing in creases and crevices. By the time she reached her front door, the fog was beginning to lift.

On her way to the tea kettle, Lily passed by the framed pictures of her family. The oldest was a 1908 portrait taken at the Minnesota State Fair, where she sat with Louis upon her lap and Jean beside her. *A good day.*

Next, she saw a photograph taken by Superintendent White Wolf of her friends and allies: Migisi, Fawn Chevreuil, Blackfish LaBiche, John LaBiche, Pierre LeDuc, Christine LeDuc, Martin and Dolly Nielson, Bjorn and Emily Forsberg, Farrell and Florence Luning, Kermit and Mabel Crain, and her husband Jean. *The calm before the storm.*

The faces of her grandchildren followed: Michelle, Charlotte, Erica, Cameron, and her youngest, Nicole, now seventeen.

How did I get so old so fast?

A few minutes later, a cup of tea kept her company as she read her newspapers. The big house came to life around seven o'clock, which was when she set her newspapers on the edge of the porch. Inside the kitchen, her daughter-in-law Hannah prepared breakfast, and a few minutes later, three bedroom lights came on.

Just after breakfast, her son Louis and grandson Cameron went to do chores. Louis gave a nod and Cameron an enthusiastic wave. Cameron, unlike his serious father, was slovenly and awkward. His leather boots shuffled as he crossed the yard, and his shirt was untucked despite the suspenders that tried to keep his large pants from slipping past his waist. On the backside of his head, tufts of black hair defied the orderly pattern of his right-side comb-over. *The poor boy can remember any conversation ever spoken to him yet is considered a fool by society. Nicole must be the one.*

Her youngest granddaughter came to the porch shortly after breakfast and gathered the newspapers. Even though Nicole was a quarter Native, she looked nothing like the girls from Turtle Island Jesuit School. Her chestnut skin and dark hair revealed her Anishinaabe heritage, but she wore makeup and lipstick as if mirroring a Hollywood starlet, and her cheaply made red dress screamed for attention.

Back inside her cottage, Lily glanced at a six-inch mirror. Her white hair was pulled up in a bun, and she wore a cheap floral print dress. She had heavy dark shoes and nylon stockings that hung loosely below her knees.

Somehow, she still expected to see her sixteen-year-old face despite the accumulation of scars upon her heart. Lily remembered how she'd rejected her ancestry at the same age.

Her pleasant routine was shattered by the arrival of a shiny red car that parked between the two houses. Lily observed it from a small gap in the curtains of her house.

Her grandfather's voice whispered the warning found in the Seven Fires Prophecy:

'Beware, the light skinned race comes wearing the face of death.'

'You must be careful because the face of brotherhood and the face of death look very much alike.'

Luckily, the man who stepped out of the car did not fit the prophecy, for his skin was dark yet not Native American. *But his face is familiar.*

At the big house, Hannah appeared first. She untied the apron she wore and set it down across the porch railing, then she descended the three steps that led to the walkway.

"Good afternoon. My name is Charani Bessant, and I'm an anthropologist from Tribhuvan University. Is this the home of Lily Guerin?"

"No," Hannah answered and folded her arms.

Bessant smiled. "It isn't? I was led to believe that—"

"She lives over there in the old house." Hannah lifted her arm to point. Lily shifted despite being almost invisible to those outside.

"Ah, yes," Bessant said, pivoting as the rest of Lily's family came out of the woodwork.

Cameron stood at the screen door, hunched and nervously clasping his hands. In one of the windows shaded by the roof of the porch, Louis, holding a bottle, stood peering out. Nicole emerged still holding a newspaper.

Bessant waved and only Nicole waved back. He asked Hannah, "Are you relatives of Lily Guerin?"

"She's my mother-in-law. I'm Hannah; I'm married to her son Louis."

"Ah, so these two must be her grandchildren?"

No, this can't be happening yet. It's too soon.

"Yes, this is Cameron, and that's Nicole," Hannah explained, but then glanced over her shoulder to the window Lily peered from. "What do you want?"

"Oh, I spent the past week meeting with tribal elders up at the Leech Lake Band of Ojibwe, and her name was brought up on several occasions when I discussed the Battle of Sugar Point. I was told she was a witness to the event."

Yes, I was there, and I saw much more than a battle. Lily had purposely become a recluse decades earlier, yet her family didn't follow her lead.

"I don't know about all of that," Hannah continued. "I suppose it's possible. Why do you want to talk to her about something that happened so long ago?"

"I'm a historian, and I am putting together research into the history and culture of the Anishinaabe people."

"I see. I'll go check with my husband to see if he wants a stranger talking with his mother. Just wait here."

Hannah retreated up the porch steps and past the screen door, where Cameron stood. He said, "I'm part Indian. Do you want to talk to me?"

Just go back inside, Cameron.

Bessant grinned. "Cameron, is it? I'm looking for some insight into the Midewiwin religion, do you still practice it in your household?"

Cameron shook his head. "We're Methodists. We go to the United Methodist Church in Wadena."

"Ah, well, as much as I'd love to speak with you, I'd rather speak to your grandmother about the religion in which she was raised."

"She's Catholic; that's how she met Grandpa Jean, but they were both kicked out of—"

"Cameron," Nicole called out, "Mr. Bessant doesn't need to hear that story."

With his feet placed exactly where they'd stopped, Bessant pivoted back to where Nicole stood.

Lily had seen enough. She stepped away from the window, rushed to the kitchen, and then took a new observation spot at the crack of the front door.

Hannah returned, this time with Louis a few feet behind. He stopped in the doorway and whispered something to Cameron.

"You can see if she'll talk to you," Hannah explained, "but Cameron needs to be with you."

"Absolutely," Bessant agreed.

"Nicole, it's time for you to come back to the house," Hannah finished.

Nicole stomped away as Cameron led Bessant to Lily's front door.

Bessant called out, "Mrs. Guerin?"

Jean warned me this day might come.

Lily took ten steps into her kitchen and returned with a ten-inch butcher knife blade. She whipped open the interior door and gestured with the knife level to his face, forcing him to let go of the screen door and take a few steps backward. Knowing she was a sad spectacle, she let her knife speak for her.

"Mrs. Guerin, my name is Charani Bessant, and I represent—"

"I know who you are, and I know why you have come, thief," Lily said to him as he retreated down the front steps. She continued to flash the knife toward his face.

"I'm not here to rob you, Mrs. Guerin. I wanted to have a conversation with you about—"

"The Manitou? Go back from where you came from, Servant of Biboonike! I might be old, but this old witch is not ready for the grave yet. Tell your dark master the time has not yet come, and if you break the accord, I will turn all his plans to ash. Is that understood?"

Back at the Thunderbird, the driver put his hand in the inner pocket of his tweed jacket and moved to leave the car. Lily saw that Louis still held a bottle of whiskey in his left hand, but now his right hand held a double-barreled shotgun, aimed in the general direction of the car.

That's better.

Charani Bessant raised both his hands and began walking backward. "There is no need for alarm. I came to ask only a few questions. That's all. I'll get in my car and be on my way."

He exchanged an uncertain glance with the driver before stating, "Stay in the car, William. Mrs. Guerin does not want to speak at the moment. Perhaps we'll come back another time when she feels different about the situation."

Bessant walked around the car, putting himself in the shotgun's line of fire. He politely nodded to Louis, whose deep-set eyes withheld emotion. With a nod to Hannah and Nicole, he slipped into the backseat.

A few moments later, the car slowly drove away.

The family congealed in the space outside the gated garden, with several excited questions asked at once. Their voices were only four in a great chorus of voices filling her mind. Overwhelmed, Lily surrendered the big knife to her daughter-in-law who held out her hand for it, and Louis cracked open the shotgun for safety. Cameron put his hand on Lily's shoulder, but it was Nicole who looked angriest.

"Why would you do that?" Nicole asked, her brow furled.

Lily looked down. *I need to protect my family. It's too early, which only means…*

She turned around and went back inside her house. Past all the heirlooms, past the dreamcatchers, she opened a drawer in the end table where she found the journal.

Tell me what to do, Jean.

Raven Feather

Old Copper Road
June 10, 1961

NICOLE GUERIN HID from the world in the folds of her Bible. Her eyes followed one word after another, one column after another, and one page after another until her father's angry, drunken rants could no longer be heard.

"Honor your father and your mother, that your days be long."

Why isn't there a commandment about how to treat your kids?

Something about the appearance of the fancy stranger sent him into a rage, and he began cursing his father, his ancestry, and everything else about his lot in life. Her mother made matters worse by challenging him, and soon, the storm centered around their numerous marital issues.

Nicole kept reading.

Her room was neat and orderly compared to everything else in their home. She collected pictures of Paris, and her imagination sometimes allowed Minnesota to disappear entirely. Charlotte had left her record player, but it sat untouched. Nicole had once made the mistake of trying to drown out her father's drunken tirades only to have the record ripped off the player and shattered against the door.

Now she sat in the corner of her room, wrapped in a wool blanket. Instead of picking a novel, she grabbed her Bible, letting the prophet Isaiah take her to a different time and place. It comforted her to know that Isaiah's world was a pit of chaos, and that he, too, turned to the Lord for comfort.

She'd flipped familiar pages until she found herself in Isaiah 26, a Song of Salvation. Even though she tried to concentrate on the promises of peace, she could not help but notice repeated descriptions of the dead living again to join in the song.

By the time she reached Isaiah 27, she closed her Bible when Isaiah talked about a serpent named Leviathan who lived in the sea.

Even in the Bible, she could not hide from destiny. Lily had often referenced evil serpents and pending doom, but only in vague comments. Her mother considered such talk akin to paganism. Yet the Bible also had serpents, witches, and other foul creatures.

A gentle knock sounded, and Nicole flinched as the doorknob twisted. The door opened to reveal her older brother Cameron. "Nokomis needs you to drive her somewhere."

Cameron had the grace of a beaten dog, thanks to her father and the relentless bullies at school. Although only twenty-one, Cameron looked a decade older, with his nondescript crew cut, basic white t-shirt, and heavy green work pants. Lean and muscular but bent, Cameron looked at his boots as if a servant in his own house.

"The word is grandma, Cameron. If you keep using Indian words, people will always treat you like an Indian. It's grandma."

"Nokomis needs you to drive," Cameron repeated.

"But why," Nicole began but then remembered her father was already drunk and her brother had epilepsy. She grabbed her purse from the dresser and walked past Cameron with a huff. The creaky stairs announced her arrival despite her cautious steps.

Her mother was cleaning up her father's mess in the living room, but her father was nowhere to be seen. Her grandmother stood in the doorway, undefeated and resolute. *She looks serious.*

"What's this all about?" Nicole asked once she reached the bottom of the stairs.

"I'm too old to walk all the way up the hill," she said. "I need to speak with my oldest friend."

Nicole understood, and just the suggestion changed everything. She escorted her grandmother to the car, adjusting the mirrors and seats. Grandma Lily's oldest friend was also the wealthiest man in Hiawatha County and their friendship stretched back to the turn of the century. While Nicole lived in a musty old house on the edge of a swamp, Albert Fisher lived in a mansion overlooking the town.

Driving past the MacPherson farm, she saw the men gathered together along the railing of a cattle pen. *Gavin will be my classmate—but will he be a friend or an enemy?*

Despite growing up on Lake Manitou, she didn't know many of the teenagers that would soon be her classmates. Following in her grandmother's footsteps as a babysitter for families with money, she knew many of the younger kids. On a couple of occasions, she'd watched over Brian and Julia Forsberg, but for her seventh and eighth grade years, she babysat young Christopher Luning when his parents went on trips to visit their new grandchild.

She'd once thought Marlin and Betsy Luning lived in a mansion, but the three-story home had been a "hand-me-down" wedding gift for Albert's daughter after he finished the construction of his own mansion overlooking the town.

"This used to be a convent," Lily said once they entered the pillared driveway. "I stayed with the nuns for a while after my mother died. Everything has changed except for the bricks and that big willow tree."

On a previous visit, Eunice Fisher explained how they'd used the bricks of the old convent to build the mansion

"Drive to the garage. Go past the front doors," Grandma Lily commanded.

The driveway divided with one lane looping toward the front door and another lane leading to the two garages.

"Stay here," her grandmother said once she parked in front of the garage. A stout man wearing bib overalls and rolled up sleeves stepped out to speak with Lily, who nodded as he wiped grease from his hands. A moment later, she retreated to the car.

"Albert's not home," her grandmother said. "Which means I'll need you to take me to my old home."

Her old home?

This is serious.

The Mizheekay Band of Ojibwe Reservation was so small it often did not appear on maps. The larger reservations in Minnesota, like White Earth, Red Lake, or Leech Lake, were formed around existing settlements and towns. The MBO, however, was a narrow stretch of land along the Blue Knife River between Lake Manitou and the town of Nimrod, which had a bridge that allowed settlers to cross the river instead of having to drive far to the northern reaches of Hiawatha County.

Nicole's family had been the original Chippewa inhabitants of the land when the government distributed lots, and in the years that followed, the land at the delta was turned into a state park, and the lot upstream was leased to the Triton Corporation, which dammed the river, stealing half of the worthless land from her family.

For the past ten years, Nicole had taken the same road to Turtle Island Jesuit School: up Old Copper Road into Split Rock, a left turn out of town, a right turn at the Nimrod road, and a left at Lyons road.

The village of Lyons did not exist anymore, but apparently, its foundations could still be seen near the property line of the state park. The road led from a potato field to the wooded ravine along the Blue Knife River. A small cemetery, a grim welcome, marked the entrance to the reservation. Beside the road that paralleled the river, a dozen houses appeared in random locations along the trees. Some belonged to the TIJ staff members while others belonged to families that answered the call to return to their homelands. There hadn't been a new house built since the 1930s.

But in all that time, Lily had never visited her brother.

"So why are we here?"

"I need to warn my brother about the visitors."

Her granduncle Migisi managed to maintain ownership of his original lot, and north of that, the lot had been bequeathed to the Catholic Church, resulting in the creation of the Turtle Island Jesuit School.

"Take me to the office."

The winding road finally opened to the campus of the aging school.

It's a Saturday during the summer. Will anyone even be there?

Even though the school had struggled financially in recent years, in yesteryears the pocketbooks of the Catholic Church had been opened widely, sparing no expense. A cluster of ten small houses had been built at the entrance to house the staff with a dozen ornate but aging stone buildings. Nicole stopped at the former girls' dormitory, which had been converted into a retirement home for a dozen year-round residents.

When Lily did not so much as reach for the door handle, Nicole took the hint and got out to open the passenger door for her grandmother..

"Well, Nicole Guerin, have you changed your mind?" Sally Gray Sky, the school secretary, called out from the doorway of the dormitory.

"Um, no. My grandmother wanted to speak with Superintendent Riel. Is he in?"

"He should be. His car is parked out back," Sally replied pointing to the smaller building.

Her grandmother started walking toward the small office. "Your grandfather Jean once lived here," her grandmother said. "Later, Paul White Wolf ran the school from this office, but that was ... long ago."

Superintendent Riel appeared at the door. Even during the hot summer months, he still wore a gray suit jacket with a turquoise turtle bolo tie that draped down over his crisp black shirt. His long black hair was pulled tightly into a ponytail that ran down his back. He was large and fit, an intimidating figure for all the troublesome boys at the school. "Ah, Nicole, how lovely to see you. Tell me you've returned to register for fall classes."

Nicole looked to her toes for a moment and shook her head. "My grandmother needed to speak with you."

Riel's smile slid away. "Of course, of course. Come into my office."

"Just the two of us," her grandmother said, her eyes glancing to the empty chairs across from the secretary's desk back to Nicole. "I need to speak to you about important matters."

She walked past him to the chair in front of the desk and sat down without invitation. Riel raised his eyebrows to Nicole. "You and Sally need to have a conversation about coming back to Turtle Island this fall. I want things settled by the time I return."

"I'm not sure that's going to happen; I've already registered at Split Rock High School for all my junior classes."

"It's never too late to change your mind," he said, turning towards his office door. "Did Mrs. Lange treat you well during the registration process?"

"She did. All of my classes transferred, but they took issue with my G.P.A. Mrs. Lange came up with some weighted scale that dropped some of my grades to an A-. It was either that or I had to retake the course."

"Well, why would they do such a thing?"

"To avoid having a TIJ end up as the valedictorian, I suppose. I'll give them a run for their money, though."

"I'm sure you will, Nicole. It won't be the same around here without you."

"Yes, I'll miss everyone, but you know how much I wanted to be part of their music program."

"Oh, I understand. Just know you're always welcome here."

When her grandmother tapped his desk, Superintendent Riel sent Nicole a brief smile before he closed the door.

Nicole replayed the incident with the red car, trying to understand why it escalated so quickly.

After several minutes of waiting, the front door flew open, banging loudly against the doorstop. A bare-chested Ojibwe boy with short black hair and blue jeans blinked wide-eyed at Nicole.

"Hello, Sakima. How are you doing?"

The boy ran over and threw his arms around Nicole. "I thought you were going to another school."

"I am. I'm attending Split Rock High this coming fall. What happened to your shirt?"

"I forgot it," Sakima said, showing her a white cowry shell on a leather band around his neck. "One day I'm going to be a Mide for our people."

"Really?"

Sakima nodded proudly. "I'm learning from the same elder who taught my father. I was helping him build a new lodge."

"No wonder you're so filthy," Nicole said, fixing his hair. "Have you been keeping up on your reading over the summer?"

"I have. I read each night before I go to bed. Migisi is teaching me how to read the Teaching Stones. They're picture-words."

"Migisi? Is that who is preparing you to be a Mide one day?"

"He's very old."

"Yes, I know. Did you know that my grandmother is his sister?"

"Really?"

"She's very, very old; she's older than he is!"

Sakima Riel kept the focus of the conversation on the adventures he'd been having over the summer, and while the boy talked, Nicole realized that he knew far more about her granduncle than she did. Somewhere near the cemetery, a narrow road led to where Migisi lived a simple life. Nicole's older sisters and mother had referenced him on several occasions, but never around her grandmother, who never explained what had broken their relationship.

Half an hour passed before Superintendent Riel appeared at the door and was immediately gobbled up by his high-strung child.

Nicole's grandmother shuffled straight out the door without speaking, leaving her to follow.

Once back in the car, Nicole asked, "So, did things go well?"

Her grandmother sighed.

"Does this have to do with those men who showed up in the red car?"

She pursed her lips.

Nicole drove out of the school campus and down the long road that paralleled the river. As she neared the turn by the cemetery, Nicole's thoughts returned to her mysterious granduncle. "Why don't you speak to your brother Migisi?"

"I do speak to Migisi. What do you think I was doing all that time in Riel's office?"

"He was … there?"

"I don't speak directly with him. He is too … stubborn and bitter. It works better if we speak through a mediator, and both of us trust Norval. The Riels are our Canadian cousins."

Cousins? "How so?"

"Ah, it was long ago, prior to the Battle of Bleeding Rock. My brother traced our family tree to *my* great-grandfather's grandfather. Two siblings formed two branches. We are descended from the brother Makadewa and the Riels are descended from the sister Kishkedee." Lily huffed like a frustrated teacher. "Now, put my brother out of mind and trust that I know what I am doing. Can you do that?"

A few hundred yards down the road, she saw a shiny green and black LaSalle—Albert Fisher's car. *Trust? You haven't told me what's got you agitated.* "Of course," Nicole answered and drove back to Split Rock.

Honor your father and mother.

Honor your family.

Past the LaSalle, Migisi hid in the woods.

But what if you don't trust your family?

What if your family keeps secrets?

Eye of the Thunderbird

Mizheekay Band of Ojibwe Reservation
June 10, 1961

MIGISI ASIBIKAASHI AND Albert Fisher sat under the shade of the pines and smoked their pipes. For Migisi, he smoked from a pipe given to him by PJ White Elk at his wedding to Fawn LaBiche. His favorite part about it was the authentic red pipestone bowl.

With his eyes closed and ears listening to the sounds of life in the forest, he ignored the departure of a car that drove past the cemetery. One day, he'd joined his relatives in that plot of ground. *But I won't go to the grave without a fight.* At his side, an instrument of death waited to be called upon.

Beside him, Albert finished his offering of tobacco from a ridiculous looking pipe that curved down from his lips to his chin and then opened into a bowl that looked like a giant mushroom.

"Where did you get that pipe?" Migisi asked.

"I bought it in London. It's a Calabash pipe, like the one used by Sherlock Holmes."

"You should never buy a pipe. If you are meant to have a pipe, the Great Spirit will provide you with one."

Albert was the same age as Migisi, but a lifetime of living in luxury left Albert strangely withered and weak. Despite having more wrinkles on his face, Migisi still felt as strong as he'd been decades earlier.

Although Albert had surrendered to old age long ago, his eyes still twinkled with mischief. "Okay then, let's trade pipes."

"We'll need more tobacco," Migisi said, handing his pipe to Albert before standing and brushing off the pine needles.

In front of him, cool breezes lifted off the surface of the Blue Knife River.

His grandfather Nanakonan had once told him these words: *'Listen to the wind; it talks. Listen to the silence; it speaks. Listen to your heart; it knows.'*

A mile downstream, he could hear the screams of leisure, as dozens of alien families played in the waters of the Blue Knife delta and the beaches of Lake Manitou. A mile upstream, he could hear the occasional slam of doors at the Turtle Island Jesuit School he'd once attended decades earlier. A few hundred yards away, he could hear the whine of gears and engines and the steady rush of water down the log chute of the Nicollet Dam.

Yet for all of this, Manabozho was silent. Instead, Albert Fisher received dreams and omens. *Why does Manabozho bless a rich white man with visions yet ignores his most loyal servant?*

Finding another bag of tobacco, Migisi returned to the big pine, climbing under it like he'd once done as a boy. "Now tell me more about this dream."

Albert looked up to the boughs of the pine tree, then stuffed the pipestone with fresh tobacco. "I was lost inside of the willow."

"The old one at Jiibay Hollow?"

Albert shook his head. "No, the one in my front yard. I sit under it, waiting for the nexus of past, present, and future to cross. Its branches wrap around me, and I feel it enter the veins of my arms, drinking my blood like some vampire."

"Or wendigo." Migisi found himself shaking his head. "No, the willow was made to help us, not to harm us."

"I know, which is why I said it was a bad omen. I felt my manido leave my frail body and enter into the tree, and I flowed upon its branches like I was going down a river. I could travel down into the roots and see the past, or I could go up into the highest branches to see the future."

"And what did you see during your vision?"

"I saw the Omodai."

Migisi gave voice to his disapproval. "Did you speak with the Omodai?"

"Why?"

"The Omodai is dangerous!"

"Lily told me the Omodai could defeat the Wintermaker."

Lily sees things as she wants them to be. "Yes, that is true, but the Omodai has the potential to be even more powerful than the Wintermaker. Remember, at the end of the Seventh Fire, the Omodai will be given the power of choice, and his decision could either destroy the world or bring in the blessed era of the Eighth Fire."

"That certainly explains why I saw so many of them."

"What do you mean?"

"I saw differences in them; different branches had different versions of the same person."

"Our choices today create different futures."

"Why do you think the Omodai is a boy?"

"It's what is told in the Seven Fires prophecies. Why?"

Albert withdrew for a moment. "I've seen different women within the willow tree. At first, I thought the willow was a woman, but then I realized different women were found in different parts of the tree."

"Tell me about the women."

"Well, one I knew—your sister."

"Mmm, yes, of course. And the others?"

Albert touched his face. "She was … wounded. Half of her face had been disfigured or mutilated. But then I saw another woman, looking back at me, with brilliant green eyes and crimson hair."

"The color of blood."

"The strangest woman, though, changed forms."

"Manabozho transformed himself during his visits to earth. A shape shifter seems to be a good omen. What shape did she take?"

"She was first a chubby teenage girl, but then she changed into a willow, with branches for arms, and then, the branches turned into the wings of a raven."

"A raven," Migisi repeated, remembering his father. "My father said ravens were bastards, and you should never listen to them. He told me ravens would drive you mad."

"I'm not sure what to make of that." Albert finished smoking. "It's a good pipe. Can I keep it until the next time we need to talk about dreams?"

"Manabozho meant for you to have it."

The two old friends parted, but as Albert drove away, Migisi saw a second visitor approaching by foot.

He put away Albert's pipe and retrieved his father's hat, stuffed with raven feathers. Next, he grabbed the other relics that Manabozho had given him through the years. Properly armed, he waited for Norval Riel upon a boulder.

"Your sister just left," Riel declared. He had sweat along his hairline from the long walk. "She came with dire warnings."

Albert's dream might be a premonition of things to come.

"Men have come wearing the face of death," Riel stated.

Albert isn't the only one with bad dreams. "Was it the Wintermaker?" Migisi teased.

"Not sure. It sounds like the same men who stopped by the school yesterday."

"Did you extend them trust?"

"Of course not, I politely sent them on their way, but I never mentioned a breath about your sister or her family, yet they somehow found where she lived."

All of this time, and we are still not ready for a fight with the Wintermaker.

"It was kind of my sister to warn us, but we have not even entered into the time of the Seventh Fire. Your son will be safe."

"Yes, well, Lily has always been a bit eccentric. Even so, I told the others to stay vigilant. She wanted me to express her concerns about these men."

"My sister does not trust the prophecy, which is why her heart is always filled with fear." *Riel is here for another reason though.* "Your son is a gifted student, but that is all. Sakima is neither Jessakkid nor Wabeno, but will certainly make a fine Mide."

"I would still like you to perform the Gii'igoshimo."

Lily has filled him with fear also. "It could cause him to turn away from the path he is on. Are you willing to risk such a thing?"

"Sakima is strangely wise for his age. Don't we owe it to our ancestors to at least find out for sure?"

Migisi hesitated and chose not to answer. Instead, he asked, "What do you see when you look at me?"

"I see a mentor and a friend, a dedicated warrior guarding the light."

Migisi shook his head and lifted his left arm. "Do you see this turtle shell? When I was a boy, I thought I saw the Manitou moving through the depths of the Blue Knife River. Believing I was the Great Thunderbird, I pounced upon it, ripping a snapping turtle as large as I was from the bottom of the river. This is the shield of a fool. I am a great fool, but my sister is dangerous. You must be careful of her dire warnings. Have I told you about this hatchet?"

Riel shook his head.

Migisi reached for the instrument of death. "It once belonged to the man who killed my mother and grandfather."

"Why would you keep such a thing?"

"It is a reminder that prophecies cannot be controlled. Led by dark spirits, the man who killed my family created a bloody violent mess because he believed he was an agent of fate. Yet he did nothing to stop the prophecy from unfolding the way it needed to unfold." Migisi paused for a moment to listen to the silence. "Do you want to know why my sister and I no longer speak?"

Riel nodded.

The angry words spoken by Fawn filled his mind. "For all of her good intentions, Lily Guerin serves chaos. It doesn't bother me that she has rejected the religion of our ancestors to become a Christian. At every opportunity she is given, she fights for her own best interests. She is no different than these two men who have shown up, who did indeed wear the Face of Death."

Migisi watched to see how Riel would react to his assessment of his sister.

"No, I refuse to believe that about Lily."

"It is true. As young woman, her choice was easy. Now that she is old, she finally understands the horrible consequences of her decision."

"What horrible consequences?"

"She did not end the prophecy. She only delayed it. We must hold steady or make matters worse."

Riel's face twisted in frustration. "So, your counsel is that we do nothing?"

He wants to be a hero. "Are you greater than Kitshi-Manidoo?"

"No, but—"

Migisi raised his voice. "Ah, I think your modern clothes and power over others have given you the arrogance to believe you can control the future and the lives of others. I have contemplated much about your son, Sakima, and have determined that he is not marked by Manabozho or the Great Thunderbird. Yet you think your knowledge is superior to not only mine but also the Great

Spirit Kitshi-Manidoo! You would ruin him to satisfy your ego and to stretch a prophecy that simply does not fit."

"I think I finally understand your point."

Migisi took off his father's black hat and set it upon his lap. "We are both guardians, you and I, but I guard more than just knowledge. Do you know what I guard?"

Riel shook his head.

My family's curse—the sacred Water Drum, the White Egg, and the Philosopher's Stone.

Migisi picked up his father's hat and set it back on his head. "I will take the knowledge to my grave, knowing that the will of the Great Spirit will find a way, with or without me. Only by carefully balancing upon the path of the Great Spirit can I fulfill my destiny." He paused. "So, on my left arm I carry the shield of the Chippewa, those who sought to fulfill the prophecy; and on my right arm I carry the hatchet of the Dakota, those who were meant to guard and delay the prophecy. If I am so lucky, perhaps I will be able to hand these weapons to the Great Thunderbird before I die. If not, I will continue to walk the path."

"I've sworn an oath, Migisi," Riel argued. "You know that."

Migisi shook his left arm. "Then be the shield instead of the hatchet. Sit down. Tell me what my sister told you, and perhaps we can walk down the path together."

Riel relented and shared everything, remaining his ally instead of becoming a pawn for his sister.

As Migisi listened, he prepared for the worst. After the disaster in 1910 left them leaderless, he knew it was his responsibility to prepare the Isanti Lodge for war. Christian priests could be found in any village, and there were two Forsbergs still living in the same house once owned by Bjorn, but Fawn …

If Lily is right, then I need more allies.

Migisi interrupted Riel's story. "I need you to send a letter. Go fetch paper."

King of the Castle

Haggard Quarry
June 15, 1961

BIFF FORSBERG IMMEDIATELY sensed something was wrong. The gatehouse of Haggard Quarry was closed. He'd grown used to arriving hours before the rest of the workers, but today, his patience was tested, and after sitting quietly with his lunch box for half an hour, he began to walk around. The rolling gate had barbed wire at the top and was fitted to within three inches of the ground, but a good pair of pliers could open a hole in seconds.

If only I had pliers.

Past the posts that held the gate, a larger fence encircled the entire facility. Near the highway, a guardrail and large steel panel fence paralleled the road, and having seen the quarry from its bottom, Biff would hate to see the damage if either the guardrail or steel fence failed to stop a car from plunging over the edge of the abyss.

He studied the fence. The posts of both the chain link fence and steel paneling had been placed in solid rock, with a bit of concrete poured into the boreholes for alignment. Both types of fencing had been fitted so that not even rabbits could slip under, and above, concertina wire prevented thoughts of climbing over the chain link. Near the highway, the fencing changed to over-lapped steel panels, which certainly couldn't be scaled. Biff noticed then a bathtub-sized boulder had leaned forward from its position atop the wall, and years of runoff from the ditch had created a small channel around it. He put his foot over the gap.

Could I fit through?

A car approached.

Now, almost a hundred yards from the gatehouse, Biff pivoted and casually began walking past, but the car sped by him so quickly that the headlights barely illuminated him. It was not the man who ran the gatehouse, nor was it his uncle. It was Morgan Marquette.

During Wednesday's lunch, Uncle Ewan invited Biff up to the office building; there he introduced his cousins and business part-ners—Marquette and Stewart—who formed Triton Corporation in St. John. Marquette owned the local mortuary and had recently tried teaching Biff about the different types of gravestones quar-ried in Hiawatha County.

Biff watched as Marquette fumbled at the gate for a few minutes, rolling it open, and then stomped off to the gatehouse to raise the arm. He returned to his car, and instead of continuing to the office, he sped down the path to the bottom of the quarry.

What's going on?

Biff looked back to St. John to see if anyone else approached, but with the gate wide open, he picked up his lunch box and en-tered the quarry. He went over to the steps of the office and sat down. Normally, the gatehouse operator let him in, but none of the regular quarry employees were arriving.

Did the demolition go wrong?

Instead of an answer arriving, the mystery thickened when a pickup truck emerged from the pit.

Is there security for the quarry? Why would a quarry need a guard?

While stone certainly wasn't worthy of overnight protection, the equipment was worth millions of dollars, which did justify the security fencing and even the dozens of floodlights surrounding the quarry. The truck didn't slow as it drove past the office building where Biff sat.

No other workers showed up for the next few minutes. It was clear that it wasn't business as usual. Biff didn't want to walk all the way home, but he also didn't want to wait for Wally Crain to pick him up in the afternoon. He was about to start home when the red Thunderbird arrived.

As it passed, Biff stood. *What the heck is going on?*

Biff began walking down the road that led to the belly of the quarry. When he reached the slope, he was able to look over the edge, and there he saw the two vehicles meet at the fueling station.

Hey, those are the guys who were looking for the Guerin house. Even though the morning light was dim, the light pole allowed Biff to see the red Thunderbird and its English driver and fancy Nepalese passenger. They joined the other brother-in-law, Sean Stewart.

Where is Uncle Ewan?

Sean Stewart, the tour guide, owned several local businesses. Prior to this summer, Biff had seen him at several Boy Scout meetings with Rory, the spoiled son. Now, Stewart led the two guests right up to the deck where Red Dobie normally operated, but today, Marquette joined them at the door. All four men entered the supply office before Biff reached the floor of the quarry.

Stone fragments once again littered the floor of the quarry, which meant the blasting had not been a total ruse, but instead of the quarry being set into motion, everything was still. The interior lights added even more detail to the scene, and as Biff reached the vehicles, the men inside of the office stepped behind Dobie's counter and entered the back room.

Unsure of what to do, Biff found his wheelbarrow, flipped it over, and retrieved his gloves and hardhat. The sooner the floor was cleared, the sooner he could learn another trade, so he walked the wheel barrel toward the back wall to begin his sweep.

Near the vertical wall of stone, the shadows were thickest, but today, a strange sliver of light illuminated the ground. It came from the space between the supply building and the wall. Biff heard something similar to a barn door opening just before the sliver of light appeared.

He could also hear voices.

The first Biff knew to be Marquette. "Honestly, most of the Sioux Quartzite here is exhausted. Ewan's been digging laterally to the west for fifteen years, but the deposit is thinner in that direction. Most of the good stuff is closer to Lake Manitou, which is pretty much off limits."

"For fear of flooding?" Charani Bessant asked.

"Oh, no. The shore is higher in the west than it is in the east. Plus, we've got enough solid rock between us and the lake bed to hold back Lake Superior without fear of flooding, but as it turns out, our little pet project is found there also."

"I forget how impressive it can be," Stewart added, and a shadow made the beam of light flicker. "To think, our fathers began digging way up there sixty years ago. Now look at us."

My uncle did all the digging, not the two of you. Biff kept working but staggered the pace so he could hear the conversation.

Bessant's voice grew louder. "The Ojibwe named this place Flat Rock. According to some of the stories, they fought the Dakota so that they could mine the stone like down at the Pipestone quarry in southern Minnesota. How do you suppose they planned to do it?"

"Dig? Beats me. Sioux Quartzite is a bitch to cut. My uncle told me stories that the Indians had somehow managed to dig down ten feet before he began blasting. He said it was a smooth cut, like they had rubbed it instead of hammered it away."

"Strange. Perhaps they used the legendary Water Drum."

"The Philosopher's Stone?" Stewart chuckled. "Reality is far stranger than legend. You want to see something strange? Come with me, Mr. Bessant."

Biff watched as they passed by the threshold.

"The entire shed is built on wheels, allowing us to push it out of the way when needed. Since our discovery three years ago, we bring in a hired European crew who come in at night to take care of the more delicate work that Haggard's local boys are not equipped to handle."

The voices grew fainter as Biff stood balancing the wheelbarrow.

"What happened three years ago?"

"We found something," Marquette said. "When I was a boy, I thought Santa Claus was real, and when I learned it was all a lie, it pissed me off. It made me jaded, which made it easy to question what they dished out in Sunday school as well as what the public schools taught me in textbooks. What I'm about to show you will make you question more than just Santa Claus. You ready?"

"I have a pretty good idea of what I'm about to see, Mr. Marquette. Lead on."

"Don't say I didn't warn you," Marquette chuckled.

Things grew silent until the sound of an angry truck engine interrupted. Headlights splashed the far side of the quarry.

Someone's coming.

Biff quickly bent down and picked up a few softball-sized stones, letting the stone clunk loudly in the bottom of his wheelbarrow. By the time the truck reached the floor of the quarry, he had several stones collected.

It was Red Dobie's truck, followed by the night security man's truck.

The headlights flooded the supply building, and the Englishman in the tweed jacket appeared on the deck, pistol in hand. But the men from the trucks, including Uncle Ewan, all stepped out with shotguns in hand.

Biff froze.

"Morgan!" Uncle Ewan shouted out then loaded a shell into the shotgun.

"He's inside with the others," the Englishman replied. "Your brothers invited Mr. Bessant."

"He's not my brother, and both are fucking morons," Uncle Ewan retorted.

Dobie cleared his throat. "Leave your pistol there on the railing and go fetch your boss."

Will he start shooting?

Biff watched the Englishman ponder the command for a moment, and when he did set his pistol down, his fingers gave it a slight twist. As he walked into the office, his hands slid into his pockets making Biff suspicious of what else he may have on him.

"Is this the young prince's way of testing us?" Uncle Ewan asked Dobie as they waited.

"Could all be an honest mistake, or something more sinister? Either way, your brothers should have cleared it with me first. Goddamn bloody amateurs."

Biff saw shadows pass by the threshold, and a moment later, Marquette came out of the supply shed. "Oh, for Pete's sake, put the guns away. We're just giving our friends a tour."

"Who said they were friends?" Uncle Ewan asked. "They show up at our door and you let the fox in the henhouse? We have protocols and procedures for this very reason."

Charani Bessant stepped forward with his hands raised at the elbow, as if mocking the entire ordeal. "For any offenses, I deeply apologize. It was my belief that both Mr. Delhut and Mr. Gunn cleared my visit in advance. We came to Hiawatha County at their request." Then he turned directly to look at Biff. "Who's the boy?"

Oh, shit. Am I going to get in trouble?

"Son of a bitch," Uncle Ewan groaned. His shotgun lowered for just a moment before rising back up. "He's my nephew. Never-you-mind him, he's supposed to be here. The two of you are not."

That's right. I'm just doing my job.

Stewart appeared behind Bessant. "Ewan, if I could explain—"

"Shut the fuck up, Sean!"

"Sean and Morgan," Dobie called out, "I want the two of you to step off the deck and over to the right. Now!"

Stewart and Marquette listened, and for a moment, Biff thought the command might have been to clear them out of the way for murder and execution.

Uncle Ewan stepped forward, and even in his short-sleeved plaid shirt, suspenders, and baseball cap, he was a menacing figure compared to the foreign Bessant, clad in his white suit. "A college friend of the new boss, huh?"

"Yes, we met at Yale."

Yale ... I'll remember that.

"And now you're some sort of spiritual adviser for our illustrious leader?"

"Ross had a few questions and asked if I could give him an independent account of matters," Bessant explained.

"Young Mr. Delhut and the boys in Detroit might see their family legacy as a novelty, but here in Minnesota, men have been guarding the legacy for centuries. There's a right and a wrong way to do things, and my partners had no right bringing you here without proper vetting."

"Ewan, I called Detroit and spoke with Henry Gunn," Stewart countered.

"Proper vetting!" Uncle Ewan repeated, his voice echoing against the quarry walls.

Dobie cleared his throat. "I'm going to need you to get into that shiny red car of yours, and then I'm going to escort you back to the airport in Brainerd. You're leaving Hiawatha County. To-day."

"And if we see either of you snooping around Hiawatha County without prior consent, we'll view it as an act of aggression, and treat you the same way we treated those Nazis a few years back," Uncle Ewan added. "If you want to see a hole in the ground, we'll show you one."

Nazis?

Uncle Ewan is a bad ass.

Charani Bessant walked with his hands in his pants pockets, leading a slow retreat from the deck to the Thunderbird, where he nervously paused. "I respect your efforts, and quite obviously, misjudged the situation. Mr. Stewart, I thank you for your hospitality, and Mr. Marquette, I thank you for this opportunity to visit the 'roaring waters' here at Lake Manitou. Mr. Haggard, I apologize for my overstep, and on behalf of Mr. Delhut, I apologize for our enthusiasm and indiscretion of misunderstanding Nidhogg. I shall not return again to the quarry or Hiawatha County without proper vetting. *Alivida.*"

With a smirk, Charani Bessant slipped back into the Thunderbird, followed by the Englishman.

Dobie got into his vehicle and followed them as they left.

Uncle Ewan turned to his business partners. "Didn't we talk about threats? The body of Pierre Delhut is not yet cold, and we have foreign guests at the quarry? Clear out, and I don't want to talk about this until Red's had an opportunity to sort through this mess."

Stewart retreated to Marquette's car, following the other two out of the quarry. The night security guard did not lower his shotgun, even after Uncle Ewan sighed loudly and kicked at the ground.

He focused on Biff. "What in the world are you doing here?"

"No one was at the gate, and when Mr. Marquette arrived, he left the gate open. After a while, I just came down here. There's a lot of rock to move after the blasting."

Uncle Ewan laughed.

"Guess he didn't get the memo either," the night guard said wryly.

"There's a lot of that going on," his uncle muttered. "Okay, Biff. Clear out the debris, and I'll come back for you after I've had a shower and some breakfast. We'll be back to normal tomorrow."

Biff shrugged, bringing more chuckles from his uncle. His flat shovel scraped loudly against the quarry floor as his deposit echoed loudly into the wheelbarrow.

Uncle Ewan left with the night watchman, leaving Biff alone.

Still on the deck railing, the pistol called to him.

Soul Catchers

Old Copper Road
June 15, 1961

NICOLE GUERIN UNDERSTOOD she was poor, but unlike her brother and sisters, she did not want to play the part. In order to have a functional wardrobe before her junior year at Split Rock High School, she needed to earn money, and to do that, she woke up at 4:30 a.m. to go work at Dutch Boy Dairy.

Walking to work was a bit spooky, but she had the comfort of having both the MacPherson and Forsberg farms within her sight at all times. Just before the Doc Jenkins Bridge, she turned at the driveway to Dutch Boy Dairy. The first shift began at 5:00, which meant her walk had to be steady and brisk.

Nicole worked near the end of the processing line with four other women. Nicole and her team made sure each truck was filled to order, allowing the milkmen to efficiently drop and go before many residents even woke for their breakfast.

It was frenetic loading bottles, stacking cheese, and counting cartons, but by 7:00 a.m., she was free to return home with some money in her pocket.

This day, however, ended a little differently than normal.

Most of the workers parked in the lot near the Crow Wing River, and the big trucks circled behind the creamery for pick up and drop off. A flatbed truck full of empty jugs parked near the entrance of the lot along the shoulder.

As she walked by the truck, she saw a handsome young farmer sitting behind the wheel, eating a sandwich. He glanced at her through the large side mirror.

It was Gavin MacPherson.

"Good morning," he said politely as she passed by his open cab window.

She softly returned his salutation and kept walking, fearing taunts might follow.

"Hey, you're Nicole Guerin, right?"

This question forced her to stop and turn. She nodded.

"I hear you're going to be attending school with us this fall, is that true?"

What's his deal? Again, Nicole nodded. She felt her heart flutter, knowing that her new peers already had her on their radar. "I'm going to be a junior."

"Really? Me too." He looked in his rear-view mirror. "Hey, would you like a ride home? My dad finally trusts me to make the deliveries, and since we're neighbors and all, I can give you a lift."

"I don't mind walking," Nicole said.

"It's no problem at all, I swear."

Nicole knew she needed friends and allies at school, and Gavin seemed sincere. "Okay," she said and walked around to the passenger side of the truck.

Gavin suddenly became a discombobulated mess, fumbling to open the door for her from across the cab and then sweeping crumpled wads of wrappers off the seat.

"Sorry about the mess; I wasn't expecting company this morning. Let me make sure the seat is clean before you sit down. I wouldn't want you to get your clothes dirty."

Nicole suddenly became aware of how ridiculous she must have looked. Like all the other women at the creamery, she wore a white dress, white nylons, and a white hat. "I probably smell like cottage cheese."

Gavin laughed. "I probably smell like cows."

Nicole slid onto the bench seat, swallowed by the strange space within the cab. She closed the door and stayed as close to it as possible.

"Would you like a cheese sandwich? One of the old ladies always gives me one since I'm the youngest driver." After she shook her head, he asked, "How long have you worked here?"

"Since last March. It's just a two-hour shift, which lets me have the rest of the day to myself."

"Yeah, it's the same for me. Rain or shine, sleet or snow, I'm up each morning with Pa doing chores. What time do you report each morning?"

"5:00."

"Oh, shoot. I'm helping in the barn at 5:00. I usually make my delivery around 6:30. If you want, I can wait around and give you a ride home when your shift is done."

"Oh, you don't have to do that."

"It's the neighborly thing to do. Besides, I've heard you're really smart. Maybe you can repay it later if I need some help with homework."

"Okay," Nicole said with a shrug. "Sure."

"It's settled then," Gavin said, firing up the loud truck engine. The gears ground a bit and he stomped on the clutch until it engaged before the truck began rolling down the road.

The conversation came to an awkward end, but luckily, the radio played some old crooner from the 1940s.

Gavin bobbed a little to the music. "I don't normally listen to this stuff, but it's the only station that comes in on this old truck."

"What do you like to listen to?"

"I'm a big fan of Elvis Presley and Buddy Holly."

"Oh, me too," Nicole lied, wanting to impress him.

Before she knew it, they'd passed the Forsberg farm and were already to Gavin's driveway, but instead of stopping to let her out, the truck kept going.

"You don't have to take me all the way home," Nicole protested, suddenly afraid of Gavin seeing her house. Even though they were neighbors, she knew what a dump her house was compared to his farmstead. As they approached her driveway, she mustered a stronger defense. "You can just let me off at the end of the driveway. There isn't much room to turn a truck around."

The truck slid to a stop beside the entrance to her driveway, and, relieved, she opened the door. "Thank you," she said. "It's Gavin, right?"

"Yes, it is." He smiled. "Any time, Nicole. Have a good day."

While Nicole walked down the long driveway, Gavin struggled to turn the truck around. It took about five angles before the nose of the truck turned toward his home and bounced down the gravel road.

Twice she glanced toward the distant hill even though the truck had vanished from sight.

As she neared the house, Nicole noticed her grandmother emerging from the reeds of the shore, carrying half-a-dozen dreamcatchers. "What are you doing with those?"

"Bah," her grandmother said and walked around Nicole.

Nicole had the choice between helping with breakfast or following Lily—she chose her grandmother.

Nicole caught the door before it slammed in her face. A strange humidity filled the house, and upon the stove, four large pots boiled and steamed. The curtains were drawn, leaving the inside dim as her grandmother slipped off her shoes without letting go of her haul of dreamcatchers.

"Grandma, what are you doing with all—" A foreign sight caught Nicole's attention. Dozens of dreamcatchers, big and small, hung from doorways, windows, and walls. Although beautiful, the sight terrified her. "What is going on?"

"Didn't they teach you anything about our heritage at the school? You are the great scholar. Isn't it obvious what I'm doing?"

"You're having bad dreams?"

"Bad dreams? No, that's not it. Try again."

Nicole knew the answer. "The dreamcatcher was first made by Grandmother Spider back at the original Turtle Island. Wanting to protect the children, she hung the nets above the cradles. The bad dreams would catch on the threads and when morning came ... Are you trying to protect us?"

"There are things you cannot understand from books and classrooms," her grandmother answered as she hung each new dreamcatcher around her living room. "But yes, I am trying to protect you."

"From what? Those men in the red car?"

"An ancient evil lives in Lake Manitou. I know, because when I was your age, I woke it from its eternal sleep. Now like moths to the flame, evil is drawn to this place because of the old magic here. Something is stirring before its time, so I am trying to understand what is amiss before it is too late. What you said about dreamcatchers is partially true. When properly made, a dreamcatcher will ward off evil, allowing only good dreams to pass through the hole at the center. My grandfather Nanakonan taught me old magic from the dawn." She paused, looking down at her wrinkled hands and then at Nicole. "These are not dreamcatchers ... these are soul catchers."

Nicole felt her heart constrict, and for the first time, she saw another woman behind the mask of her grandma. "What does that mean?"

"A soul is meant to leave a body at death and travel to the afterlife. Those who die at Lake Manitou are trapped here. This place is an abomination of nature."

Her grandmother turned and found another place to hang one of her delicate dreamcatchers.

"Are you saying there are—"

"I know it must look horrifying to you to see all of them hanging within my house, but if I am to find answers, I must ask many questions of many souls. I set them out each evening, and while dew still hangs on them, I bring them in before the sun dries them out, and they return back to the depths. Don't worry, they are all quite harmless. I just need answers.

"When I was your age, I saw visions of the future. I saw an old woman with a broad, green hat, and I also saw a young man with snakeskin upon his feet. This boy will fight the Horned Serpent, the Manitou that lives in the waters of the lake. But the time has not come, so I turn to the spirits to understand what is wrong. Would you like to speak with one of them? It is time you learn the truth about this place."

No, it's too early in the day for this.

Nicole took a step backwards. "I ... I ... I should get back. I need to help Mother with breakfast chores. I should go." She bolted out the screen door and through the wooden gate.

When her mother entered the kitchen, Nicole sat at the table, brooding over what her grandmother had just revealed.

"How was work?" her mother asked, immediately jumping into her typical line of questioning.

"Fine," Nicole said, joining her at the counter to help with breakfast preparations.

The mundane conversation continued without mention of chivalrous Gavin MacPherson or Soul Catchers. Just like her mother, Nicole used routine to hide her feelings.

Like normal, she and her mother tended to the men, who tended to the farm before going off to work at Carousel Park.

A little before eleven, Nicole and her mother went outside and weeded the garden, so the little vegetable sprouts were not overwhelmed by vigorous weeds that never stopped emerging from the soil.

As they worked, going down one row after another, Nicole finally asked, "Do you know that Grandma Lily has dreamcatchers hanging all over the inside of her house?"

Her mother frowned. Unlike her Native grandmother, Nicole's mother was a third-generation Norwegian immigrant, born to Micah Mortenson and Sylvie Berg. The city girl from Split Rock had married a bad boy from the country.

"It doesn't surprise me. Lily has always been a bit eccentric, which explains your father. One moment, she'll seem like a devout Christian, and the next, she is muttering pagan chants under her breath."

"I want to be respectful," Nicole said, "but it just…"

"Your grandmother was a pretty devout Christian when I first met her, but in her old age, she's been returning to the old ways of her ancestors. I don't think she'd try to convert you."

Nicole laughed.

"It's good to know your heritage, but you're growing up in a modern world. I'm very happy you'll be going to school in Split Rock this fall. I wish Cameron had stayed in public school, but I was afraid the other students would tease him."

What's to stop them from teasing me? Nicole worried. She pushed her nightmares from her mind. "Grandma Lily seems ... um ... concerned about those men that came to the house the other day. You know, the ones in the fancy red car."

"Yes, your father was agitated by that also. Don't give it too much thought. They are both a little paranoid. Your grandmother was shunned by her Sioux relatives for being Chippewa and by her

Chippewa relatives for being Sioux. Your father felt shunned because his own father was a disgraced priest who left the church."

"Was he kicked out because of Grandma Lily?"

"I've heard numerous stories about when their relationship began, which is why your father is always so concerned about the opinions of others. By the time I met your father, Grandfather Jean had been dead quite a while. I guess that's why they say let sleeping dogs lie."

NICOLE WAS READING *Doctor Zhivago* to prepare herself for the rigorous literature classes that awaited her in the fall. She hid away in Russia until her mother called her down to help prepare supper.

Her father returned in the truck without Cameron, explaining that he'd be working until 10 o'clock. The three sat down to watch *The Alvin Show* and then *Father Knows Best* before Nicole excused herself to read more in her room.

Even though she was tired, she could not stop thinking about work the next morning and the possibility of another ride from Gavin.

The screen door slammed loudly, and Nicole realized she'd fallen asleep against the wall while reading. Normally, Cameron would come and wish her a good night, yet a few seconds later, the door slammed again, followed by a third slam.

A terrified wail pierced the illuminated protection of her bedroom—it was Cameron. Whenever anxieties or emotions overwhelmed him, he would drop into a sitting position, wail, and beat upon his head with the palm of his left hand. Hearing the cry, Nicole immediately stood and was greeted by a strange glow out of the window—her grandmother's house was burning.

Flames rose like angry serpents, high above the house, ready to strike. Her father stood in the path like a bewildered squire searching for a weapon after his knight had been slain. Cameron sat wailing in the middle of the gravel parking lot while her mother was frozen a few paces closer to their house.

Nicole flew down the stairs and into the kitchen, where the telephone hung on the wall. Picking up the receiver, she heard voices on the shared party line before she could even form a sentence. "We need help. We need help. Her house is on fire. Lily Guerin. Her house is on fire."

"Slow down, slow down," said the anonymous woman who'd been sharing gossip with the other women. "Whose house is on fire?"

"Lily Guerin. Old Copper Road. Rural Route 1 Box 4. Please, we need help."

A dozen voices began to speak at once, and the others had to yield the line, so having made known their plight, she hung up the phone and bolted outside.

Nicole stared into the eyes of the dragon and froze a few paces from Cameron. Fountains of flame flowed from both windows, and the open door billowed with black smoke.

"Where's Dad?" Nicole gasped, realizing she could see only two of her four family members. "Dad!"

Her father had rushed into the pyre, which is why the door had opened to the fiery furnace inside. She ran to it, only to be grabbed by her mother, who held onto her wrist.

"No. Don't go in there," her mother shouted, using her dead weight and vice grip to stop Nicole from moving.

In the distance, a siren wailed, but much sooner than that, a truck came roaring up her driveway, its lights blinding. Duncan MacPherson and Gavin MacPherson both burst from the truck holding axes instead of fire hoses.

"Louis went inside after her," her mother said over the roar of the fire.

"Where is her bedroom?" Duncan asked.

"In the back. Southeast corner."

The elder MacPherson rushed into the gaping mouth while Gavin ran around to the back of the house.

Before either MacPherson could win or lose, two more trucks appeared, and with the headlights of their trucks, they illuminated the fire and smoke of her grandmother's small house. Two men and a boy jumped out of the trucks. One of the men Nicole knew as Glen Forsberg, which meant the young boy was his youngest son, Brian. The other man had wild orange hair and a beard that dipped down onto his chest. In a matter of seconds, they, too, were attacking the fiery beast.

"We have to save it," Cameron insisted, suddenly at her side. "It's our only hope."

Having finally grasped the reality of the situation, her emotional brother went from victim to would-be savior in a matter of moments when he went running toward the front door.

The hairy man caught hold of Cameron just outside of the door, and her brother violently flailed away. With the help of Brian, they kept Cameron from following Glen Forsberg into the furnace.

She wanted to rush in, but fear prevented it.

"Dad!" Nicole shouted when she saw three forms coming from the portal to hell. Glen Forsberg balanced Duncan MacPherson with his left arm, and with his right arm, he dragged her father behind him.

Once past the wooden fence, the men fell on the ground, wheezing and coughing.

Meanwhile, Cameron continued to try to wrestle free to run inside the building. Cameron was soon grabbed around the chest, and like Hercules lifting Antaeus the giant orange-haired man had him off the ground and was carrying him away.

"He's burned," her mother exclaimed. "Oh, sweet Jesus, his shirt's on fire."

While Forsberg and MacPherson coughed violently, her father just groaned. Half of his plaid shirt had burned away, revealing black and blistered skin on his chest and left arm.

Two more vehicles came up the driveway, and soon men were shouting at them to clear out so the fire trucks could get through.

"Help!" a young man's voice called out. "I need help!"

Nicole turned to see Gavin MacPherson stumbling out from behind the house. In his arms, he cradled her grandmother.

Strangers rushed to help him and lifted her from him as the fire truck and more vehicles arrived. Some men attacked the fire and others gathered around the burned and wounded.

Nicole found herself clutching her mouth, both in shock and repulsion, for the smell of burnt clothing drifted up from her grandmother through the shield of emergency workers.

More sirens called out from Old Copper Road.

Suddenly, she felt someone at her shoulder, and with a glance, she saw the blackened figure of Gavin MacPherson gazing at her grandmother.

Overcome, Nicole threw her arms around him, holding him tightly. Then she found herself weeping uncontrollably against his neck.

She did not let go for the longest time, and when she looked up again, men were dousing the burning cottage with a hose from a tanker truck. An ambulance opened to take in both her grandmother and father, who were coughing violently. Medics from a second ambulance tended to both Duncan MacPherson and Glen Forsberg.

Her brother Cameron appeared at her side. He moaned and groaned, uttering incoherent syllables.

When Nicole finally let go of Gavin, he stepped back and offered a small object to her. "She told me to keep this safe."

Nicole took it, but in the darkness, all she could discern was that it was some sort of journal.

Good Counsel

Split Rock, MN
June 16, 1961

LBERT FISHER HUNG up the phone, leaving his hand on the receiver for a few moments before withdrawing it. *Why am I still alive and the others dead?*

How will I help in the coming fight?

Albert leaned back in his chair and looked at his watch. His wife would have breakfast ready soon, even though he'd barely slept a wink. He still wore his pajamas with his spring jacket over the top, and his soiled slippers, muddy from his evening walk to the willow tree.

Eunice will not be happy.

Albert stood up and walked out of his private office, then down the hall to the main part of the house. He could smell bacon, blueberry muffins, and other savory morsels long before he reached the kitchen.

"Good morning, love," he greeted and slipped into the barstool at the counter, where coffee and the local newspaper awaited him.

"Did you sleep last night?"

"No, I didn't. There was a fire at the Guerin farm. Lily and her son Louis are both in the hospital. Lily's in serious condition."

"Oh, dear Lord. Is that why I heard sirens all night?"

"I plan to visit the hospital later this afternoon, but I have a meeting first. Could I trouble you to put on an extra pot of coffee?"

"I had a—yes. I made a whole tray of muffins also. How many are coming?"

"That will be enough," he said.

After eating, he showered, changed clothes, and gathered himself on the couch until the meeting started.

ONE BY ONE, the men of the Isanti Lodge arrived.

Sipping coffee in front of the cold fireplace, Ed Nielson, Glen Forsberg, and Marlin Luning sat quietly in his private study, summoned by the ghosts of Martin Nielson, Bjorn Forsberg, and Farrell Luning.

I must be cautious. These men are not their fathers.

When Wally Crain drove up in his pickup, Albert felt relief. In more ways than one, Earl "Wally" Crain filled the shoes of his father Kermit and acted as the leader of the group despite being the youngest at 34. Albert's heart sank when he saw Crain arrived alone.

"No Migisi?" Nielson asked when he came into the office with a cup of coffee and a muffin.

Crain shook his head. "He's more convinced than ever that he needs to stay on the reservation and protect it from enemies wearing 'the face of death,' as he put it."

"How's Lily?" Luning asked.

Crain winced. "To be honest, it's almost a miracle. She lost all of her hair, but her flesh barely had a mark. It's her lungs that have the doctors most concerned. She's got tubes of oxygen in her nose, but her lung tissue is so inflamed that they're worried about organ failure due to lack of oxygen. She's in rough shape."

"After seeing her last night, I'm honestly surprised she survived," Forsberg commented. The gruff dairy farmer winced as if the thought of having seen her caused him pain. "Let's talk about that red Thunderbird. What's happening with that?"

Perhaps there is a little Bjorn in him after all. "That's the most curious aspect of this," Albert began.

"Aside from attempted murder," Luning muttered.

"Is that what we want the fire marshal to say?" Crain asked.

"Hell no," Nielson added.

Do I mention the Wintermaker?

Or the Omodai?

"Gentlemen," Albert chastened. "We are the Isanti Lodge, and our matriarch was attacked last night, regardless of what the rest of the world determines. We've all taken oaths as 'guardians,' and I believe that in the coming days, our community will come under attack. Even though our suspected enemy came with a foreign face, our real enemy resides on the other shore. Expect daggers in the smiles of our neighbors. We must be vigilant if we are to protect our children."

"Are you still angry about the quarry, Albert?"

He's still a clueless boy.

Edna Haggard, before becoming Split Rock's pastry queen, had once been a beauty, Albert remembered. The entitled beauty queen from St. John met a handsome, hardworking dairy farmer from Split Rock, and the rest was history. Forsberg wouldn't listen to advice then, and he certainly didn't listen when it came to his youngest son.

Yes, I'm still angry, but tread carefully.

"If not for Biff working at the quarry, our clue might not have even been discovered. In this regard we are fortunate. I made several calls last night, and our red Thunderbird has been located."

The men shifted in their seats.

"It's back at a car lot in Minneapolis, but it left behind a paper trail. Our enemy loves symbolism, which is why the Thunderbird was requested specifically. A few weeks ago, the Ford was purchased brand new by the Brainerd Shuttle Company, owned by our very own Sean Stewart of St. John."

"So, it is the work of Triton," Forsberg assessed.

"However, there is also an all-points bulletin that was issued by the Minnesota Highway Patrol on Monday night, which led to the car being found in the Minneapolis car dealership. Our suspects are no longer in Minnesota, it seems."

"What are you saying, Albert?" Nielson asked. "That Thunderbird showed up at the Rez, Old Copper Road, and then Haggard Quarry two days before Lily's house went up in flames. Is this Triton's way of washing their hands clean of suspicion?"

Albert felt so tired that he was almost lightheaded. "Charani Bessant and his henchman certainly had Lily in their sights, and the car connects things to Triton, but why now?"

"The summer solstice is coming," Nielson offered. "You said they love symbolism."

"What's different about 1961 than 1960 or 1959? Lily has been living in peace for decades, so why would Triton suddenly feel threatened by her?"

"Are you saying it wasn't Triton?" Forsberg asked.

"I was just a kid back in 1898, but the body count left an impression on me. Father Jean Guerin was blindsided by an enemy that he barely knew existed. We can't afford to jump to conclusions."

"I just want my son safe," Luning stated.

"Me too," Nielson added.

"Are our boys in danger?" Forsberg asked. "I know what happened in 1898."

The Tak-Pei need a blood sacrifice to wake, and with Lily in the hospital, who's going to protect Lake Manitou from the evils that slumber?

"We were all asleep at the wheel a few weeks ago, and that red Thunderbird could have snatched up all three of our boys if it wanted. But it didn't. Now, I've got my friends in St. Paul chasing down this Thunderbird connection, and I'll get an investigator to find out more about this Charani Bessant fellow, but we must take precautions."

Forsberg was shaking his head. "I'm just a dairy farmer, Albert, which is what I said twenty years ago when you set this in my lap. With Paul serving overseas, I agreed to come today, but I'm not a soldier."

Neither was Bjorn, but he still fought.

"I agree with Glen," Luning added. "Neither of us really can wrap our brains around this, which is why we let Chuck and Paul get trained."

"But Chuck and Paul aren't here now, are they?" Crain asked tersely.

"Your boy scouts cared more about merit badges than home, it seems," Luning retorted.

We've lost an entire generation.

Chuck Luning had been an All-American prospect with a scholarship to the University of Minnesota, but after getting Helen Ellis pregnant, he joined the service and took his young family to Georgia. Paul Forsberg had also been trained by veteran and scoutmaster Wally Crain, yet now, when they needed him, he was serving as a tank commander in Asia.

"I'll speak with Sheriff Betzing," Crain said. "Without giving details, he'll help keep an eye out."

"Sure he's not already in Triton's pockets?" Luning asked.

Crain glared. "Are you doubting me in—"

"And I'll use my contacts in St. Paul," Albert interrupted. "No one has died yet, and now we're ready."

But are we?

After Luning and Forsberg departed, Albert pulled Crain aside. "I saw Lily last night."

"At the fire?"

"No, under the willow tree. She was sixteen years old."

"A dream?"

Albert shook his head. "Somebody dropped a knife under the tree, and I can't tell if it's from the past or the future. You can go look if you want."

"No," Crain said. "I've got my own willow sitting in my front yard. I know all about that damn old tree. My wife writes under the stupid thing. She says it's a great inspiration."

"I'm sure it is. My point is that we've closed a loop, Lily and I. Apparently, I visited her in 1898, and she visited me in 1961. Adult Lily told me the visit was coming, to comfort me that we were on the right path. I also saw the boy with the snakeskin boots."

"Ah, the one Lily talks about."

Albert nodded. *The Omodai?* "He warned me about the Wintermaker waiting for me at the sawmill. He was under the impression that the Wintermaker was trying to change the future by attacking the past. If Lily dies, the larger loop will be broken. An Old Lily won't be able to guide a sixteen-year-old Lily, will she? This thought kept me up all night."

"My wife tried to explain this 'Grandfather Paradox' to me once, but it hurt my head." Crain scratched his scalp. "So, you're trying to say the Wintermaker is trying to kill Lily to stop a future where he is defeated … I guess that's encouraging."

"How so?"

"Well, our list of enemies is long. The quest for the Philosopher's Stone seems like a nuclear arms race. It could be the Jesuit Order, who figured out the double-cross by Father Guerin, or it could be the Periphery, who finally saw all this mumbo jumbo as a threat to humanity. Hell, it could even be some devout Pillager elder who sees it as a sacred right to kill the last members of the

Wijigan Clan. If the Wintermaker's involved, that means Order of Eos, doesn't it?"

Only he could find good news in such chaos. "I'm glad you're optimistic about this news, but I need to go speak to Migisi."

"What about?"

"We're not ready, Wally. When Lily faced the Wintermaker back in 1898, the Isanti Lodge had two priests, eight totems, and even two warriors to watch over us. When Fawn left, no one replaced her. When Father Guerin died, no one replaced him either. Sure, Marlin and Glen can sit in for Chuck and Paul, but they're not going to help us. If I was the Wintermaker, I'd pick now to attack also."

"I'll call Chuck down in Georgia. He's not on active duty like Paul, so if it hits the fan around here, I can find out if he'd be able to come. You going to speak to Migisi about Fawn?"

"I don't see what other choice we have. What about Paul?"

"I put a lot of time into getting Paul ready, and now Glen is sending his other son into the lion's den, thanks to that wife of his. The kid's a bit of a thick-skulled thug, but perhaps I can work with him."

"Can we trust a kid his age? I know Chris isn't mature enough."

"Brian Forsberg might surprise all of us."

CHAPTER THIRTEEN

The Lion's Den

Haggard Quarry
June 20, 1961

BIFF FORSBERG LEANED against the aluminum siding of the Haggard Quarry office. His shift had ended an hour ago and he'd refused Wally Crain's ride home.

I need to know if Paul is right about them.

Unfortunately, his brother Paul was on the other side of the world.

Shortly before 3 p.m., Ewan Haggard drove up, parked, and before Biff could even get to his feet, stomped into the office.

Is my uncle a villain?

Biff rose, but only to turn around to kneel. At the base of the aluminum siding, he pulled at the seam and reached in his hand for the pistol. At first, he wrapped his fingers around the grip, coveting the power of an instrument of murder. He turned the pistol to cradle it sideways in his hands.

Has this gun been used to murder people?

Biff felt as if he'd seen Uncle Ewan and all the others without their masks on, something Paul had tried to explain to him.

Two years ago, Paul Forsberg returned after his first tour in South Korea with news that he was reenlisting for another four years. Four years in the Army had turned Paul into a chiseled superhero, but during a morning of fishing down at the Crow Wing, Paul tried to warn him about their mother's relatives.

What else did Paul know about them?

Biff's leather boots kicked gravel as he walked around to the deck stairs. When he opened the front door, the secretary only glanced at him before returning to her phone call.

Biff walked past her desk and to the last office.

Uncle Ewan sat at his desk in a state of disarray. When he saw Biff, he gave an upward nod as he continued a conversation about pea rock for a construction site on the phone.

Biff waited several steps from the front of the desk, now ignored by Uncle Ewan, but when Biff shifted his hands from cradling the pistol to holding it by the handle, Uncle Ewan cleared his throat and said, "Something's come up, I'll call you back."

Uncle Ewan's eyes didn't leave Biff as he struggled to find the phone cradle. "Something on your mind, Brian?"

Biff nodded and took a few quick steps to set the pistol on the edge of the desk, yet he kept his fingertips on it.

"I suppose I owe you an explanation, don't I? Have a seat and we'll talk."

Uncle Ewan doesn't seem like a villain. Biff took his fingers off the pistol and sat. *The men in the Thunderbird felt like the real villains.*

"I forgot about the pistol, didn't I?" His uncle sighed. "I just left it there for any Tom, Dick, or Harry to find. Honestly, I assumed Red had dealt with it. You've been holding onto it all this time?"

Biff nodded. He'd put it behind the aluminum skirting that day in case anyone accused him of theft. He didn't steal it. He just put it in a place where it wouldn't get wet.

"You can keep it if you'd like."

"Pa wouldn't let me."

"I suppose he wouldn't, but I can see that you want it. I'll keep it for you if you want—until you're older."

Biff nodded, and Uncle Ewan grinned, reaching forward to slide it across the desk and then dropped it into a desk drawer. "You're a lot different than your brother. That boy would have raised a fuss the second he even saw a gun."

"He's overseas now."

"Ah, yes, I know all about that big brother of yours. For the longest time, your ma thought you were slow-witted, but it turns out you're just watching and keeping your yap shut. Did you tell anyone about our little incident?"

The incident about the Thunderbird had been shared, but no one else knew about the early morning standoff.

Biff shook his head.

"You like working here at the quarry?" Uncle Ewan asked with a different tone.

He's testing me. "I'd like to run the machinery one day."

"I'm sure. You'll be strong as an ox for football in the fall. I don't have any kids, so I'm not really comfortable being around them. I hope you understand, but you're trying really hard not to be a kid anymore. Bringing me a loaded pistol … I suppose you want me to see you as an adult, huh?"

"Who were those guys with Mr. Marquette and Mr. Stewart?" Biff flinched. *Why did I say that? Why did I cross that line?*

Uncle Ewan's brow tightened. "Haggards come from central Scotland, and our name roughly translates to 'son of the priest.' I'll let you stew on that paradox for a moment."

Mom thinks I'm slow-witted. Is he making fun of me too?

"Haggards," Uncle Ewan continued, "for better or worse, were peasants. We were farmer folks, just like your pa. No shame in rolling up your sleeves to shovel some shit or shovel some rock, right? Your ma and I, however, also have royal blood in us. You have this same royal blood. We're descended from the Sinclair

Clan, who in one way or another, have been rulers for countless centuries. Now, I ask you, young Forsberg, can you explain the paradox of your mother's maiden name?"

Biff pondered the royal blood comment for a moment, and then tucked away the name Sinclair for later contemplation. Uncle Ewan had a smug expression on his face, so Biff solved the paradox. "Priests are celibate. They don't have wives, so they shouldn't have sons."

Uncle Ewan's crooked smile appeared for a moment. "I was much older than you when I learned about my ancestry, and this paradox led me to believe all Haggards were bastards, born out of wedlock. It turns out, both my Haggard and Sinclair ancestors worshiped the old gods long before Christianity came to the shores of Alba. Haggards were not Catholic priests, it seems, and even though we went to the Christian church for weddings, funerals, and such, our religion existed thousands of years before Christ."

Uncle Ewan crossed his arms before asking, "Do you know what Monday, Tuesday, Wednesday, Thursday, and Friday have in common?"

"They all end with 'day,'" Biff mused before delivering the point Uncle Ewan wanted. "They're all based on Norse gods: Mani, Tyr, Odin, Thor, and Freya."

"When I saw you there holding that pistol, I didn't see your father, or your mother—I saw the Sinclair blood in you."

"So, you secretly worship Norse gods?"

Uncle Ewan laughed, loud. "Not exactly, Biff, but it's a lot closer to the truth than you'd imagine. Our Sinclair blood is old, and if you were my son, I'd have told you all the old legends and lore by now. In fact, you'd be shipped off to a summer camp to really train you. The old highland Haggards would explain it a hell of a lot better than I'm doing now."

Wow ... Paul was only scratching the surface. I'll have to tell him all about this the next time he comes home. "So, what does any of this have to do with those guys in the red Thunderbird?" Biff pressed.

Uncle Ewan hummed. "Our family legacy is important, Biff. There is a burden to being an official member of the Sinclair family. Here in Hiawatha County, the family is represented by the Stewarts, Marquettes, and myself, but our family tree is much larger than just those here on the shore of Lake Manitou."

"Triton Corporation," Biff said, and when Uncle Ewan seemed a bit alarmed, he added, "I've read about it in the newspaper. They own a bunch of businesses in Minnesota, including the quarry."

"I thought this "baby boom" generation was supposed to be a bunch of entitled lazy halfwits. You certainly pay attention, don't you?"

Biff shrugged.

"I won't bother bullshitting you. I might not tell you everything, but I won't bullshit you. Triton currently is made up of three ruling families: the Delhuts, the Sinclairs, and the Terronts. We all share the same Sinclair ancestry; however, the Terronts are French, the Delhuts are American, and the Sinclairs are Scottish. On paper, Triton Corporation owns steel mills, rubber plantations, and entertainment companies, but privately..."

Uncle Ewan rolled his eyes. "There is a bit of a power struggle happening at the highest levels of the company. Here in America, our most recent leader, Pierre Delhut, died and his son inherited a billion-dollar steel company. The head of the Sinclair family, Aleister Sinclair, is a paranoid old man who doesn't trust young Ross Delhut. You following so far?"

Biff nodded. In May, the Morrison family moved to Split Rock from Colorado, and nobody in sixth grade talked to the kid. "Nobody trusts the new kid."

"Our loyalty is to the Delhut family, and it's been that way for centuries. Now that Pierre Delhut is gone, old Aleister Sinclair is trying to steal power away. He doesn't trust the new American boss, so he sent his guys to poke their noses into our business. My partners, Stewart and Marquette, foolishly allowed strangers to visit. If it was a test of our defenses, we failed miserably. If it was for nefarious purposes, we failed miserably."

I guess that explains the shotguns.

Uncle Ewan shrugged. "You have more of a right with your quarter Sinclair blood than either of those men had stepping foot in my quarry. I swore an oath, and it's a blood oath. If I freaked you out by coming in with guns, I hope you understand why."

"I do." *This is what Paul tried to warn me about.*

"And I hope you understand why I need secrecy."

Biff nodded.

"See, it's that royal blood of yours, Biff. Don't be thinking you're just the son of a lowly dairy farmer. You've got grit, and combined with your blood, you might make something of yourself. Do you have any more questions?"

Who was Charani Bessant?

What's up with the Nazis?

What kind of gods do you worship?

What's in the tunnel?

Why would anyone guard a rock quarry?

Biff shook his head.

Uncle Ewan stood up, and Biff stood also. "Whenever you want that gun, it's yours. I'm going to talk to Red, also. After lunch break, I want you to be my wingman for the rest of this summer. I want to show you what it takes to run this quarry, and if you want, we can talk more about your birthright. Would you like that?"

"Yeah, I was already a fan of Norse mythology ever since I read *Lord of the Rings.*"

"*Lord of the Rings,* huh? I'll share some stories Mr. Tolkien never heard of at Oxford."

Where There's Smoke

Old Copper Road
June 20, 1961

IN HER WHITE work dress, Nicole Guerin carefully climbed past the protective metal rail and, after brushing away a spot, sat down on the wooden planks of the bridge, her feet dangling over the edge. She opened her father's old lunch box and unpacked the little meal beside her.

The Crow Wing River flowed fifteen feet under her, and the birds went about their business as if nothing had happened.

It had become her new routine following the fire.

From Split Rock, a boy on a bicycle came flying down the hill. He pedaled along with intensity, making him fly as fast as many of the cars that went by. Chris Luning gave her a little wave and then kept peddling, most likely to Biff Forsberg's house on the other side of the river valley or all the way to Carousel Park.

Nicole longed to have a twelve-year-old's free heart.

A familiar maroon Chevrolet truck passed by Chris, descended the valley, shook the bridge, and then slid to a stop as it began its ascent into town. It pulled off the road into the grass, leaning awkwardly into the ditch.

Gavin MacPherson emerged from the truck. He wore a pair of denim overalls without a shirt underneath and a red International Harvester hat. His thick leather boots kicked up rocks as he jogged to the bridge. "Hey, how have you been?"

"Been better."

"I've looked for you at the creamery after dropping off my loads, but I haven't seen you."

"Yeah, I took a job in the bottling line to help make ends meet until my dad can go back to work. It's an 8-5 shift. I'm on my lunch break right now."

"How is your dad?"

"It'll be a month before the burns on his arms heal, so he has to keep them wrapped with special gauze. He's in a lot of pain, but my mom is taking care of him. Until he can work again, I have to help put groceries on the table."

"That's a tough way to spend your summer," Gavin said. "I work every day, but at least I get some free time when my chores are done. How's your grandmother?"

Nicole held back tears, thinking of her most recent visit to the hospital. "Not good."

Gavin climbed past the railing and sat down on the side opposite the lunchbox. Without invitation, he picked up *Doctor Zhivago* and began thumbing through it, which felt as personal as if he'd started unbuttoning her blouse.

Flustered, she added, "She's in the hospital at Brainerd. They have her on a ventilator because of all the damage the smoke did to her lungs. Because of a lack of oxygen, she hasn't really regained consciousness yet."

"I'm sorry," Gavin said softly, setting down her book.

"What are you sorry for? If it weren't for you, she would be dead."

Gavin merely looked at the river flowing below his feet.

"I'm serious. You're a hero. I saw you run around to the back of her house with the ax. You must've cut a hole right through the wall and pulled her out, didn't you?"

"It seemed like the quickest way to get to her. It was only some lathe and plaster, and fire was already burning in front of her window."

Nicole moved her hand from her lap to touch the denim near his knee. "I know you and your father don't want any credit, but you'll always be a hero to me." She withdrew her hand. *How can I flirt while talking about the fire?* "Would you like a slice of chocolate cake? I packed way too much food for dessert."

"Oh, no. I couldn't."

"Go ahead. I probably would have left it here for the birds anyway."

"Well, if you're not going to eat it," Gavin began and accepted the tinfoil wrapped slice of cake.

"Here, put the tinfoil back in the lunchbox," Nicole said as she watched him eat the cake with his fingers.

Gavin MacPherson smelled like a barn, his forearms were riddled with a hundred red marks, likely from hauling hay bales, and he had a layer of dirt upon his face where rivulets of sweat made channels through it—it terrified Nicole how gorgeous he was to her. Watching him eat made it worse.

He glanced over at her and smiled.

"Would you like a drink?" She poured water from the thermos into the lid and offered it to him. She watched his lips wrap around the bottom of the cup where her own lips had recently been. He'd been on her mind almost as much as the sinister red Thunderbird.

"What did your grandmother give me that night?"

"It was Grandfather Jean's notebook. It was a journal he kept."

"A journal? It must have been pretty important. Once I broke through the wall and found her, she crawled back into the fire to get it. I had to pull her back by her foot or else she might have never come out."

"My grandfather was a missionary in the Philippines," Nicole said, thinking of the first few pages she'd read. "He died a long time ago, so I guess she wanted to save some memories of him."

"Well, I hope she gets better soon," Gavin said and then nervously bobbed his head. "Say … if you're working each morning, I could give you a ride to work instead of bringing you home."

"That's nice, but now that my dad is unable to work, I'm actually using his car. I came out here because it's better than sitting in a cafeteria with a bunch of old wives."

"Oh, sure."

Her ears felt hot. *Am I blushing?* "But I like having my lunch break with you. Are you usually free this time of day?"'"

"Usually, yeah. My dad often sends me to town to run some errands. Is this normally your lunch hour?"

"Noon to one, every day, but if it's raining, I eat in the cafeteria with everybody else."

"Well, I'll look for you then," Gavin said, rising. "Save me a spot, would ya?"

"I'll do that."

Nicole watched him walk back to his truck and then almost flip it over as he drove precariously along the side of the steep ditch. She let out a deep sigh of relief once he was gone, wary of her own desires. She picked up her book to read more about the illicit affair happening between poor Lara and the wealthy Komarovsky.

Life imitating art?

AT THE END of her shift, she quickly returned home and helped her mother prepare supper.

Once supper was over and dishes were done, Nicole ended up standing at the charred ruins of her grandmother's home.

The hundred dreamcatchers and their secrets had transformed into ash along with the walls, and the only metal that remained was the old iron stove which stood naked amongst the rubble. Even days afterwards, she could still see smoke from some of the old beams and feel the heat as she walked.

Her father had been born inside the ashen square she now stood beside, and he had almost died in there as well. The little wooden fence that encircled the house had been mostly knocked down along the front by volunteer firefighters who responded to the call, but Nicole could see the back of the fence contrasted with the dark foliage of the woods leading toward Carousel Park. Somewhere on the other side of the woods, kids were screaming and enjoying their summers as they rode rides and gorged on sugary treats, but Nicole felt as if the theme park was a million miles away.

A few feet from the big cottonwood that towered over the other trees, a thin trail entered the woods. When her older sisters lived at home, all of them would walk the trail and sneak into the park rather than pay admission.

The trail ended at the Venetian Romantic Rowboat Ride, where couples would cross the bridge over Kanaranzi Creek. Faux-Italian singers serenaded those who waited in line. Couples took the floating path around the shallow waters behind Carousel Island, which was far more exotic in the night than in the day.

Nicole and her siblings would magically appear like fairies out of the woods and run across the bridge to the main part of the park. Now she realized the park attendants ignored them in patronizing sympathy for their poverty, which is why she rarely went there anymore.

Gavin MacPherson's words had troubled her for most of the day, and when she reached the backside of the charred house, she stood for a moment trying to remember where the window had once been. A few feet away, she saw Gavin's ax, where he must've tossed it aside once he'd made a hole.

She knew she was falling for Gavin, not only because he was a hero but also because he didn't treat her like a poor half-breed the way the rest of the town did.

The fire showed Gavin's true character.

Nothing grew behind Grandma Lily's house since the house shaded the eastern sun and the big cottonwood shaded the western sun. Even at its tallest, the sun could filter only through some thin locust branches to cast light upon the back of the house. She and her grandmother had once transplanted ferns to the back, but they died by the end of summer. A dirt swathe almost five feet wide permanently existed behind her house—there was nothing to burn.

Some of the back wall had fallen onto the dead patch, and it had also turned to brittle gray ash. Within the ash, she saw a small object. Nicole used her toe to inspect it.

At first, she didn't recognize the silvery object, so she crouched down and picked it up with her fingers. From the distinct four-hole pattern of the steel hood to the round flint wheel still connected, Nicole held the lighter, realizing suddenly that the supposed accident might have been arson.

Why would there be fire on a patch of dirt?

Dirt doesn't burn.

Yet on the night of the fire, fire had encircled the house, trapping Lily. Gavin went around the corner, where the flames were smaller under the window, which meant gasoline or kerosene had been used to turn the small house into an inferno before anyone could even smell smoke.

Nicole looked back to the house.

Confronted with this fact, her father would react irrationally and grow even more paranoid. The same fact would undoubtedly be ignored by her mother, who would never be able to understand ill will.

Grandmother Lily had greeted the strangers in the red car with a knife in her hand, and then immediately went to T.I. for help …

What does this mean?

What should I do?

Nicole turned her back on the burned house and took a few steps toward the forest.

Even though the branches scratched and clawed at her, she pushed through, still clutching the head of the lighter. Once under the canopy of the woods, she could see the lake to her right and Old Copper Road up the hill to her left.

After just a few extra steps into the woods, she found an empty five-gallon gasoline can leaning against the trunk of an oak tree, confirming her worst fears.

Crushed Cans

Split Rock, MN
June 23, 1961

CHRIS LUNING BLAMED Biff for ruining the summer. After all, if he hadn't eaten the lunches, he wouldn't have gotten in trouble, which resulted in him working at the darned quarry. And because of him, his father had insisted Chris also get a job instead of "screwing around the house and fishing the summer away."

Chris took the last few bites of supper and stood up. His mother stopped her work in the kitchen, buttoned the top button of his shirt, and kissed him on the forehead. "Be a good listener tonight."

A scout is obedient. "I will."

His mother had wanted him to stay at home for another summer, but between Biff working at the quarry and Jimmy helping on the farm, she lost the argument to her father and husband.

Outside the house, Grandpa Albert waited in the running car, but in the distance, Chris saw his father walking across the road from the lumber mill.

"Good luck on your first day of work," his father called out from the edge of the road that separated the big warehouse from the house. "Do a good job."

A scout is trustworthy. "I'm just picking up garbage, Dad. Any idiot can do that."

His father had lost his battle also. If up to him, Chris would have been given a broom to sweep the sawmill, but his mother worried too much about the danger of the machines. Daddy's little girl went to her father, and soon Grandpa Albert came up with a new solution—working at Carousel Island. Chris knew this option was better than being the boss's kid or a momma's boy.

I miss being a kid already.

"Ready to go, Champ?" Grandpa Albert asked as soon as Chris opened the door.

"Why's everybody making such a big deal about this?"

"You're growing up, Christopher. A job means responsibility, and our world needs responsible people who can be trusted. You'll get to show everybody what you're made of."

Instead of playing at Carousel Park, Chris now had to work there each Friday and Saturday night. Even though the job would be potentially humiliating, it meant he'd earn his own money.

A scout is thrifty.

He'd already met his manager and went through the job description, but for his first shift or two, he'd work as an apprentice to the main custodian—an odd duck known as Can Man.

As soon as Grandpa Albert parked, he got out of the car too.

"What are you doing?" Chris asked.

"I'm going to have a few drinks and listen to some music in the roof garden. Come and find me when your shift is over."

The two had barely left the parking lot when a man came up to them and gave his grandpa a hug.

"Good to see you, Cameron," Grandpa Albert greeted.

"You too," Cameron "Can Man" Guerin said, avoiding eye contact with Chris. "How's Chuck?"

"Chuck's good," Grandpa Albert answered. "He's in Georgia learning how to be a helicopter pilot. Can you believe that?"

Cameron nodded. "He used to like climbing trees. He's not afraid of heights."

"I supposed that does make sense. How's your father doing?" Grandpa Albert asked.

"He's home now."

"That's good to hear. And your grandmother?"

"She's still in the hospital in Brainerd."

"You might not believe it, but your grandmother taught my Sunday school classes when I was a boy. She'll be in my prayers. When you see her, tell her that Albert Fisher sends her his regards." Grandpa Albert turned to Chris. "Cameron, this is my other grandson. This is Christopher. He's going to be your apprentice."

A scout is kind. Chris extended a hand. "Pleased to meet you, Cameron."

"Any friend of Chuck is a friend of mine."

"Yeah, well, he's my brother, but sure, I understand."

Is this why Grandpa Albert wanted me to work here? Because of Can Man?

Grandpa Albert went his separate way, leaving Chris to his apprenticeship.

Chris already knew Cameron Guerin, but only from a distance.

Cameron "Can Man" Guerin was odd. Chris didn't want to be mean about it, but the twenty-one-year-old had the mentality of an elementary student. His eyes were nervous, his gait was hunched, and he shuffled like his shoes weighed ten pounds more than regular shoes. His dark chair was combed over from one ear to the other, held in place by a thick hair gel that left a coating of dandruff on his shoulders.

"Friday nights are the worst," Cameron said, handing Chris a pair of gloves.

"Oh yeah, Can Man, why is that?" *Remember to be kind.*

Cameron didn't notice the nickname. "On Saturday nights, folks don't quite drink as much because they don't want to attend church with a hangover. Fridays—they know they can sleep it off."

That was all Cameron had to say for almost an hour as they made a sweep of the park. By the time they finished, the sun had set, allowing park-goers the luxury of just dropping the trash on the ground instead of finding a bin, and the teenagers that came on Fridays often drank and caroused.

Chris helped empty a garbage can into the dumpster at the front corner of the parking lot and let the lid slam down loudly. He placed the garbage can back into the cart built with plywood and repurposed bicycle wheels and tightened the strap around the belly of the can.

Growing up sucks. I should be playing instead of working.

Chris walked beside Cameron, who rolled his cart down the middle of the pathway, hunting for stray wrappers or empty bottles. Cameron paused in front of the crazy mirrors, smiling as they made his body long and twisted. He nudged Chris to do the same.

Chris looked down, refusing.

Cameron raised his arms, and they became octopus tentacles reaching out of the water.

Chris saw a group of kids' glance at them. *A scout is loyal.* Chris indulged him and moved his arms, bringing a belly laugh from Cameron.

Cameron's smile quickly left, and he continued pushing his cart. "Mr. Shoemaker said we're not supposed to talk to any of the customers, especially the children. Just keep your head down when you work."

Chris didn't care; his head was on a swivel as elementary kids tried for the prizes at the midway.

At night, the illuminated carousel was more magical than ever, and at the garbage can near the gate, both paused to watch the majestic horses leaping high into the air, followed by cats, rabbits, and other equally beautiful creatures.

"I like the songs it plays," Cameron said sadly.

Chris waited patiently for them to continue.

Next came the large buildings that housed the bumper cars and roller-skating rink. The line for the bumper cars was filled with middle school kids.

Chris remembered Biff taunting Can Man with pelts of "Bucky" and "What's up Doc" because of his teeth. Now, Biff was too tired to play. Jimmy Nielson, also, was worked like a man. The smirks of fifth grade boys were directed at Chris, shielding Can Man from overt teasing. This time.

Cameron retreated, moving to the roller-skating rink filled mostly with middle school girls who circled and twirled in packs. They waved at Chris before whispering and giggling to each other. Chris worked feverishly just to move on. Together, he and Cameron swept through the benches, changing area, and the dining tables surrounding the skate rental booth.

Unlike the rest of the park, which seemed more fantastical in the night, the peony gardens became a maze of waist high shadows, and the large flowering blossoms turned into shadowy faces. The paths led to the Roof Garden where live bands performed for the adult crowd. Even though the Roof Garden had the most garbage, it was the most genial crowd.

"If it isn't the working man!"

Grandpa Albert stood with two drinks in his hand. Chris ignored all protocols and rushed forward, wrapping his arms around his grandfather. "Hey, Grandpa."

Cameron looked down, nervously.

"We're not supposed to talk to the customers," Chris said with a grin at his grandfather.

"Then I'll let you two get back to work," Grandpa Albert whispered, with a nod to Cameron.

Cameron nodded back and kept moving through the tables facing the dance hall, pulling Chris away.

"I'll be right here when your shift is over," Grandpa Albert called out.

He'll probably have cotton candy waiting.

After sweeping through the two-story building, Cameron and Chris returned to the cart, pushing it toward the beach, where the water rides were beginning to close for the night.

Just behind the beach area, the grandest attraction of Carousel Island—the Python—stood towering above the oak trees. Built in 1947, the wooden roller coaster had been painted green and was visible from almost any shore of Lake Manitou, including from distant St. John on the opposite shore of the lake, seven miles away. Standing eighty feet tall at its highest peak, the eighteen-passenger roller coaster would shoot across the waters of Lake Manitou before looping around in the woods of Deadwood Island and returning back to the mainland. The popular three-thousand-foot track reached speeds of fifty miles an hour and took two minutes to complete.

"My father normally maintains the roller coaster," Cameron said.

Instead of Louis Guerin, another man sat on a stool behind chatting away with the young woman collecting tickets.

Beyond the Python, an illuminated path fro the Venetian Romantic Rowboat Ride led to the arched cement bridge that spanned Kanaranzi Creek. Cameron quickly passed by all the young lovers and took the wooden bridge that floated upon the surface of the water. Chris paused to test the buoyancy of the floating bridge, hastening the crossing of his mentor.

At the center of the island, the trees had been cleared away for a second carousel, this one with only horses, and for a large stage, where bands would provide music for the local teens from Wadena, Park Rapids, and even Brainerd.

"My sister is somewhere in that mess." Cameron grinned. "Do you know Nicole Guerin?"

Do I? Chris had fallen in love with her back in third grade, and whenever he saw her, his heart fluttered. *Is it good or bad that I'm working beside her brother?* "She used to be my babysitter."

The noise of the band, the crowd, and the passing roller coaster made Cameron proceed with total focus while Chris lost all of his. The cart was full of garbage, and after the sweep around the back of the concert stage, they returned to the front of the park.

As they reached the other side of the stage, the drums exploded, and screams filled the air.

Chris started to look around but paused when his eyes landed on Cameron.

"Can Man, what—"

"Something's wrong," Cameron interrupted.

The cacophony Chris had heard had been too loud for the circular drum set. A pulsing gasp and the crackle of instruments flowed through the crowd and then—a different kind of terror.

The crowd of teenagers divided: some ran toward the bridge and others ran from the stage and into the woods.

Others stood or dropped to the ground on the dance floor, but all of them looked toward the trees opposite the stage.

Chris suddenly realized what sound was absent—the familiar noise of the roller coaster.

"Let's go, Cameron!"

Once they reached the rollercoaster dozens of onlookers stood looking up into the trees, where bodies hung from the branches. Some writhed and screamed while others hung limply like raggedy dolls.

"We need bandages! Get us some cloth to help with the bleeding!"

A scout is brave. Heroes bolted past them toward the floating bridge, but Chris could only take a single step closer.

Boys were climbing trees like monkeys to reach the figures caught in the branches. Flashlights and lanterns quickly brought the details of the scene into the light.

At the curve of the track, where the Python banked and turned back toward the lake, the railing had been sheared away and one of the steel tracks stuck out like a finger, pointing toward the swath of destruction through the trees.

Blood rained down onto a boy climbing one of the trees.

In another tree, three boys lifted a body from the crook, the limp arms doing nothing to help the descent.

"Nicole!" Cameron shouted, and then like a lost calf, continued to bellow her name.

Almost unable to breath, Chris wrapped his arms around his chest.

A third tree held a frantic young woman, whose long hair had somehow been caught in the branches of a tree, causing her to spin and dangle as two boys tried to lift her legs while another tried to free her hair. Chris grimaced as her plaid dress lifted to reveal her panties and long socks–it wasn't Nicole though.

He couldn't swallow and almost gagged at the bile surging up from his belly.

Looking away from her awkward rescue, Chris spotted the overturned rollercoaster cars. One car contained four passengers, still buckled in, sitting wide-eyed upon flat ground.

The passengers in the other two cars were not so fortunate.

One had rolled and twirled, leaving it looking like a crushed tin can. A group of shirtless boys stood around a bloody corpse where they had used their shirts to sop up the blood from an unseen wound.

A few feet from that, another group wept around a dead body.

Beyond that, Chris could see a group of young men gathered around an overturned car, whose smooth, silver wheels rotated freely, unbound by their normal track.

When the boys finally flipped the car, a collective gasp and groan came from the crowd, for under the car were two severed bodies, cut in half when the car hit the ground and slid to a stop. From the blood and gore, a third body moved, and despite the carnage, hands pulled a young girl, a sole survivor, from the backseat.

"Cam—"

Cameron had vanished, leaving Chris alone and frightened.

Adults came running to the scene, trying to bring order to the chaos.

The wounded were treated right there on the cold ground of Deadwood Island, and the remains were quickly covered with shirts and jackets.

Hundreds stood around the scene of the accident, watching helplessly as bodies were gathered under lantern light.

Chris felt his knees weaken, and soon he joined the others who openly wept. Behind the whisper of prayers, Chris thought he heard singing and chanting coming from the darkness of the trees, and when he looked toward the sound, the shadows grew darker and began to move.

Am I seeing things? Am I about to faint? What is that?

The wail of sirens soon replaced the sound of chanting, but even when the flashing lights arrived, the ordeal was not over, for none of the vehicles could cross the footbridge to the island. Men with stretchers came pushing through the crowd, carrying off the worst of the wounded.

Chris crouched as the world revolved around him.

The hazy details spread through the crowd quickly.

Four passengers had been killed instantly. Gladys Kruger of Walker, Minnesota, died when her body came free and hit a tree. The parents of Leona and Mary Brady of Sisseton, South Dakota arrived on the island along with the swell of other adults from the park, only to realize their girls had been the two killed when the front car flipped over. Walter Zibas of St. Cloud had been in the seat behind them, died from a broken neck, yet his sister Ruth had miraculously survived.

In the crowd, one of the onlookers threw arms around Cameron—it was Nicole. Chris took a few steps closer. Nicole didn't say anything but simply clutched tightly to her brother as she wept. Finally, she said, "They're going to blame Dad for this, and he wasn't even here. Let's go, Cameron. Let's go."

Wait, take me with you.

A moment later, Grandpa Albert emerged from the crowd, gathering Chris up in an embrace that was too futile to shield him from the trauma he'd already seen.

A scout is supposed to be prepared.

I wasn't prepared.

CHAPTER SIXTEEN

Fuel for the Fire

Old Copper Road
June 24, 1961

D EADWOOD ISLAND GREW silent as the sun began to rise above the horizon. Wally Crain stood along the western shore, the toes of his boots pointed out toward the main body of the lake. As anticipated, looky-loos were already jumping in their boats to see for themselves what had happened the previous night. A Hiawatha County sheriff's deputy anchored his boat a hundred yards offshore, which kept the other boats at a distance, for the time being.

Wally wore his LMFD jacket and yellow helmet to further convince onlookers that the scene of the accident had been tightly locked down.

Now that the sun had come up, he could view the arched back of the roller coaster and the two tracks reaching out from the mainland. A few yards behind him, the silvery polish of the uninterrupted track suddenly stopped at the place where the track had broken and had sent the riders smashing into the trees.

Over at the park, a dozen emergency vehicles still flashed their red lights, but on the island, all the bodies had been taken away and the crowds were dispersed, leaving Wally alone with the congealed blood and trees.

He heard footsteps and turned toward the heart of the island. Ed Nielson, also wearing LMFD gear, walked toward him carrying two cups of coffee.

The long night seemed to have little effect on the leathery farmer. "The state BCA investigators have arrived to replace us. This coffee is a friendly fare-thee-well."

Wally took the offered cup. "BCA? Are they going to be treating this as a criminal investigation?"

"Don't get ahead of yourself. The BCA is here to do a forensic analysis of what happened," Ed said after taking a sip of his coffee. "My bet is that governmental agencies were fighting it out in St. Paul, and somebody gave it to the BCA to keep it on neutral turf. This is gonna get pretty ugly."

Wally could see teams of investigators being led from the parking lot to the little concrete bridge that spanned Kanaranzi Creek. "Follow me," he said, turning away from the beach and into the woods. "There's something I want to show you."

"I was dreading this conversation."

"It's not what you think."

Wally looked at the trees to get his bearings until he found the big oak tree. Walking to the northern side, he found a bare patch where the bark had been cut away to the lighter pulp beneath. He pointed to the message that had been carved there with an old Barlow knife: Earl loves Nancy.

"Earl loves Nancy," Ed repeated. "I take it *you* carved this? That's your given name, isn't it?"

Wally nodded. "Nancy is the only one who still calls me Earl. It's been here almost two decades now. I came here a lot after I got back from the Pacific. It's where I first met Nancy, and on one of our first dates, we snuck away from the concert, kissed under this tree, and I carved a declaration of my love."

Wally smacked the tree as if it were his trusted steed. "I tried to find a little silver lining after the nightmare I saw last night."

Never sentimental, Ed cut to the chase, "So…?"

"I don't know what to think."

"Something's happening, and we're just standing here holding our dicks in our hands. First, they stole our queen, and now this. The Isanti Lodge is a mess. Even if we were at full strength, who are we fighting, Wally? Just point me in the right direction."

"I need you to hold steady, Ed. If we get emotional and carried away, we might just make matters worse. Father Guerin said our enemy will wear false faces and will only remove the mask at the last moment. Let's see what the state inspectors say first. Maybe we're just looking at two accidents."

"Bullshit." Ed bristled. "A bunch of kids are dead, and the Guerin family was hit hard, Wally. The Isanti Lodge needs to convene. All of us."

"Paul Forsberg is stationed in Vietnam. How am I supposed to get him to show up?"

"That's why we should have chosen Glen instead of your wunderkind Eagle Scout. What good is he to us if he's not here when we need him."

"You know why we couldn't pick Glen to replace his father."

"Careful, Wally. He's my brother-in-law."

"Yes, and Bonnie comes from good Forsberg stock. Glen chose to marry that Haggard woman, and he was already married before his father passed. We couldn't risk it. Now, I'm sure Paul will somehow find out what happened without me needing to raise alarms. My biggest concern is Albert."

"Albert Fisher might be old, but have you heard Marlin Luning's cough? That damn lumber mill is killing him. How can we rely on either of them when the going gets tough? With Paul in Germany, we're just a bunch of old men."

"Father Guerin wrote that the battle would be both physical and spiritual."

"And with Lily gone, what does that leave us with? Norval Riel? What do we know about that man?"

"First of all, Lily's not gone. Get that through your head, Ed. Norval knows more about this stuff than any of us."

"But we didn't pick him, Wally. He was sent to us after Paul White Wolf died. There was a reason Jean Guerin left the Jesuits."

"Norval Riel wasn't sent by the Jesuits," Wally retorted. "What do you want from me, Ed? Huh?" Wally asked, raising his voice so loudly that he looked around to see if they'd been noticed. "Let's go. Maybe I can make sense of things once I get a little sleep."

Wally began walking, not even checking to see if Ed followed. By the time he reached the clearing at the dance hall, he saw the rest of the Lake Manitou Fire Department volunteers clustered together sipping coffee.

Deputy Charlie Roy led the BCA inspectors into the clearing, where they began to set down their gear.

Fire Chief Ken Uselman stood a few paces from the rest of his crew. He nodded when he saw Wally and Ed.

Glen Forsberg stood with Dale Sundby, Otto Waln, Warren Lorentz, and Dean Hoemberg.

Uselman declared, "Well, I should probably get you fellows home to your wives. Until the investigation is done, keep your traps shut. Rumors will only make matters worse, and people in the community will take whatever you say as Gospel."

Chief Uselman led the Lake Manitou Fire Department back the way they'd come hours earlier, and when they reached the walking bridge, their boots echoed across the waters.

Ed left for his own truck, but Wally, having come from St. John, joined the others at the ladder truck.

After returning the ladder truck and medical truck to the station, Wally looked at his watch to realize it was only seven o'clock.

He sat in his green GMC for a few moments before starting it up and heading north instead of south. He took Highway 34 west, and when he reached Nimrod road, he let his foot off the gas before he decided against heading up to the Rez for answers he didn't want to hear yet.

Instead, he stayed in routine.

Ulman Oil Co-Op was located on the western side of St. John on the Sebeka Road. Wally had been supplying gas, oil, propane, and fuel oil to farms, houses, and businesses around Lake Manitou for more than a decade through worse weather than a postman could possibly imagine. During the winter, lives were often on the line, and because of this, Wally delivered regardless of what life threw at him.

"I've been listening to the radio about the accident at Carousel Park," Gene Ulman said as soon as Wally stepped through the doors of the office. "How bad was it?"

Wally grabbed a clipboard from the wall hangers and checked the delivery slips. "Pretty bad, Gene. Pretty bad."

"I always thought it was a bad idea to put that coaster over water. Those footings are bound to move in the mud every time the ice comes off the lake."

"It wasn't the footings, Gene," Wally said, flipping through orders. *It was sabotage.* "Is this slip wrong? I just stopped at Haggard Quarry on Wednesday."

"It's correct. They've been burning the midnight oil, so to speak. Apparently, business is booming and they're striking while the iron's hot.

Upon arriving at Haggard Quarry, Red Dobie stepped out to greet him. No matter the season, Red wore a Detroit Red Wings stocking cap over his spaghetti-colored hair. Red had also been born and raised in Hiawatha County. Although Red was a bachelor, his family tree connected back to the Sinclairs through a line in

Albany, New York. For all intents and purposes, though, Red Dobie *was* Haggard Quarry.

Red waited at the big fuel oil tanks while Wally prepared the discharge hose. "Heard all about the disaster at Carousel Island. How many folks died?"

"Too many for one night."

"Agreed. So did I hear correctly that the roller coaster came off its tracks?"

"I helped only with securing the scene of the accident. I didn't get to do much as far as investigation goes," Wally admitted.

He handed the job clipboard to Red, who signed the slip, took his copy, and handed it back. "I suppose you've been up since yesterday morning."

"I'll be sound asleep by this afternoon, that's for sure."

"Wish I could catch a break. They've been working me to the bone over the past few weeks."

"I've noticed the oil orders have doubled. You guys supplying every road between here and St. Paul?"

"It's not the pink quartz." Red shrugged as he worked on the valve of his storage tank. "We reached the bottom of the seam, but apparently, there is some special type of granite below the quartz. You ever curl before?"

"Of course."

"You might not know it, but each curling stone is mined on an island off the coast of Scotland, Ailsa Craig. Haggard has a team of quarrymen come all the way from Scotland to work this seam of granite."

"Is he looking to get into the curling stone business?"

"Who knows? Apparently, it's some rare stone, so he's trying to capitalize on it, which means I'm working overtime this summer."

"I see." Wally felt his body burning on fumes. "Well, hang in there, Red. We can both sleep when we're dead."

After leaving Haggard Quarry, Wally returned to Ulman Oil, turned in his clipboard, and arrived home by mid-morning.

His three daughters were playing on the swing set when he pulled into the old farmstead. All three ran up to his truck to greet him with hugs.

"Is your mother inside?" Wally asked.

"She's writing. She told us to stay outside and play. Can we go inside now?"

"I suppose that would be fine."

The girls dashed ahead of him, throwing the screen door open so that it slammed loudly as it closed.

His wife reached the door before he could open it. "How are you doing?"

"A lot of shook-up folks," Wally said. "Pretty messy scene."

"Anyone we know?"

"I don't think so. Mostly folks that drove in for the weekend."

"Come on in; I brewed up a fresh pot of coffee."

"I already made my oil run, so I'll pass on the coffee for now. I think I might need something a little stiffer than coffee to get me through the day."

"I promised the girls I'd bring them into Brainerd to do some shopping. Do you want to come with us, you know, to keep your mind off things?"

"No, I think I could use a little time for myself," Wally said, stripping off the denim shirt he'd worn for two days.

At the dining room table, he saw Nancy's typewriter and a stack of completed pages. "I'd appreciate the solitude. We'll talk about it more when you get home."

Oshiimeyan

Mizheekay Band of Ojibwe Reservation
June 26, 1961

MIGISI ASIBIKAASHI WEPT after Wally Crain left his front porch. Not a single tear had been shed while the oil delivery driver smoked with him as they faced the evening sun. Migisi sifted the news, holding it in his heart and mind without emotional reaction. He would pray before acting or speaking, and then he would give Wally his opinion on matters.

Migisi wept in relief.

Wally delivered an update from the hospital about Lily. While losing her hair in the fire, her flesh was remarkably unharmed, but her lungs remained a grave concern and kept her on oxygen for the near future.

"Louis is looking at a nursing home up at Leech Lake once she's released from the hospital," Crain had explained. "Given Lily's age, the recovery is going to take quite a while. I can drive you to Brainerd if you'd like."

Migisi had shaken off the idea. "The Tak-Pei will know she's gone, and the Wintermaker will certainly sense it. I must stay here to make sure the Horned Serpent does not rise."

He wept for lost youth.

Now in his 70s, Migisi was older than his own grandfather Nanak had been the year the Wintermaker rose from the depths of Lake Manitou. Migisi's fingers were crooked and tremulous, his back bent with time, and his left eye twitched, leaving his vision uncertain from hour to hour. Lily had also become something ancient and weak.

It didn't help that his mind still painted a perfect picture of him and Tew playing along the shores of the Blue Knife River as children. It was a time before boarding schools changed them both; a time before they faced the ancient evil that slumbered in the water near their home. As a boy, he believed he'd stare into the eyes of the Horned Serpent and thrust a fatal blow to any darkness that stood before him. Now he struggled to defecate in the morning.

He wept in anger.

The murders of his mother and grandfather still festered in his heart, and he now blamed the Tak-Pei more than he blamed Adam Thunder Face for the heinous deed. The Tak-Pei didn't care about race, age, or religion. The four victims at Carousel Park provided the same sustenance that his family had provided six decades ago, and just as Grandfather Nanak had been the first of many, the deaths in the roller coaster accident would only give the Tak-Pei strength to create more accidents. The timing was too perfect. Death within days of the summer solstice—at exactly the spot where Tew had defeated the Tak-Pei previously.

He angrily wiped his tears from his wrinkled face, chewed on his bottom lip, and wished he could cover his hands in the blood of the man responsible for the accidents.

Migisi left the porch to cook a simple supper upon the cast iron stove in the center of his cabin. Unlike his grandfather, who filled his ceiling and walls with the relics needed as the keeper of the Wijigan, Migisi's cabin was plainly lined with cedar, from his bed to the cupboards that kept his own secrets covertly filed away. In the cedar-framed portraits, the faces of the past stared at him.

He wept in remorse.

His pride broke the family apart in a time they needed to band together—at the return of the Serpent Star.

For a decade, the Isanti Lodge had prepared itself for the return of the Serpent Star and the arrival of the Wishwee, the one destined to defeat the evil in the depths of the lake.

Father Guerin felt confident that the Creator (regardless of name) guided them to a righteous confrontation with a force of darkness. The team was complete, its members were strong, and they had been unified in purpose.

Halley's Comet, the scientists declared, would arrive in May of 1910. The Serpent Star, Guerin explained, would usher in the next era of the Seven Fires. Just like a solstice gave strength to the spiritual word, the comet would bring with it the power to defeat the Horned Serpent. Armed with the Wintermaker's own weapon, Guerin believed the Wintermaker would be vulnerable enough to be destroyed by the Great Thunderbird.

And I was supposed to be the Great Thunderbird incarnate.

Despite his confidence, the Isanti Lodge's leader fretted about little details. A week before the comet came closest to earth, Jean Guerin decided a return trip to Mankato was in order, so he hopped in his car and drove the 200 miles from the Blue Knife River to the Blue Earth River.

"Why do you run off to confirm what we already know?" Superintendent White Wolf asked what they all wanted to ask Guerin. "We know how the Philosopher's Stone was found at Mankato and brought here to Lake Manitou."

"If anything is missing, my trip to Mankato will confirm it. The last time I went was winter, and I was rushed. This time I'll make sure. It's only a day's drive."

Jean Guerin returned in a coffin.

Instead of fighting the Wintermaker with the Water Drum, the Isanti Lodge buried its leader next to Nanakonan, Winnie, and Big

Squeak Weber. The Blue Earth County Sheriff's department informed them that Guerin had been fueling his car at a gas station in LeHillier, MN when a near collision at the nearby intersection sent a car crashing into the pumps where Jean was crushed into his own vehicle.

In bitterness and despair, Fawn challenged the plan to confront the Wintermaker. Instead of being allowed to mourn, Lily vented her rage at her cousin.

In that moment, instead of bringing healing to the family, Migisi repeated the words of Nanak, that they were only witnessing the end of the Fifth Fire and the lighting of the Sixth Fire—that it would be at the end of the Seventh Fire that the Wintermaker would be vulnerable. This drove away both Lily and Fawn.

For Lily, she could not get over the loss of her husband, especially with their only child Louis being so young. "It was a trick," she muttered. "It was all a lie."

For Fawn, wounds created in 1898 suddenly reopened, and when she pressed Lily about her encounter with the Wintermaker, the conversation turned into a violent fight between the two. Fawn left with Blackfish LaBiche for the Turtle Mountain Chippewa Reservation in North Dakota before later vanishing into the Canadian Rockies.

Migisi suspected the reason they fought, which is why even though he studied to become a Mide, he lived like a Catholic priest, siring no children.

As evening passed to night, Migisi burst out of his cabin to face Lake Manitou. There on the high bluff overlooking the lake, he could see the shadow of Deadwood Island, now called Carousel Island.

He wept with fear.

As a child, he pictured himself stabbing the Horned Serpent as if it was a sturgeon or flathead catfish swimming in the channel. Then Wijigan priest Joseph Little Toad offered him as a living sacrifice, an Omodai, to the Wintermaker. His soul was pulled from his body and held by the deathly hands of his nemesis. If not for his sister, Migisi's soul would have remained in the depths until his body withered and died.

Now, having seen the real Wintermaker, he knew Father Guerin was most likely right: The Wintermaker was an ancient evil with roots in the mythologies of all nations. Not only did it have ties to the past, but it also had connections to the apocalyptic prophecies of the future.

Migisi put his hands upon his knees and let out a groan from deep in his soul.

He wept now with anticipation.

He knew the Tak-Pei had been woken by the blood of the four slain teens. Had Lily been safe at her watch post on the shores near Kanaranzi Creek, the foul spirits would have been quickly put back to rest. Instead, she'd ironically been defeated by smoke instead of fire. Now, the embryos of evil would grow stronger by the day.

The servants of the Wintermaker had one purpose: to protect and serve their master. If it was his will to rise, the Tak-Pei would make it happen. If the Wintermaker needed protection, they would provide it. Both possibilities meant one thing: more deaths.

A fight was coming, and the Isanti Lodge was either absent, wounded, too old, or too young to muster a proper defense.

Finally, he wept for those who would face the Seventh Fire.

A Pledge of Allegiance

Haggard Quarry
June 27, 1961

BIFF FORSBERG COULDN'T help but smile as he pressed the starter button on the yellow 1961 Caterpillar 922B. The big engine had so much power that the hairs on his forearms could feel the vibration.

The beast wasn't much bigger than a normal tractor, yet it had twice as much metal and twice as much power.

Red Dobie took his arm and pointed, shouting over the motor, "You need to turn the switch to disengage the starter motor once it's running. Hop up and give it some gas."

Biff climbed up into the cab, filling the quarry with the sound of his new machine.

Uncle Ewan stood next to his truck, arms crossed. Dobie stepped back to stand beside Ewan and the two exchanged a few words.

Biff lifted and lowered the bucket just to confirm the instruction he'd been given. "Can I get to work?"

Uncle Ewan nodded. "Just don't run into anything."

Biff put the loader into gear, lifted the bucket an inch off the ground, and took aim at the closest bit of rubble as Uncle Ewan drove back up to the office and Dobie went back into his machine shed.

AT LUNCH, INSTEAD of reading his Norse mythology book given to him by Uncle Ewan, Biff's curiosity drove him to hang out inside of the shipping building with Dobie.

"If it isn't the dragon rider. How's that yellow bitch ride?" Dobie asked without even glancing up.

Biff shrugged. "It's a lot better than a shovel."

"I bet it is. You're a company man now. Keep working hard and you'll get rewarded. You've got to earn it, kid."

Biff approached the counter cautiously, his eyes peering down the hallway for just a split second then back to the clutter surrounding Dobie. "Uncle Ewan said you're flying out with us for the Fourth."

"Yeah, I thought about just fishing, but the lakes are so crazy on the Fourth that I figured I should make an appearance at the company picnic."

"Uncle Ewan said it was a family reunion." *I wonder if Paul ever went.*

Dobie flinched. "And I ain't family?"

"Are you?"

"Have you looked at yourself in the mirror lately? Where do you think you get those freckles and ginger hair from? Your Uncle Ewan and I were all reared in the same playpen as babies—the lot of us: Sean, Morgan, Ewan, and I."

There's so much I don't know about the Sinclair family tree. "How do you connect to the tree?"

"The tree!" Dobie chuckled. "You are a quick learner, aren't you? Branches and roots. You're going to fly out to Nova Scotia with us and get a headache trying to understand old Yggdrasil. For generations, the tree has had its princes and its workers. My family goes back to a branch far older than this "American" branch you're part of. The Dobies make sure. We get it done."

"So have you ever flown in a plane?"

"Nervous? Don't be. We're not going to be in one of the flying buses. We'll be taking the company plane—it's fast and safe." Dobie reached under his stocking cap to scratch his head. "Little lesson for you Biff: don't judge a book by its cover. You take one look at me and assume I sit at home drinking beer and eating potato chips. I've been all over this world on family and company business. I just know my place and do my job." Dobie continued to sort his papers. "Know your place. Do your job."

Biff held onto his other questions and went back outside to his waiting lunch.

THE REST OF the afternoon left him with his thoughts: on family legacy, on Norse mythology, and of Thunderbirds and secret caves.

Like clockwork, Wally Crain arrived with his fuel truck at the end of Biff's shift. Compared to Red and Uncle Ewan, Wally moved with the confidence of a movie star. His jet-black hair was slicked back, and his mustache perfectly groomed.

Biff climbed into the truck cab while Wally dealt with Dobie and the paperwork. Biff studied Wally from the front door to the cab door. His feet were light, his gait was casual, and his whistle was pleasant. *There are no dark skeletons in his closet,* Biff thought. *Wally Crain was now Dull with a capital D.*

"Any plans for the Fourth?" Wally asked once the fuel truck began rolling toward Biff's house.

"I'm flying out with Uncle Ewan to a family reunion in Nova Scotia."

"You don't say," Wally said, a crease forming on his forehead. "Your, uh, Uncle Ewan's really taken you under his wing, huh?"

Biff nodded and watched as the quarry passed by the window.

"Hey," Wally finally said as they passed through St. John, "I've got a couple Boy Scout events coming up. Did you get the list in the mail?"

"Yeah, but I'm pretty tired when I'm done working at the quarry. Maybe I can do the camping trip on Labor Day weekend."

The conversation stalled as the truck headed east. When it descended the valley of the Blue Knife River, Wally asked, "Any news from your brother?"

Why is everyone so focused on Paul? Biff shook his head. "No, since he's been stationed in Vietnam, we haven't heard much from him. He's training the South Vietnamese to fight the Commies, I guess."

"Your brother was quite a leader in Scouts. I can see how that translated into the military."

I wish Paul were here now.

As the fuel truck climbed the hill separating the reservation and Turtle Island State Park, thoughts of Paul filled Biff's head. Everyone talked about how awesome Paul had been, but with ten years between the two of them, Biff remembered only indifference from his teenage brother when they were growing up. The only so-called bonding happened in the moments where Paul would try to scare him.

"Paul used to tell me stories about a monster that lived in Lake Manitou. He made it sound like Jormungandr, the Midgard Serpent, lived in the depths of the lake."

"The Midgard Serpent? I don't know about that, but I do know my dad used to tell me stories about a Horned Serpent that crawled out of the lake one night and tried to grab him. Luckily, he had a knife and cut his way free." Wally reached into the front pocket of his blue jeans and pulled out a short pocketknife. "Behold Mjolnir, foe hammer."

Biff took the knife, opening its two blades. Wally Crain suddenly became more interesting than he'd been a few minutes earlier.

CHAPTER NINETEEN

Oh Say, Can you See?

Old Copper Road
July 4, 1961

JIMMY NIELSON LOOKED outside to check the weather. Depending on the conditions, it meant fishing on the lake or along the river.

The light pole hid the rest of the world in contrasted darkness and the little plum trees in the front yard swayed. It was already a windy day. The only thing outside that didn't seem swayed by the wind was his father Ed.

His father stood at the corner of his pickup with a shotgun in his hands, leveled but not aimed. His gaze fixed on a spot past the barn and toward the distant wheat field.

I wonder what he sees?

Jimmy slipped on yesterday's blue jeans, a fresh white t-shirt, and his converse. In under a minute, he'd traveled from his bedroom to the screen door facing the front yard. He opened it slowly so the springs on the coil did not make a noise, and he held it as it closed behind him.

His father still hadn't moved.

I wonder if he's spotted a skunk or a badger.

Jimmy crept across the porch, down the front steps, and over the walkway that greeted the driveway. His father was now adjacent, looking off in the distance.

"What is it?" Jimmy whispered.

Wide eyes and both barrels of the shotgun spun to place Jimmy in the cross hairs.

The air in his lungs suddenly felt like he'd been gored by a bull, for his father's eyes had transformed into the eyes of a killer. Even when lashing with a belt, his father's eyes never held so much anger and hatred. Then, with a simultaneous blink and gulp, his father returned.

"What the blazes are you doing out here?"

"I was going to help with chores, remember? And then head off for the day with Chris."

His father glanced back over his shoulder to the darkness before responding. "Oh, that's right."

Jimmy's heart was still racing. "Did you see something?"

"I'd gone down to the barn to feed the hogs and thought I saw some coyotes or wolves down by the shore." His father turned back to the darkness, still deepened by the bright lamp illuminating the yard.

"Wolves?"

"Four of them, sniffing along the beach. I ran back to get the shotgun from the gun cabinet and by that time, they were coming up the hill. I lost sight of them though."

"How do you know they just weren't dogs?"

"I don't. All I saw were dark forms in the distance. Could've been four bears, but only wolves hunt in packs."

Jimmy scanned the distance. Already, the rising sun gave resolution to the entirety of Lake Manitou beyond their farmstead on the hill. "Should I go get a rifle and we'll chase them off together?" Hunting each fall was one of his favorite times spent with his father.

"No. No, my eyes aren't what they used to be. You're probably right. I probably saw four Canadian Geese." His father shrugged. "No, you've earned a day off to play with your friend. We'll get chores done, and then you can spend the day doing whatever you want."

A FEW HOURS later , Jimmy rode his bicycle through the oak woods of Old Copper Road. Normally, the only concern was a lost traveler trying to find the entrance to Carousel Park, but today, he watched the shadows of the forest for signs of the four mysterious hunters.

Once he passed through the woods, he slowed when he saw the yellow police tape that had effectively closed Carousel Park for the summer. His mother gave daily updates from the newspaper, including an explanation of how lawsuits would keep it from reopening. For the past several summers, he'd spent countless hours on the rides and playing games. Now, like his childhood, that time was over.

When he passed by the Forsberg farm, he slowed his pace.

What's his problem?

Since school ended, Biff had changed. He no longer wanted to play or even be adventurous. No fishing. No building stuff. No exploring. He'd turned into an adult the day he stole those rice crispy bars. Now, he chose to accept an invitation to travel to some creep's house in Nova Scotia rather than hang out for a four-day-weekend.

Biff's little sister Julia was standing on the second-floor porch and waved when she saw him. Now he'd have to deal with her for the whole day tomorrow as the two families celebrated the Fourth of July together. Jimmy was half Forsberg, yet Biff chose to celebrate with his Haggard blood.

The betrayal caused him to bite his lower lip as he sped down the hill to the Doc Jenkins Bridge.

Luckily, his friendship with Chris Luning remained intact. From Old Copper Road, he could see the rooftop of Chris's house, but to reach it, he needed to cross the bridge, ride down Market Street, and then cut back over at the Fisher Lumber Mill.

Chris lived in a monstrously large Victorian-era house. Even though Marlin Luning managed the lumber mill, the house was grander than his salary could afford. Marlin earned the house with a sex-scandal that was still talked about decades later.

They can keep their money for all the trouble it causes them, Jimmy decided as he dropped his bike in front of their picket fence.

Chris came stumbling out the door with a tackle box, lunch box, and a fully rigged fishing pole.

At least Chris still has time for me.

BY MID MORNING, the boys were set up along the eastern bank of the Crow Wing River, lines in the current. Fishing was terrible because every ten minutes vacationers in canoes passed through the clear water.

Jimmy began to evaluate new options for fishing.

Above his head, he could see the treetops getting blown by the strong northwestern wind, which meant the only calm place to fish along the lakeshore was several miles away at St. John. Yet Carousel Island would block the northwestern wind if they fished along the shore near Biff's house.

Jimmy knew the perfect spot.

He began reeling in his line, but Chris didn't so much as flinch. The sinker came bouncing up to shore, and still Chris, his eyes fixed on the trees, didn't notice.

Jimmy picked up a stone and tossed it at his friend.

Chris flinched. "Cut it out!"

"What were you looking at? Seeing wolves?"

"Wolves, no, I, um … Are there wolves around here?"

"I think they're farther up north in the old pine forests. Too many dogs and farmers around here."

Chris began to reel up his line. "Do you want to try another spot?"

"One smallmouth in an hour isn't going to cut it. There's a spot near Biff's place that should be sheltered from the wind and waves."

The line reeled all the way up to the sinker and the pole bent before Chris took notice. He pushed the button on his reel to release a little line before he asked, "What's on the opposite shore?"

Jimmy studied the old trees and shadows, afraid of what might be there. "Did you see something?"

Chris shook his head. "No, I'm just trying to understand whose land that is on the western shore."

"I'm pretty sure it's all MacPherson land. You know that big hill where their farm is built, and how the ditch is so steep on the east side of the hill? We're looking at the bottom of the MacPherson hill."

Chris hummed.

"Why?"

"And Lake Manitou is on the other side of the ridge, right?"

"Yep. What are you thinking?"

"Never mind. But you know … it's too bad there's not a bridge right here. Going back to the Doc Jenkins Bridge has to add a whole mile onto the trip, doesn't it? We should build our own bridge."

"Either the DNR or floods would take it down."

"How about a rope swing?"

"And every idiot in a canoe would stop and use it."

"Okay, let's pack up and go then," Chris said, giving one last glance to the opposite shore.

TWENTY MINUTES LATER, THE boys descended the gravel road leading to the Doc Jenkins Bridge. The first thing Jimmy noticed was music. A doo-wop song with a female chorus sifted through the air in fragments, growing louder the closer they came to the bridge.

Then Jimmy spotted a maroon Chevy, which he knew belonged to Gavin MacPherson. Gavin had taken Jimmy's sister Alexandra to a dance last spring, but nothing came of it that he knew.

That radio is probably what scared away all the fish.

"Whoa," Chris muttered loud enough to be heard from the bridge.

One of the unique features of the Doc Jenkins Bridge, besides the canopy of steel that formed the trestle, was its wooden plank flooring, which extended past the rails of the bridge to create a three-foot-wide platform along the side of the bridge. There, stretched out on a blanket, was a certifiable babe.

In a scene from a California beach, the babe wore a yellow, floral print bikini that would have rivaled Brigette Bardot. Her skin was copper, and her bobbed hair was as black as the sunglasses she wore. One of her knees raised from the blanket and she pulled herself up onto her elbows to speak to the river below, "Company."

Afraid his jeans might not be able to hide his thoughts, Jimmy felt like turning around. The babe, now sitting up with her flat stomach, had cleavage that, by Jimmy's standards of measurement, was somewhere between grapefruit and cantaloupe.

"Well hello, Christopher," the babe said with a slight smile on her crimson lips.

Her voice felt like Superman's super chilled breath: it sent shockwaves through Jimmy's heart.

"Hi, Nicole," Chris answered sheepishly, yet he had big enough balls to steer his bike toward her side of the bridge.

"You've grown up," Nicole noted. Jimmy, using his buddy as a shield, stopped behind Chris.

"I'm a teenager now."

"I'm going to be going to Split Rock this fall. I'll probably see you in the halls."

Of course, it was Nicole Guerin. The reclusive Indian family that sent their kids to Turtle Island Jesuit School had produced a babe almost unworthy of public school.

Chris turned to explain to Jimmy, "Nicole used to be my babysitter when I was an ankle biter."

I had my older sisters. Damn.

A moment later, Gavin MacPherson came up from the southwestern corner of the bridge, wearing swimming trunks. The lucky bastard looked like a Ken doll to Nicole's brunette Barbie. From his perfectly cool wet hair to his muscular chest and rippled abdomen and defined arms, he made Jimmy want to jump off the bridge like old Doc Jenkins had once done.

They deserved each other.

"The fish biting?" Gavin asked, slowing his pace like a golden lion ready to protect his lioness from a couple scabby hyenas.

"I caught a smallmouth," Chris answered, leaving Jimmy speechless. All he could do was to step onto his pedal and continue on his way.

Behind him, Chris said, "Well, it was nice seeing you again, Nicole. I'm glad you'll be a Bulldog."

Chubby Checker's "Twist" playfully mocked their retreat.

Just five years older, junior Gavin MacPherson doubled Jimmy's muscle mass, and if Jimmy were ever going to earn a babe like Nicole Guerin, he needed to pack on some muscles like Biff was doing.

Perhaps there were some advantages to growing up.

A Wind Age, A Wolf Age

Oak Island, Nova Scotia
July 4, 1961

BIFF FORSBERG INVENTED A mental machete—not a real blade, of course—which would chop off each hand that held him by the shoulder or tousled his hair. At first, there had been so much manhandling that he worried about the real possibilities of a sex cult. For this reason, he kept an aluminum pen in his side pocket in case he needed to slam it into some pervert's neck. Alas, it truly was just a family reunion.

He sat, now on the final day of his trip, along the shore overlooking Mahone Bay and the Atlantic Ocean. Although the older relatives freely intermingled, their children formed into small gangs of common interest. Biff sat with the Albany kids, with the Portuguese kids to the left and the French kids to the right. All totaled, there were about forty kids watching the fireworks reflect off the waters of the bay.

Sinclair Mansion was built on one of the two dozen islands in Mahone Bay, with a concrete bridge connecting to the road that led back to the city of Halifax. The stone building looked like a large hotel: three stories tall with fifty windows on each side of the long rectangle. It had been built in the late 1800s by William Sinclair, brother of St. John's founding father Scott Sinclair. While Scott produced a son and five fertile daughters, William produced only a solitary daughter who vanished in the mountains of Colorado, something still whispered about decades later. After William's death, the house became a vacation home for the families that owned Triton Corporation.

During his four-day vacation, Biff learned the place's history and met two billionaires. Even though he couldn't remember Mr. Terront's first name, they talked openly for a good five minutes about the threat of communism to South Vietnam. The Terronts owned rubber tree plantations, which were used to create tires. Mr. Terront had assurances from President Kennedy that the communists would not steal his prized trees from him. That is when Uncle Ewan stepped in to explain how Paul had joined the U.S. Army leaving Biff to serve interests at home.

The second billionaire was Ross Delhut, who got super drunk on Saturday night and was knocking stuff over to the consternation of the old women. Ross made Biff smile. A recent college graduate, Ross was far more interested in Biff's football acumen than talking about his steel empire in Detroit. For the next three days, Ross gave Biff six-shooter gestures whenever they passed.

Along with meeting billionaires, Biff met several doppelgangers. Never in his life did he blend in with a crowd, but at the Sinclair Mansion, half of the kids had freckles and red hair, including Dobie's nephew, Tomas Dobie from Albany. Ross Delhut had dubbed them "the lollipop guild," which brought laughter from the adults and fear from the other kids who knew bullies. Away from the adults, none of the kids laughed at the brooding cousins.

Tom sat next to Biff and spent more time pulling tufts of grass from the yard than watching the colorful explosions overhead.

When a barrage of cannon fire signaled the grand finale of the light show, all three hundred visitors clapped for whoever had set it up.

A hand grabbed Biff by the shoulder—Uncle Ewan. "Mr. Sinclair is going to tell stories by the bonfire. You've been invited to join him."

Tom looked at Biff and shrugged. "They'll have you playing the bagpipes soon."

While the crowd flowed back to the illuminated back porch, where music and desserts waited, Uncle Ewan walked Biff to a secluded area, past the helicopter pad and through a manicured path lined with the trees. Biff assumed it to be the center of the island, for when they reached it, not a glimmer of water could be seen—only stars above their head.

Four or five elementary age kids already sat at a table-sized bonfire. In a larger chair, an old white man sat with vibrant white hair and a chin capable of making a turkey jealous. Sitting in a smaller chair beside him was a woman, her head wrapped in a shawl that seemed to envelop her entire body. And completely out of place was Dobie—sitting beside the billionaire Aleister Sinclair.

"Don't embarrass me," Uncle Ewan whispered in Biff's ear before leaving.

Biff sat down with the younger kids and waited until the last few were escorted to the private bonfire.

He remained the oldest by three or four years.

"Did you enjoy the fireworks?" Aleister asked to resounding acclaim. "Good, good. I'd like you to meet my very good friend. This is Saara Olavintytär. She is a storyteller. She is a 'knower,' which makes her far more qualified to tell the stories from the dawn than me, but when I was your age, this is how I began to learn the legends of our family."

"Thank you, Mr. Sinclair." Her voice was melodic, even when saying something simple. Her eyes studied them for a moment, and Biff looked down. "You see an old man in front of you whose twilight is coming. He was once young like you, and one day, if you are lucky, you'll live to a ripe old age also. Life and death is a cycle. Do any of you know the story of 'The Twilight of the Gods'?"

Yes.

Before Biff could raise a hand or verbalize the answer, a young girl shouted, "It's the Ragnarök."

"Good, good. Now tell me what you *think* you know."

"It begins with a triple winter," a boy blurted.

For the next several minutes, Biff kept his mouth shut as the kids told the stories about Loki's escape and betrayal, Odin getting eaten alive by the great wolf Fenrir, Silent Vidar avenging Odin's death, Thor killing and then tragically dying in a battle with the Midgard Serpent, and how Heimdall and Loki died at each other's hands. The shawled woman smiled, nodded, and corrected each account.

How do these kids know these stories so well?

Even though she was almost entirely covered by her shawl, her face and hands were stunning, beautiful. Biff found himself focused entirely on the playful nature of her lips. "What was the signal that the Ragnarök would begin?"

"The Midgard Serpent would rise."

"Heimdall blows Gjallarhorn."

"The ship of the dead breaks free."

"Loki escapes."

Miss Olavintytär navigated the answers before giving her own. "It is Fimbulvetr—the terrible winter. Before any of it can happen, the worst winter in the history of the world is triggered. Only then will the great tree Yggdrasil shudder and groan. When the tree is destroyed, the doom is sealed."

Biff hated school, even those around bonfires.

Then she did something he hated most—she called on him. Her gaze settled on him, forcing him to look up for her question: "Did all life perish in the great battle Ragnarök?"

Biff cleared his throat and offered, "No. There were survivors. Two humans survived by hiding in a tree."

"Go on, child."

"The fire giant, Surtr, ends the battle when he destroys the world in flame, but in destroying it, he is buried in the rubble. And even though Asgard is destroyed, there are four survivors: Vidar and Vali—the sons of Odin, and Modi and Magni—the sons of Thor."

"Surtr's Bane," Aleister Sinclair mumbled under his breath.

"And what is their purpose, Mr. Sinclair?"

Biff studied Mr. Sinclair, wondering the answer.

"They will avenge the destruction of the world by Surtr and bring a new spring to the world. They will help restore things to the former glory of the old world."

"But where are the heirs of Asgard?" Miss Olavintytär asked rhetorically. "Some say they are buried, just like evil Surtr is buried and dormant. Others say they are disguised and living in the world of men. Other tales say they passed their strength onto their heirs. Can any of you tell me how the stories described Thor?"

She fielded a variety of answers until she heard the one she wanted. "Yes, he is known for his red hair. It is the feature unique to the northern lands, isn't it? The red hair of our forefathers is a link back to the days of the dawn, our connection. Be proud of who you are, children."

Dobie, still not having said a word, crossed his arms and nodded.

Miss Olavintytär continued, asking, "Was the Ragnarök a loss? A failure by Odin?"

"No," Biff blurted out.

"Explain."

"Hope remained after his death. The battle is not over."

"What is your name, child?"

"Brian."

"Our brother Brian has the heart of the answer. In the dawn of the gods, Odin learned a terrible truth—the world was in a terrible cycle of destruction. Ice and Fire, again and again, destroyed the world before it could blossom. The doom of mankind, the giants, and even the gods was complete, a twisted play that continued generation after generation. Odin was determined to break this cycle. Do any of you know how he learned this secret knowledge?"

"He gave up his eye at the Well of Mimir," someone answered.

"In a way, yes. At the Well of Mimir, he learned the future—the fate of all living things. Yet upon learning his destiny, and the destiny of all, he did something to change it all."

"He killed himself," Biff answered so bluntly that some of the children gasped. Even Dobie snapped his head to stare at Biff.

A smile crept onto Miss Olavintytär's face.

Biff continued. "It was a sacrifice. Odin hung himself from the great tree Yggdrasil, and there, his spirit journeyed into the dark waters. He returned from this journey with a plan to destroy the destiny given to the world. He found a path that would claim his life but ultimately give life a chance to survive its destined doom. He did it so the next generation would survive."

"And that is why you are all here at my bonfire," Aleister Sinclair said. "One day, I will die, like Odin, and you will be asked to lead in the fight against Death. You will be champions of life, fighting for the Free Will of all. Your parents bring you here because we all share in this fight.

"When Odin temporarily died at the tree, not only did he see the future, but he also saw the past, he saw the mysteries of the universe written upon the foundations of our world. When he came back to life, he knew an ancient language, which we now call runes. He taught this language to his people, but many of us have forgotten how to read it. My friend, Saara, has been learning this old language. Did you know that it was once a song?"

Aleister paused to let them ponder before asking, "Would you like Saara to sing some of it for you?"

Biff felt a chill run down his spine. *This is bad. Very bad.*

"I can sing some of it in English since I doubt any of you will understand the old tongue. I'll sing the opening verses describing the beginning of the Ragnarök, so that like Odin, you might guard your hearts and prepare yourselves for the coming battle."

And she began—

"'It sates itself on the life-blood of fated men,
paints red the powers' homes with crimson gore.
Black become the sun's beams in the summers that follow,
weathers all treacherous. Do you still seek to know? And what?

Brothers will fight and kill each other,
sisters' children will defile kinship.
It is harsh in the world, whoredom rife
—an axe age, a sword age—shields are riven—
a wind age, a wolf age—before the world goes headlong.
No man will have mercy on another.'"

As she sang, Biff closed his eyes, and pictured himself, an old man, fighting in a great battle, his friends around him. He was wounded. Crawling. Crawling with his last heartbeats to destroy the enemy standing over him.

The Turtle Shell

Invermere, British Columbia
August 4, 1961

LEONARD WHITE ELK tried not to think of his dreams, especially while at work. He focused on the five sizzling hamburger patties in front of him, waiting for the right moment to flip each. His red bandana caught the sweat from his brow, and his long hair was braided down the middle of his back. After a week at the grill, he'd need to soak in the hot springs for an entire day to purge his body from all the grease.

My last burgers of the summer.

He flipped the patties onto buns and rang the bell in front of him. Although his skin was pocked from the grease that plugged his pores, the rest of his body was the pristine model of health. His weight-lifting regimen each morning left his arms and chest looking like those of a football player. Compared to the rest of the kitchen staff at Copper Valley Golf Club, he was taller by a foot—his Lakota blood, his brothers told him.

He wiped his hands on a clean towel and stepped away from the grill, peeking through the small window that looked out to the restaurant. Most of the golfers were off the course, and those still sitting at the restaurant had been fed. Leonard returned to the grill and began scraping.

It was time to go home.

HIS SUMMER HOME was only a quarter mile from the club-house. He lived in an aluminum trailer parked in an open lot unused by the local Shuswap people.

Leonard lived alone. He quickly changed out of his white pants and shirt and slipped on a pair of blue jeans and a black t-shirt. He stuffed his dirty laundry into a basket, grabbed his keys, and hopped in his big truck. His permanent home was a twenty-minute drive down BC-93 to Fairmont Hot Springs.

Leonard lived in the Canadian Rockies at the Great Continental Divide. A crease ran down the spine of the Canadian Rockies from Sinclair Pass to Columbia Lake, which turned the narrow valley into a summer vacation destination for Calgary ranchers, adventurous travelers, or the wealthy elite.

Fairmont Hot Springs, another resort town, provided his four brothers with steady employment, and like himself, they all lived in cabins on the remote slopes of Indian Head Mountain that overlooked the resorts below.

Before he could go home, he had to make a stop.

A block off the highway, Leonard had purchased a small two-bedroom bungalow. Wanda Laurier, a widow at forty, took one of the rooms free of charge on the condition she cared for his invalid mother. Leonard spent three months working at the resort to pay for the nine months he wouldn't have to work.

He knocked lightly on the front door before slipping in his key. Wanda had left a light on in the kitchen, casting the living room with enough light to see. A moment later, she appeared in a robe.

"I have all of her stuff sitting there beside the door," Wanda said with her arms crossed. "I'm still going to get paid for the rest of August, aren't I?"

"Of course, but I might need you for a few weeks after my Vision Quest. Once I know the path I need to walk, I might need to bring her back down the mountain if I have to leave."

"You? Leave? Where in the world would you go?"

"I might need to travel to Minnesota for a few weeks to deal with some family matters."

"Ah, that's right, Fawn is originally from Minnesota, isn't she?"

He ignored the question and asked, "Is she ready?"

"She's rested, if that's what you mean. I'm not sure how much of this plan she even understands."

"Could you help put her stuff in the truck?"

"You're leaving tonight? Stay. Sleep on the couch."

"Ma's going to sleep regardless of the time of day. I'd rather get going and wake up in my own bed."

With a huff, Wanda came for the bags at the door and Leonard walked back to his mother's room.

"Aaniin, Nimaamaa," Leonard whispered. *Hello, mother.*

He only knew Fawn Chevreuil from the stories told by his family. On Leonard's birth bed, Fawn had a brain aneurysm that left the mother of five young boys with permanent brain damage and the inability to walk. Surprisingly, she survived, first nursed by her Lakota husband White Elk, and then years later by Leonard, who felt guilt and responsibility for her.

Fawn felt no heavier than a sack of rice in his arms as he scooped her from her bed. His kiss on her brow woke her from her slumber.

The stroke had paralyzed the left side of her face, leaving her right eye, cheek, and corner of her mouth to express her emotions. Fawn smiled as a little tear came down her cheek.

Although Wanda insisted on a short haircut for Fawn, she made sure to keep her hair brushed and her nails polished.

When Leonard reached the bed of the truck, he effortlessly laid Fawn on a bed of comforters and covered her with another. He told her, "You can see the stars on our way."

With his mother situated, he turned back to the house. "Thank you, Wanda. If I don't come back, you can keep the house."

"What is that supposed to mean?" Wanda asked.

I shouldn't be going anywhere near Lake Manitou.

Leonard closed the door without answering.

As he drove from the foothills of Fairmont Hot Springs and up the mountain road that led into the Akisqnuk First Nation reservation, he caught glimpses of the stars through the trees. He was fluent in four cultures—his mother's Anishinaabe, his father's Sihasapa Lakota, and the local tribes, the Shuswap and Akisqnuk . All four had stories about the constellation known as the Big Dipper. All four had tales involving the constellation Orion also, but Fawn's version told of the Wintermaker.

Leonard reached his cabin a little after midnight. He immediately tended to his mother's needs, setting her up in her wooden rocking chair to face the morning sun. After bringing in her belongings and medicine, he flopped into his bed for some rest.

Tomorrow will be a long day.

HE WOKE TO an ogre looming over his bed.

"Are you really going through with this plan of yours?" Russell White Elk had two inches and a hundred pounds on his brother, but little of it was muscle. The casino bouncer was all bark but little bite.

Leonard groaned and rolled out of bed. "When did you get here?"

"Dennis got all of us on the radio this morning. He said he saw you get back sometime after midnight. He got another letter from Migisi."

"Did he?"

"We're all waiting to talk some sense into you."

"If Ma agrees, there's no changing my mind," Leonard said and got up. He still wore his blue jeans and black shirt, even though he left his boots where they'd been kicked off upon entering the cabin.

Outside, all three LaBiche brothers waited by their various steeds. Dennis, the eldest at 49, had an open-top Jeep; Clyde had saddled his horse; and Vernon, the youngest LaBiche brother at 46, had a rusty yellow truck. The grandsons of Blackfish LaBiche all had sullen eyes but the fat cheeks of their mother Fawn. Their father, John LaBiche, had died at the Turtle Mountain Chippewa Reservation in North Dakota when all three boys were young.

Instead of going home, Fawn and her father-in-law Blackfish took them to the Standing Rock Indian Reservation in South Dakota, where she met her second husband, White Elk. For five years, the family lived in South Dakota before they continued Fawn's quest to "the top of the turtle shell" that she'd once seen in a dream. Four years after settling on Indian Head Mountain, Fawn had her aneurysm giving birth to Leonard.

"Tell me about the new letter," Leonard said.

"Migisi asked for us to send two of our boys to him so they can be properly trained."

"Wa-wa-shesh-she and Be-nays," Leonard explained. "He wants representatives of the Deer Clan and Bird Clan to learn the rituals."

Russell huffed. "We know what Migisi wants, but we're not sending any of our children to Lake Manitou while Lily Guerin lives."

"She ... survived the fire?"

"She's still recovering in the hospital, but she's getting stronger by the day. It was all a false alarm. We were right to ignore it."

Leonard's dreams came flooding back, hardening his resolve. "None of us know. If Migisi is right, and the Servants of the Wintermaker are attempting to wake the sleeping evil while the Isanti Lodge is at its weakest, then we not only fail him but also our ancestors.”

“While you’ve chosen not to have a family or children, the rest of us have something to protect. Ma has twenty-three grandchildren and five great-grandchildren living in these hills. She brought us here for our protection. You know this to be true. You know what is special about this place.”

“We can’t hide from a fight—because if we lose, there will be no place on earth to hide. You all know this to be true.” Leonard sighed. “What else am I supposed to do?”

“Ma’s a feeble old woman. You know what this trip will do to her.”

“I do. She’s held on for thirty-six miserable years, and if we could talk with her one more time, for one more day, wouldn’t you trade those thirty-six years trapped in a broken body?”

“There’s no guarantee this will even work.”

“If it doesn’t work, I’ll return to Lake Manitou. I’ll learn whatever Migisi wants to teach me, and I’ll look after the others.”

“I can’t let you do this to our mother.”

“Then let her decide.”

“Does she even know what’s going on?”

“Let’s find out,” Leonard said, returning to the cabin. Fawn was looking outside, and he kissed her on top of the head before pulling the rocking chair backwards out the door and onto the porch.

“Ma, tell the others where you want me to take you.”

Fawn’s head began to bobble, her right hand twitched, and her throat cleared. A rivulet of drool came down her chin, which Leonard gently wiped away. “Cave.”

Leonard looked up and pointed to the higher peak of Indian Head Mountain.

“And why are we going there?”

Again, Fawn took a moment, as if winding up her strength, to mutter a slurred single word. "Quest."

Leonard nodded. Mother and son had rarely communicated effectively through verbal communication, but their kindred spirits united them in purpose.

"And of all your grandchildren, which one should come with us up the mountain?"

Fawn's eyes looked to Vernon. "Ben."

Vernon muttered under his breath and shook his head.

"The folks at Lake Manitou did not ask for this to happen to them, nor do any of us want it to happen. But we must act, and if a Vision Quest will help guide our path, then why do we delay?"

Clyde burst into a sudden sob, pinching the bridge of his nose to hide his emotions.

"Migisi sent a package with the letter. He reminded us that he and Fawn were always allies and that he misses her wise counsel. He said this will help guide us." Dennis handed the opened package to Leonard and walked to put a hand on Clyde's shoulder.

Vernon stood his ground. "I'm glad it's Ben. I'll go fetch the boy, and then he's all yours. But I swear Leonard, you're not taking him back to Lake Manitou while that witch is alive. Understood? You can bring him up to that mountain cave, but that's it."

Leonard nodded.

Russell White Elk lingered as the others departed. "Do you want help bringing Ma up the slope? I know you're strong as an ox, but that's one hell of a trip."

"I'll have time to catch my breath once I reach the cave. I'll have the boy to give me a hand, too."

Russell lowered his head and walked away.

Leonard opened the four leaves of the box. Inside, he found freshly cut willow fronds, feathers, beads, and animal sinew—materials for a dreamcatcher.

For a final conversation with Ma.

Guardian of the Knife

Turtle Island State Park
September 1, 1961

WALLY CRAIN SLIPPED HIS hand into the front pocket of his blue jeans and pulled out the Barlow pocket knife entrusted to him by one of the founding members of the Isanti Lodge. If Migisi Asibikaashi was correct, his role was that of only a storyteller—not a warrior. If Lily Guerin was correct, the boys surrounding him were all in danger.

Wally cleared his throat. "On your marks, get set, go!"

The boy scouts from Pack 88 had been given ten minutes—the hypothetical time of an impending rainfall—to collect materials for a fire-starting competition.

Two decades after being a young man serving on the USS South Dakota, he now mentored young leaders as a Scoutmaster. After a summer that began with fire and blood, things had grown quiet. Nothing crept out of the shadows of Lake Manitou.

Even so, we're still not ready for a coming fight.

With many of the local farm boys attending the Minnesota State Fair or vacationing with families during the last weekend of summer, only eight boys had been able to join him at Turtle Island State Park along the northern shore of Lake Manitou. The junior high boys from both Split Rock and St. John went through short training sessions like knot-tying, fire starting, knife sharpening, life-saving measures, and first aid.

With Ed Nielson a devout disciple of Lily Guerin, he didn't need to worry about training Jimmy, but he needed to test the others. None of them took to the badges like Paul Forsberg had done several years earlier, but Wally saw potential in some of them.

Brian "Biff" Forsberg had the same skills as his brother but none of the charm. He was grim and bitter, more prone to hurting one of the other boys than saving one. Biff hated his red hair and freckles, but his thick shoulders and powerful arms had turned him from the butt of jokes into the bully.

Rory Stewart displayed the most social charm in the group, but despite his flashing demeanor and manners, Wally could not bring himself to trust the boy from St. John, especially with his Triton heritage. He often vocally led the other boys, but whenever Wally stepped away, Rory would become verbally abusive, and they would simply ignore the loudmouth.

Christopher Luning, who seemed untouched by puberty though heading into seventh grade, proved to be the natural leader. The dark-haired boy had skinny arms and, despite wearing a tank top, had a hard time stretching the fabric across his chest. Yet whenever Wally threw a new task at them, Chris not only soaked it up but also helped the other boys figure out how to do it.

If Wally could take Stewart's charm, Forsberg's strength, and Luning's leadership, he could have shaped a suitable member for the Isanti Lodge, but by the time he took out the packets of marshmallows, he knew it would be years before any of the boys were ready for the mantle of leadership or inclusion in the Isanti Lodge.

After watching the boys compete to start a campfire with flint and steel, Wally kicked his feet up on a rock as he sat on a big maple stump. His job as pack leader was finished, but his role as a

Guardian was just beginning. Jimmy Nielson, Ed's only son, won the competition and had a blazing fire going while the others were still producing smoke. When Wally produced the marshmallows, graham crackers, and chocolate bars, the boys—all except Biff— abandoned their failed fires to stuff their bellies.

Wally kept a guard over the supplies until an orange flame illuminated the slight smile on Biff's face.

Some, like Chris Luning, were so tuckered out by the activities of the day that they were sound asleep by the time Wally finished telling his basic ghost stories. For a while, the boys tried, and failed, to tell their own horror fests, but they mostly ripped off B-movie plots. Wally's second round of tales shifted to Tales of the Haunted Valley, which featured gruesome Indian ghost stories he'd read when he was a boy. By midnight, the embers of the fire radiated heat, and logs set on it would blaze up faster than a new story.

When only Jimmy, Biff, and Rory remained, he knew it was time to tell stories about Lake Manitou.

"Do you boys know why this place is called Lake Manitou?"

Jimmy jumped to answer, "There is a big water serpent like the Loch Ness monster that lives in an underwater cave somewhere at the bottom of the lake. It's probably a plesiosaur."

"You think there's a dinosaur living in the lake?" Biff mocked.

"I heard Manitou means spirit," Rory commented. "So, Lake Manitou means spirit lake."

Wally nodded. "Manitou is a Chippewa word, and Rory is right, it does mean spirit, but the Dakota who lived here before the Chippewa didn't call it Spirit Lake; instead, they called it *Wanagiyata*, which means *Place of Souls*." He studied them. "What does that tell you?"

"I thought the Manitou was some sort of Horned Serpent," Jimmy defended.

Rory jumped on the point Wally was making, "It means both of them thought it was haunted."

"Right. Do you guys know the name Joseph Nicollet?"

"The Nicollet Dam," Rory again answered.

"He was an explorer," Biff softly followed.

Wally continued, whittling a stick as he spoke. "A long time ago, a Chippewa holy man by the name of Chagobay, along with his son Nanakonan, led Joseph Nicollet's expedition up Kanaranzi Creek—"

"The one by Carousel Park," Rory interrupted.

"What does Kanaranzi mean?" Biff asked.

"I'm not really sure what Kanaranzi means … anyway old Chagobay led Nicollet up the creek and into the lake, but he warned the scientist and the members of the expedition to not touch any of the water lilies or they would risk waking the evil spirit that lived here. On his map of Minnesota, Joseph Nicollet called this place Lake Manitou. Before it became the Nicollet Dam, the place was called Nicollet Rapids."

"Why?" Biff asked.

Before Wally answered, he made a mental note that while the Forsberg boy was a brute and did not follow orders like his older brother, Biff was naturally inquisitive.

"I was told all of these stories by the grandson of Chagobay, who is now a very, very old man just upriver at the reservation. Migisi is his name. If I remember correctly, Nicollet and Chagobay were trying to go up the Blue Knife River when they were abducted by Pillagers, who took them as hostages and brought them up to Chief Flat Mouth at Leech Lake."

"My dad has an old cabin on Bear Island," Biff added, only to see his fact hang awkwardly on the air.

Until Jimmy asked, "Why is the river called Blue Knife?"

"Nicollet was a scientist who made geological notes about all the areas he traveled. Blue Earth County in southern Minnesota was named by Nicollet just like the Blue Knife River owes its name to him. It has something to do with copper vitriol."

"But there's no copper around here," Jimmy said.

"I've seen some blue ooze coming out of the rocks below the Nicollet Dam," Rory commented.

Did he go on his own, or was he taken? Migisi was the only one that could patrol the eastern shore, which belonged to the reservation. The western shore was owned by Triton.

"Before the dam covered up Nicollet Rapids, the blue vitriol was a bit of a landmark, which is what Chagobay intended to show Nicollet."

"The rocks by my house bleed green and blue," Biff said. "My dad said that's why it's called Bleeding Rock."

Wally hesitated, remembering the boys would soon be in seventh grade English with his wife, who would scold him for telling gruesome tales to impressionable boys.

But he told his next story anyway, how the evil shaman Wiyipisiw sacrificed twelve children, along with twelve mothers, who still haunted the woods of Old Copper Road seeking their children. He ended it by talking about how Chief Black Horse of the Dakota personally avenged himself against the man who'd killed his mother and brothers, which seemed to take the edge off the boys.

This time, all three sat there for a few minutes without a question. "Do you believe Lake Manitou is really haunted?" Jimmy asked.

Wally's hands grew still. "I've heard some strange stories in my life, but I've never seen a real ghost."

Then Wally sent the three boys to their tents.

He now stared at the fire, holding the Barlow knife and wondering if he'd have the courage to face the darkness.

Long ago, Lily Weber stood on Turtle Island with the Isanti Lodge and used her magic to save her brother. Having just battled the Manitou, she knew the immortal creature would outlast her, so she created a spiritual alliance to fight the evil. The forces of light had triumphed over the darkness.

Sixty years later, Wally knew the mantle of leadership had fallen to him, even though he'd never seen a Horned Serpent, Tak-Pei, or even one of the Jiibay ghosts that reportedly haunted the water.

Now he, Ed Nielson, Norval Riel, Marlin Luning, and original member Albert Fisher had to get organized without being at full strength: with Lily in the hospital, Chuck Luning in Georgia, and Paul Forsberg stationed in Germany.

Kermit Crain, Bjorn Forsberg, and Albert Fisher had been boys when they battled the Manitou. Lily hadn't been much older. Wally wondered if battling monsters was best left to the youth, like Biff, Rory, Jimmy, and Chris.

Wally rose from his spot beside the campfire and slipped into his hammock a few feet away.

CHAPTER TWENTY-THREE

Hunting Ghosts

Turtle Island State Park
September 1, 1961

JIMMY NIELSON WOKE IN his tent, and, upon hearing Wally Crain snoring, walked down to the empty dock. He stared out at Lake Manitou as if trying to solve a puzzle.

Jimmy then walked back to his tent and nudged awake his best friend Brian Forsberg as well as Rory Stewart. "I call bullshit," he whispered so only those in the tent could hear him.

"I'm sleeping," Rory said in protest.

"Fess up then."

"I'm not lying," Rory said slightly louder. "It's there. I swear."

"I call bullshit. Prove it."

"Now?" Rory whined. "It's the middle of the night."

"Exactly. Everyone is asleep. No one will see us. We'll paddle across the lake, jump the fence, and we'll find out if you're telling the truth or not."

"We'll get in trouble," Biff reminded.

"Only if we get caught." Jimmy grinned in the muted light of the tent.

"Let's do it." Rory slipped out of his bag.

"Should we wake Chris?" Jimmy asked.

"No, he'd probably tell on us. Let him sleep," Biff said.

A moment later, the three boys tip-toed out of the camp and back to the sandy beach where they'd left their canoes. In a matter of minutes, all three absconded a canoe and left behind the other scouts in the middle of the night.

Rory led Jimmy and Biff from the western shore of Lake Manitou to the edge of the highway. Once at the highway, Biff took over the mantle of leadership. "We'll cross one at a time. If all three of us cross together, they might see us. Stay low. The security guards might be able to see this far."

"Why would there be security guards?" Jimmy asked.

"Those machines are more expensive than some farm tractor," Rory rebuked.

"You go first, big mouth," Biff insisted. Once Rory crossed the road, Biff told Jimmy, "For the record, this is stupid."

After Wally's ghost stories, Rory argued that Haggard Quarry was actually a cover story for a secret treasure hunt. When Biff hesitated, Jimmy knew part of the tale might be true. After his dreams, Jimmy needed to know the truth.

"What's the worst that can happen?" Jimmy asked Biff.

"They'll shoot us for trespassing."

"Oh, come on … they're not going to shoot kids." With that, Jimmy hustled across the road and jumped into the ditch with Rory.

"This is fun," Jimmy admitted. "It's just like *The Guns of Navarone*."

"Yeah, it sure is. Except I get to be Captain Mallory. You can be 'Butcher' Brown."

"But he gets killed in the movie."

"Yeah, but he's cool. Biff can be Andrea."

Almost on cue, Biff jumped into the ditch, landing on top of Jimmy, who quickly shoved him off.

"You're going to be Andrea. I'm Butcher, and Rory's Captain Mallory. We're going to blow up some Nazis."

"Andrea's a girl's name. Why can't I be Captain Mallory?"

"Andrea gets the girl at the end, right?"

"Yeah."

"So shut up and take orders."

Biff pointed. "There is a spot up ahead where the water has created a little ravine. We can sneak under the fence."

"Ready men?" Rory asked.

Jimmy hesitated. *What am I afraid of? Obviously, Rory isn't worried about a thing.* "Ready, sir."

Twice hiding because of passing cars, Rory led them through the ditch and quickly found a spot where the soil had washed out from under the fence.

Although not the official officer, Biff again took charge. "Okay, now be careful because it's almost a two-hundred-foot drop to the bottom of the quarry. This side is pretty steep. Watch your feet and don't say a word because the quarry will echo the smallest noise. There's a ridge about ten feet from the lip of the quarry. That'll lead around to the area where we can get deeper."

"If one of us slips and falls, we'll die," Rory protested.

"The ridge is ten feet wide. They drive trucks on it. Just keep your hand on the wall and you'll be fine."

When the boys reached the lip, they formed a precarious human chain that linked each other over the ten-foot drop-off onto the first ledge. Even in darkness, the scope of the quarry was breathtaking. The pink quartzite quarry extended for hundreds of yards in all directions. On the far western edge, the quarry flattened for the trucks and machines to extract the quartz, but on the end closest to the lake, the walls were almost sheer.

Once they walked around the side of the quarry, they came to where years of digging had created a series of giant-sized steps.

Quickly they learned how to scale down the sides from one step to the next.

Why does it feel like we're crawling into an open grave?

When they reached forty feet from the bottom of the quarry, Biff stumbled, sending a shower of quartz gravel over the side of the next step.

"Get down," Rory quickly ordered, and the boys dropped to their bellies. Rory shimmied over to the corner, followed by Jimmy and Biff.

True to Rory's prediction, a floodlight from the top of the quarry shone light into the bottom. It panned across the floor and stopped at the wall. It was then that Jimmy saw the tin shed that Rory and Biff discussed.

With the spotlight over their heads, its scan left them in the shadows. But on the western side, a man with a flashlight appeared in the darkness. He walked toward the center of the quarry and then flipped on a panel of lights that illuminated the floor.

The security guard had a shotgun over his shoulder.

Earlier in the tent, Rory had insisted that the park had armed guards. His father had told him that Nazi spies had shown up once before WWII, and that since then the quarry had been guarded.

"Having lights on all night would create suspicion," Rory had whispered to Jimmy. "That's why they keep it dark and use spotlights only when needed."

Now Jimmy believed part of the story. For ten minutes, the lights remained on while Biff muttered profanities.

Rory insisted on waiting another ten minutes before moving from their spots. It took considerable "non-verbal coaxing" to get Biff to leave.

When the boys believed the coast was clear, they finished their descent to the bottom of the pit. Dodging between heavy equipment and rock piles, the boys steadily made their way to the tin shed on the far side of the quarry.

Before they could make it, the spotlight turned on and cast a beam thirty yards behind them. The boys split in two directions—Brian and Rory ran left to some equipment, but Jimmy sprinted straight ahead and threw himself into the shadows beside the tin shed.

Both Rory and Biff stood a chance with a security guard: Biff had worked at the quarry all summer and Rory was the nephew of its owner. Jimmy knew getting caught would mean his father's belt on his backside.

The spotlight stayed on the big bulldozer, trapping Rory and Biff in its shadows. As soon as the floodlights were turned on, Rory stood up and walked out.

To Jimmy's horror, he heard the shotgun load. *Biff! Be careful!*

He pressed into the darkest shadows formed by the tin building and the edge of the wall. Although just a few inches wide, a gap existed between the straight back wall of the shed and irregular face of the quarry wall. At the bottom, the shed butted right up against stone, but two feet up, a ten-inch-gap allowed Jimmy to slide his foot into the cavity, and with a shimmy of his hip, his torso followed. Once hidden, his hands felt the smooth surface of a sliding door, and the thick floor beam of the shed, but below it, he felt the lip where a space existed.

Crouching down into the space, he produced a match from a box stored in his front pocket, which illuminated the underbelly of the tin shed, built upon big metal wheels like a toy train.

So they can slide it out of the way.

Turning back to the quarry wall, he looked at stone at the base but two feet up, just where the shed met the wall, the cavity existed.

A second match revealed a tunnel.

Holy shit. Rory was right. What are these guys hiding?

Jimmy entered the space headfirst but backwards, using his feet to push himself. When the scraping against his head and back ended, he spun around and lit a third match.

A tunnel, large enough to drive a truck through, lined up with the back wall of the tin shed. Having just climbed down from the reed-filled shore of Lake Manitou, Jimmy knew he was two-hundred feet below the surface of the lake, and more than a hundred-and-fifty feet below the lakebed.

Steel tracks ran east from the opening at the quarry to a place where a chain link gate filled the tunnel from top to bottom. The posts were cut and cemented right into the stone. If he'd had a wire-cutter, he could have cut right through the flimsy defense.

Biff's theory about curling stones now sounded pretty lame.

And Nazis?

During his World War II phase, in which he tried to understand the bitter adult men in his life, Jimmy read all about Heinrich Himmler and Dietrich Eckart and their occult obsessions. But what would Nazis want with Native American legends?

Jimmy stood and began walking between the rail tracks. By his sixth match, he had his face pressed against the fencing.

Biff's theory suddenly held water. The pink quartz that filled the entire quarry abruptly ended at the chain link, and in a hewn cavity where the rail tracks went in three directions, the opposite wall, twenty yards away, was a much darker stone, cut—not blasted. The tools left it almost smooth, even though Jimmy couldn't run his hand over the curve.

The sixth match burned his fingers, and in the shock of pain, his hands became clumsy, and the matchbox tumbled to the ground, leaving him blind.

Oh shit, not good. Definitely not good.

His hands quickly brushed over a few of his remaining matches, but without the striker on the edge of the matchbox, he—

Jimmy desperately tried to light a match against the rough wood of the railroad tie, only to feel the head break off the match.

With his second attempt, he tried snapping two matches together.

In total darkness, his hands felt for the matchbox while collecting any spare match he came across.

His breathing and own heartbeat filled the cavity and his ears. The panic caused his chest to beat so loudly that it almost became an annoyance. Then the hairs on his neck stood on end.

An echo of his heartbeat thumped. Not fast, but almost simultaneous.

Goosebumps grew on his neck and arms and fear climbed up his cheeks and into his ear. He heard a whisper:

"Is it time?"

Family Matters

Haggard Quarry
September 2, 1961

BIFF FORSBERG KNEW the guards were not about to kill them, but the danger was far from over.

"It's a couple of kids," a man had shouted.

In the distance, a truck started. Biff stepped out of the shadows and could barely see with the bright spotlight shining on him. But as he looked around, he couldn't see Jimmy anywhere.

"Don't say anything about Jimmy or I'll kill you," Biff muttered to Rory as the man approached.

"Face down on the ground, boys."

Half an hour later, Biff and Rory were in the waiting room of the office building. The four guards that had converged on them and frisked them also waited. One of them had even searched the area around the tin shed but came back without Jimmy and claimed that he hadn't seen anything.

The door opened and Red Dobie, not Uncle Ewan, stepped inside. "Son of a fucking whore," Dobie muttered and stood over the two boys for a few moments of silent judgment. Then he plopped down in the secretary's chair and began asking questions.

Rory stuck to the story that it'd only been him and Biff, and after thirty minutes of questioning, Dobie called Rory's father.

When Sean Stewart arrived, he unleashed his anger on his oldest son, but Biff noticed how he gave Dobie a strange handshake first, like the adults at the Sinclair family reunion had done.

"What the hell were you thinking?" Mr. Stewart asked then smacked Rory hard across the back of his head with an open hand.

"We were having an adventure," Rory tried.

"You're breaking the law by trespassing here. Do you want me to let these men throw you in jail?"

Rory shook his head and glanced at Biff.

"Aren't you supposed to be camping right now?"

Both boys nodded.

"Did Forsberg put you up to this?"

Asshole. Biff glared. *Where is Jimmy?*

"No." Rory kept his cool once again. "We were pretending we were secret agents like in *The Guns of Navarone.*"

"*The Guns of Navarone?*"

The men finally laughed.

"Is there anything I need to take care of, Red?" Mr. Stewart asked.

Dobie scratched at his bearded chin. "Forget about it. The shame is on me and my men for letting a couple of kids sneak in like this. Obviously, we'll need to tighten things up around here."

"I'll make sure Rory knows his place," Mr. Stewart added.

"The kid knew a lot about the quarry. Do *you* know your own place?"

"Of course," Mr. Stewart snapped. "So, are they clear to go?"

"Get them out of here."

As Mr. Stewart led him and Rory to the waiting Mercedes, he smacked Rory several more times before shoving him in the backseat.

"I'm tempted to just bring you straight home, but then I'd have to explain things to Crain as well as your parents, Forsberg." He glanced at Biff then Rory. "So, let's be clear. This did not happen? Understand?"

Biff nodded.

Rory nodded.

Mr. Stewart sighed. "Where did you boys leave the canoe?"

"We hid it in some cattails next to the road," Rory answered.

"Do you boys understand that we'll never speak of this again? You'll paddle back across the lake and when you wake up, it was all just a bad dream. It never happened."

"Yes, sir," Biff answered.

Again Rory nodded.

The guards closed the big gates behind the car.

WHEN BIFF AND Rory reached the canoe, it was empty—Jimmy was still nowhere to be seen.

Both boys walked over to the canoe. Nearby a car engine purred. *We're still being watched.*

"What about Jimmy?" Rory whispered.

Biff shoved Rory forward. "Just get in."

Biff and Rory pushed off and began paddling, and a moment later, Mr. Stewart's car drove off.

He's gotta be hiding back in the quarry. "Okay, turn around. We gotta wait for Jimmy."

This is my fault. I knew better. I never should have let them leave camp. Biff was on the verge of returning to the eroded ravine when Jimmy came scrambling over the road.

"Okay, hurry up, get in the canoe," Jimmy said, almost out of breath. "I think someone is following me."

After several strong paddle strokes into the lake, Biff stopped paddling and asked, "What the hell happened to you?"

"Don't ask."

"Where were you?"

"I found the tunnel Rory told us about."

"See, I told you!" Rory exclaimed.

"Did you go in?"

"There was a locked gate."

"So did you see the Manitou?" Biff asked sarcastically.

Jimmy hesitated. "I don't think so. No. But I heard something."

"Probably the security guards," Rory said.

"Did they get your names?"

"They called my dad, so yeah, they know who we are, Jimmy." Rory shrugged. "But we were told that no one was ever going to speak of it. It's all good."

"So, what did you hear?" Biff asked.

"Um, nothing. I just hid."

He's lying. What's he trying to hide?

CHAPTER TWENTY-FIVE

David and Goliath

Turtle Island State Park
September 2, 1961

CHRIS LUNING CRIED when he realized the source of the noise that woke him. It wasn't a monster or a ghost; Jimmy, Biff, and Rory had snuck out of camp without him. At school, his homework alliance with Biff helped him socially, but at a Boy Scouts events, he felt in his element. Being left out hurt, which is why he cried.

Do they all think I'm a rat? Am I not trustworthy?

When Jimmy, Biff, and Rory returned in relative silence to avoid Wally, it also felt like a slight to Chris.

After sorting through his emotions, Chris wiped his tears and slipped out of his tent and took two steps to where Wally Crain slept.

A Scout must be morally straight.

Jimmy and Biff failed the code. Rory too.

They were sneaky and deceitful. Yet telling on them … would that be morally straight?

According to the handbook, being morally straight meant living life with honesty (which they didn't do), to be clean in your speech and actions (which meant not telling lies or cursing), and to be a person of strong character (like telling on them).

For most of the summer, he felt like the pariah for telling on Biff for the rice crispy bar incident. *Is this another test of character? Am I doing this to be hurtful to them?*

A scan of the camp confirmed three things: it was still night, Wally still slept in his hammock, and his friends were either sleeping or pretending to be asleep.

Then he heard the same noise that had woken him—sniffing.

He returned to his tent and found his flashlight and slingshot.

Whether rabbit or black bear, his sling shot packed enough of a nonlethal wallop to send the sniffer running.

Chris glanced over at Wally and the other tents, which were illuminated in the soft glow of the dying fire.

He slipped the flashlight into his back pocket while he readied the sling in his right hand and the large rock projectile in his left.

The sniffing came from the darkness formed between his tent and a large tree on the edge of camp. He took four steady steps around the tent to peer into the darkness.

Chris pulled the elastic rubber all the way to his ear but then released it without firing the shot. He bent down and picked up two more stones in case he missed with the first. He put the stones in his mouth, holding them in each cheek, then turned his gaze to the darkness.

When he heard the sniffing and a shuffle of feet, he let the rock go, the twang of the slingshot echoing loudly.

He heard a ricochet on the ground, but a shadowy form bolted from the darkness, heading toward the lake.

Chris quickly loaded, aimed, and fired at a distance of only fifteen yards. The second rock hit the animal squarely in the side, producing a strange rattle instead of a thump.

Quills, Chris quickly realized, and spit the third rock into his waiting fingertips. By the time he took aim again, his theory was confirmed.

From the small head to the humped back, the shape of a stunned porcupine could be seen in the starlight. Chris wanted to call out to Wally and the others, but that might scare away the porcupine and only leave him with a story no one else would believe.

A head shot, however …

Chris was about to release the stone, the porcupine turned toward him—and stood up on two legs.

A pair of skinny arms, with long fingers, extended from the quill-covered torso.

"Will it be you?" the creature asked him. "Your blood would taste as sweet as any of the others. Come down to the lake with me."

The rock in the leather cradle of the sling vanished from his fingers, and in a heartbeat, it traveled from his hand all the way to the creature's forehead—with no effect.

Chris gasped, out of ammunition.

He bent low to the ground to find another rock, but as soon as he took his eyes off the creature, it rushed right at him. He raised his forearm to shield the brunt of the charge, but just before impact, a dark shape swooped down from the sky.

In a rustle of feathers, the porcupine man retreated for the water, galloping upon its long arms and short legs.

Another dark creature had taken its place.

The beady eyes of a big raven studied him for a moment. Chris let go of the rock at his fingertips.

A guttural click came from the raven's throat. Then two distinctly human syllables followed, "Found you."

Chris spun his head to find Wally, who remained sleeping. He turned to his friends' tent—nothing. Even the tent behind him remained silent.

Found me? What does that mean?

Despite his beating heart, Chris settled onto his knees and heels, surrendering to the moment. "Hello," he whispered to his hero.

Is this just a dream?

"Dream," the raven uttered. The ebony bird stood almost as tall as Chris knelt.

It read my thoughts. It's trying to have a conversation with me.

A scout should be mentally awake.

A scout should be curious.

A scout should ask questions.

"Who are you?"

The raven growled for a moment before uttering a peculiar word, "Robin."

A bird named after another bird. Weird. Chris looked past the raven for a moment, to make sure the creature was gone. *What was that?*

"Tak-Pei," the raven answered.

Just like the stories. The Little People are real. Chris reached into his front pocket to find sunflower seeds, which he tossed forward. The raven glanced at them, insulted.

Why are you here?

"Help," the raven answered.

Be prepared! Chris felt a flutter of excitement. *Are you here to help me, or do you need help?*

"Help," the raven answered again.

Show me what you need. Show me how to help.

The ebony bird struck the ground with such force that Chris felt the impact in his knees. Again and again, the bird struck, producing a crack in the ground that began to spread.

A chasm to the underworld opened, and Chris had to step away. Like shattering ice, the earth broke apart, swallowing his tent, the tent with Biff and Jimmy, and even the trees that held Wally's hammock.

A rumble filled the air, and when Chris looked toward the Blue Knife River, a wall of water came rushing at him.

It lifted Chris into its embrace, and he felt his body being carried into Lake Manitou, tumbling and spinning as if he was in his mother's washing machine.

His dream changed Lake Manitou into a big bathtub, with all the water leaving through a single drain that made a strange sucking noise as a vortex formed. He found himself spinning, spinning, spinning…

His hands grabbed hold of something.

A rock in the middle of the vortex.

Both hands managed to clasp it in a desperate hug, and despite his torso and legs being caught in the current, he moved his head and shoulders out of the water.

"Chris! Chris! Hold on!"

Grandpa Albert stood on the shore, frantically waving.

The raven swept down from the air, landing upon the stone that Chris clung to. "Help!" the raven mocked. "Help me!"

It needs my help. It wants me to help it. What do you need me to do?

The ungainly fowl turned its head before answering, "Let go."

But Chris couldn't let go.

Letting go meant certain death.

On the other shore, a man wearing a black slouch hat, deerskin pants, an unbuttoned denim shirt, and leather boots held a pistol, which he pointed to the raven and fired a shot. Blood came oozing out of the raven's breast muscles.

"Bastard," the man muttered and turned to face Chris. "That's how you deal with bullies, son."

Chris woke in his tent with a gasp, prompting the others in the tent to shift and grumble.

Dawn had arrived, and outside, a raven croaked.

CHAPTER TWENTY-SIX

A Sticky Start

Old Copper Road
September 5, 1961

FOR THE FIRST time all summer, Nicole Guerin woke before the ravens. By the first "caw" of the morning, she was sitting in front of her repainted vanity and inspecting her attire.

Nicole, now Nicki in her mind, had a reputation to establish, after all. She adjusted her brown headband that matched her shoes. Unlike at Turtle Island Jesuit School, her hair was now cut in a bob that floated just above her shoulders. A year ago, she would've simply pulled it into a ponytail, letting loose strands end where they wanted.

Next, she inspected her outfit: a plaid skirt crisscrossed with yellows and browns and a turquoise sweater-jacket worn over a light blue blouse. At TI, she'd been an aloof, slovenly nerd who looked down at all of her less-talented classmates. *Now I'll be fun. Now more showing off.*

Her golden beige skin tone could easily be the result of a successful summer of sunbathing, but Nicki knew that to the kids at Split Rock High School she'd be a "wild Injun." At Turtle Island Jesuit School, she'd seen scholarship winners from all over the

United States and Canada go running home to their reservations in tears because of treatment from returning students. As a freshman, she'd even joined in the cruel sport of bullying. *Smiles today … knives will come out by Friday.*

An argument in the tree outside of her window continued until one of the ravens flew off, followed by another, leaving a solitary bird to stare back at her from his perch.

Here goes nothing.

Nicki collected her packed school bag, turned off her light, and bounced down the stairs to the kitchen where she received three distinct reactions. Her mother gasped then clasped her hands at her chest and smiled broadly. Her father furled his brow, shook his head in silent condemnation, and immediately sipped his coffee. Cameron opened his mouth widely at first then asked, "Are you wearing makeup?"

"Of course," Nicki said, stopping at the table to pick up a poured glass of orange juice. "Remember what we agreed upon, Cam?"

Cameron chuckled as her father muttered, "Ashamed of who you are?"

"I'm a realist, Dad. Those kids at Split Rock will look for any reason they can to hate me and torment me. It's bad enough that I'm mixed blood, poor, and the new girl, but if they find out my brother is the new custodian—I'll stand no chance at all." She huffed. "And why am I going through all this turmoil?"

"A music scholarship," her mother answered.

Nicki nodded. "Let me fight my battles the way I know how, Dad."

"While you were out waging war with your new friends last night, we got a phone call from the hospital. They've taken Grandma Lily off the respirator. She's breathing on her own now, and in a few days, her voice should be strong enough to speak."

"Oh, thank God. That's wonderful."

For most of the summer, Grandma Lily was unresponsive, struggling just to take a breath as her body grew weaker and weaker. In August, her lungs finally began to fight back against the damage inflicted in the house fire.

It's almost a miracle.

But somehow, the thought of her grandmother returning to live with them filled her with dread. Duty and responsibility could spoil her future plans. This rattled Nicki, shaking her confidence before she headed off to school.

Her mother motioned at the table. "Sit down. Eat."

"I don't want to spill anything or have seeds stuck in my teeth for the first day of school. Gavin is picking me up on his way to football practice, so I don't have to ride the bus. I'm going to wait out on the steps."

Gavin MacPherson's test was about to begin. As the only witness to the nefarious accident involving Grandmother Lily, his sincerity lacked reproach. Over the past few months, Nicki had encouraged their relationship, which involved kissing and touching above the waist, but hands needed to remain outside of the clothing at all times.

Her virtue intact, she now needed him to help secure her reputation. The way he talked about her to his friends would matter. The way his friends reacted to her would matter. So far, she felt genuine feelings for him, but it could all turn on a dime if he felt social pressure in dating an "Injun." It made Nicki's stomach a bundle of knots just contemplating it.

But when he pulled up to the house, she played the part. She hopped into his truck, pecked him on the cheek, and let the conversation be all about him.

In minutes, they transitioned from isolated Old Copper Road to busy Market Street.

Following World War II, Split Rock, like so many other districts, experienced a population boom, prompting a new school to be built. With massive financial donations from local philanthropists Albert Fisher and his business partners from Triton CorporaCorporation in St. John, the new school was built in 1952.

Compared to the old stone buildings at Turtle Island Jesuit School, Split Rock Public School looked like a Manhattan skyscraper.

The three-story glass facade greeted all students, whether they walked across the parking lot or were dropped off in the horseshoe lot by the buses. Gavin drove past the cheery exterior and the big gymnasium to the sports parking lot on the south side of the building.

At 6:35, there were several vehicles already parked in all three lots. Nicki apparently wasn't the only one nervous for the first day of school.

"You're going to do just fine," Gavin said after taking the keys out of the ignition. He leaned over and kissed her gently on the lips. "Stand your ground, and I'll see you after morning practice."

Nicki walked in through the south doors nearest to the agriculture building and sports complex. The central doors remained where most kids would enter, running the gauntlet of social judgment. Nicki and Gavin had already toured the building, and she knew her turf well. Her domain—the auditorium, band, and choir rooms—was on the opposite side of the building at the north doors.

Instead of going there, Nicki chose the stairs.

The ascending staircase faced the grand commons and deposited her on the second floor where the glass windows of the central offices looked out over everything. The secretaries were also preparing for their first day battles, but Nicki already had everything she needed.

Built on the slopes of the Crow Wing River valley, Split Rock Public School had a unique feature—skywalks. The main part of the three-story building stood at the base of a hill that flattened out into the parking lot and sport fields before continuing to down-town and the river. From both ends of the library, forty-foot tubes extended like two outstretched arms to reach the top of the hill, where a single-story wing had been built.

Nicki had done her homework before setting foot in the build-ing. Having interviewed Cameron and studied Gavin's 1961 yearbook, she felt ready for her own test.

While the north tube was claimed by the freshmen and sopho-mores, the southern tube, always a bit warmer and sunnier, was claimed by the juniors and seniors. For the past decade, the seniors would line the tube, often sitting against the electric radiator panels as they judged the students who ran the gauntlet between build-ings.

Her first day couldn't have started better. She met senior cheer-leader Alexandra Nielson, who was nice to her. She held her ground with junior classmate and potential rival Leslie Christian-sen. With a crowd of upperclassmen around her, Mrs. Crain went out of her way to greet her (and commend her transcript grades).

It was nearly perfect.

Nicki shared all four morning classes with Gavin, and by lunch, she'd experienced victory after victory, including sitting at the popular junior table with several other couples affiliated with foot-ball players.

Then disaster struck.

There were gasps.

Then laughter.

And apologies.

At least fifty kids watched with various reactions to what Gavin, of all people, did with ten minutes remaining in the lunch hour.

For Nicki, it turned into a surreal blur. From the bathroom, she heard the bell ring and pushed down the tears, deep down, and walked out with her head held high.

"Nicki, I … I'm sorry."

"Just go to class and let me deal with this," she snapped loudly enough that others were certain to hear her.

For a few moments, the crowd of students ascending the staircase left her invisible, but instead of going to her locker, she had to meet with the high school secretary, who empathetically listened while Nicki explained what happened.

Within a few minutes, a plan was hatched, and kind Jane Anderson handed Nicki the pink tardy slip to excuse her to Mrs. Crain's fifth hour class.

Mrs. Crain's room was in the far southeast corner of the upper wing, and the hall was empty as the bell rang. Just seconds later, Nicki stepped into the room full of her peers. She boldly walked across the front of the room and placed the tardy slip on the podium before pivoting around to claim an empty desk in the front row.

She felt her damp blouse sticking to her shoulder and back, so she didn't lean back in her chair.

It took only a glance at several of the girls to see the joy in their eyes, and a few of the guys smirked as Mrs. Crain read the late slip.

The hazing had begun.

Gavin's not going to shelter me this hour, Nicki realized as Mrs. Crain began her introductions. *At least he's not here to make matters worse.*

During the introduction to the course and distribution of materials, Nicki stayed focused, ignoring the nightmare that happened during lunch.

When it came time for the speeches of introduction, the seas parted to leave Nicki Guerin all by herself for a moment. Mrs. Crain spotted Maurice Williams lingering in a pack of three boys.

"Maurice, I said partners, not trios. You and Nicki can partner up."

Maurice was too slow-witted to muster a defense stronger than a reluctant sigh, and while Nicki took copious notes, Maurice kept his eyes on his desk more than he looked up. When the timer sounded, Mrs. Crain avoided starting with them, choosing several other pairs before selecting Maurice and Nicki.

Eventually, Maurice stood in front of the podium with Nicki flanking him.

"Um, so, this is Nicki Guerin, and she's kinda new. She was a TIJ last year and—"

"Maurice," Mrs. Crain stopped him as a couple chuckles came from the audience.

"What? She said it."

"I did say it, Mrs. Crain. It's just an acronym. Last year, I was a TIJ, and now I'm a proud Bulldog."

Maurice nodded as Nicki defended him. "Nicki likes music and reading. Her favorite memory from the past summer is seeing a Minnesota Twins game, and her goal for the school year is to meet new people and get good grades and to stay dry."

Again, the class burst into chuckles at Maurice's answer, but before Mrs. Crain could muster up a fierce scolding, Nicki smiled and did a little curtsy while saying, "It's true."

Maurice stepped away, and Nicki stepped to the podium, still putting up poised armor. "The gentleman standing beside me is Mr. Maurice Williams, and he is definitely not a TIJ. His proudest accomplishment over the past three months is catching a thirty-eight-inch musky at Leech Lake, and his goal for the coming school year is and I quote, 'Not failing Public Speaking class,' unquote."

Life had taken a swing at Nicki Guerin, and she danced right around a potential disaster with Maurice.

Seventh hour study hall, however, proved to be much more of a challenge. Nicki had to be fierce while also fixing an unexpected problem.

Mrs. Crain had a small library of novels and magazines against her hallway wall, and after going through all seventy-seven study hall rules, she watched from her podium to make sure each and every student either began working on their homework or found something to read.

"You need to earn your library privileges first," Mrs. Crain finished. "Focused behavior today will bring those privileges sooner rather than later."

To set the tone, Mrs. Crain patrolled the rows for the first ten minutes. The study hall was a mixture of 6th-12th grade students, which meant Nicki was being watched by a sampling of the entire student body—including Gavin, who made it worse by wanting to apologize nonverbally.

Nicki kept her nose in her collection of textbooks and sat in the front of row five, with smelly Biff Forsberg and a freshman girl between her and Gavin. Beside her, Jimmy Nielson, another neighbor, sketched pictures in his notebook.

Whenever she looked up from her textbook to stretch, Gavin was staring. When Gavin's relentless focus became unbearable, Nicki walked up to the podium to request a bathroom pass, which Mrs. Crain allowed with an empathetic nod.

Nicki hadn't even left the room when she saw Gavin stand from his desk to make the same request.

Luckily, Mrs. Crain denied it.

Nicki did not go to the bathroom, however, and instead went directly to her locker. As promised, secretary Jane Anderson had taken the messy jacket to the laundry room, quickly washed it, and put it in the drier for the better part of fifth and sixth hour. Nicki took the jacket and went to the restroom to re-dress.

When Nicki returned, she once again wore her turquoise sweater jacket and tried to forget what happened at lunch. Gavin, however, held a folded note in the palm of his hand, and when he rose to go to the bathroom, he dropped it on her desk.

Nicki left it there.

Mrs. Crain saw it also, but she waited until Gavin returned. He eyed it with horror as he returned to his desk without the ability to make it float back up into his hand.

A moment later, Mrs. Crain began patrolling the desks again, and as she passed by, she swept the note up into her hand.

Nicki gave no reaction.

Mrs. Crain returned to her podium after the pass, and along with the rest of the class, waited for the hand to reach three. When the bell finally rang, the students all but jumped from their desks to bolt toward the door, but Mrs. Crain called out, "Miss Guerin, a word."

Despite the sudden flush in her cheeks, Nicki held her head high as she walked up to the podium. "Yes?"

"I was surprised to learn that the girls' bathroom is now a full-service laundry. Care to explain?"

Nicki did not so much as quiver a lip. "Mrs. Anderson told me she would leave my sweater jacket in my locker after it dried, and since I was only a short distance away, I checked my locker before going to the restroom. A boy at lunch accidentally spilled his lunch tray on my back when he tripped standing up. Do you want me to fetch Mrs. Anderson to verify my story?"

Mrs. Crain was silent for a moment. "That won't be necessary."

"Is there anything else?

"That's all," Mrs. Crain said, and then handed her the note, "Don't be too harsh on Mr. MacPherson."

Nicki nodded in affirmation. The tests of the first day had been passed, but the rest of her junior year might not be so easy.

CHAPTER TWENTY-SEVEN

The Sacred Flame

Mizheekay Band of Ojibwe Reservation
September 6, 1961

L EONARD WHITE ELK extended the empty dreamcatcher
to Migisi, who hesitated for a moment before taking it.

"So Fawn is dead?" Migisi asked from the doorway of his
cabin.

Leonard looked at Ben LaBiche before answering. "Her spirit
lingered for a while, long enough for us to speak one last time. My
brothers and their families then joined us to help guide her on the
River of Souls. They gave her a proper Anishinaabe funeral."

"And where was she buried?"

"Far away from here, which was her wish. If there is a place beyond the grasp of the Horned Serpent, it is the place where I
buried her."

"Sit, both of you," Migisi said to Leonard and Ben LaBiche,
stepping out onto his porch. He looked down at the dreamcatcher
for several moments, but like an empty bowl, it held nothing for
the old man.

"Your mother saved my life," Migisi said, gesturing off to the
distance and the shimmer of Lake Manitou. "If not for her, I'd be
another trapped soul. My young body would have withered and

died, and that would have been my story. Certainly, she told you her dream of the turtle."

Leonard again looked over to his nephew. "Are you listening? You need to remember everything you hear during our visit."

The chubby boy nodded sincerely.

"During the battle with the Wintermaker, Fawn had a vision sent by Manabozho. In this vision, she saw the hero from legend, Iyash, but her assumption was that it was you, trapped on the island by the Horned Serpent."

"Indeed, and when she gathered the others together like in the first Midewiwin Lodge, Lily found a way to restore this sick boy back to health, just like in the tale. But that wasn't the only thing she saw in her vision from Manabozho, was it?"

"No," Leonard answered. "Fawn realized she'd misinterpreted the vision to be about you. It was a vision about the Seventh Stopping Place, and that in order to save the real Iyash, she needed to fulfill the prophecy."

Leonard turned to Benjamin. "The Anishinaabe people left the Atlantic coast to fulfill the prophecy. They stopped in Montreal, Niagara Falls, Detroit, Manitoulin Island, Sault Saint Marie, and Madeline Island, but the Seventh Stopping Place remained elusive. Some felt it was Spirit Island by Duluth, others thought it might be Mille Lacs, and there were some who felt it was here, at Lake Manitou."

"My sister and I found the sacred megis shells just a short walk from where we sit today," Migisi added.

"Your grandmother's vision showed her a turtle, a symbol that represents the Seven Fires prophecy, the story of creation, the story of the great flood, and for a brief while, it represented Lake Manitou, but Fawn revisited her vision again and again, realizing her mistake. She knew the turtle represented the vast continent of North America, and the journey of the Seven Fires. While Iyash was found on the edge of the turtle, the Seventh Stopping Place was not here in Minnesota, but high upon the ridge of the turtle's back. That is why your grandmother left her home."

"And did she find the Seventh Stopping Place?" Migisi asked.

"For you to learn the answer, you'd have to leave Lake Manitou and come back with me," Leonard explained.

"Me? Leave here? No, I have summoned you. We are in danger again. All of humanity is in danger."

"Fawn read your letters and instead chose to stay. She believed this new threat was a trick devised by your sister."

"A trick? I have seen the Tak-Pei prowling the dark shores. Evil has woken. I have kept my silent vigil for decades, and something is happening."

"I don't doubt that 'something is happening' but my mother told me not to trust anything that happens here as long as Lily Guerin lives, and she lives, doesn't she?"

"Her battle with death is over, but she has a long road to recovery."

"Her flesh might be weak, but her spirit is strong. Fawn told me what Lily did in her battle with the Wintermaker. I've brought my nephew Benjamin to be trained, but at the end of the week, we'll be leaving and returning home."

"A week? I can't possibly pass down what I know in a week."

"Fawn understood, perhaps better than you or your sister, the power of prophecy. Her vision of the bear, marten, crane, loon, fish, eagle, raven, and the deer will certainly come to pass, which is why my nephew and I have come. I will learn the role of the was-wa-shesh-she, and Leonard will learn the way of the eagle directly from you."

"But just a week? A battle is coming. You can't leave."

"I am not an ignorant man, but the autumnal equinox is coming, at the same time as a full moon, and with Lily still taking breath, there is no way on earth I would let Benjamin stay here. I don't doubt the Tak-Pei are prowling, which is why you will only get a week."

Migisi's face seemed to compress in angry wrinkles. "Your mother and I were allies. We are not the ones who spoke with the Wintermaker. For the better part of ten years, we prepared to fight the Wintermaker when the Serpent Star returned. First Lily was betrayed, and then we were betrayed by Lily. Remember that before you pass judgment."

I want to trust you, for my mother's sake. "If I did stay, what do you think would happen?"

"Something has stirred the darkness, and for reasons I do not understand. The last time, my sister accidentally woke the Tak-Pei and the Wintermaker, and we must make sure it does not happen again."

"Accidentally? While I share your blood, I know what Lily is— she is Wijigan. Her fate was to bring death, which she has brought again and again. The Creator shaped her for that role. Her actions were inevitable, not accidental."

"No, Father Guerin spoke of delaying the prophecy. He said our role in the Isanti Lodge was to stand against the darkness. That is what I would do. I must stay and guard against the darkness."

Admirable but misguided. "The unstoppable force meets the immovable object. You do know that this prophecy is a tapestry of beliefs. The Anishinaabe are not the only ones who know of it. For generations, the Oceti Sakowin, my father's Sioux, stood as guardians while the Anishinaabe, my mother's Chippewa, searched for the end of the prophecy. Both were instruments of the Great Creator. Who are you to impose your will?"

Migisi chuckled. "You sound like my grandfather. You have the spirit of an old man, and I still feel like a boy."

"I am your ally, even in disagreement."

"So, you would do nothing?" Migisi asked.

"I am here, aren't I? Fawn explained several things to me."

"Fawn had a stroke giving birth to you. She was incapable of speech."

Leonard looked long into Migisi's eyes, and then down at the dreamcatcher. "Fawn told me that the Water Drum is very real, and while Lily used it to defeat the Wintermaker, it is still too powerful to trust. Yet you stay here? Why? You are the sixth generation to claim it as … what? An heirloom? You see yourself as a guardian? What could you do to stop me if I wanted to take it?"

"Is that why you are here? Are you a murderous Sioux? Is that it?"

Leonard ignored Migisi's agitation. "The Water Drum is key to the unlocking of the prophecy, and whether in your possession, or in the possession of a Frenchman, it will serve its purpose when the Creator determines. What about the Ironwood Scrolls?"

"What about them?"

"Fawn told me they contain ancient magic, a song written upon them. So, do you have birch bark scrolls hidden in a nearby cave? Or do you have copies of copies?"

Migisi grew sullen. "What is your point?"

"We are in the Era of the Sixth Fire. Isn't it plain? It began with the arrival of Halley's Comet in 1910, and it will end with its return in 1986. You and Lily act as if the great battle is about to begin any day, when it most likely won't happen until … what … 2061? You and I will be dust by then. Even if we held the Water Drum in one hand, and the Ironwood Scrolls in another, and stood upon the right spot, at the right time, you're still missing something."

"The Sacred Fire. Did Fawn find it?"

"We need to pass our knowledge to the next generation, Migisi, and pray that your sister's betrayal does not doom all of mankind. We must trust in the future—that the boy in the snakeskin boots and the scarred woman—that they will find a way to defeat evil."

"You underestimate our enemies," Migisi stated. "Father Guerin knew all about them, and they seek to control the prophecy, which tells of a glorious Eighth Eternal Fire, but it also tells of fire and destruction. Your faith is foolish. You said that it was Lily's destiny to wake the Wintermaker, but if Father Guerin and the others had not fought, Joseph Little Toad would have given the Wintermaker his victory over death. Humanity walked upon the razor's edge that night."

A paradox of fate and free will. I trust fate, and Migisi believes in shaping his own destiny. "I understand."

"But you will not stay?"

Leonard shook his head. "Train us. Hell, come back with us, Migisi, where it is safe."

"No, I've felt the touch of the Wintermaker, and I'll do what I can to fight against him and his servants."

After a moment Migisi handed the dreamcatcher back to Leonard.

And I'll pick up the pieces when this is over.

Someone must trust the ancient prophecies.

A Road Less Traveled

Split Rock, MN
September 24, 1961

THE FULL MOON peeked in through the bedroom window of Chris Luning as he dreamed about the dead boy. His pillow was damp from crying, and he'd prayed himself to sleep after hearing the awful news.

Isaac Larson had been found dead shortly before noon along the cliffs of Bleeding Rock.

No foul play.

An accident.

A misstep on a shortcut home.

The TV news flashed up a picture, and in that moment, Chris knew he'd most likely been the last person to speak to the boy.

The Split Rock High School Homecoming was held Friday, September 22, and after a raucous pep fest, the high school kids streamed out of the gym to get ready for the parade and the junior high boys flooded out the door for an extra fifteen minutes of football before the buses arrived.

Isaac Larson had been with them, unaware that they lingered because most were staying for the game later that evening.

"Dang, I missed my bus," Isaac said to Chris, who'd just fumbled the ball, leading to a pileup of bodies a few yards away.

"That sucks," Chris said, and turned back to the pile.

It was the last time anyone saw Isaac alive.

In life, he'd turned his back, but now, in his dream, he watched the fourth grader continue toward home.

Isaac grabbed his book bag from the line of bags that formed the out-of-bounds sideline, let out a whimper, and bolted another ten yards before surrendering to his situation.

A handful of aides still stood in front of the school, helping the younger kids onto the buses, but Isaac didn't approach any of them.

It was a beautiful September day, with clear blue skies, warm temperatures, and no wind. He stood for a moment, weighing his options.

He turned and began walking.

Instead of walking in public, Isaac took a short cut.

Once across the intersection, the route became clear to Chris: Isaac Larson intended to follow the railroad south until it crossed the Division Street Bridge, where he would walk through the pine woods of the big granite bluff between the river and the lake, which ended at Old Copper Road.

With Fisher Sawmill on one end, and Fisher Lumber Mill on the other, and from his numerous visits to Biff Forsberg's house, Chris knew the territory well.

Now Chris watched helplessly as Isaac chose a road less traveled.

North Division Street was a major road in town, but past Highway 19 and the railroad, it turned into a gravel road that skirted the northern edge of the bluff and descended to the lake and the boat ramp. Isaac looked toward the dock, but he turned to the bluff halfway down the hill.

The pine forest was wild and free. The granite outcropping was actually difficult to climb, and he had to ascend it on all fours as he scaled thirty yards of elevation in a distance of only twenty yards.

Once he reached the top, the view was grand. The dome of the bluff was covered in old pine trees towering above his head. Unlike the pines in his grove, these trees had few lower branches, which allowed him to see the patches of exposed rock emerging from the rusty blanket of dead pine needles. To his right, all seven miles of Lake Manitou stretched out before him, drawing him closer for a peek over the edge.

No, you fool, don't do it, Chris called out.

Below Isaac's feet, the granite sloped away to the water's edge, but a few hundred yards ahead, the incline became a sheer cliff. Isaac had no problem keeping proper pace as he made a beeline for the highest point of the bluff.

When he reached the cliff, he paused, dropped to his belly, and cautiously crawled forward until his chin stuck out over the drop off. The granite was solid, allowing him to place both hands on the sharp edge as he looked to the rocks below.

The summer had been dry. Most years, fishermen cast jigs where the water met the perpendicular stone, but now, a pile of rubble and rocks angled down to the water's edge. Drawing saliva and mucus from his nose and throat, Isaac hocked a big loogie, listening as it splatted on one of the stones below.

What is he doing? Chris wondered from his bed.

Standing back up, Isaac unzipped his jeans and peed over the cliff. Even though he stood two paces from the edge, he could hear the urine creating a mini-waterfall. Once done, he zipped up and hustled on his way.

Isaac crossed a bald area of exposed granite so uniform he could walk over it like a paved parking lot. Even though it undulated in areas, it was almost level, except for an area where stones were stacked up in man-made columns. There were a few beer cans and bottles to indicate bored teens had come out drinking. There were about a dozen piles of stones, each consisting of about a dozen flat stones that had been carried onto the top of the bluff. Some were toppled in piles, begging to be stacked again. As Isaac passed by one of them, he kicked it over, topping the pile but also causing the top stones to come crashing into his ankle.

Isaac winced when he found a bloody scrape. His mood spoiled, he continued, limping slightly.

As he descended the bluff, the forest changed. The northern slope of the bluff had only pines, but downhill thick bushes grew between the pines along the southern slope, and the shadows thickened.

From these bushes, Isaac heard a whisper that stopped him cold in his tracks.

Chris Luning heard it too, an echo from the previous day.

Isaac turned in all directions; nothing but trees and dark bushes surrounded him.

He took a few steps forward.

Another whisper.

"Who's there?" he called out defensively. He could see a hundred yards all around, yet nothing explained where the source of the sound had come from.

Run, you fool. Get out of there, Chris cried.

Isaac's legs wobbled.

The only threat seemed to be in the obvious uncertainty of the shadows.

Indecision caused him to simply sit where he'd stopped. He whimpered with fear. His body shook uncontrollably as he stared at the growing shadows in the bushes.

Then one of them moved.

"Help," Isaac whispered.

"Follow us," the shadow from the bushes said. "We will help you find your way home."

Isaac's eyes grew wide.

Chris, also, could see several shadows separate from the bushes to stand in front of him. Even though there were few features, Chris somehow knew they were female.

"Do not stay in this unholy place. Evil spirits haunt these woods," another shadow said. "Come with us before it is too late."

Too late.

Isaac looked to his right, and in the western sky, stealing both light and warmth, a cloudbank swallowed the bright September sun.

The shadows grew.

"Now, little one," the shadowy faces of a dozen women called out together. "We will show you the way."

Isaac stood up.

With his eyes fixed on the shadows, he began to shake his head.

His legs turned, whisking him from the danger of the strange women who hid in the bushes at the bottom of the hill.

Run back to the sawmill. Men will still be there, Chris instructed and for a moment, it felt as if he was going to save the boy from the nightmare.

But as Isaac passed by the stacked stones, one of the shadows kicked out a leg to trip him, and Isaac slammed onto the granite floor so hard that his front teeth shattered.

Wailing started from the shadow women behind him.

His hand inspected the damage and dabbed at the blood, but when he looked up, another of the stone stacks began to change shape. A small troll stepped right out of a fairy tale and into the reality of Hiawatha County. It was gray as granite with long arms and short little legs. Instead of hair, it seemed to have quills like a porcupine. The creature stood straight up–long fingers began to twitch and reach.

Another black troll approached, blocking the sawmill.

In the distance, the wail of the women grew louder.

Now he only had two paths, two choices.

Isaac chose to run toward the river.

Just like his entrance to the bluff, the granite dropped away in massive steps as it descended sharply to the river below. He ducked around a few trees before another porcupine man jumped out from behind a tree and slammed his gray hands into his chest.

Isaac tumbled so hard his backpack went flying off his shoulders.

A fourth face emerged from the needles gathered in a pocket of granite. The little troll climbed out of solid earth, and soon long fingers were grasping at his leg.

Isaac crab-crawled backwards for a moment, seeing all four creatures closing in on him.

He turned his back on them for a moment so he could rise again to run, but with the lake looming in front of him, the creatures corralled him like a lamb to the place where he'd peed off the edge a short time earlier.

With a shove, Isaac was knocked off his feet.

Then the creatures attacked.

His body rolled.

And rolled.

Then Isaac Larson fell to the place where a fisherman had found him on Saturday.

Chris Luning felt as if he'd been murdered also. Once his sobbing stopped, he threw his blanket from his bed and walked to his window, where he could see the slope of Bleeding Rock across the river.

They can't get away with this.

Somehow … I need to stop them.

Lost in the Woods

Brainerd, MN
September 30, 1961

PATCHES OF WILLOWY hair grew between the long strands of gray that remained unharmed by the flames. Despite her clothes catching fire, only a few discolored patches gave indication Grandma Lily been in the house fire.

"Why is that mask tied to her face?" Nicki Guerin asked when the busy nurse returned to the room. "I thought she was better."

"It helps her breathe. Because of all the damage the fire caused, her lungs haven't healed yet, and she has developed a bad case of pneumonia. Even though she struggles to breathe, the mask makes sure each breath she takes is full of rich oxygen that helps her recovery."

"Can she take it off?"

The nurse hesitated. "For a while. All the talking she did last week gave her this cough, so we're just taking precautions. At her age, recovery will take much longer."

With that, the nurse left the room again, leaving the three of them to share the silence. Nicki sat in a straight wooden chair beside the bed, where she caressed the top of her grandmother's hand above the spot where the IV needles had been inserted into her veins.

Is she sleeping? Or too weak to open her eyes?

In the corner near the closet, Gavin MacPherson sat clad in his heavy denim jacket, clutching the newspaper. He locked eyes with Nicki across the bed as if prompting her to say or do something, but then his head drooped as he solemnly stared at his feet.

Nicki listened to the ventilator pumping air through the tubes and into the mask and watched the blankets slowly rise with each breath her grandmother took.

On her lap, Nicki had a folded sheet of messages from her family that she decided to read. Cameron's message had brought her to tears, prompting Gavin to get up from his chair. She affectionately gave his hand a squeeze as he stood beside her. As soon as she let go, he went back to his chair. Nicki folded up the sheet and slid it into the purse beside her feet. She paused when she saw the leather-bound journal inside.

"The homecoming dance was last weekend, Nokomis," Nicki said softly but her voice felt like a shout in the sterility of the hospital room. "I've made lots of new friends at school. I'm getting all A's despite working in the delivery room at the creamery. Dad has a new job at the lumber mill where he works on the motors. It's just a few hours a day, but I think it helps that he's out of the house. Even though Carousel Park is closed, they still pay Cameron to visit each day to make certain everything there is secure."

Her grandmother's hand rose from the side of the bed to pull away the mask. "You must protect him."

Nicki felt her heart quake in her chest. "Cameron? What's happening, Nokomis?"

"I'm sorry. This is all my fault."

Nicki quickly reached into her purse and found the silver tip of the melted lighter. "Did someone start the fire? Does someone want to hurt us, Nokomis?"

Her grandmother took a breath to answer, but a thick cough stole her words. She tried to keep it down, but the coughing fit became more violent, causing Gavin to sit forward as if he were going to bolt down to the nurses' station.

After some fumbling, the mask was back over her mouth and after a few shallow breaths, the coughing fit stopped. Tears ran through the deep creases in the corner of her eyes to drop onto the pillow. Her grandmother nodded slightly and then closed her eyes again.

Nicki's hand clenched the piece of metal for a few moments before she put it back in her purse. She picked it up and stood.

"What did she say?" Gavin asked.

"Let's get out of here," Nicki said, ignoring the question.

OUT IN THE truck, Gavin forced the answer by keeping the keys in his hands instead of putting them into the ignition. "What did she say?"

"She apologized, that's all."

Gavin calmly set the newspaper down between them and waited.

Nicki glanced at it, seeing the picture of the little boy who'd recently drowned on his way home from school. "She said I need to protect him, okay?"

And I don't know what to do.

What should I do?

Gavin slipped the keys in the ignition but then leaned back into the seat. As always, his face hid his emotions from her and his thoughts were his own, so she waited for him to make his point. "We need to tell someone about the lighter. I just feel that the fire, the roller coaster accident, and now the Larson boy—it's too much to ignore."

It's so easy for him to be a hero, isn't it? "It's been more than three months since the fire, and everyone has decided the fire was an accident, like they decided Isaac Larson died accidentally. No one's going to believe us."

"We have the journal."

"It's not proof of anything."

"Your grandmother almost died trying to retrieve it. We've both looked at it. You can't deny it is important."

He doesn't get it. "I didn't say that it wasn't important, I said it wasn't proof. What are we going to say if we give it to somebody? 'The Manitou did it.' We will look like idiots."

Gavin's lips tightened. "We could tell them about the red Thunderbird and those men that stopped by your house."

Nicki sighed.

"If your brother is in danger, you're in danger. We need to tell someone, especially if those men are out there killing kids."

"Isaac Larson fell to his death," she sarcastically repeated the official account back to him. "No one killed him."

"What about the tooth?"

"What?"

"They didn't put it in the newspapers, but my dad was one of the men who found his body near Bleeding Rock. Isaac's front teeth were broken."

"Of course they were broken, he fell off a cliff."

Gavin shook his head. "They found his backpack before they found his body, and a few yards from where they found it, they found blood and a piece of tooth. It was like Isaac fell while running from something."

"The men in the Thunderbird?"

"Possibly. Either that or…"

"Or what?"

"What did your grandpa Jean call the porcupine monsters in his notebook?"

"Tak-Pei."

"Tak-Pei" Gavin repeated flatly.

"You suddenly believe in the Porcupine Men? Are you telling me that the Porcupine Men stopped at a gas station to fill up their gas can, and while there, picked up a lighter?"

"Your grandfather's journal said there would most likely be—"

"Twelve deaths," Nicki interrupted. "Yes, I've read it also, but I am not ready to believe that Tak-Pei loosened the bolts on the roller coaster."

"Everybody knows your father hadn't worked at the park for weeks, Nicki. It wasn't his fault. It just happened."

"Of course it wasn't his fault. I think someone sabotaged the roller coaster knowing he wasn't there to check it. You can't arrest something supernatural. Someone started the fire, someone loosened the bolts, and if I was to guess, someone pushed poor Isaac Larson off the cliff."

"Right, which is why we must say something to somebody."

Nicki reached down and picked up the journal from her purse. "How much of it did you read before you gave it back to me?"

"I went through the whole thing. Your grandmother said we need to protect Cameron. It's because of the prophecy, isn't it?"

"Yeah, but you're getting a C+ in English because you flip through the stories instead of actually reading all the words."

He sighed.

"In the stories, Iyash is always described as a young boy, and in the Seventh Fire, it again describes a young boy with a strange light in his eyes. This is why my grandfather thought the zealots abducted Migisi—because he was a boy. Cameron is twenty-one years old, which makes it unlikely he is the reincarnation of Iyash, or the boy with the strange eyes, or even the Omodai, whatever that was supposed to mean."

"Then why did your grandmother say we needed to protect him?"

"She…" Nicki held her tongue to avoid saying something cruel. "Are we going to spend the whole day talking about this? We're supposed to be shopping, aren't we? I shouldn't have asked you to swing by the hospital. There was a reason my mother insisted that my grandmother live in the guest house, okay? Crazy people can look at something and see answers that simply are not there."

"What about the lighter and the gas can? Do you have some rational answers for them?" Gavin pressed.

Nicki spoke sternly yet softly. "We both believe it was not an accident, and without the paranormal or conspiracy theories, it leaves us with the simple fact that Lily Guerin is an Indian living off the reservation."

"What?"

Is he honestly this naïve? "You don't see the way everyone looks at me at school. Some of those girls hate my guts, Gavin. Do you know why?"

"You're the new girl."

"No, I'm 'Injun.' I'm a TIJ. I might cut my hair short, and wear nice clothes, but they see an Indian. Nothing I can do will change that, and for all I know, some drunk from the Crow Bar wandered off the road with hatred in his heart and tried to finish off what his white ancestors failed to do."

"You don't believe that." Gavin finally turned the keys, firing up the truck engine. "So, where do you want to go?"

Nicki stared down at the journal. There was a piece of paper inside it with the addresses of several shops in Brainerd, but she couldn't bring herself to take her hands off the leather binding. Tears formed in her eyes, and she found herself biting her bottom lip.

"Nicki?"

"Why do you care about any of this?"

"Lake Manitou is my home, too, and since the fire, five people have died."

It was a safe answer, but it was enough. "If we can't go to the authorities, then I need you to bring me to the reservation so I can give this to someone who can figure it out."

"So, no shopping?"

Nicki shook her head.

"Where are we going?"

"We're going to find my great-uncle Migisi."

Busting Heads

Split Rock High School
October 3, 1961

BIFF FORSBERG LOVED busting heads, especially on defense. He didn't have to think about football, for it allowed him to hurt with impunity, which he did on each play.

He held out a hand and helped the Pine River running back off his feet, savoring the second groan as the kid rose unsteadily. Biff looked to the sideline, where Coach Spicer signaled the alignment. As middle linebacker, Biff ran the defense. The other 10 Bulldogs gathered around him to take instruction. With four blubber butts in front of him, Biff could unleash his strength and speed on any Tiger daring to cross the line of scrimmage. Now it was 3rd down and eight yards to go for Pine River.

"They're going to run a slant play. Arms up on two. Chris, don't get fooled by the juke move. Jimmy, keep him in front of you. Break."

Jimmy and Chris trotted out to the sideline, with Biff remaining right where the huddle had broken. Pine River's offense took time. Most junior high teams didn't pass, but eight yards was too far to run again.

Pine River threw a slant.

The receiver juked, Chris bit, and then was shoved aside for an open slant across the middle. Jimmy hit him with a shoulder, spinning both. Jimmy fell down, and the receiver turned back for the end zone.

Biff punched the ball out from behind, which Chris recovered before being buried in a pile of bodies.

Biff looked to the sideline. His father, keenly aware that milking needed to begin in twelve minutes, looked at his watch. His mother stood, stopping her clapping only to point to him. Beside her, Uncle Ewan clapped as enthusiastically as the other fathers who weren't dairy farmers.

"What did I tell you about the slant?" Biff said as Jimmy returned to the sideline following the turnover.

Jimmy didn't answer.

Most of the eighth-graders started on offense, letting Biff catch his breath to look at the scoreboard.

Home 36 and Visitors 6.

The Split Rock Bulldogs were crushing the kids from Pine River with seven minutes left to go in the game. After three feeble runs up the middle, the offense punted.

Biff slapped his helmet, then took Chris by the facemask for a head-butt. "Keep them in front of you."

The junior high football season was already half-done, and it worried Biff what would happen when he could no longer take out his anger on the padded kid across from him.

How did Isaac Larson really die?

Thud.

What is hidden in that tunnel?

Smash.

Who was that slick fellow in the red Thunderbird?

Crunch.

What is Uncle Ewan's deal?

Punch.

What's got Jimmy and Chris so rattled?

Shove.

Is all this mumbo-jumbo about Lake Manitou being haunted real?

Late hit. Fifteen-yard personal foul.

Damn it.

CHAPTER THIRTY-ONE

Those Who Roast

Mizheekay Band of Ojibwe Reservation
October 7, 1961

MIGISI ASIBIKAASHI SAT alone, weighing how much honesty to give his guests when they arrived. He'd had more people visit him over the past three months than he'd had in the past three years.

On his shelf, he found a book: William Warren's *History of the Ojibway Nation*. Inside the green cover, he found Fawn's letter.

June 9, 1912

Dearest Migisi,

Protect the Children! Now that I've given birth to my firstborn son, I fully understand the terrible choice made by Lily. I hope you understand why I could not stay. One of us is wrong, and nothing I say or do can change her mind. While I prepare for the future, you must be ever vigilant at Lake Manitou. If Lily learns she is wrong, she might make matters worse. In fact, I fear that …

Migisi folded the letter, tucked it back in the book, and set it aside.

Fawn was right and now the children come to me for advice.

While he waited, he processed the burlap sacks full of raw wild rice. Three big bags gave him enough food for the rest of the year. Superintendent Norval Riel had taken a busload of students up to the rice fields around Leech Lake to teach them the skills of harvesting in canoes and then drying the rice on tarps. Behind him, in the shadow of the porch, all three bags waited for preservation.

In front of him, Migisi had the big black kettle that had once belonged to his mother Winnie. It sat upon the coals of a wood-fed fire in the middle of his yard. With a yardstick-sized paddle, he stirred the wild rice to ensure it roasted evenly.

Over the course of his life, the term used for his people had changed from Chippewa to Ojibwe to Anishinaabe, which Riel preferred. Riel explained the meaning of the word Anishinaabe ranged from "Beings Made from Nothing" to "Original Man" to simply "the People." The previous word, Ojibwe, had more sinister definitions, translating commonly to "those who roast until it puckers."

Riel had recently taught his students that definition referred to a curing method for new moccasins that required a little heat to treat the leather. Stirring the kettle of roasting wild rice, Migisi wondered if the word might've referenced the method of preparing the "food that grows on water" stated in the Seven Fires Prophecy. But after what befell his grandfather and great grandfather, he knew the horrific practice of roasting referred to captured enemies upon pyres.

I wonder if Riel teaches about burning enemies alive?

An enemy had returned to Lake Manitou, even if Migisi had not seen its face. Leonard White Elk had dismissed it, and Wally Crain listened but took little action. Now, like the terrible year of 1898, children had begun to take notice.

Using thick mitts, Migisi lifted the black kettle from the fire and walked it several steps to the chaffing pit. He poured the hot rice into the small pit he'd dug in his front yard, which was lined with smooth wood. A spare chair waited in front of it.

A few feet from the chaffing pit, the winnowing tray rested against a third chair, with boxes of empty jars and cans behind it.

They are late.

Migisi slipped off his boots and slipped on a pair of hardened old moccasins kept for use once a year. He found his dancing stick beside the chair and had just set one foot upon the warm rice when he heard a voice.

"Aaniin, Uncle Migisi," Nicki Guerin called.

In truth, he was a great-uncle, brother to Nicki's grandmother Lily. He'd met her on several occasions over the years, but only as a student at Turtle Island Jesuit School.

Seeing her made him almost sick to his stomach, for despite her efforts, she looked so much like his sister. A strapping young farmer followed beside her, a crooked grin on his face.

"First, we will work, and then we'll talk."

"Of course, Mr. Riel made it perfectly clear," Nicki said as she approached. "Show us what we need to do."

FOR THE BETTER part of the afternoon, the teenagers worked diligently. Gavin MacPherson, with 180 pounds of lean muscle, wore the moccasins and crushed the cooked rice under his feet as he attempted the "dance" used to separate the chaff from the kernel. At the next station, Nicole used the tray and the air to separate chaff before she packaged up the grain in vessels that would protect it from pests over the course of the year.

Together, they finished a sack and a half of harvested rice.

Finally, Migisi pushed aside decades of anguish to say, "Tell me what you have seen."

Each of them retrieved an object.

In Nicki's fingers, she held the metallic striking plate of a lighter.

Gavin, however, ripped Migisi's heart from his chest when he showed him the leather-bound journal of Jean-Nicholas Guerin.

How much different would things have been if he'd lived?

CHAPTER THIRTY-TWO

Dracula and the Headless Horseman

Old Copper Road
October 16, 1961

JIMMY NIELSON KNEW the moment it happened even though he didn't learn of the murder until the following day. The overcast, dreary October day seemed to slam the door in the face of summer. Meteorologically, a strong low-pressure system and upper-level disturbance approached central Minnesota and pulled moist and unstable weather right up to Hiawatha County. The warm, humid air lifted above the cold front and violently returned back down to Lake Manitou shortly before midnight.

Just north of Nimrod, a funnel cloud dropped down from the colliding system, ripping through woods for almost a mile. Along the southern shore of Lake Manitou, a bolt of lightning struck the tallest pine on Turtle Island and rattled the windows of his home.

When it struck, Jimmy had been dreaming of missed tackles on the football field. The cannon blast of thunder almost flipped him out of his bed, where he quickly took measure of his reality.

For a moment, he almost ran to find comfort with his sister Faye but then remembered she'd left for Mankato State College back in August. Of his three sisters, Faye had been the most maternal. His eldest sister, Rachel, had been gone for four years, and was now married with an infant. Alexandra, only five years older, openly despised him.

Jimmy calmed his heart and laid back down, pulling his pillow over his head in case the storm tried to wake him again.

Soon Jimmy found himself back at Haggard Quarry in the godforsaken tunnel. This time, the chain link gate was left wide open. At the spot where the seam of quartz ended and the dark, dense granite began, the underbelly of Lake Manitou had been magically cleared away to reveal smooth, polished walls, formed without joints.

Jimmy's hand touched the smooth surface and followed it several yards until he found an entrance with a vaulted cut. As soon as he stepped in, he knew where he'd seen the room before.

From the cobwebs and the waxy candelabras to the great descending stairs and tall pillars supporting the ceiling, the chamber was unmistakable for its most prominent feature—a sarcophagus. The stone tomb belonged to *Dracula*, and the stake and hammer beside it left Jimmy with no other choice: he had to kill the monster.

His fingers tingled as he took hold of the cold iron.

Would the monster have slicked Bela Lugosi hair, or would it be furry like the wolfman? With a shove, Jimmy pushed aside the lid and found Rory Stewart.

"Help me," Rory gasped, and from within the burial bed, a pair of arms came up from around the pillow to clasp a white rag over his face.

"If you've come to kill me, you've chosen the wrong weapons."

The iron in Jimmy's hands melted into useless pools upon the floor.

Rory Stewart continued to struggle inside of the coffin as black hands pulled him through the bottom of the coffin, and no sooner did he vanish than a black, inky cloud began to flow out of the space, causing Jimmy to step away.

Weird! It didn't happen like this in the movie!

The villain in the shadows was not Count Dracula either. "Do you think my servants would allow my sleep to be disturbed? Do you think they would serve your will or mine? Fool!"

The voice came from behind one of the towering pillars that stretched to the ceiling, the very foundations of Lake Manitou. Instead of a Romanian nobleman, a bronzed figure stepped out. Instead of clothes, he wore beaded fabric upon his ankles, knees, loin, neck, and wrists. Without a hair upon his body or face, the hair upon his head was shaved to the scalp, except where it formed two horns of hair.

The Horned Serpent? Or just a coincidence?

The first horn formed above his forehead, where it was entwined with beads that protruded several inches. Atop his head, a great red braid formed a second horn, lifting from the top of his head more than a foot before cascading down to the middle of his back. "Have you forgotten my name, boy? Isn't it written upon the stars? You should not have come here."

Jimmy had heard enough.

He'd seen enough.

He bolted through the vaulted entrance and back to the tunnel.

…. Except now, the gate was closed.

"Do you think I could be killed? Me? I am the Master of Death!"

Turning Jimmy saw Red Horn grab his own neck, and with a violent tug, tore his own head from his shoulders.

"I will rise from my own death and smash your prophecies to pieces!"

Red Horn, with the athletic grace of quarterback Johnny Unitas, took his own head and threw it into Jimmy's chest. The force of it took him through the gate and tin shed and out into the center of the quarry.

Back here again?

Rising to his feet, Jimmy frantically looked around for Red Horn's severed head but instead only found pieces of shattered pumpkin in the rubble of tin and lumber.

A demonic growl sounded in the darkness. From the shallow end of Haggard Quarry, six hunched creatures approached, waddling awkwardly like a pack of hyenas, but when they came into the light, they rose upon their hind legs to reveal arms that stretched from shoulder to their toes.

The Tak-Pei.

"You should not have come here. We won't let you take him from us."

Jimmy ran for the steep end of the quarry, remembering a path that had previously allowed him to escape unseen. The Tak-Pei snapped at his heels as he climbed up a level, forcing them to run around to the shallow end. By that time they cleared the first level, he'd climbed up another level.

"Do you think you can run from us? There is nowhere we can't reach you if our Master wills it."

Jimmy soon reached the surface, but instead of climbing up onto the highway, he found himself standing on a location vaguely familiar—the top of the Nicollet dam.

Three inky Tak-Pei appeared on both sides of the dam, slowly trapping him with malice on their slender faces. "There is only one choice for you."

On one side of the dam, Jimmy saw Red Horn's open tomb waiting below. On the other side of the dam, he saw the raging waters of the Blue Knife River—and a rope.

Jimmy took hold of it, placing his feet against the surface of the dam. With one hand over another, he began his descent.

"You can't escape us," the Tak-Pei hissed.

Their inky hands touched the rope, but instead of severing it, they commanded it. It coiled itself around Jimmy's neck, strangling him until he felt his feet slipping and his hands losing strength.

Why does this dream seem so real?

When Jimmy woke, he was out of breath.

His fear turned to immediate anger that a dream had rattled him, and he tossed his sheets aside.

His alarm clock read 1:02 a.m.

Knowing sleep wouldn't come, he rose and walked to his window to see something far more surprising than Red Horn, Dracula, or the Headless Horseman: his father.

Ed Nielson sat crossed-legged in the middle of the farmyard with a pole across his lap and a shotgun at his side. His gaze looked out at Lake Manitou.

His father had confessed once that he'd never slept a night away from home. During World War II, he had a house full of women to care for, including his wife, widowed mother, widowed grandmother, and two daughters. Yet even in days of peace, he remained a homebody focused on his fields and flocks.

What is he hunting?

A few moments later, Jimmy slipped his feet into a pair of his father's snow boots and trudged out to the light of the lamppost.

"The storm woke the living, too," his father greeted, flicking a stubby cigarette butt into the gravel in front of him, joining a dozen cold butts.

The shotgun spoke for itself. Countless times, the animals in the barn sent out an alarm whenever badgers, coyotes, wolves, or even a stray black bear prowled too close, and his father jumped into action. The pole sat beside him now like an afterthought. The pole was neither a shovel nor hoe, both good weapons for smashing varmints; instead it was a woven tangle of willow branches with a jagged stone blade tied to its head.

A caveman's weapon. A spear.

"Something prowling, Pa?"

Ed scoffed. "Quite the storm, huh?"

Jimmy nodded.

His father stared off in the distance. "Your mother hates storms, but I find them to be wondrous. You can almost feel the magic in the air. Sit. You can help me keep watch."

Jimmy obeyed, sitting on his father's left side opposite of the shotgun. "What are we expecting to see?"

"He never told me, specifically." His father slid the willow spear over to Jimmy, letting him inspect it. "He made this. I keep it tucked away in the stone foundation of the barn. Just before you came out here, do you know what I was thinking of?"

Dracula? Jimmy shrugged.

"I was awake, but it's like my mind shifted into neutral while still going down the road at full speed. I saw my grandfather and my grandson come walking up that hill to offer counsel. I'm not sure how I knew it was my grandson, but—you never met him, did you?"

Jimmy was still rattled by thoughts of a son. "Grandpa Sig?"

"No, not *my* father. My grandfather Martin. I never knew my father. You've heard the reason from Grandma D, right?"

"She was married a month before Grandpa Sig left to fight in World War I."

"By the time I was born, he was dead and buried. My grandfather Martin was the only father I knew. He was the one who made this. He told me I'd need it in a battle with monsters. For a few minutes, I thought the time had come."

"The Manitou?"

His father chuckled. "What do you know about the Manitou? Don't let those good Lutheran women hear you talk about stuff like the Manitou, okay?"

"Wally Crain told us campfire stories."

"Ah, Wally … of course." He sighed loudly. "Grandpa Martin taught me while we worked. I'd be plowing a field, chopping firewood, and these instructions would come out and then were never spoken of again. I remember to this day, though. 1986 … Shit, I'll be old by then. Almost 70, and you … you'll be my age. I suppose I need to share, but I need you to keep it secret. It's more than just trying not to sound crazy to our neighbors. You have allies and enemies in this world, and you never know when they wear a false face, so keep our secrets until you know for certain."

Jimmy's throat tightened. "So, does this have something to do with the Manitou?"

"What do you know about being a Nielson?"

"We're Norwegian."

"You are French, Swedish, Norwegian, and Faroese."

"Egyptian?"

His father laughed. "With an F. Martin was born on the Faroe Islands and grew up in Bergen, Norway, where he met your great-grandmother Dolly."

Jimmy remembered she had white hair and a flabby chin.

"In Faroese, the name Nielson means Cloud Champion, which I suppose partially explains why I love storms. Before coming to America, we Nielsons were sailors. Mast men. We'd climb up to the top of any ship to hang sails or make repairs, regardless of the weather. Weather doesn't frighten us. We live in the clouds and lightning is our companion. I've let you grow up like a normal American teenager, but our hands are sea faring hands. Do you see the skill that went into the pole you're holding? Your grandfather wove a hundred willow branches together to fashion it. He claimed it was as strong as steel."

"Why? Why'd he make it?"

"I don't even know where to begin." His father sighed, but then he pointed west. "You know Jiibay Hollow, right? The swamp between our farm and the Bergs? There's a big willow tree that grows there. That's where he harvested the branches for this. Now I'm not sure if it's just this one tree or all willows, but there is something special about it. There are tools for all sorts of situations. A shotgun is good on an angry badger, and that staff will help with—the rest. One day in the future, you'll take my place as a Guardian."

Suddenly, shadows appeared in front of them, black and long.

A light had been turned on in the kitchen, and the dozen bulbs created a strong enough light to flood out into the darkness. Jimmy and his father saw their own shadows upon the ground.

"One of the gals is awake. We'll talk again. You take the shotgun."

But I have more questions.

Whetstone

Sterling Junction
October 18, 1961

RORY STEWART'S BODY was found beneath the Blue Knife River bridge. Wally Crain reread the front-page news article, focusing on the details after the shock wore off from the headlines. Everything written in the *Minneapolis Tribune* echoed what Wally had already learned yesterday when the boy had been found.

The dining room was strangely silent, and despite his wife sitting in front of her typewriter—there would be no writing this "writing" Wednesday.

Most Wednesday mornings over the past decade, Nancy carefully stacked the finished chapters of her novel to the right of the typewriter and placed her notebooks of ideas to the left. She took time once a week to nurture a role as an aspiring novelist.

During the summer, his wife filled notebooks with ideas under the big willow tree in their backyard, her love of symbolism, metaphor, and mythology led her to create a series of novels inspired by famous stories placed in a modern setting. Wally had seen cover pages for at least three of these works: *Hamlet's Ghost, Cassandra's Curse,* and *Ulysses' Bow.*

Today, the sheet of paper she slid into the typewriter held the same two sentences they held at 5 a.m.

Wally gave her space, putting aside the paper and moving to place his cereal bowl in the sink before heading out to the garage to arm himself for battle.

When was the last time I saw Rory?

The camping trip?

The Blue Knife River was two miles east of St. John, so the boy had either walked out of town of his own volition or was abducted and brought there. The reports could not yet identify whether the boy had been killed first and then dropped over the edge of the bridge or if he had been killed by the fall.

Regardless, authorities admitted that two boys falling to their deaths near Lake Manitou in the span of one month was more than coincidence, especially since Rory Stewart's backpack was found tossed in the bushes just outside the Stewart property on Monday night. His body was found on Tuesday morning.

Semper Fortis, Wally thought as he searched for the small can of oil in the garage. *Always courageous.*

Back in the kitchen, Wally heard the paper torn from the typewriter. Wally moved to the counter, where he'd spread out three kitchen towels to clean his weapons: a small jackknife, a horrifying hooked blade with a wooden handle, and a disassembled pistol. With his small can of oil, he finished cleaning the pistol and began reassembling it.

Unfortunately, Nancy finished writing an hour ahead of schedule.

"What do you think you are doing?"

"The lighting was terrible in the garage," Wally said as he worked on the old pistol.

"The girls will be waking up in an hour, and I do not want them seeing this exhibition displayed on the kitchen counter; it will alarm them."

"Are you still taking them to school?"

"Of course I am taking them to school. We're going to keep on living, regardless of what happened to the Stewart boy."

"They're going to want to talk to the children today, especially with the MEA break beginning tomorrow. Are you going to speak with the girls or wait for their teachers to do it?"

"I was going to speak to them before, but I don't want to have to begin the conversation because they saw their father oiling a pistol in the kitchen. Where did you even get that?"

Father Jean Guerin. "It's a Colt 1872 Open Top. It's an heirloom. My dad gave it to me after Lily Guerin gave it to him after her husband Jean died." He finished putting the chamber back together, spun it, and slapped it into place. "Someone is killing kids, Nancy."

"Who suddenly made you a deputy?"

"If I'm driving around Hiawatha County and see something strange happening, I need this with me."

In fact, he'd been "on the job" when Rory Stewart vanished after school Monday. He'd even spoken personally to Sheriff Betzing on the phone to let him know that he'd driven the road between Split Rock and St. John during the late afternoon. According to Red Dobie, who logged the delivery, Wally arrived at the Haggard Quarry at 3:35 for a fuel delivery.

St. John dismissed at 3:00.

Rory Stewart had not gone home after school.

His body had been…

Again and again, Wally replayed his route on Monday, hoping to remember something that would identify what happened to one of his boys.

Nancy took the newspaper from the table and put it in the garbage. "Well, put the pistol back together and get it out of sight. I understand what you are doing, but I do not want this in the house again."

Wally shrugged.

He knew what had happened back in 1898. Lily Guerin claimed she'd woken the Manitou when she practiced the ancient rituals taught to her by her grandfather Nanak. With the floodgates opened, the evil spirits, the Tak-Pei, that guarded their master, fed on the deaths that happened around Lake Manitou. With each death, the creatures grew stronger and stronger, until they were capable of taking on corporeal form. Twelve folks died that year in random fashion, from murder to tragic accidents.

Four dead at Carousel Park.

Now two boys.

They're halfway there.

"I'll drive you and the girls to school today. I'll just shift my deliveries back a few hours. Why don't you go get them and I'll tell them what happened? It's certain to be talked about at school."

A few minutes later, Nancy herded the girls into the kitchen. *They're too young to deal with this stuff,* Wally hesitated. *But they have to know.*

"Girls, there's something I need to speak to you about. You'll certainly be hearing about it at school, but I want to talk to you about it first. A boy from St. John died yesterday, Rory Stewart. The police are searching for the person who hurt him."

Janet's brow furled. *Damn, they understand the killer is still on the loose.*

"You will certainly be safe while you are at school. Your teachers will probably talk to your classes about strangers and being safe. There are a lot of brave people out looking for answers, so you don't have anything to worry about, okay?"

Margaret looked to be on the verge of tears, and Cindy seemed to be processing the details, but Janet quickly connected the dots, asking, "It is the same man who killed Isaac Larson?"

"We don't know exactly what happened to Isaac Larson, just like we don't know what happened to the Stewart boy who died yesterday. I am certain the police will figure it out and keep us safe.”

“Wasn’t Rory in Pack 88?” Margaret asked.

Nancy’s eyes commanded him to stop but Wally nodded.

Yes. Yes, he was.

AS ANTICIPATED, OTHER fathers accompanied their children to school. Wally stayed long enough to learn that the Split Rock superintendent called the faculty together to distribute a press release prepared by the Hiawatha County Sheriff’s Department. After that, he retreated to a discreet distance, where Ed Nielson sat on his tailgate sipping coffee.

“While I was filling up with gas, Bill Jensen told me he had a theory about a serial killer. He said he saw some sinister looking Indian, tall muscular fella, lurking around the Blue Knife River in recent days.”

“Leonard White Elk?” Wally asked. “He left a month ago.”

“Exactly. Albert was right about folks looking for a monster.” Nielson looked around the neighborhood beyond the school. “Any theories? Aside from … you know?”

“I keep replaying it in my mind,” Wally admitted. “Rory had to have been abducted right outside of his house. If he’d walked out to the Blue Knife, I certainly would have seen him walking down the highway as I came into town.”

“No sinister red Thunderbirds?”

“Marlin Luning said he spoke to a deputy about that incident back in June, but hell, that car vanished like a fart in the wind. I think it would be a tad bit conspicuous for a kidnapper to be driving around in it.”

“Why would Rory Stewart get in a car with a stranger?” Ed asked.

Wally shook his head. “The guy must’ve grabbed him right outside his house, which explains the backpack being tossed in the bushes. I saw Sean at the exact same time his son was getting nabbed. I had to sign some new work orders at the quarry, and there they all sat: Haggard, Dobie, Marquette, and Stewart."

Nielson dumped the last of his coffee onto the ground. "I hate to think of it, but the pervert who took Rory kept him somewhere. Dumping the body at the bridge was like taking out the trash for this creep."

But it was strategic, too. "Even so, folks are going to put a lot of heat on the reservation. I should let Riel and Migisi know what's being whispered on the winds."

"We're probably making matters worse sitting here," Nielson said, preparing to leave, "but I'm coming back at 3 to make sure some kid doesn't wander off and that my kids go straight home."

"I'll see you back at 3 too. I'm going to speak with Albert and then drive around a bit. See you later, Ed."

Wally left and drove just a few blocks away from the school to Albert Fisher's estate.

He parked at the garage instead of in front of the house to avoid having to talk with the man's nosey wife. Behind the glass in the garage doors, Albert had a collection of classic automobiles, but none of that mattered to Wally right now.

Rory Stewart had been murdered. It's the only theory that makes sense.

A few minutes later, the lights inside of the garage came to life and the big garage door opened.

Albert Fisher's face held the grief of an entire community.

He thinks this is his fault. Wally got to the point quickly. "What am I looking for?"

"I wish I could give you a clear answer. Back in '98, a young boy drowned. There was an explosion at the creamery. Three people were murdered, and the death of the killer made it four."

"The Weber murders," Wally recalled. Yet Rory Stewart was not an ally. "Did anything ever happen to the folks from Triton?"

"Now that you say it, I don't think ... No, wait, I remember hearing something about one of them drowning in his bathtub. He was a businessman from out east, so no one knew him well. Folks assumed he had a bad heart. Before the incident at Deadwood Island, there were several random deaths."

Perhaps my father was right about the Manitou. Or could it be something else? "I've been thinking about speaking to Dobie about this red Thunderbird the boys saw. Obviously, none of the guys at Triton would do something to endanger their own children, but in '98, it was Joseph Little Toad who tried to wake the Wintermaker."

"You're not trying to implicate Leonard White Elk, right?"

"No, of course not. What if this guy the boys met in the red Thunderbird was a 'false face' to those guys at Triton? Human hands set the fire at Lily Guerin's cabin, and human hands caused the rollercoaster to collapse. While we don't know what happened to the Larson boy, I'd bet his body was tossed from that cliff. Something had to have woken the Tak-Pei."

"The night this began, I had a vision," Albert revealed. "The young man in the vision warned me that they were fighting the Wintermaker in the future. Lily stood toe-to-toe with the Wintermaker and his Tak-Pei back in 1898, bringing the darkness to an end. What if this puppet master exists in the future and is manipulating events now?"

"I don't know what to even say about that, Albert. I want to take hold of some son-of-a-bitch by the throat, okay? Give me somebody to bloody."

"A fight is coming, but it might not be that kind of fight. I do know one thing: we need to protect our children."

"I can get behind that notion."

Wally Crain went to St. John, loaded his oil truck for deliveries, drove around Lake Manitou for a few hours, circled back to St. John where a television crew filmed, and returned to Split Rock by the end of the school day.

Like several other fathers, he waited, leaning against his door at the back of the lot.

One by one, the girls came rushing to him. Twenty minutes after the bell, Nancy came out the side doors also.

She told him the elementary teachers overreacted with fear while the teenagers were swept away with anger. "Your boys concern me though. Chris seemed reasonably focused, but Biff had obvious anger, and Jimmy seemed withdrawn. He seems frightened too."

"What about the older kids? The Guerin girl?"

"She's a hard nut to crack. She puts on a good show, that's for sure. I have no idea if any of this is bothering her. I think the MEA break will help."

Wally doubted four days off of school would let anyone forget about the death of two boys. If anything, it would make matters worse.

B.O.H.I.C.A. Blues

St. John, MN
October 23, 1961

ALL OF HIAWATHA County seemed to mourn the death of Rory Stewart, and the gloom continued past the boy's funeral.

A thick blanket of clouds hid the sun for an entire week, and during much of the time, a steady rain fell, turning the gravel roads to a muddy maze for Wally. At several places along his delivery route, he had to back up to avoid water that filled the ditches and passed over the roads. While his truck had plenty of clearance, its weight threatened to sink it right into the muddy base of the gravel roads.

Both the Blue Knife and the Crow Wing rivers raged so wildly that Wally worried they would cut the county into three islands, forcing him to drive far to the north to safely pass over the waters, but, like the hearts of its residents, the waters swelled but did not break.

At most stops, the residents came out of the houses to chat while he filled their fuel tanks. Many kept the conversation superficial and polite, but several openly talked theory and conspiracy about the recent deaths. Wally shrugged off most of it, all the while keeping his pistol in his glove compartment.

His inherited pistol almost brought the Manitou back to life in 1898, Wally realized. From what his father told him, Jean Guerin had come face to face with cult members from the Wijigan Clan, and even though he gunned them down in cold blood, the murders acted as a blood sacrifice to the Manitou, who surged to consciousness.

Father Guerin's heroism backfired, and we must be careful not to repeat the same mistake.

Lily used magic from the dawn to battle the evil entity to a draw. She subdued the Manitou and his Tak-Pei, and for decades, the evil slumbered.

Now Lily battled for breath.

He'd visited her for guidance and to seek information about the mysterious visitor that both Migisi and the boys had seen prior to the fire. He didn't get much more than what Nicki Guerin had told him already.

AT HAGGARD QUARRY, Wally found some sure footing. Normally, the quarry road terrified him, but the narrow road cut out of stone was the sturdiest delivery he made all week.

Having spoken to Jimmy Nielson, Biff Forsberg, and Chris Luning about their strange encounter with the fellow in the red Thunderbird, he came away with insight. While Jimmy and Chris both felt the paranormal danger, Biff focused on predators, and when asked for a recap of the details, he alluded to the fact that the red Thunderbird had been coming from Haggard Quarry.

It didn't make any sense.

Not even Wally's job made sense right now.

Wally looked to the far side of the quarry where the machines were buttoned up for the winter as he stood for several minutes putting hundreds of gallons of fuel in the tank nearest Red's office.

"Looks like you boys are closed down for the season," Wally said in passing.

"Indeed, we are. As soon as I get done with this paperwork, I'm doing my best goose impersonation and flying south for the winter."

"Ah, that's right, you're a snowbird, aren't you. Florida?"

"Hell no. Swamp? I'm a rockhound. Arizona."

"So, if the quarry is closed down for the winter, and you're off in Arizona, what's the deal with filling these tanks?"

"I told you about this. Road construction is certainly done, but Haggard has this contract for the blue hone granite."

"Ah, yes, the knockoff curling stones."

"Haggard has some small crew working now that construction season has paid the bills."

"You know these guys?"

Red stared over the tops of his gold rimmed glasses. "Playing detective? Ah, I don't blame you after what happened to the Stewart boy. No stone unturned, huh?"

Wally shrugged.

"The head engineer has visited a few times over the summer in preparation for the winter harvesting, but there's no 'stranger danger' with him. He's got a tight alibi, also. Is that the theory now? A stranger? I'd have put my money on someone local, but, you know, they could be random incidents also. Who the hell knows?"

"When I was in the Navy, we had a saying: 'Bend over—here it comes again. Bohica.'"

"Bohica. Yeah, I feel like that also."

Wally had known Red most of his adult life. He was part of the landscape of Hiawatha County. "I didn't mean to implicate your granite engineer. Sorry about that."

Red blew it off with a huff. "Sad shit, kid that young dying. It would be irresponsible not to ask questions."

"Right, so I hope you don't mind another, but you wouldn't happen to know anybody that drives a red Thunderbird, would you? A brand new shiny one."

"A car like that would stand out, wouldn't it? Why do you ask? Got a lead or something?"

"A few folks I know remember seeing one driving around earlier in the summer, and it approached a group of boys. Probably innocent, but now it seems suspicious."

"Where did you see this Thunderbird?"

"Old Copper Road."

"Sorry, Wally. It was probably just someone who got lost looking for Carousel Park."

He blew that off pretty quickly. "Yeah, you're probably right. You have a good time in Arizona this winter."

"Yeah, I'll think of you each time I read about a blizzard."

After leaving Red's office, Wally parked along the narrow isthmus of road between the quarry and lake. Out the driver window, he could see the pink wound in the ground. Past the passenger window, Lake Manitou rippled innocently.

Because he felt like a frightened boy, Wally got out his father's castration knife and held it before him. While he'd told the boys the story of the Barlow knife, he didn't tell them what happened after his father was bullied in dreams by the Manitou. When it all became too intolerable, little Kermit returned, with a sharpened castration knife in hand, and stood fearlessly on the shore, pissing on the water with one hand and the castration knife in the other.

The Manitou claimed a dozen souls in 1898, yet Lily and her original Isanti Lodge had somehow defeated the evil. Now, it was time for the new Isanti Lodge.

Lord, guide my thoughts and deeds in the days to come.

Wally put the knife away then left the shore of the lake.

As he drove toward St. John, he reviewed the facts. BCA medical examiners had taken their time with the body of Rory Stewart, but once they finally released him for burial, and even though the funeral had been held, little more was known about the crime a week later.

Wally stayed on the main road that led into the heart of St. John. His eyes wandered to the wooded shore where the Stewart house overlooked Lake Manitou. His truck crossed the path Rory would have taken to get home and a chill ran down his spine.

Soon enough, he reached the Blue Knife River bridge that connected the communities of St. John and Split Rock. The massive project had been completed prior to the Great Depression and allowed residents to make the trip in ten minutes rather than the thirty it took to go around Lake Manitou to the south or cross far to the north at the Nimrod bridge.

The steel girder bridge passed over the Blue Knife River a little less than a hundred feet in the air. Even though Highway 34 dipped slightly while approaching the deep gorge, the bridge ran for almost five hundred feet over the river so that modern vehicles like his fuel truck did not have to expend much energy crossing the formidable natural obstacle.

Wally didn't bother to slow down or look as he passed over the bridge. He'd seen the river a thousand times in his life, with the Nicollet Dam reservoir to the north and the sand bars that formed at the confluence of Lake Manitou to the south. Rory Stewart's body had been dumped onto the exposed rock, which was now covered by raging waters from the recent rains.

Once out of the Blue Knife River valley, he came to the intersection that led to either the state park to the south or the Nimrod road to the north.

He turned north.

The Turtle Island Jesuit School, like other businesses and residences in the area, had allowed their fuel supply to dwindle in the long spring, leaving its tanks almost empty as winter approached.

After filling their tank, Wally drove out of the small reservation but parked his truck alongside the road where it turned back east toward the Nimrod road.

Migisi Asibikaashi lived like a hermit along the Blue Knife River, and Wally's boots were heavy with mud by the time he reached the small shack. The flooded Nicollet Reservoir had swallowed four feet of shore and now approached the bases of the old trees.

"Migisi," Wally called out as he neared the old man's residence, "it's Wally Crain."

Migisi didn't appear.

When he reached the porch, he saw a stack of willow branches and rolls of sinew—Migisi was constructing dreamcatchers. Wally rapped loudly on the front door, but with scarcely a glance into the window, he could see that Migisi was not there.

A dying fire burned in the middle of the yard, and past it, sheltered by tall pines, a freshly built sweat lodge stood a few feet from the edge of the river.

If Wally hadn't seen other lodges in his life, he would have assumed a gigantic beaver had swallowed a tree and taken a crap, leaving a random pile of bark and branches. For all of its aesthetic ugliness, the sweat lodge did its job, exuding heat from the flap that marked its entrance.

"Are you coming out, or am I coming in?" Wally asked as he gently knocked on the birch bark structure.

The flap flew open, and Migisi, looking like a wet rat, stared at him. "What have I done to make Manabozho hate me so much?"

Wally extended his hand, and Migisi took hold to climb out of the lodge. "Why does Manabozho hate you, old man?"

"He taunts me with signs of my enemy but will not show me the path to take to fight him. I've waited my whole life to fight the Horned Serpent, and now that he again rises, I am an old man. Why would he be so cruel?"

"You've heard what happened to the Stewart boy?"

"Ed Nielson told me a few days ago. I have been in prayer ever since."

"That's good. The authorities have no answers. Do you?"

"I have more questions than answers," Migisi said. He wore only a pair of boxers, and from inside the doorway of the lodge, he pulled out a wool blanket that he draped over his shoulders. He led the way to the shack, threw open his front door, and walked directly to the old cast iron stove in the middle of the room. He spent a few minutes stoking the cold coals until flames began to appear.

Once satisfied, he walked over to his small bed and picked up a leather notebook, which he carried to Wally, extending it to him.

"What's this?"

"Death. Take it away from here."

Wally found the notebook in his fingers, but instead of opening it, he watched Migisi dress himself and then begin to brew some coffee. "Are you going to explain?"

"Children brought it to me, more likely than not, children who will be the next victims of the Tak-Pei, for the contents of the notebook contain secrets that have long been guarded by the Midewiwin, Jes'sikkid, and Wabeno. Now white children possess the secrets and carry it around like an Algebra book."

"Who brought this to you?"

"Nicole and her little puppy, the MacPherson boy. He wouldn't follow her so willingly if he knew the truth about the blood that flows in her veins. The Men of the Dawn heap piles of children upon the altar, knowing evil will come to feast."

For all of his bluster, Migisi wasn't offering a plan. *How can he just sit here and let all this happen?* "What am I supposed to do?"

"Get rid of that notebook. It was wrong for Guerin to have written down secrets that should only be whispered in a sweat lodge. For his arrogance, he had to die twice where most men need only to die once. My sister suffers because of the same arrogance."

Migisi's hands fluttered with agitation. "I don't care what you do with it, but know that as long as you have it, evil will be drawn to it, for it is both a threat and a prize to them."

"Why are you afraid to keep it? You claim to be a warrior yet seem to avoid a fight."

Migisi's wrinkled face seemed to constrict with hatred. "The Tak-Pei sneak up to my cabin at night. I can hear them whispering and plotting, but when I rush out to battle them, they flee like smoke in the wind. They won't fight me."

"Why?"

"Because they know that their master is under my blade. I hold the knife to his throat, and with a word from my sister, I could destroy all of the plans of the Wintermaker."

Wally's fists clenched as he fought rage to ask his question calmly. "Why don't you?"

"Bah!" Migisi dismissed him with a flail of his hands. "You are still an ignorant boy in the skin of a man. Would you destroy your house to put out a fire on the stove? Lily made a choice, and now I must defend it to my last breath, even if I wouldn't have made the choice myself."

I'm not sure what that means. "So, what do I do about the fire on the stove?"

Migisi ignored him long enough to gather two tin coffee cups and pour steaming coffee into them. Even though he was a bitter old man, Migisi showed his affection by bringing two cubes of sugar for Wally.

Wally put his hand over the cup. "How could you end this all right now, Migisi? What did you mean with your comment about a knife to the throat?"

"The Wintermaker cannot rise without three sacred items. My sister and I guard one. As long as we live, we will hold back the waters."

Wally removed his hand and Migisi dropped the cubes into the coffee. For a few moments, both men sipped away at the coffee in silence.

"Fawn Chevreuil is dead," Migisi said to break the silence. "Her son Leonard and grandson Benjamin came and visited me for a week in early September. Benjamin. What kind of name is that?"

Did he forget he told me already? Wally restrained himself from cruelty. "Benjamin is from the Bible. He was the beloved son of Jacob."

"Well, he and Leonard have both begun their training in the secrets of the Wijigan and the Song of the Manitou. They know enough should I die this winter."

"Do you know something that I don't?"

"It is not my health that worries me."

"You worry about the Wintermaker and his Tak-Pei?"

"For being a young man still, Leonard is surprisingly wise, and it was prudent that he left Lake Manitou when he did."

"Why is it prudent? Won't we need his help in fighting the Wintermaker?"

"We do not fight the Wintermaker," Migisi said flatly.

"I don't ... what do ... what do you mean?"

"Why do you come to me for counsel when you don't listen? I just told you that we do not fight the Wintermaker, yet you want more information about an enemy that is irrelevant. Fine. Let me speak to you as if you are a child.

"The Horned Serpent that torments Iyash—that is not our enemy. The Manitou that lurks in the waters—that is not our enemy. The great shape-shifting Bear that is known as No Soul—that is not our enemy. This enemy with many names is the concern of future generations. We'll be bones and dust before we have to concern ourselves with this evil being."

Wally was losing patience, but he knew Migisi was an important ally. "Okay, Migisi, I understand your point. Who do we fight?"

"We fight summer," Migisi said with a smirk. "Guerin came to us because the Black Robes understood the true face of evil far better than my grandfather did! The Wijigan stood too close to the fire to understand the difference between the light and the darkness. I remember hearing the tale from Nanakonan, but only now that I am old do I understand it."

"Fighting summer is impossible," Wally surmised. "The seasons change, and there is nothing that can be done to stop it."

"Not necessarily. Long ago and still to come, there once was a man, the Wintermaker, who wanted to stop time, and after studying the truth about the world, he noticed how the Summerbirds would come and go with the changing of the seasons. Did the Summerbirds arrive because of the seasons, or did the seasons arrive because of the Summerbirds?"

"I think—"

"So the Wintermaker began to collect the Summerbirds. At first, no one even noticed, for who would miss a single Summerbird? But after a while, the Wintermaker had so many birds in his trap that the seasons could not change, and a terrible winter fell upon the world. The animals were bewildered, so the Fisher Cat was sent to the lands of the north to investigate. He found the Summerbirds locked away in a cage, and the herring watched over them. While the Fisher Cat was not strong enough to battle the Wintermaker, he was able to fight the herring, and during the fierce battle, he found enough time to unlock the cage and free some of the Summerbirds. Even though some remained in the cage, enough escaped to usher in a new summer, and time continued to move."

"So that's what is happening here?" Wally asked. "The Summerbirds are slowly collecting in the cage."

"When I was your age, I wanted to fight the Wintermaker too," Migisi replied. "It is easier to fight the herring than the Wintermaker.".

"I must find the herring," Wally said, even if he wasn't sure he understood the metaphors. "The herring is my enemy."

"The herring is the servant of the Wintermaker, but the enemy of the Wintermaker is the coming summer. He collects the Summerbirds in his cage to keep the summer from arriving, for in his great wisdom he knows that a terrible summer of Fire and Water will come to destroy him. It is good to save the Summerbirds from the cage, but you must also understand that the Creator sends Summerbirds north knowing they will be captured. For the Terrible Summer can only arrive once the Fisher Cat has freed all the Summerbirds from the cage."

Wally sighed loudly enough to end the lesson.

Migisi began tending to the empty coffee cups. As he collected Wally's cup, he said, "You asked me who we fight, but I must speak in metaphors. If you fight the herring, you may free a bird or two, but if you leave the gate open, and all the Summerbirds escape without being led back south, all will be lost."

This is ridiculous! To keep his frustration in check, Wally focused on the leather notebook in his hands. "Have you read this?"

"Mostly half-truths, but then again, I might be wrong, and Father Guerin might be right. Who knows? I would have thrown it in the fire myself, but then it occurred to me that the Men of the Dawn burned Lily's house to either kill my sister or destroy the notebook."

"But why would Eos wait so long to act? Triton men have known about Lily for decades now."

Migisi's hand went to a metal bowl and retrieved a small metal object, which he tossed sharply at Wally. It bounced against his thick canvas jacket, but Wally caught the rebound. In his hand, he held the metal head of a lighter.

"Care to explain?"

"The MacPherson boy told quite a tale. He said that when he ran around to the backside of Tew's house, the ground in front of her house was on fire as if someone had poured fuel around the house. Nicole said she found this lighter on the edge of the fire, and not far away in the woods, she found an empty fuel can."

"Ed and I already suspected arson. Why did they wait—" Wally knew it was too late to make accusations, and even if he'd been the one to find it that night, he knew tangling with Eos or Triton meant he needed concrete evidence.

"This is *not* the act of a servant," Migisi said.

The Wintermaker bought a Bic lighter? "What do you mean?"

"The Wintermaker and his servants know they can outlast Lily and me. They understand the truce forged so many summers ago. Something changed, and instead of waiting for my sister to die, an enemy struck first. Whoever set the fire is acting independently of their master."

Migisi looked directly into Wally's eyes. "Your enemy is not Eos. As Father Guerin once explained to me, evil is often a house divided."

The red Thunderbird?

What's the saying? The enemy of my enemy is my friend?

"Father Guerin argued that the Isanti Lodge needed to make a stand against evil. Leonard White Elk recently tried to convince me that the prophecy will not be fulfilled for another century and that I should do nothing. You and I must walk the line between these two philosophies."

"To save the Summerbirds?"

Migisi nodded. "Souls are like fuel to the Tak-Pei. When Tew battled the Wintermaker long ago, she trapped the Tak-Pei on Deadwood Island. If Leonard is right, the Wintermaker should simply wait, but instead, someone is purposefully waking the Tak-Pei before the proper time. I just don't understand why. But I know this: the Tak-Pei are again growing stronger, and when they grow strong enough, they will rally around their master like hornets protecting their nest."

Wally slipped the leather notebook into the pocket inside his jacket. Then he reached into the front pocket of his jeans and pulled out his small Barlow knife. "My father used this blade to stab the Manitou, yet you keep talking about Tak-Pei. What am I dealing with, Migisi? Men or monsters?"

Migisi studied the knife for a few moments. "Perhaps both. Both men and monsters came for me back on Deadwood Island, and I would gladly lay down my life to stop the killing, but we must weather the coming storm. The final fight will not happen this generation."

"I'm not willing to wait a hundred years to do my part," Wally said, standing up. He embraced Migisi before leaving.

A few minutes later, when Wally stopped at the Nimrod road, a 1950 Plymouth, dark blue, drove past his stopped truck at full speed, heading north.

Its driver wore a derby hat.

A herring?

CHAPTER THIRTY-FIVE

Blood Brothers

Split Rock High School
November 3, 1961

THINGS DIDN'T GET better after MEA break. The two murders clouded everything. Chris Luning even noticed angry flashes exchanged by his friends as he approached them at their lockers. "What was that all about?"

Jimmy looked over to Biff before answering, "Nothing."

Sure looked like something, Chris thought as the three walked to the cafeteria together.

By the time they arrived in the lunchroom, half of the student body was sitting at tables with trays and the other half was standing in line. Jimmy and his friends punctuated the end of the line. While they waited, Chris chirped out theories about the coming NFL games, especially about the Vikings. Jimmy nodded to keep Chris going.

What are they hiding from me?

When they sat down, Chris finally stopped talking, mainly to eat. Classmates Carey Jensen and Dale Nase had shoveled down their food, and before Chris had taken a few bites, the two bolted toward the side door of the commons for recess, leaving the three buddies almost alone.

Normally, Biff led the charge outside to play football, but today, he took his time eating crinkle-cut fries one by one.

"So, what do *you* think happened to Rory?" Jimmy finally asked.

"Charlie Morrison thinks it is some sort of pervert," Chris offered. "Some weirdo who lives by himself, and from time to time, he gets in his car and drives around looking for a boy who's all alone."

"Somebody like the janitor?" Biff asked.

Jimmy glanced across the dining room to the senior high tables and Chris followed the glance. Standing behind the rolling garbage cans with a push broom propped in his hands, Cameron Guerin meekly watched the students.

Chris shook his head. "Can Man? He's harmless."

"He's always staring and watching," Biff retorted. "Think about it for a minute. What if he was a psycho? He's hiding in plain sight. Lily Guerin's house burns down. The accident at Carousel Park, and Isaac Larson—all three things happened around Can Man."

"But he had nothing to do with Rory Stewart," Chris countered.

"You're just defending him because you've got the hots for Nicki Guerin," Biff challenged.

"Do not," Chris said, his ears suddenly hot. But it was true. His former babysitter had become a babe.

"Do too," Biff pressed. "Just last week you were talking about her hair."

"I was just noticing it. For crying out loud, she's a junior and I'm a seventh grader. Besides, I worked with Cameron at Carousel Park. He's odd but—"

Jimmy came to his rescue. "I've got to agree with Chris. Can Man might be a bit creepy, but he had nothing to do with Rory."

"That we know of," Biff added, pressing his point.

"It's not him," Jimmy insisted.

Biff gave up with a shrug. "Who's your suspect then?"

Jimmy looked around to make sure no one sat near them. Most of the kids had slipped out the doors for the final ten minutes of recess. "What if it's not a person doing all of this?"

Thoughts of the spooky shadows lurking in the trees and the raven back at the state park entered Chris's mind. *He's right. Something more sinister is behind this.*

"What, like the Wolf Man?" Biff teased and then hit Jimmy hard in the fleshy part of his shoulder.

"Ow, what was that for?"

"For being a dumbass."

Has Jimmy seen something too?

Jimmy didn't cower to a bully though and turned his conversation to Chris. "What if Wally Crain was trying to tell us something," Jimmy started. "And I'm not talking about survival skills or tying knots. What if all those stories about the Manitou and such were meant to warn us?"

"Warn us about what?" Chris suddenly became aware of his full bladder, and the contents of his stomach churned. This conversation made him want to run away.

"You know ... all those Indian legends. The story about the Sioux women looking for their lost children. The story about Wally's dad getting attacked by the Manitou when he saw those men performing a ritual. The Porcupine Men who hide in the woods."

Chris felt his throat constrict. "The Tak-Pei," he said softly.

"Yeah, the Tak-Pei," Jimmy repeated. "What if those stories weren't meant to scare us before bedtime? What if they were meant to educate us?"

"Did you see something?" Chris asked almost in a whisper.

Jimmy hesitated and looked down.

Biff grew sullen and looked away.

He saw something.

"What did you see?" Chris asked.

"We probably shouldn't tell you," Biff said, glancing from Jimmy to Chris.

Chris grew angry, remembering how he'd been abandoned that night. "You're my pals. Pals aren't supposed to keep secrets."

Jimmy sighed and looked at Biff, whose mouth tightened as he shook his head.

"We swore we'd never talk about it," Biff revealed.

"Hey, hey," Chris said, holding out his hand and then bending his thumb to display a white scar at the knuckle joint. "We're blood brothers, and not some pansy thumb prick, either. Each of us have the same scar on our knuckles so we won't forget our pals. My knuckle overrules any verbal promise that was made."

Biff looked away.

"We made the promise with Rory," Jimmy clarified.

"Oh," Chris said, shamed and suddenly jealous. "This doesn't have anything to do with his death, does it? Cuz if so, we gotta tell somebody."

"I don't want to tell you because I don't want to involve you," Jimmy said, avoiding his first question.

They don't trust me with their big secret. "Well, I give you permission to involve me, then. Neither of you are smart enough to figure this out, apparently, so you either need to tell an adult or you need to tell me."

Biff suddenly relented with a nod and immediately Jimmy leaned in to whisper, "When we were camping at Turtle Island State Park, we snuck out in the middle of the night and broke into Haggard Quarry."

"Wh—"

"We planned on waking you, but you were sleeping in the tent beside Wally, and we didn't think we'd be able to wake you up without waking him," Biff said.

No. They thought I'd rat on them. Biff is still upset about the rice crispy bars incident.

Jimmy continued, "We hopped in a canoe and paddled across the lake, and before we knew it, we were sneaking under the security fence and into the quarry."

"Why?" Chris asked.

"Rory said there was some sort of treasure that they were guarding. I knew better but Jimmy called bullshit," Biff explained. "Sure enough, security guards came out of nowhere. They were watching the quarry as if it was a bank vault. We got separated, though, and they only found Rory and me."

"Where were you?" Chris asked Jimmy.

Again, Jimmy looked around before lowering his voice. "At first, I threw myself in the shadows beside some shack, but then I crawled into a hole in the lattice and hid under it. I saw the armed guards come and take Rory and Biff, so I held tight, but while I waited, I heard something whispering to me in the dark. It came from behind me, and I found an entrance to a tunnel. The shack was built right up against the stone wall, but from underneath the foundation, I was able to slip out from under it on the other side of a locked door."

"Was it a cave?"

"No, it was man made. See, they're hiding the entrance so that no one knows what they are doing. The rest of the quarry is just a distraction. They're digging under Lake Manitou."

A tunnel to what? "Where did…" Chris almost formed another nervous question but knew the answer. "And you heard a voice come from the tunnel?"

"What voice?" Biff asked, agitated.

Jimmy didn't tell Biff this part, Chris realized.

"It was a whisper, but it was more than my imagination. It came from the tunnel, I swear. For a while, I didn't believe it myself, which is why I didn't tell you what I found," Jimmy said, glancing at Biff. "But I've been having really weird dreams lately, and there are times when I can hear the voice whispering to me in the dark."

Biff muttered a profanity under his breath.

Chris now had to squeeze his thighs to control his full bladder. "What are we going to do?"

"We? You didn't go there. It was me, Biff, and Rory, and now Rory is dead, along with Isaac Larson, and those four other people who died in the roller coaster accident. That's six people, and if Wally's stories are true, there will be six more before…"

"Before what?" Chris prompted Jimmy.

"Before the Manitou wakes."

Biff shook his head. "I don't believe the Manitou killed those people."

"Are you saying I'm a liar?" Jimmy asked.

"No, I'm not saying you're lying. I'm saying … Old Copper Road is haunted by Sioux women looking for their twelve children, right? Wally didn't say the Manitou killed them. He said some Chippewa cult leader sacrificed them at Bleeding Rock, the same place Isaac died. What if someone is trying to wake the Manitou?"

The lunch hour was almost done, and Chris needed to use the bathroom, so he rose, but not before saying, "That's why they are targeting kids."

"That's right," Biff said. "Now that you know the secret, you need to promise me something."

"What?" Chris asked, shifting his legs.

"Maybe Jimmy's right. Maybe there is some monster causing all this to happen, but if I'm right, and it is some psycho cult leader out there doing this, then Rory died because we snuck into the quarry. There were five or six adults there that night, but none of them knew Jimmy was there, right? So, if something happens to me, then you know the killer is a real person. If something happens to both of us, then you need to get the hell out of Hiawatha

County, even if you have to run away and live on the railroads like a hobo, okay?"

"We need to tell somebody about this," Chris insisted, glancing at the restroom.

"Promise me," Biff repeated.

"We should talk to Wally about this," Chris dodged. "He seems to know about the Manitou, right?"

"And what if the Manitou is real?" Jimmy asked. "What then?"

"We need to tell him about the tunnel, don't we? Maybe he'll know what to do."

"We're blood brothers," Jimmy said sternly. "Make the promise, Chris."

His bladder demanded attention. "Okay, if something happens to either of you, I'll become a hobo and leave, but I'm not going to let anything happen to either of you. We're going to stick together and not let anything come between because … I made a promise, too."

Jimmy and Biff were caught off guard.

"When you guys snuck out, I think I saw a Tak-Pei … and something else. I think I had a vision."

"You've kept that to yourself all of this time?" Biff asked, a wrinkle of concern appearing on his forehead.

"I was mad that you didn't wake me up to come with you."

Biff sighed. "If we brought you, it might be you dead now instead of Rory."

Chris offered his hand, with his pinky extended. "Pinky swear?"

Jimmy looked around, and at the second-floor railing, he saw Mrs. Crain looking down at him. "People are watching, Chris. We'll pinky swear some other time, okay. We'll talk some more after school."

Chris withdrew his pinky and rushed off to the restroom.

CHAPTER THIRTY-SIX

Protective Gear

Split Rock, MN
November 11, 1961

ALBERT FISHER STOOD at the window in his study, examining the old brick wall as a cold wind came through the window panes. At one end of his study, a brick fireplace held the embers of the fire that had warmed the room for his morning coffee break at his mahogany desk. The fireplace also contained the ashes of the morning newspaper, which updated Hiawatha County about a possible serial killer preying on young boys.

As a boy, Albert knew the fear of death. His fear of Lake Manitou and the Tak-Pei motivated him to reuse the bricks from the old convent to build a new mansion that not only looked over Split Rock like a watchtower but also stood beside the old willow tree.

He felt safer knowing that some of the bricks had once belonged to a house of God, for across the Crow Wing River, on the other side of the valley, the Manitou still whispered to him in his dreams.

But I can't hide here all day.

I have to see if my dreams are warnings.

His gaze shifted from the bricks to the world outside of his sanctuary. A dusting of snow covered the lawn. The weeping willow in the center of the yard bowed low, its tendril branches touching the ground. The fall snow had come before many of the trees lost their leaves, and while several oak and maple branches snapped off from the weight, the willow simply drooped as it bore the burden. If he had his druthers, he would not step outside for the rest of winter—or else simply go south for the winter with his wife Eunice.

But with Lily recovering from her ordeal, Albert knew the responsibility as the eldest member of the Isanti Lodge fell upon his shoulders, and since the burden was heavy, he needed to move or be crushed by its weight.

Eunice and her book club members were having tea in the parlor, but none of them took note as he slipped out of his study through the main dining room and out into the garage. Even though he paid for a maid and a groundskeeper, either of which were willing to drive, Albert knew he had to go alone today.

The attached garage had the two newer cars, a Buick Roadmaster and a Mercedes Benz, which he and his wife frequently used, but Albert went through that garage until he reached the side door. Elmer Johnson, the groundskeeper, had shoveled the path to a storage garage, leaving him no excuse but to keep going.

The storage garage was the last vestige of the old convent that sat tucked away by the trees planted behind the estate. When he reached the door, he found it unlocked.

Johnson jumped when the door opened, hitting his head against the motor shield of the snowblower he was working on. "Mr. Fisher, is there something I can help you with?"

"Yes, I'd like to take the LaSalle out for a spin. Could you pull it forward and help me with the door?"

My father's car. It was a symbol of decadent wealth, and Albert couldn't bring himself to part with it.

"Do you want me to take you someplace Mr. Fisher? I'm only fine-tuning the motor on the snow blower before winter arrives."

"Absolutely not. Keep tinkering. I simply want to take the car out for a spin. If all this October rain had been snow, I'd be buried in my house until it melted in March."

"Well, I'd say it is safe to take it out now, Mr. Fisher. I think it would cheer folks up to see it cruising around the streets of Split Rock."

"Is it ready to go?"

"Should be. I serviced all the engines back in July and was just about to rotate through them prior to winter until this snow-blower gave me fits. Let me get the door, and I'll bring it out for you."

THE GREEN AND Black LaSalle purred. A little smoke came from the tailpipe, but for as long as it sat, that was to be expected. As soon as he settled upon the seat, the magic of the LaSalle turned him from a seventy-year-old man into a teen. Hoping Eunice and her friends did not see the car sneaking down the driveway, he gave Johnson a nod and crept away from his estate.

In spite of there being no stop sign, Albert paused at the intersection of North Division and Seventh Avenue, a new street built along the ridge overlooking the valley.

Owning twenty acres of wooded land at the top of the ridge did not prevent the new houses to the north of his driveway from seeming like intruders. They gave the impression that Split Rock was vibrant and growing when in reality, old houses rotted like tumors on the aging town.

Not wanting to put the brakes to the test, Albert turned south. He hardly needed to put his foot on the accelerator for the LaSalle wanted to be out on the town. A block from his driveway, Lyons Park looked much as it did when he was a child, yet the young oak trees had grown into adult oak trees to replace the thick canopy that covered the merry-go-round, swings, and the tallest slide in all of Hiawatha County. There wasn't a single child playing in the park, and it occurred to Albert that he wasn't sure if it was a weekday or weekend.

The park ended at Chicago Street, and Albert slowly passed by the three-story house that had belonged to Hazel Sloan. Once, the house had belonged to Doc Jenkins, but when he hung himself from the trestle bridge during the Great Depression, the rich old woman purchased the home for herself. For three decades, nary a repair or improvement had been made to the estate, and if Hazel Sloan hadn't been as old as he was, Albert would have suspected her of the foul deeds happening around lake Manitou.

But Albert knew better.

Hazel Sloan wasn't to blame. He knew a real sorceress named Lily. Her absence allowed evil to return.

Evil clings to the bricks of this community like lichen.

Are my dreams echoes of the past or omens for the future?

In his dream, the creamery and lumberyard were destroyed. He let off the brakes and continued rolling down the hill toward the Crow Wing River. He paused at the railroad tracks that once sent thousands of dollars of lumber out to southern Minnesota each day. Now, the lumber left on trucks and the trains would stop here only once a week during the summer and once a month during the winter.

At the bottom of the wooded ravine, he passed over the old iron bridge now known as Doc Jenkins Bridge. His recent dreams about the creamery proved unfounded. *It's still standing. No explosions. No disasters.*

An echo from the past?

The parking lot was full, the milk trucks came and went, and the smokestacks from the boilers puffed away as they'd done for decades. Albert never took the LaSalle out of gear as he made a leisurely loop around the factory and went out the way he'd come.

At the entrance of Dutch Boy Creamery, he gave a long glance at Old Copper Road. He wanted to patrol the old road that led to distant Turtle Island, but he knew the heavy rains would have turned it into a muddy mess, so he chose discretion over valor and went back toward town.

After passing over the bridge and railroad tracks, he turned south onto Market Street and to Fisher Lumberyard.

Past the tracks, the train depot allowed the lumber cars to be brought to the back of the massive warehouse building. More than a dozen men were still employed full-time to fill the local orders and organize the factory for a building boom that most likely would never come again.

Perhaps my dreams of doom were economic, Albert speculated.

Fisher Lumberyard was built upon a jut of land caused by a loop in the Crow Wing River. On the flat piece of land, his father had built several small docks and chutes to collect lumber from the sawmill on the north side of the town at Split Rock Creek. Smaller buildings housed saws that turned the raw lumber into smaller pieces of wood.

The road came to an end at the house Albert once called home but now belonged to his son-in-law, Marlin Luning. Before Albert parked the car, Marlin opened the front door and stepped out onto the deck. Robust for fifty, Marlin Luning had a full head of silver hair swept over to one side. His thick mustache and goatee matched his silver hair. Behind him, Christopher had the jet-black hair his father once had.

"Good morning, Al," Marlin said, and then loudly cleared his throat. "What brings you all the way down here on this fine Saturday?"

"I needed to get out of the house while the weather held."

"Little gloomy today, but at least it's not raining anymore." Albert stood twenty yards from the front door, and the roar of the

Crow Wing River caused both of them to almost shout. "Do you want to come in for a cup of coffee?"

"Actually, I was wondering if you could give me a little tour of the plant. I want to see the new equipment you told me about."

Marlin looked at his son. "Chris, run inside and pour two cups of coffee for your grandpa and me. Pick the mugs with the lids. Ask your mother for help if you can't find them."

Chris vanished from the doorway, and Marlin stepped down from the porch to where Albert stood on the other side of the painted picket fence surrounding the yard.

"Hear anything from Chuck?" Marlin asked.

"Eunice wants to fly down to Fort Benning for either Thanksgiving or Christmas."

"Well, that would be lovely. Georgia is certainly going to have better weather than Minnesota. If you're making the trip, could Betsy and I send some presents for Karson with you?"

"Certainly. It's hard to believe my great-grandson is already in kindergarten, isn't it?"

"It certainly is. Chuck is learning how to fly helicopters. When he's done with his stint in the service, he'll have a very lucrative career in aviation. The military has at least got his head in the right direction now."

"Helen and Eunice are still walking on eggshells. I worry my great-grandson is going to grow up not knowing any of us just because Eunice doesn't know when to keep her mouth shut."

"I'm glad Chuck and Helen are finding a way to make it work."

"So am I."

Chris Luning came through the door with two cups of coffee. "This one has milk and honey in it for you, Grandpa."

"Betsy certainly has a memory, doesn't she?"

"She has her moments." Marlin sighed and then turned his attention to Chris. "Go ahead and keep watching the Gophers game without me."

"Is your football season over?" Albert asked before Chris left.

"Yeah, junior high doesn't have playoffs. Our seventh-grade team went undefeated this year."

"Well, maybe you boys can bring Split Rock another championship, like your big brother Chuck did."

"I'll sure do my part."

"I bet you will."

Chris bolted back to the house, jumping over all three steps on the porch to show off a little. *I'd give my life to keep him safe. Wally is right; we must protect these children.*

The previous generation had grown up too quickly: *Paul Forsberg and Chuck Luning were supposed to take our places.* "Would this have been Chuck's senior year at the U of M?"

"You're not here to talk about Chuck or football, are you Albert?"

"No, I'm not," Albert admitted and walked toward the plant.

Both men put on their protective gear: hard hats, ear plugs, and goggles. The sound of the saw blades replaced the sound of the river, bringing comfort to Albert. Water chutes still connected the two sawmills, and once winter froze everything solid, work would come to a complete halt at the northern plant.

Inside the warehouse, Albert and Marlin were greeted by the familiar faces of men who'd worked for the company for decades. The large rectangular building had a receiving chute at the northern side, where the finished lumber would arrive from the smaller saws to be sorted, stacked, and dried. On the southern end of the building, a semi-truck with a large flatbed trailer waited to be filled. Albert walked up the stairs that led to the old factory office near the ceiling.

By the time he reached the third level, Albert had to clutch the railing that overlooked the warehouse while Marlin patiently waited for him to remove his protective gear and get to his point.

Albert reached inside his jacket to fumble at his collar, and when his fingers found the leather band, he pulled out the wooden cross hidden against his chest. "Your father gave me this cross. He made it himself."

"Yes, I know the story well. He used to tell me the story when I was a kid."

"He gave it to me to comfort me when I was a boy, but now I am an old man, and the same fears keep me up at night. What has Sheriff Betzing learned about the death of the Stewart boy?"

Despite his incredulity towards anything paranormal, Marlin still was a valuable asset to the Isanti Lodge, especially with his connections to the Sheriff's Department.

"They have a few leads and a person of interest. Betzing said they're looking for a blue Plymouth. It was another rental car checked out by someone matching the description of that fellow in the red Thunderbird."

"The Indian fellow?" Albert asked, realizing how the word meant something else to most of America.

"No, the English smoker that the Guerins described. The driver."

"Ah. A blue Plymouth."

"It might be just a rogue predator."

"Might," Albert repeated. "Do you know each tree that goes through this warehouse feels like a little victory for me? I know the environmental groups speak of responsible harvesting, but none of those experts have ever stood in the old forest and heard the whispers in the pines. If I had my druthers, we'd rip out every tree between Lake Manitou and Leech Lake, leaving no place for the shadows to hide."

"The shadows would simply find new places to hide, Albert."

"My father became business partners with Triton Corporation, and since that day, I've lived most of my life in fear. I worry about those people."

"Those people? Edna Forsberg is a Haggard."

"We can't see the strings of the puppet master. Something is happening, Marlin, and I know in my heart that Triton Corporation is behind it. I had a dream about the creamery exploding, and a flood of children came out of it, pouring into the Crow Wing River."

"Wasn't there an explosion there years ago? Perhaps your brain is just reflecting on childhood fears."

"When I was a child, I saw monsters. Real monsters, both in the woods and in the water. You've spent your whole life blissfully unaware of the truth about this place, but I know different. Even though you weren't born when your father gave this to me, I feel as if it should be yours. Or give it to Chris for protection."

Albert pulled the pendant over his head and handed it to Marlin, who accepted it reluctantly. "If it is a family heirloom, shouldn't I give it to Chuck?"

"Chuck is far away from Lake Manitou; Chris isn't. I know you think I am a foolish old man, but I can feel evil growing by the day, and it is our children who will pay the price for our lack of vigilance. Stay watchful, Marlin. Stay watchful."

WHEN ALBERT RETURNED TO the LaSalle, he did not head back up the hill to his house even though it was late in the afternoon. Instead, he turned north on Market Street and drove to the Old Mill. At the adjacent hill, the old log chute passed twenty feet above his head and descended all the way back to the lumberyard.

Descending the bluff, he saw the towering red building of the Fisher Sawmill. Marlin had recently suggested they close the Old Mill and turn it into a historic park.

For the first time in sixty years, Albert returned to the place where he almost died.

Omodai.

The word echoed in his memories. He'd seen the Tak-Pei. He'd been hunted by them for weeks before one pulled him into the waters of Split Rock Creek right out from under the noses of his father and Triton businessmen. Only Farrell Luning had acted, jumping at great personal risk into the raging current to save him.

Why?

The Omodai.

Once, Lily Weber believed the evil spirits in the water were trying to claim him, to use him as a vessel for resurrection. Lily and the Isanti Lodge fought to keep that from happening. Ultimately, the bad guys snatched Migisi, sparing Albert another brush with death. Years later, Albert understood the Wintermaker would never want him.

But do I have another part to play? Lily and Farrell once saved me, and now I must repay the debt.

Without Lily, the loops could be broken.

Albert parked his car in the empty lot. He checked his coat pocket for his keys and walked over to the main door.

Once he reached the fourth level, he walked over to the hinged window shutter, and with the support bar, lifted it open so he could peer out onto Lake Manitou. A ring of ice extended from the shallow waters along the shoreline between Deadwood Island and the steep bluffs of Bleeding Rock. In the distant channel, he saw a solitary fisherman standing beside a bucket on ice that could only be a few inches thick.

Life and death will hang in the balance of the sawmill, an apparition under the willow tree had told him. Albert knew and loved Lily. He trusted her. He trusted everyone in the Isanti Lodge, but the boy in the snakeskin boots? He wasn't sure.

His gaze finally fixed on the rock and concrete dam that had been built along Split Rock Creek, the namesake for the town. Defying the laws of physics, the creek seemingly cut right through granite in a series of falls before reaching the Crow Wing River.

Although the main outlet for the lake, his father had built a small dam that powered the mill and lifted the water level at the mouth of the creek to allow logs to be wrangled from the lake. Thick metal planks across a channel not much wider than ten yards held back the entire lake.

Albert turned around and walked to the eastern side of the mill, lifted the same hinged window shutter, and looked down on the angry creek.

Without Lily, the loops could be broken and all their efforts—past, present, and future—would be destroyed.

Someone must destroy the Wintermaker or...

Lily would survive to be an old woman, but they all assumed she would live until the Serpent Star, commonly known as Halley's Comet, returned in 1986.

The Wintermaker and his servants had been caught off guard years ago when Lily and the others stood up to fight. The Isanti Lodge might have been ready to put up another fight in a quarter of a century, but evil had other plans.

The great battle can't be happening now. How do I fix this?

Even though he would be reprimanded by Eunice for his unexplained absence, he lingered at the window an hour as the October sun set. If the Tak-Pei were to appear, they would come out at twilight, yet only the water stirred.

Albert returned to the LaSalle slightly morose but also relieved. The engine purred with just a twist of his wrist, and the headlights lit the faded red paint of the Old Mill. He turned widely and slowly, bouncing over the diversion tracks built into the parking lot.

He saw a solitary truck parked at the boat launch; undoubtedly, the vehicle belonged to the reckless fisherman back at the channel. As the old LaSalle climbed up the steep hill of the bluff, its lights illuminated the old log chute over the road. As a boy he always wanted to get a sled and rocket from the mill to the lumberyard.

A gray shadow came out of the thick trees.

At first, Albert thought it was a deer, but when he saw another come out from the left side of the road, he knew what he saw.

The third hunched Tak-Pei, with strange hair like porcupine quills, elongated fingers, and squatty legs, came over the hill toward him.

The three creatures with long snouts like wolves snarled as they blocked his passage.

Albert gripped the steering wheel, knowing his LaSalle was more of a weapon than any knife or gun. Yet he'd stopped halfway up the hill, and if he gunned it, he might stall the engine.

Behind him, at the boat launch, he'd be able to turn around and then gun it for a hundred yards, scattering the ancient creatures that could not comprehend the power of a GMC engine. Calmly stepping on the clutch with his left foot while keeping his right foot on the brake, he shifted the car in reverse.

Glancing in his rear mirror, the boat launch lit up in a soft red glow.

Suddenly a fourth Tak-Pei slapped at his window.

In a panic, Albert stomped on the accelerator, and while he left the fourth Tak-Pei behind, he was sent hurtling down the hill. When his good sense returned, his foot shifted back to the brake, but the snow and ice on the landing provided no friction for his tires, and in a heartbeat, he saw the landing and truck pass by his windows.

He heard the cracking of ice and felt the LaSalle lurch backwards, its headlights pointing toward the stars. As water rushed around his windows, Albert clutched at his chest, only to remember the oak crucifix was no longer there to protect him.

A False Face

Split Rock High School
November 27, 1961

NICKI GUERIN KNEW how to hide, but Cameron didn't. The greatest danger to her popularity always came during lunch, for after a day of whispers between classes, Nicki revealed herself to the student body as she stood in line with Gavin and the rest of the popular juniors.

Nicki kept the spotlight into November, and the Monday before Thanksgiving break, she stunned the student body with her "Blonde Bombshell" transformation. Since school began, Nicki's sweaters became tighter, her skirts became shorter, and the recent coup-de-grace: her hair became blonde, dyed and cut short.

Any boy who had reached puberty took notice, and girls who hated her for being an Indian now spit nails as she hugged up close to her man.

Being a tramp, even a monogamous one, was far better than being an Indian at Split Rock High School.

Nicki knew the rumors swirled about the killings, and although her father and grandmother had been victims of the same bad fortune, all eyes turned to her misshapen, and far more obviously Indian brother.

She glanced at him occasionally and suddenly regretted the rules she'd established in September about never speaking to her in public.

With a crooked grin on his face, Cameron, armed only with a mop and the security of Principal Carlson, stood against the windowed wall.

Cameron couldn't help but smile.

When he was thirteen, an outbreak of meningitis swept through the county, killed two girls from Split Rock High School, Wanda Rosenberg and Sharon Jorgenson, and left him hospitalized for the better part of a year. He survived, but the left side of his body was partially paralyzed, robbing him of the next three of his teen years. Eventually, he regained control of his arm and leg, but his left cheek stayed perpetually flexed, causing him to smile even when he didn't mean it. Cameron held the mop with two hands to keep his left arm under control.

After filling her tray, Nicki had to walk past both Principal Carlson and her brother. Since the two deaths, Principal Carlson had become much more of a visible presence. Luckily, they were busy talking about Thanksgiving plans.

Cameron did his part by ignoring her, and once Nicki sat down with Gavin, she glanced back at her sweet brother. Nicki refused to let Gavin hang out at her house, mostly because of her father. But also because of her poverty. And her brother. *Does Gavin even know Cameron is my brother?*

He must know, right?

Nicki chatted away with the others like normal until a crash was followed closely by a round of laughter.

"Ten o'clock," Carlson said in reference to the junior high tables.

Cameron took hold of one of the rolling trash cans with his weaker left arm and held the mop in its bucket with his right hand. Two rows over and three tables down was a tray abandoned by a sixth-grade girl, who was running toward the bathroom as a table of seventh grade boys kept laughing.

"What a loser," Biff Forsberg said loudly.

Nicki fumed but did nothing.

Cameron went to work picking up the larger items on the floor, the milk carton and bread. A dustpan hung from the side of the garbage can, which he unclipped and used to scoop up the scalloped potatoes and ham. Next, he picked up his wet mop and slopped over the whole area until little remained of the mess except the wet spot on the floor and some spilled water on his pant legs.

"Don't slip on the water," Cameron said to Jimmy Nielson when he rose from the end of the table.

"Nice job, Cameron," Chris Luning said as he also got up to walk around the slippery spot on the cafeteria floor.

Nicki knew the junior high kids always ate faster so they could get outside to the playground, but the sophomore boys were another story.

The sophomore boys filled a table a row over, and their whispers were followed by chuckles, all aimed at Cameron who rolled the garbage can to one side of the slippery spot and then moved the mop bucket to the other. He carefully set the handle of the mop across the width of the puddle so that no one would accidentally walk through it while he went to retrieve the wet floor sign, but while he was bent over, a tater tot struck him in the ribs, bouncing back under the empty table.

Nicki felt ready to gouge out eyes but looked away instead. When she looked back, she saw Charlie Morrison grinning and another, John Thaxton, glaring at Cameron. *None of these sophomore creeps know he's my brother.*

Nicki prepared herself to do something incredibly stupid—defend Cameron. She took hold of a half-finished milk carton, widening it for a quick dump over Charlie's head. Any sass after that would be ended by Gavin, who would defend her without thought.

But Cameron hustled off toward the custodial closet near the washroom, and by the time he returned to the puddle, the sophomores had gone to empty their trays as Cameron fumbled with the plastic "wet floor" sign.

Finally, the lunch bell rang again, sending Nicki and the rest of the students off to the teachers.

WHEN THE SCHOOL day ended, Nicki tried to forget all about what happened to her brother, but he was all she could think about as she left.

I should have done something.

She looked out the window to where Cameron parked his old F1 Ford pickup truck behind the gym near the dumpsters. Although dented and rusting, it had been part of his severance package from Carousel Park management. The truck came with strings attached. Cameron was given the utility truck purchased by the park so he could do a security check of the park twice a day. Although everything had been boarded up, it still invited vandals, so each day before he headed to school, he stopped at the park and walked around the grounds. Then he went after his shift at the school as well.

He's my brother. Next time, I won't let those racist jerks pick on him.

Claiming she had to work on homework, she gave Gavin the cold shoulder on her ride home.

HOURS LATER, NICKI was working on homework when she heard honking.

I'm sorry, Cameron. Whenever Cameron finished his shift at school, he passed by the house, honking twice at the end of the driveway before continuing down Old Copper Road.

She turned her guilt into focus on her homework. She was so focused that she didn't give the sound of snowmobiles much thought. The new recreational sport was all the rage, and Gavin's family owned one. He'd even taken her on a short ride, wrapping his arms around her as he sat behind her.

Is he the one?

How far do I take our relationship?

It can't be serious if I won't even let him meet my family.

Thoughts of riding snowmobiles with Gavin ended her homework efforts, and she decided to go to bed so she could finish in the morning.

First, Nicki said a prayer for her brother.

She next prayed for healing for Grandma Lily.

For her father, she prayed for contentment.

For her mother, she asked for needed patience and strength.

Finally, she prayed for all the people on her paternal side, realizing her anger stemmed from the sight of her brother being harassed by adolescent white boys.

Nicki was almost asleep when she heard Cameron's old truck. Then she heard her mother's scream.

By the time Nicki threw on her robe and raced down the stairs, a pool of blood formed on the linoleum. Her father cradled Cameron in his arms while holding a blood-soaked dishtowel to Cameron's eye, where the eyebrow dangled vertically.

"Call the Sheriff!" her mother shouted at Nicki, returning with more towels.

CHAPTER THIRTY-EIGHT

Cut Off

Leech Lake, MN
December 4, 1961

LIGHT DECEMBER SNOW fell across Hiawatha County as Lily Guerin looked out the passenger window of the hospital van. Behind them, her son followed in his own car.

Just a moment earlier, it had been a youthful summer. Now, old man winter had arrived. Between the towns of Pine River and Backus, Highway 371 bent into Hiawatha County for a span of ten miles, bringing her the closest to the battle as she'd been in months. Lily, however, was in full retreat, and the big van soon crossed into Cass County on its way to Leech Lake.

…Where I can heal in relative safety.

Jean had taught her all about watersheds. Nimrod Hill, for example, was a watershed that fed two rivers on either side. A snowflake that fell on the eastern slope of Nimrod Hill would melt into the Crow Wing River, yet if the snowflake fell on the western slope, it would melt into the Blue Knife River, which would pass by Lily Guerin's childhood home along the Turtle Island Reservation.

Both rivers eventually led to the ocean.

If the snowflake dropped anywhere within an area of 1.2 million square miles in the adjacent 32 states, the fate of the snowflake would be the same—the Gulf of Mexico.

For Jean, rivers and watersheds were synonymous with the afterlife. His studies of the Jewish concept of Sheol, the Greek concept of Erebus, and the Anishinaabe concept of the River of Souls led him to believe that a human soul had a spiritual connection to the flow of water that led to the primordial Underworld. When Jean's body was crushed by a runaway car, his blood and soul spilled at the LeHillier gas station but still found its way to this spiritual river.

It was a journey she almost took a few months earlier.

Only a few places in the world did not flow into what the Greeks called Oceanus, the River of the Dead.

"It's an endorheic basin," Jean had again explained in 1910. "They form in a depression on the top of plateau, like with Devil's Lake in North Dakota; or as in the case of Salt Lake in Utah, between two mountains with no outlet."

"I still don't understand why you're driving all the way to Mankato," Lily had said to him.

"I just realized that Lura Lake, the lake you were named after—Tewapa Tankiyan—is in an endorheic basin. It's only a few hundred yards from the Maple River, but it's cut off. I believe your ancestors chose to camp along its shores because it was spiritually protected from the evil water spirits lurking around the Haunted Valley or even here at Lake Manitou. It's a spiritual blind spot. No water flows in or out of this place. Do you understand?"

Lily didn't understand then, but she did now.

I'll be unseen by the Wintermaker and his servants.

Lake Manitou, in contrast, had an inlet and outlet that connected it to a web of rivers and lakes that flowed all the way to the Gulf of Mexico. On the whole of North America, only a few places like Lura Lake existed.

Fawn had fled to an endorheic basin after Jean's death. First, she spent a few years at the Turtle Mountain Reservation in North Dakota before continuing all the way to the "spine of the turtle" deep in the Rockies, where her high mountain home was cut off from the great watersheds.

Now, Lily fled to a man-made endorheic basin.

Once the home of her paternal grandfather, Leech Lake was fifty miles north of Brainerd. Although the Mississippi River looped around it on its eastern, northern, and western borders, it was not directly part of the chain.

In fact, aside from several lakes and rivers that drained into it, Leech Lake was essentially cut off from the Mississippi thanks to a government made dam. In times of drought or winter, it acted like a concrete moat.

For Lily, living at Leech Lake would allow her to slip into one of the spiritual blind spots to recover.

At the intersection of Highway 371 and 200, the hospital van turned toward a place familiar to Lily and her Anishinaabe people. Since defeating the Dakota centuries earlier, Leech Lake was the hub for Ojibwe culture in Minnesota. While the rest of the lake now belonged to sportsmen and vacationers, the central peninsula held the community of Onigum, where government annuity payments were once distributed. It was also the center of the Leech Lake Indian Reservation and her temporary home.

The van stopped at Wanakiwidee Retirement Home, where the greeting sign read "Aaniin" instead of "hello."

"There is nothing wrong with my legs," Lily protested when the sliding door opened to reveal a nurse with a waiting wheelchair.

"Ma, it's just so you don't slip and fall on the ice," Louis said, approaching from his car.

Her son took her by the arm and helped the nurse guide her back into a sitting position. The cold air caused her lungs to restrict, and she began to cough. Without prompting, the nurse put the oxygen mask over her nose and face, restricting a good view of her recovery home.

The interior of the nursing home didn't look much different than a hospital except for the aviary at the corner of two hallways.

Binesi. Good birds.

Louis walked alongside them. "I've already moved your belongings and bought you a few things you didn't have. You've got a lot more space than the room in the burn unit."

"How is Cameron doing?"

Louis soured. "They still don't know who attacked him at Carousel. Sheriff Betzing tried taking photographs of the snowmobile tracks, but the wind destroyed the evidence. They were all wearing ski masks when they attacked, so I doubt there will be any arrests."

"I asked about Cameron."

"The brain swelling is gone, so he's talking again. They busted his eye socket and broke several ribs, so he's going to be on bed rest until at least Christmas. We brought him home on Tuesday, though."

I wasn't there to protect him.

Lily knew how evil worked. While the Tak-Pei had the power to manipulate the elements and bring all manner of death, their magic could also darken the thoughts of humans in the same way the New Testament demons did. Cameron had been attacked by a gang of snowmobile riding thugs, undoubtedly spurred on by the evil surrounding Lake Manitou.

"Well, home sweet home, Ma. What do you think?"

Lily had been so lost in thought that she hadn't even noticed where her room was located.

Her window overlooked Leech Lake; a football field sized yard was between her new home and the wooded lakeshore. Her bed had a big oxygen tank and a tangle of tubes coming off of it. A crucifix and a framed picture of the late Pope Pius XII hung on her wall. A small loveseat, table, and chair filled out the rest of the room.

"Where is the willow that Eddie Nielson brought for me?"

"I think that was thrown away when they cleaned out your hospital room."

"I need that. I need him—" Lily began coughing, and she focused on taking deep breaths to avoid getting lightheaded. The ride had stolen away all the energy she had for the day, and after taking a few moments to collect herself, she allowed Louis and the nurse to help her to bed.

Louis stayed for a few more minutes and gave her a notepad to write down requests for her new room.

Willow branches

Sinew

Feathers

Cowry shells

Leather

Beads

Lily tore off the page and handed it to Louis before he left.

LIKE LEECH LAKE was cut off from the Mississippi, she felt spiritually cut off from God. Although her sorcery and magic once worked near the shores of Lake Manitou, her physical and spiritual blindness continued after her migration from Brainerd to Leech Lake.

A punishment for my arrogance.

Just as Job was cursed with tragedy and physical ailments, Lily also felt herself in the crosshairs of the Evil One.

Luckily, she began to regain her strength. And although spiritually cut off from the world, she was able to read the many newspapers brought in from around the state and country.

She just finished reading about the Wadena fisherman who died on Lake Manitou. Young Wesley Thorgaard fell through the ice, leaving behind a widow at home and a red Jeep parked near Carousel Island. *A sacrifice.*

Feeling defeated, Lily closed her eyes and did not open them again until the next morning. But during the night, God granted her a dream.

Her first dream involved Charani Bessant and his henchman, driving down highways like wolves hunting through the timber. For months prior to the fire, she'd seen Bessant's face in her dreams, unable to comprehend why. Now, his somber face transformed into a frosty blue mask—Biboonike, the Wintermaker.

Now that the season had turned to winter, the Wintermaker's constellation, known to the western world as Orion, appeared upon the horizon. His outstretched arms shattered the glass of heaven, and he stepped from the dark cosmos onto the wooded edge of the horizon. A shadow, he crept from tree to tree, and like the thugs who'd attacked her grandson, his face was masked.

Biboonike pulled a sled behind him, and on the sled, Lily saw the souls of the departed: Wesley Thorgard, Rory Stewart, Isaac Larson, Gladys Kruger, Leona and Mary Brady, and Walter Zibas. He stopped the sled in front of Deadwood Island, now known as Carousel Island. Five black spirits——the sleeping Tak-Pei—still waited for death to bring them life. The masked Biboonike chopped a large hole in the ice, shaking the souls of the dead into the water.

Then with an empty sled, he continued his trek toward the shores of Bleeding Rock.

When Lily woke, she wept.

Three Tines are a Trike

Split Rock High School
December 15, 1961

THE SNOW CONTINUED to come down hard, but it was too late on a Friday afternoon to bother closing school early. Chris Luning, like most of the other students, watched the world turn white as he walked through the tube to his locker.

Winter arrived too quickly.

"Hey, what are you doing this weekend?"

Chris looked up to see Jimmy Nielson standing beside his locker.

"I don't know. Why?"

"There's a problem," Jimmy said, glancing at the busy hallway full of students preparing to leave.

Does he believe me now? The nervousness of Jimmy's glance drew Chris's attention to the cut along his eyebrow. "What's wrong?"

"Coach Webster scheduled a scrimmage on Saturday."

Really? This is about wrestling? Neither of his blood brothers believed his theory that something foul had caused Grandpa Albert's accident. Both chalked it up to Grandpa Albert being old. "So?"

"A varsity scrimmage."

My grandpa is in the hospital and your biggest worry is practice? Jimmy remained sincere, so Chris prompted, "And?"

"Biff's still wrestling JV, and they're not expected to be there, and even if they were, he's gotta stay home and do the milking chores this weekend because his dad's going to Leech Lake for some fishing tournament or something." Then Jimmy's face grew somber. "We can't let Biff be alone."

Chris suddenly understood the unspoken message: The Manitou was coming for Biff. "What do you want me to do?"

"Invite him over to your house."

"But … he's got chores."

"Exactly. Invite him over to your house for the weekend, and when he tells you no, ask if you can go to his house. It's just him, and his ma, and his little sister. He's vulnerable, okay? If something's going to happen, it will happen this weekend: It's the Winter Solstice."

"Did something happen with you guys? Why aren't you two talking?"

"It doesn't matter."

"Yes, it does. If he's sore about not making varsity, that's one thing, but if there is something else, then I need to know. We're blood brothers."

Jimmy's fingers went to the cut above his eye. "He told Emile Berg his stupid theory about the custodian being the serial killer, and Emile told his older brother, and those assholes were the ones that put Can Man in the hospital."

"I heard Can Man was arrested."

Jimmy's mouth tightened. "They had to bring him to the hospital. The cops wanted names so they could press charges, ya dimwit. They didn't arrest him."

If they're fighting, then I'll be the one to help both of them.

"Figure something out, okay?" Jimmy said and drifted away with the current of the crowd.

Chris finished stuffing his bag with homework and began walking toward Biff's locker. It was easy to spot Biff with his orangish-red hair and distinctive plaid shirt. Before Chris reached the locker, an older girl ran right by him in her loud white gogo boots and skirt. Curious, he watched her run toward the tubes until someone crashed into him from behind, sending him spinning into the freshmen lockers and a nearby girl.

"Sorry," Chris told the ninth-grade girl he crashed into, and when he looked up, he saw Gavin MacPherson glance back at him. "Sorry," Chris repeated before heading toward Biff.

"So … there's going to be some good football games this weekend. Who you got between the Vikings and the Bears?"

"Bears."

Biff is going to see right through this. "Yeah, you're probably right. You know, you should come over and watch some games on TV with me."

"I can't. I've got chores."

"Oh," Chris said, almost wincing. "Hey, I've got an idea. Why don't I come over after school, spend the night, help you with chores tomorrow morning, and then we can watch some games together? I'll even help you with the afternoon milking as well."

"You wouldn't know what the heck you're doing around dairy cows."

"Yeah, but I'd be better than your little sister."

Biff turned, revealing a bruise on his right cheek. "How did you know my dad was going to be gone?"

"Um … Jimmy told me."

Biff began to angrily toss books around, with old worksheets and papers flying everywhere. "You going to walk out to my house? Alone?"

"I could get my dad to bring me."

"Whatever."

"So, is that an invitation?" Chris asked, but Biff was already walking toward the wrestling locker room.

AFTER SCHOOL, CHRIS knocked on the front door of the Forsberg house while his father turned around in the driveway.

Chris and Biff, who lived less than a quarter of a mile from each other, lived in different worlds, separated by the Crow Wing River. The Forsberg farm was one of the oldest in the county, built by Gustaf Forsberg, of Swedish descent. Although the house had been modernized over the past hundred years, the barn remained largely unchanged. Unlike the large red barns with high, domed ceilings, the Forsberg barn was built with rock walls on the southern and northern ends and a high foundation along the long walls. Much of the central barn was now skirted with lean-to additions that gave it more space for the animals.

With the farmstead built atop the rocky ridge separating the Crow Wing River from Lake Manitou, the feedlot had an irregular shape and was immaculately clean. Two smaller outbuildings, one for hay and one for straw, were tucked away in the trees higher on the ridge.

Julia, Biff's younger sister, answered the door.

"Mom, Chris Luning is here."

Mrs. Forsberg stepped into view, wearing a flour-coated apron over everyday clothes. "Hello, Christopher," she said, her mouth agape. "It doesn't look like you're selling anything. You planning on staying a while?"

"Um, yeah. Didn't Biff say anything about our plan? Me helping with chores?"

"No, he didn't. He's still at wrestling practice," Mrs. Forsberg said. "But you can sure help with chores. Go, sit. I'll bring you something to eat."

Julia glanced at him from her spot in front of the RCA radio as Mrs. Forsberg continued to the kitchen. After Chris took a seat at the table, he looked at the family pictures on the wall. The largest picture was taken when Biff was a toddler and Julia was an infant; it also included Paul, who looked older despite being the same age as Biff was now. On the piano, Chris saw a dozen pictures featuring Paul in military uniforms. Some of the oldest pictures on the wall were of men with wild facial hair standing beside horses with tangled manes and hairy legs. *The Forsbergs have been at Lake Manitou for quite a while.*

"So how is your grandfather doing?" Mrs. Forsberg asked, setting a plate of snacks in front of him.

I think he's dying. When Chris visited him in the hospital, Grandpa Albert had been wearing an oxygen mask, limiting their interaction to only a squeezing of hands. He repeated what his parents told him: "Better. The bump on his head is healing, but he's got pneumonia now. The doctors are keeping a close eye on him."

"I heard he drove right into the lake," Mrs. Forsberg stated. "Lucky for him, an ice fisherman rescued him before the car dropped through the ice."

BIFF ARRIVED SHORTLY after five o'clock and Mrs. Forsberg had a few private words with him before Biff jogged up the stairs toward his room ignoring Chris.

"Julia, come help me in the kitchen. We need to prepare supper."

"But I'm playing," Julia said from her toys set up in front of the old RCA radio.

"Julia!" Mrs. Forsberg barked, and Julia kicked away her toys before answering the command. She stuck her tongue out at Chris.

Chris headed upstairs. Although he'd been friends with Biff since Kindergarten, he'd never slept over.

Besides a crucifix and a picture of an old man praying over a loaf of bread, Biff had no other decorations on his wall. His bookshelves were filled with knives, belt buckles, animal skins, fishing gear, a few tools, and four books: The King James Bible, The Boys Scouts of America Handbook, J.R.R. Tolkien's *Lord of the Rings*, and Snorri Sturlson's *Prose Edda*.

Where are his toys? Chris wondered.

"We've gotta go do evening chores before we can eat."

Guess we're not playing—we're working.

Just the sight of Biff sent the two dozen dairy cows into a frenzy.

Biff clearly knew what he was doing in the barn. "Okay, I need you to fill this wheelbarrow with feed, and starting on the north side of the barn, fill each trough and then lock the cows into their stalls. I'll take care of the milking. When each one is done, you can release them. Try to keep up."

Once Biff slid open the barn doors, the cows immediately divided themselves into the two-dozen stalls within the barn. The first cow stepped into the stall, looking up at Chris in anticipation of her food, which Chris dumped into the trough with a large scoop. At the rear of the stall, Biff pulled the strange metallic octopus contraption to the swelled udders of the cow and went to work with deft hands.

It's like the cows know what to do, Chris decided.

Silent and steady, Biff milked each cow while Chris kept each one happy and distracted with its food.

It took Biff five minutes to milk each cow, and in an hour, the barn had been emptied.

"That wasn't so bad," Chris said.

Biff handed him a pitchfork. "Go open the north doors. You'll see the shit pile at the back of the lot. Clean up the big stuff with the fork and then shovel the rest into the cement troughs."

"The whole barn?"

"I do it twice a day. You'll be fine."

Jimmy owes me for this!

Biff stood by the silver milk machines and watched Chris work the first few stalls. "Hey Chris, if a regular pitchfork has four tines and is called a four-k. Wouldn't a pitchfork with three tines be called a *trike?*"

"It's a trident, Biff."

"Ah, like Poseidon. You're the God of Shit, Luning. Part the seas."

He thinks he's so tough for doing this each day. I'll show him…

It took Chris another hour to clean the barn while Biff processed the milk through the holding tanks. When he finished hauling away the day's fodder, Biff had all the milk processed and the machinery cleaned.

Chris's shoulders ached, but it was a good ache.

Mrs. Forsberg had a meal of fried-chicken ready when they walked through the doors. After supper, Biff let Chris sit in his father's chair and the Forsberg family watched *Bonanza* together.

At eight o'clock, Edna proclaimed, "Well boys, you'd better get to bed. The morning milking will be upon you before you know it."

Instead of playing cards or talking, Biff did just what his mother said and was snoring less than ten minutes after his head hit the pillow.

What a hard, boring life he lives, Chris thought even as he appreciated the soft pillowcase against his cheek.

BIFF NUDGED CHRIS with his foot the next morning, and when Chris tried to sit up, he could barely move his arms.

"A little stiff?" Biff asked as he slipped on a plaid shirt over his white undershirt.

Like a zombie, Chris followed his friend through his routine.

Mrs. Forsberg greeted them with a cup of coffee at the kitchen table. "I'll have bacon, eggs, and cinnamon rolls ready when you finish."

As the two boys were about to step outside, Biff snapped his fingers. "I need to find a small crescent wrench. One of the tubes is leaking on the milker. Go get things ready and I'll be right there."

"Where are you going?"

"I gotta run to the garage for a minute."

The exterior light on the house lit the way to the barn, and the cows seemed to know they were coming, for he could hear them calling out. He opened the gate to the feedlot and, starting with the eastern doors, let the cows out into the holding lot. Going back through the main lot, Chris walked around to the north side of the barn, where he entered through the sliding door. His hand reached around the corner for the light switch, and when his fingers found it, something reached out and grabbed him.

An arm came out of the darkness and wrapped around his face. He felt a damp cloth cross his face, and when he took a deep breath to scream, he coughed and immediately saw spots.

His legs turned to jelly, and arms tightened around his chest.

Suddenly, concerns of Tak-Pei were nonsense, and the man who'd killed the other boys now had him … Chris slowly lost consciousness with each panicked breath.

Light blinded him, and for a moment, Chris thought he was at St. Peter's Pearly Gates.

"Let him go!"

It was Biff.

Through his blurred vision, Chris saw his friend through the dark fingers over his eyes.

A knife flashed in front of his face, but a moment later, his attacker let out a loud grunt, and Chris felt himself fall to the concrete of the dairy barn floor.

"Get out of here or I'll split your head open!" Biff shouted.

A moment later, Chris heard shouts: "Ma, get the gun! Ma! Get the gun! The gun! Get the shotgun!"

The world spun, and the yellow man standing in front of Chris slowly came into focus—it was a piece of straw between his face and the floor.

Chris turned his head slowly, and, inches from his face, he saw blood.

His hand moved up to his face, where he felt his throbbing nose. Then his fingers moved to his throat to see if the knife had slit it open wide.

It wasn't his blood.

Mrs. Forsberg's bare legs appeared between her nightgown and oversized boots. Chris looked up to see a shotgun in her hands.

Biff appeared from the open door, snatching the shotgun from her, cracking it open to check for shells, and then handing his mother an eighteen-inch machete.

"What is going on?" she asked, holding the big knife.

"Some guy tried to grab Chris. When I stepped into the barn, he had a rag held to his face. He pulled out a knife, but I jabbed him with the pitchfork before he could hurt Chris. He ran out into the woods."

"Is Chris hurt?"

Suddenly both Forsbergs were looking down at him. Chris tried to speak but his head was dizzy, and his arm throbbed with pain.

"I think he's fine. I might've got him when I threw the pitchfork."

"Oh, good Lord. What should I do?"

"Go back inside. Make sure Julia is safe and call the police, okay Ma?"

Mrs. Forsberg nodded and then vanished out of the barn.

With the shotgun in his hand, Biff knelt down to Chris and rolled him. "Sorry about your arm, buddy. You'll be fine, though. Here, sit up."

Chris felt Biff tugging at his armpits and looked down. He saw blood coming out of his sleeve and a small hole near his left elbow.

Then his blood brother set the pitchfork in his lap.

"Use this if he comes back. I'm going after him."

Despite the world spinning, Chris felt his fingers wrap around the wooden handle of the pitchfork. *What the heck just happened?*

Cold Hearted

Old Copper Road
December 16, 1961

NICKI GUERIN'S HEART leapt in her chest when the phone rang. *Could it be Gavin?* It kept ringing, and she heard her mother answer. Instead of her mother shouting her name, the phone call was for her father. Nicki checked the time.

Why's it so dark for eight o'clock in the morning?

She rose from her bed and walked to the window.

The barn had been swallowed by a thick bank of winter fog.

Hoar frost decorated all of Hiawatha County like tinsel for Christmas. With all of her plans suddenly canceled until further notice, Nicki slipped into a matching flannel outfit, put on a pair of her thickest socks, and wrapped herself in her favorite blanket.

She shuffled out the door and to the bathroom, only to find the door closed. She could hear Cameron peeing. When he was done, she gently knocked on the door and stepped back.

His eyes were still wide when he opened the door, a sign of sustained fear. The black and blue bruising had turned to even more disgusting yellows and the scar tissue around his eye added red to his face. He hadn't shaved in a few days either, adding to his frightening appearance. "What's the ruckus?"

"The phone call?"

"No, all the noise coming from the lake."

Nicki hadn't noticed a thing. "I don't know." The toilet was pink with blood, a sign Cameron's internal injuries were still healing. "Would you mind flushing?"

"Sorry," he said and shuffled back. Even before, he'd been twitchy and hesitant, but now, after the attack, he was even more so. He averted his gaze as if Nicki was a stranger.

If anyone should be apologizing, it's me. "I'm sorry for being such a bad sister. I should've stopped those boys from picking on you. I didn't know that … I … it … Gavin wouldn't do it. He … he … wasn't one of—"

"I know," he interrupted, avoiding eye contact. Then he looked up to ask, "You're not really going to change schools, are you?"

"No, I didn't mean what I said. I can't let them win, right?"

Cameron nodded. "I had a dream last night that you and I were at Carousel Park and—"

Now Nicki heard the ruckus. Of all things, it was the sound of a snowmobile getting nearer.

She turned and hustled down the stairs, only to see her father walking through the dining room with a shotgun.

"What's going on?" Nicki asked her mother, who was in the kitchen near the phone.

"Another attack. This time, it was the Forsberg boy."

"What do you mean an attack?"

Her question went unanswered. Her father loaded two shells and vanished into the entryway.

The snowmobile grew louder.

"Ida MacPherson called and said the Forsberg boy got attacked doing chores this morning and the attacker fled on foot to the north. The MacPherson boys are in pursuit, and law enforcement is on the way."

The MacPherson boys—Nicki adored all of them. Even though Gavin was an only child, a dozen MacPhersons would fill the house for supper time, or in this case, for Saturday breakfast.

Following the death of the patriarch Willem MacPherson, all four sons banded together to turn their family business into one of the more successful operations in Hiawatha County. Duncan, David, Dale, and Donnie were all born to the matriarch Grandma Olive, who lived in the big house two bedrooms down the hall from where Gavin slept. Except for the hair (from Duncan's cue ball bald head to Donnie's shaggy blonde locks), the four brothers were clones in attire, language, and physical appearance. Over the past few months, Nicki had been a part of joyous and heated debates at the big table, which could seat twenty when David brought his wife and children.

The front door opened, and the snowmobile whine reached the kitchen.

Two flashes of light stunned Nicki as she approached the ajar door. First, the single beam came from the lake, right through her grandmother's path in the wild rice and up onto their yard. The second blast of light came from her father's shotgun, which flashed a warning blast into the air.

The rider had a rifle strapped to his back yet heeded the warning. He put up both hands while the sled idled. Then cautiously, he reached for his helmet, ripping it off to reveal the face of her ex-boyfriend, Gavin.

"Back that thing up and get off my property," her father shouted.

A moment later, Nicki stepped into the doorway drawing Gavin's attention.

"The Forsberg boy was attacked; I was just coming to make sure you knew."

"My son was attacked too," her father said. "Didn't see you rushing over to warn *him*. Now clear off. We got the message."

Why am I doing this to him? He still loves me … and I love him.

But Nicki stepped back inside the house, leaving Gavin with her father.

A moment later, the shiny new Ski-Doo returned back north.

Her father seethed for a few moments before declaring, "I'm going to walk around the property and make sure no weirdos are hiding. Lock the door until I return."

Nicki obeyed and returned to the kitchen table to glean information from her mother, still at the phone. Her mother cupped the phone receiver to ask her, "What's going on outside?"

"It was Gavin. Dad's trying to act tough. Gavin just wanted to make sure we knew what had happened."

Her mother continued to cradle the phone. "What happened between the two of you?"

"I made a scene after basketball practice. I got angry about what happened to Cameron and kinda accused him of holding back. In front of the whole team, I basically told him to … um … go to heck, but I didn't say it like that."

"Nicole."

"I know."

"So that's why he's been calling the last few days?" her mother asked, and Nicki nodded. "Did he have anything to do with Cameron?"

Nicki shook her head. "No. I just wanted to make it clear to everyone that—"

Suddenly, her mother's face changed as she listened in to the party line call, which connected the housewives of Old Copper Road far better than the CB system belonging to the men.

"They found something by Bleeding Rock."

That's where Gavin was heading.

Be careful, Gavin.

CHAPTER FORTY-ONE

Son of a Parson

Lake Manitou
December 16, 1961

UP ON THE bluff, Wally Crain could see the flicker of colored lights—undoubtedly from police vehicles that had finally arrived at the Forsberg house. The fog was beginning to lift, and the scale of the crime scene grew by the minute.

A snowmobile came racing from the south. Wally, Donnie MacPherson, and Steve Knutson pointed their flashlights directly at him and waved their arms.

Gavin MacPherson stopped and asked, "What's going on?"

Donnie MacPherson shouted, "It's part of the crime scene, we think. We're watching over it until the police can get here."

Gavin climbed off his Ski-Doo and walked over the ice to where the three men stood in front of a rectangular hole about three feet wide.

"What's this all about?".

Wally noted how clear-headed the MacPhersons had been during the crisis, unafraid to jump into action. The youngest, Duncan's boy, continued to impress him. Their sleuthing had given the Isanti Lodge a clue—the Bic lighter and gas can—as well as one of its most important discoveries—Father Jean's journal. Yet Gavin didn't become an idiot. Instead of going to authorities, he took the journal to Migisi.

An ally in our fight then.

"Some of us thought the guy might have fled to an ice house, so we headed out to make sure he wasn't hiding inside one of them," Wally explained. "That tarp covered the hole. From the looks of it, he recently had a shelter over the top of this place."

"Thought it was for spearing pike at first," Knutson explained. "But nobody would leave a hole that big in the ice, especially with just a tarp over it."

"We figured he meant to dump the body in the lake after he killed the kid," Donnie added.

"So he could still be somewhere around the lake—on foot? Do you want me to keep looking for the guy?"

Donnie shot down his nephew. "Cool your jets. Why don't you drive back up to the boat landing and remind them to send some-one down here? There might be evidence or something."

"Don't drive on the line between us and the boat launch ei-ther," Wally added. "There might be some evidence on the ice."

Gavin nodded and jogged back to the Ski-Doo. He heeded their advice and drove wide of a direct line.

"Your nephew's got a good head on his shoulders," Wally commented.

"Ida tends to spoil him too much, but Duncan keeps him in line."

"If you boys have this, I'm going to head back to the Forsberg house and see if anyone knows what's going on. Take care, Don."

Now able to see his path back to where the killer had recently walked, Wally put his flashlight inside of his coat pocket. His theo-ry about the Plymouth crumbled with each new fact.

At the center of the bluff, Bleeding Rock was thirty feet of sheer cliff, but on the edge of the Forsberg property, the incline lessened, which is where sled tracks had ascended to the Forsberg barn.

The sound of an engine roared up behind him before a voice said, "Hey Wally, hop on the back and I'll help get you up the hill."

"Any word at the boat landing?"

Gavin nodded. "I talked to my Uncle Dale. Some guy tried to grab the Forsberg kid while he was milking cows. The balls on this guy, huh?"

The storytelling was interrupted for a moment as Wally and Gavin roared a few hundred yards south to the crease in the bluffs that allowed the sled to access Old Copper Road.

Once the snowmobile slowed, Gavin continued speaking. "Well, the Forsberg kid fought him off with a pitchfork, and when the guy took off to run, the Forsberg kid chased after him with a shotgun. Followed his blood and footsteps all the way back to the landing, but by that time, the guy was gone. They're trying to figure out what kind of vehicle he drove from the tire tracks. They are also trying to get some info on the guy from his footprints."

The snowmobile stopped a few yards from the house.

Gavin stood. "I'm going to run inside to let my Uncle Dave know what's going on. He's protecting the women."

As with most Scottish names, Mac meant "son of" as a prefix for whatever surname followed. In the case of the MacPherson clan, Pherson was an old Scottish spelling of Parson, which meant the Catholic family had once been a protestant family, for a Parson was the equivalent of a rural Anglican priest.

We should have made them allies long ago.

The MacPherson boy jogged up to the house, quickly relayed the information, and then jogged back to Wally.

As they neared the Forsberg house, Wally saw an ambulance pulling away toward town. Other emergency vehicles blocked the driveway. Gavin slowed and with a wave to the deputy drove around then used the snow-filled ditch. Wally spotted Duncan MacPherson's truck right beside his big Ulman Oil truck and a sheriff's car.

"What the hell is this?" Sheriff Betzing asked from the open door of his vehicle, and when he recognized Gavin and Wally, he waved them through.

Gavin dismounted the Ski-Doo and turned it off. He looked around the yard before he headed to his father. "Uncle Dale wanted me to see how things were up here."

"I thought I told you to stay with your mom," Duncan chided.

"Uncle David stayed with her. I just got back from the boat launch area, and they said the guy took off already."

Servants of the Wintermaker, just like Father Guerin described. "I'd put down money that the tracks match a blue 1950 Plymouth," Wally said mostly to himself. "But what do I know?"

"More than him," Duncan MacPherson said with a look of disdain toward Sheriff Betzing.

"Who was in the ambulance?" Gavin asked.

"The Luning boy. Chris," Duncan answered. "The attacker used chloroform in a rag to knock him out."

"I thought Brian Forsberg was the one—"

"Yeah, well, it turns out that Chris Luning was staying with the Forsbergs last night."

"Lucky he did, or else Brian would be in the lake right now," Wally assessed. *They're fending for themselves when I should be the one protecting them.*

A sharp whistle came from the barn, where yellow tape circled most of it. A few yards away, on a rock outcrop that separated the yard from the woods higher up on the ridge, Edward Nielson smoked a cigarette.

Both men obediently answered the call, and Gavin followed a few paces behind.

"I think you are wrong about your lone wolf theory," Nielson said. "Whoever did this knew Glen Forsberg was going to be gone. He thought Biff would be alone for morning chores and carefully set up things to snatch him as soon as he stepped outside."

"He used chloroform," Wally informed Nielson. "Does that sound like anybody around here?"

"It might surprise you," Nielson added. "Now, with both the Larson boy and the Stewart boy, they were coming home from school, which made them easy pickings. Your lone wolf certainly could have staked out a school and just waited for the right opportunity, but that's not what happened here."

Nielson pointed to the northern corner of the barn. The yellow tape that encircled it veered straight west to a tree on the edge of the ridge so as to create an invisible barrier along the southern side of the crime scene, which included the whole of the Bleeding Rock bluff. A series of little flags identified items to be photographed by the BCA—a red plastic sled and the pitchfork, both in sight outside the rear barn door.

"This guy ... this son of a bitch ... he knew better than to kill the kid here because it might get messy, so what does he do? He uses chloroform to knock him out so he can put him on the sled, haul him a half mile across the bluff, and then dump him just offshore of the boat landing, where his car waited so he could make an escape. Nope. I'm not buying your lone wolf theory at all, Wally. This guy feels comfortable here at Lake Manitou, and he knew Glen was going to be fishing up at Leech Lake."

"Glen goes every year," Duncan said. "Half of Hiawatha County knows it. But I gotta agree with Ed on this one, Wally. This botched abduction has to be someone from the area."

Everyone looked to Wally for leadership, but his Plymouth theory had been a dead end. He felt impotent in the face of his adversary.

Wally wanted to bring up the contents of the notebook Lily had given Gavin after the fire. He wanted to talk about the Men of the Dawn and Jean Guerin's concerns about everyone affiliated with Triton Corporation. He wanted to bring up the theories about the Tak-Pei and the Manitou. He wanted to ask Migisi for guidance.

Instead, he kept his hands in his pockets and kicked at the snow.

"Who'd want to kill the Luning boy?" Duncan asked to break the silence. "Some weirdo or pervert?"

Nielson shook his head. "He targeted Brian. He most likely didn't know Chris was going to be there. Grabbed the wrong boy by accident and paid the price."

"They said at the boat landing the guy was wounded," Gavin noted.

Nielson pointed with his cigarette between his fingers toward the woods. "Bled like a stuck pig. Brian got him with a pitchfork after he turned a knife on Chris–chucked the fork right at him and then picked up a machete. I'd run, too. The kid might be thirteen, but he's strong as an ox."

The three men all looked behind Gavin, who turned too to see Sheriff Betzing approach. Betzing looked like he should be wearing an apron in a bakery rather than holstering a pistol. His fur lined winter parka wasn't puffy enough to hide his massive gut. Nor could his jiggling cheeks and chin avoid turning bright red in the cold. "The BCA will be here any minute and they want everyone cleared out."

"Any news over the radio?" Wally asked.

"Based on the injury to the Luning kid, I don't think this guy is going to need hospital attention, unless he gets an infection."

"We can only hope," Nielson said. "Hope the bastard rots away and dies in some hole."

"Are you serious, Nielson?" Betzing raised his voice, but not because of the comment. "Are you sitting there smoking near the crime scene? Did you drop any cigarette butts?"

Nielson sighed.

"The Luning kid told me that when the guy grabbed him, he had smoke on his breath."

"You pointing the finger at me?" Nielson asked, tilting his head with a locked jaw.

"No, of course not. But when I asked you to keep an eye on the woods, I didn't expect you to light up and start smoking."

"You didn't tell me about the guy smoking cigarettes."

"You're not a deputy. None of you are." Betzing groaned. "Again, I thank you all for helping, but we have to let the professionals do their jobs now. I need you all to go home."

Nielson twisted the cigarette in the palm of his leather glove and poured the ash and tobacco into his front jacket pocket with a condescending nod before hopping off of the outcrop.

Wally and the others walked past the barn and parted ways to return to their daily routines.

Smoke on his breath? It's gotta be the Bic lighter guy.

But who is he?

Fimbulvetr

Leech Lake, Minnesota
December 31, 1961

WHILE THE REST of the world celebrated New Year's Eve, Lily Guerin watched a battle taking place in the pines. The blizzard attacked relentlessly. For most of the morning, she sat at a dining room table with one blanket wrapped around her legs and another around her shoulders, and stared through the big window in the dining hall.

Physically, she had few worries for herself, safe inside of the Wanakiwidee Retirement Home. Since arriving, her strength improved each day, and the isolation of Leech Lake was a tonic for her body and soul. At Christmas, Louis brought his wife and all five grandchildren. Like her beloved Fawn, three of the granddaughters moved far away from Hiawatha County, yet the holidays brought them back with their husbands and children for a three-hour visit.

If the Wintermaker had enough prescience to see beyond the shores of Lake Manitou, a gathering of the Guerin clan certainly could have provoked the unnatural storm.

There will be no visitors for a few days now.

Weather was the deadliest weapon of the Tak-Pei, which her maternal ancestors called *Canotila* and her paternal ancestors called *Memegwesi*—the little men of the forest. Jean simply called them demons.

"If Satan is indeed the 'Prince of the Power of the Air,'" Jean once quipped, "and demons tried to drown Christ and the disciples while crossing Lake Galilee, then attacks on us might be disguised as natural phenomenon, which explains the storm over Lake Manitou when Joseph Little Toad tried to perform the 'Song of the Manitou.'"

Now another storm was raging above Lake Manitou, dropping two-to-three feet of snow along a swath between Highway 10 and Highway 2—with Hiawatha County at its center. Leech Lake had already received a foot, and it was only catching the edge of the system.

How many Tak-Pei are now awake?

At Leech Lake, she was safe, but her knights were off fighting the dragon.

And losing.

Even though she was surrounded by her people—*the people*—she remained an outsider. Her family had lived in the shadows of Anishinaabe society, and then American society, for centuries, and even though ethnicity connected and nurtured her, her fight would be solitary.

She rose from her wheelchair, walking behind it to hold onto the handles as she headed back to her room. Her weak lungs still caused her to get lightheaded, so gripping the handles gave her enough security for the nurses to leave her alone.

Halfway back to her room, however, she stopped.

It wasn't because of dizziness. No, she felt as strong as ever. In fact, the magic in the snowstorm rekindled the God-given strength inside of her. On her shoulder sat Migisi and Jean, still debating the names of the Creator: Yahweh, El Shaddai, Manabozho, Inyan, the Almighty … Migisi represented the Eagle, the powerful thunderbird seeking the Horned Serpent; the black-robed Father Guerin represented the raven, sent to scout by Noah, sent to nourish the prophet Elijah.

Lily stopped in front of the aviary.

None of the little birds represented the symbolic power she needed, but she closed her eyes to pray in their presence.

She prayed for the recently dead—eight souls now trapped in the cold depths of Lake Manitou.

She prayed for her Isanti Lodge.

And she prayed for the Omodai.

God, forgive me, what have I done?

She pictured Jean dead on bloodstained sands, and in her hands, the cursed stone, pulsing with an eternal life unto itself.

No.

No! Quit mourning him.

Jean passed decades ago and bemoaning my choices will not bring him back this time. If the Wintermaker wants a fight, then I'll give it to him. I'll tear the web apart and destroy everything before I let him—

Sitting in her wheelchair, listening to the chatter of the little birds, Lily drifted from prayer to dream.

What should I do?

WHEN SHE FELT a hand on her shoulder, Lily jerked back to consciousness, startling the little birds. Instead of the Wintermaker's cold blue hands upon her throat, she turned to see a familiar face. "I saw him. He's hunting."

Eddie Nielson knelt down beside her wheelchair. "Saw who, Nokomis?"

The blonde Scandinavian man did not have a drop of Native blood in him, but as a boy, he'd wander from his farm home overlooking Turtle Island and spend hours learning about both Oceti

Sakowin and Anishinaabe culture. When Eddie learned the name for grandmother, he never called her anything but Nokomis.

"I saw the Wintermaker."

"On a day like today, I certainly understand why. It's a frozen hell out there."

Lily tucked her dream away for a moment. "Why are you here? Has something happened?"

Eddie's dimpled smile eased her worry. "All is well. Since tomorrow is a holiday, Wally was making emergency deliveries near Pine River, so I drove my pickup to blast through the drifts. He's topping off some tanks at Onigum right now, which gave me time to deliver you some items you requested."

Lily looked down to see a sack with willow branches sticking out. "Bless you, Eddie. You were always my favorite student."

He took hold of one of Lily's hands and kissed the top of it gently. "Now what about your dream of the Wintermaker?"

Lily looked around to ensure privacy. In her dream, the Wintermaker again walked the earth in human form—small, muted, diminished. His cold soul stood out in a city at the junction of rivers—the Missouri and Mississippi. He hunted like a lone wolf, seeking his prey in a bar full of men. She even heard a name spoken aloud. The taste of beer and the smell of smoke filled her mind as she watched him fixate on the next victim. But instead of murder, a strange ritual began.

"I'm so confused. The Wintermaker is slumbering in the depths of Lake Manitou, unable to wake until the Song of the Manitou is sung fully."

"Exactly. What did your husband nickname him? The Alpha?"

"It doesn't matter what he is called. Manitou, Horned Serpent—his name is irrelevant. Do you remember Jean's theory about the Seven Fires?"

Eddie nodded. "How could I forget? Halley's Comet has ushered in each era of the prophecy. In 1456, your people were at

Montreal, a turtle-shaped island. In 1607, the Second Fire came true. In 1682, the Chippewa pushed into Wisconsin and Minnesota. By 1758, the Chippewa took control of Lake Manitou and all of northern Minnesota. In 1835, Jean Nicolas Nicollet came with your grandfather Nanakonan to Lake Manitou. And 1910 ushered in the beginning of the Seventh Fire. The Seventh Fire is end to begin in—"

"1986, which is why I am so confused. Joseph Little Toad failed in 1898 because it was not time. For the Wintermaker to win, he needs his own prophecy to align."

"Could the agents of the Wintermaker have found the Sacred Shell?"

Is the blue man just an agent of the Wintermaker? "It's possible, but from what we learned from Leonard White Elk, the Sacred Fire cannot be lit, and the Water Drum remains hidden. Little Toad and his heretical Wijigan only knew fragments of the Song of the Manitou."

"Your husband warned us about the Order of Eos and their secrets. Perhaps there is schism in their ranks just like there was between Nanakonan and Little Toad."

The mysterious Order of Eos remained steadfast. It had been the Isanti Lodge that crumbled back in 1910. With the return of Halley's Comet, known as the Serpent Star by her ancestors, the magic surrounding Lake Manitou was heightened. A healthy debate on fate and free will turned into bitter strife between herself and her beloved cousin Fawn. Lily's secrets all but came spilling onto the floor for all to see, with Fawn correctly guessing the heart of it. *Am I once again causing these foul deeds to happen?*

Lily cleared her throat. "Do you remember our talks about Manidos?"

"Yes, but I'm not sure if I have the subtle details. A Manido is another word for spirit. Your people believe there is spirit in things found in nature from trees, to animals, to rocks. Manidos surround us. Any of the 10,000 lakes in Minnesota would have a Manido, but only one, our home, has the Wintermaker dwelling in it—an evil, ancient spirit. Your concept of God, the Gitche Manidoo, simply means Great Spirit." He chuckled. "How'd I do, Nokomis?"

Lily patted his smiling face. "If mankind is to survive the wrath of the Wintermaker, we will need the old stories. You should be a teacher instead of a farmer."

"I do alright farming," Eddie said, but then hesitated.

"What is it?"

"I'm worried about Jimmy. I think he deserves to know more than I've told him. I think this growing evil has darkened him in recent months. He's had two kids his age die, and … I think he senses the reason."

"You've protected your home?"

"Of course, I've left the dreamcatchers and the little sage dolls all over the property and Turtle Island, but Jimmy can't stay home all day."

Lily sighed. "Wally is concerned about the Forsberg boy also, but I think they are still too young to understand."

"The original members of the Isanti Lodge were children."

"Yes, they were," Lily admitted. "The old stories tell how the Creator understood the suffering of mankind, and he gave us the original clan system. These seven clans were for the healing and protection of the people."

"What do you want me to do? I'm here to serve as your warrior."

In the old tale, the original Wintermaker was thwarted by the hero Ojiig, who was represented by the Fisher Cat, Eddie's symbolic position in the Isanti Lodge. Like her brother Migisi, he only wanted a chance to fight evil. *But what if the evil is me?*

She noticed then that the birds were abnormally silent in their cage. Tears filled her eyes, and she wiped them away. "The spider was not one of the clans, was it? Am I an unknowing force of death and destruction?"

"Why would you say that? I know your story. You fight for love, you fight for family, and you fight for the future. This storm has darkened your thoughts as well. Let's get you back to your room."

Yes. It is time I start fighting back. "I have a favor to ask. I need you to bring me something."

"What? More willow?"

"Bring me my grandson Cameron."

Advantage: Wintermaker

Split Rock High School
February 17, 1962

JIMMY NIELSON FELT eyes looking over his shoulder, but he stood at the locker room door as instructed. Finally, the door flew open, and Mr. Van Slyke stood in the space.

"Ready to be champions?" Van Slyke asked, and the other seven wrestlers shouted their war yawps.

Jimmy followed his coach through the crowded hallway and to the gym door.

As soon as he saw the mat, he felt his anxiety subside. He sprinted ahead, making the others keep pace with him as he began running warm-up laps in front of the Split Rock crowd.

It was the second day of the team wrestling tournament and the fourth dual in so many days. Split Rock had upset Park Rapids on Friday, crushed St. John in the second match, and earlier in the day, defeated Motley-Staples to advance to the championship match against Walker-Hackensack-Akeley. As the youngest and smallest member of the varsity squad, Jimmy wrestled at 115, the lowest weight class. Biff Forsberg, the other junior high member now on varsity, ran three spots behind him at 154 lbs.

He spotted his mother and father, flanked by his three older sisters, Rachel, Faye, and Alexandra in the crowd. There were a lot of other faces in the crowd, but for some reason, he noticed the calm presence of Mrs. Crain, flanked by her husband Wally too.

When Jimmy finished laps, he dropped to the mat and took the team through stretching exercises. Linda Baxter, Barb Thurman, and Nicki Guerin sat at the edge of the mat in their colorful cheerleading uniforms.

Stay focused on your opponent.

Just a few yards away, Tommy Kane warmed up with his team. The ninth-grader from Walker had gone to State as a 7th and 8th grader, and now as a freshman, he was undefeated. Jimmy had already faced him twice during the season, getting pinned by him in December and then losing on points in January.

Coach Van Slyke called the team together, and even though plenty of inspirational words were shouted out of his mouth, Jimmy couldn't hear a thing he said. In fact, the entire gym went strangely quiet for him, and all he could hear was his own breathing and the thump of his heart.

Jimmy stepped out of the huddle and walked to the center of the mat where Kane waited for him.

The referee said a few words, and when the signal was given, everyone vanished for Jimmy except for Kane. Kane immediately began to stalk him, and Jimmy was fine with that, for when Kane shot forward, Jimmy bent slightly as Kane reached for his legs, and as both bodies dropped to the mat, he had Kane's inner knee in his grasp.

And it began: simultaneously they fought each other both offensively and defensively. After the last match in January, Jimmy knew Kane had a much stronger upper body, so he worked to get leverage on Kane's legs. At the same time, Kane tried to bully his way—which worked. In the span of twenty seconds, Jimmy's plan failed, and Kane scored points for the flip, leaving Jimmy no choice but to spin away in retreat.

With Jimmy moving outside the circle, the ref had the boys start again, this time with Jimmy in the down position on all fours and Kane above him having the advantage. Knowing he was in trouble, Jimmy prepared himself for his best escape move, and when the whistle blew, he turned to jelly as Kane tried to flip him onto his back.

Though Jimmy was weaker, he had another gear that Kane did not, and with each move made by Kane, Jimmy managed to slip right out. The crowd erupted when Jimmy scored a point for another escape.

As the third and final period began, Jimmy faced Kane standing as equals. The ref blew the whistle, and this time, Kane took his time, ducking low and waiting for Jimmy to make a mistake. Both he and Kane grappled with their hands for a moment until Jimmy reached out and found leverage behind Kane's head.

But Kane used Jimmy's hold for balance and threw his own hand behind Jimmy's head as both wrestlers butted heads and wrapped up each other's shoulders. Jimmy felt a throbbing pain as Kane's hand raked across his left eye. He didn't give Kane the satisfaction of a grunt, but it was a dirty move, and combined with the hard head butt, Jimmy was dizzy as well as partially blinded.

Kane released and stepped back, knowing he'd inflicted the subtle damage needed. The two circled for a few more steps before Kane went for Jimmy's knee, and then with both hands, slid down to Jimmy's ankle, lifting his left leg from the mat, forcing Jimmy to either let the ligaments in his knee be torn sideways or relent with an awkward fall.

Jimmy fell on top of Kane, but as he did so, he saw Kane's exposed leg and quickly grabbed it. He flipped his free right leg around Kane's shoulder, and despite the warnings from his mind, he locked his right ankle against the left ankle that Kane held.

As expected, Kane began rolling Jimmy onto his back, but before that could happen, Jimmy squeezed his two legs like a pair of scissors, catching Kane's neck in the crook of his left knee. The weight of Kane's own body combined with the power in Jimmy's leg left Kane in an inverted triangle chokehold.

Kane arched his back, leaving Jimmy face down on the mat but with his legs wrapped around Kane's neck and shoulders. Kane tried to rise from the move, and Jimmy used his weight and leverage to flip Kane over. With a snarl on his face, Jimmy looked down his torso at Kane, whose face had turned red.

In the span of four seconds, Jimmy had gone from victim to bully.

The ref angrily blew his whistle and slapped the mat, and Jimmy let go, but Tommy Kane remained flopped down across Jimmy's right thigh.

Jimmy slapped Kane's chest to let him know he'd released—

Kane had passed out.

The world grew louder than Jimmy had ever heard as the Walker-Hackensack-Akeley coaches screamed at him. Then he heard fans and parents screaming at him. Even the wrestling cheerleaders from the other team screamed at him.

The ref was looming over him, grabbing Kane by the shoulder to help roll him onto his side and away from Jimmy.

A wave of relief passed over Jimmy as Kane's eyes fluttered open, and his body flexed and began to move again. Instinctively, Kane rolled over and sat on his feet to catch his breath. Jimmy reached out a hand and patted Kane on the head as a show of no ill-will, but it was too late for apologies.

Why did I do that?

What's wrong with me?

The ref stood and blew his whistle. "Illegal choke hold. Disqualification."

Coach Van Slyke rushed over from his spot beside the mat but not to defend Jimmy. Instead, he went over to Kane to join the opposing coach.

Coach Daniels intercepted Jimmy before he could find his chair with the rest of the team. "Get to the locker room. Right now!"

Jimmy listened and jogged away.

When he entered the locker room, he found himself all alone, with the only sound coming from the dripping of the shower.

He sat in front of his locker, and as the gravity of his actions sunk in, he kicked the door with his feet. He'd blown it.

While the rest of the team remained in the gym, Jimmy paced, listening to the cheers that erupted from time to time. He finally stopped in front of the shower room, watching the water dripping from the faucet.

Each time a drop fell from the showerhead, it struck the floor with such impact that a strange ripple emanated from the room like a ripple upon the surface of a lake. He began to see an image form.

Beside the floor drain a young man clutched his chest where three bullet holes oozed blood. Terror in his eyes. With each drip, the boy gazed out at Jimmy in horrified amazement.

This isn't happening, Jimmy told himself. *This is the future.*

Gray shadows emanated from the boy's body. At first it appeared as if they were comforting him, but then Jimmy realized they were dabbing at his blood with their long fingers, which they brought to their mouths to taste. With bloody grins, the gray men dissolved and floated with the water down the drain.

The locker room door was kicked open, and Biff Forsberg charged in: "We lost because of you, Jimmy."

Behind Biff, the other dejected members of the varsity team entered. Biff's charge concluded with a violent shove on Jimmy's chest, which he took without mustering a defense. He went flying into the shower room, sliding across the space where the dying boy had been. He looked back, but instead of seeing Biff in his singlet, he saw a fat, balding, middle-aged man in a khaki uniform pointing a gun at him. Then another drop fell from the faucet, and he saw Biff transform back into a young man.

Glimpses of the future?

The urge to fight overwhelmed Jimmy, and he bounced back to his feet and returned with his own charge. With Biff outweighing him by forty pounds, Jimmy's shove pushed Biff back only a couple of steps, and then the fists began to fly.

For every heavy thump Biff gave him, Jimmy landed two sharp strikes. The rest of the team stood and watched, letting the boys bloody each other before the coaches came rushing in.

Jimmy found himself being slammed hard against a locker by Coach Van Slyke. "What the heck is wrong with you, Nielson?"

"I don't know," Jimmy answered, but he did know.

Doom was coming to Lake Manitou, and he could no longer enjoy living in the present.

Wrestling became stupid.

Everything was stupid.

The voice echoed in his mind … *Is it time?*

Raw Faw

Leech Lake, MN
February 18, 1962

LILY GUERIN WATCHED her grandson Cameron cross the parking lot toward the front doors of the nursing home. A fierce cold front brought subzero temperatures, making their weekly visit uncertain, but once he stepped out of the car, Cameron only winced and hastened his staggered pace for the trek between his car and the doors.

Cameron tripped as he stepped over the curb. His left leg was still unresponsive after the attack and manifested as a limp. When he saw her through the glass doors, he tried to smile.

The scar along his eye socket was no longer infected, and the tissue surrounding his eyes had turned from deep purple to a sickly yellow, but the eye itself had turned pale as if winter had somehow frozen it inside of his head. Talk of patience had turned into whispers of removal, but the doctors held onto hope that enough damaged blood vessels would regrow to save the life of the eye, which would never function fully again.

Cameron Guerin would turn twenty-two in March, but he looked like an old man. *How much more will my family have to suffer because of my sins?*

Lily also saw herself in the reflection of the glass. Her hair, once a long braid of gray and black, had been burned away in the fire to the scalp, but now, several months after the fire, it had regrown to cover her head with silvery-white. She wore a red blanket draped over her shoulders as she sat in her wheelchair.

"Hello, Nokomis," Cameron said and took hold of her wheelchair, pushing it over to the aviary, as was their new routine thanks to the loyalty of Eddie Nielson.

"How are the children?"

"Angry," Cameron said, laughing at his joke.

"What do you mean?"

"Nicki and her boyfriend got into a fight. She hit him during a music festival."

"This is the doing of the Tak-Pei. A series of small battles before the war begins. What of the others?"

"Also angry. Last night, the Nielson boy got disqualified at the region wrestling finals, and later he got into a fight with the Forsberg boy."

"Then we need to finish this today."

On cue, Cameron took out the yellow note pad, flipped past several pages, and handed it to her, followed by a pencil.

"Before we finish this song, I need you to understand something."

As always, Cameron nodded enthusiastically.

"Do you remember the story from church about the 'Armor of God'?"

Cameron grinned, a rivulet of saliva leaking onto his chin, which he wiped away. "Yeah, it sounded like a knight of the roundtable."

The words of Ephesians 6 filled Lily's mind: '*Put on the whole armor of God, that ye may be able to stand against the wiles of the Devil. For we wrestle not against flesh and blood, but against principalities, against powers, against the rulers of the darkness of this world, against spiritual wickedness in high places.*

'Wherefore take unto you the whole armor of God, that ye may be able to withstand in the evil day, and having done all, to stand. Stand therefore, having your loins girt about with truth, and having on the breastplate of righteousness; And your feet shod with the preparation of the gospel of peace;

'Above all, taking the shield of faith, wherewith ye shall be able to quench all the fiery darts of the wicked. And take the helmet of salvation, and the sword of the Spirit, which is the word of God.'

"Yes, Cameron, like a knight of the roundtable. What is happening now at Lake Manitou might be the beginning of a much greater battle, but I am old, and if it lasts as long as I think it might, I'll need you to do your part?"

"What's my part?"

"God gives each of us a specific gift, but you are not a warrior destined for battle. And you are too old to play the part of the Omodai."

"What's that?"

"We must defeat the Wintermaker. The fate of the whole world depends on it."

"Is he like … the Antichrist?"

"No, he is worse, for he is the enemy of both God and the Devil. He is trying to stop reconciliation from ever happening. In the Bible, the prophecy is for the restoration of Paradise here on earth in a place called New Jerusalem. In the Seven Fires Prophecy, there is an Eighth Fire of peace and harmony. The Wintermaker wants to destroy these prophecies. But we won't let him win, will we?"

"No, we won't." Cameron gave his crooked grin again. "How will we defeat him?"

"I think the answer lies in an old tale about Iyash and the Horned Serpent."

"The Horned Serpent is the Wintermaker."

"Yes, my dear. But the old snake is slippery and cautious, and he hates all the descendants of Iyash, especially our family."

"Why?"

"Because we have the power to destroy him, but it will be dangerous. The legend of Iyash talks of how our young hero befriended the Horned Serpent lurking in the waters."

"Why would he befriend something that wanted to kill him?"

I should have trained my grandchildren better when I had the chance. Now I understand how my own grandfather must've felt in his final months. "The only thing that the Horned Serpent fears is the Great Thunderbird, the Gitchi-Animikii. The Thunderbird will have the strength to kill the Horned Serpent and cast it into the River of Souls."

She sighed. "Long ago, the great sorcerer we call the Wintermaker cheated death, binding himself to Lake Manitou, where the powerful magic from the dawn keeps him from passing over. In the tale of Iyash, the Horned Serpent is so fixated on the threat of the Thunderbird, that Iyash is able to trick him. He lies to the Horned Serpent, who thinks he is just a weak little boy trapped on an island. The Horned Serpent lets Iyash ride upon his back in exchange for him to watch the clouds.

"You see, the Wintermaker is cautious and fearful, and will rise from the waters only when he thinks it is safe. Iyash, however, knew about the Great Thunderbird, and instead of just thinking of himself, he thought of others, and seeing the opportunity to rid the world of the ancient evil, he led the Horned Serpent into the shallows, trapping him there, where the Great Thunderbird came crashing down to kill him."

"Iyash tricks him." He paraphrased. "Am I Iyash?"

"No, as I said, you are too old. Iyash was only a child, but by risking his life, he saved the lives of others, didn't he?" *Perhaps his suffering will wake unknown gifts.* "Perhaps your accident will change you, dear boy. I think it might change you for the better."

"It doesn't feel like it."

"Our ancestors were blessed with abilities to see both prophecy and the unseen world. With your good eye, you'll be able to see the world as it is, but with your changed eye, you might be able to see the world how the prophets of old saw it. If you close your good eye, you might be able to see the truth. The Wintermaker, Iyash, the Tak-Pei … you might be able to lift the masks that hide them from the world."

"Huh."

"Let me know if you develop this skill. You are a young man, and in the distant days to come, I'll need you to watch for Iyash, for the new members of the Isanti Lodge, for the Horned Serpent, and for the Great Thunderbird in the clouds. Let the others be the shield and sword. I need you to be the watcher. You will not have a place in the Midewiwin Lodge, but you will stand outside of it, watching over them all. I need you to stay alive to be an old man."

Cameron smirked. "I'll keep an eye out for them."

"Now, let's help the others put on the Armor of God. Let's finish this song." Lily began to scratch out large letters, just as they'd done in recent weeks. "Try this phrase."

"Raw faw? What does any of this mean?"

"In truth, I do not understand any of the words myself. It is an ancient language lost generations ago."

"Then how do you know it?"

"The Wijigan Clan, our ancestors, were not blessed by the Creator with a gift meant to help humanity. We were different from other humans, who were given touch, smell, taste, hearing, sight, and even intuition. No, we were given a burden instead of a gift—a seventh sense, the ability to see the future. I've seen Iyash in the future, as well as two other spiders, who spoke to me about things still to come. I learned the song from a woman with a damaged face, and for her also, it wasn't a tragedy but a blessing."

"When life gives you lemons, make lemonade."

Lily laughed but then grew serious. *Do I let this sweet boy join in the fight?* "Yes, Cameron. She taught me the song, which had many verses, including a verse I misunderstood. Now, I'm going to use this verse to protect your sister and the others." Lily looked it over one more time before handing it to him. "Give this to your sister. Have her practice singing the words. Promise me you will give it to her."

"I promise, Nokomis."

If the servants of the Wintermaker manage to wake their master, Nicole is in grave danger. All of my plans have turned to ash. "I'm sorry I did this to you. I am a selfish, horrible woman."

"You didn't do anything to me. Those redneck assholes did this to me."

Fawn was right about me. "I had a chance to defeat evil, but I threw it all away to save your grandfather's life."

"But if you hadn't saved him, I wouldn't be here today. I still have a good eye to see you with," Cameron said with complete sincerity.

"Yes, you do, and I need you to begin your watch. You will be our scout. Our enemy is preparing for war and will try to crush the young Thunderbird while he is still a chick in the nest. Watch for him, Cameron. Find him before they do."

Only the Great Thunderbird can make this suffering worth the cost.

A House Divided

Split Rock High School
February 20, 1962

NICOLE GUERIN SEETHED after taking her spot in detention. She chose the front row, closest to Mrs. Crain's desk, just to avoid having to look at anyone else in detention, especially Gavin MacPherson.

At first, Nicki tried to do her homework, but she couldn't focus on the calculus book in front of her. Any noise from the hallway caused her eyes to dart to the left as if Cameron's monsters would walk right through the doorway. At other times, she would study the wall and board in front of her, and when most daring, she would look over to Mrs. Crain's desk to study its contents or gaze out through the window behind where she sat.

Mrs. Crain was grading a stack of essays in front of her; the stack of pink slips sat by the edge of the desk nearest Nicki. John Hensely, a chronic skipper, sat staring at the eraser on the end of his pencil.

Two seventh-graders, Biff Forsberg and Jimmy Nielson, sat on opposite sides of the room as a consequence for a fight in the locker room following the wrestling tournament the previous weekend. Nicki had seen part of the unfortunate event unfold, with Jimmy Nielson being disqualified in the first match and heavyweight Gregg McCue getting pinned in the final match to give the team victory to their rival school, Walker-Hackensack-Akeley.

Gavin sat somewhere behind her, and she refused to look in his direction.

She shuffled her books, retrieving the yellow notepad. Even now, after a few days of deciphering it, it flustered her. It had bonded her and Cameron for hours each night, but outside of him, she had no one else to talk to about it. So, she studied the phonetic syllables written upon the page as if it could fix what had happened at the All-State Music Festival.

As recently as December, Nicki and Gavin sang a duet at the Christmas Concert that wowed the audience, and despite breaking up over Cameron's attack, Gavin handled the situation maturely—in public. Unfortunately, Joyce Lee, the music director, had the honor of selecting four of Split Rock High School's finest musicians to take to the All-State Choir festival in St. Paul. Both Nicki and Gavin were chosen. At first, Gavin played it cool, and Nicki stuck to the side of Alice Lodwell just so there couldn't be any private moments.

But all hell broke loose at Happy Chef following the performance.

When Nicki went to the restroom, Gavin followed, cornering her in the hallway with his puppy dog eyes and lame proclamations of love. After he brought up snowmobiles and Cameron, Nicki snapped. She didn't quite remember what she said, but there, on Mrs. Lee's pink slip, she could see what earned her detention:

*Outside of the restroom, Miss Guerin slapped Mr. MacPherson hard across the face and then loudly proclaimed that she would "castrate him" if he ever came near her family again. She also loudly used the phrase "son of a b**ch" and "b*stard" in public.*

Poor Gavin served detention for a reason other than profanity or threats.

Gavin's pink detention slip read:

Mr. McPherson knocked over and broke a stand holding menus and also shattered a door when he flung it open with great force.

Mrs. Crain glanced up, and Nicki looked back down at her yellow notepad.

How did my world get so crazy?

Growing up, she'd heard the stories about the place she lived, but she took them for tall tales. Now, her grandmother and brother tried to prepare her for a battle.

Accepting this challenge meant … she was a weirdo, a kook, a nutjob. No popularity, no music scholarship next year, no respectable husband with a five-bedroom house. She'd either have to deny her brother or deny herself.

Mrs. Crain set one of the essays aside and using her right hand as a prop against her brow, Nicki stealthily shielded her face so she could read the essay without being seen.

The essay belonged to Biff Forsberg.

The prompt was fairly basic: Whose mythological adventure would you want to personally endure and why?

I'd want to be Orion. Orion was a hunter. He had an awesome hunting dog named Sirius. He uses a bronze club when he is hunting. It is said that there wasn't an animal or monster on earth that Orion couldn't hunt. He was so good that the gods had to invent a monster, a giant scorpion, in order to kill him. I like hunting monsters. That is why I'd want to be Orion.

Nicki glanced over at the rugged farm boy. If ever there was a "Biff," it was Brian Francis Forsberg, yet for all of his simplicity, she also sensed inner strength. He'd come face to face with a killer, a child molester, and stared down his monster. For weeks, it was all the state of Minnesota could talk about. Biff had saved the life of his friend by throwing a pitchfork. And now he liked hunting monsters.

A few minutes later, Mrs. Crain set another essay aside. This one belonged to Jimmy Nielson.

Jimmy Nielson was visibly struggling, and it was more than the tedious time spent in detention. Cameron insisted on protecting the children, and from what Nicki read in the paper, the anonymous serial-killer was targeting kids.

Mrs. Crain leaned back in her chair and studied them. Nicki averted her eyes and quickly flipped to a blank page when she realized her teacher was fixated on her yellow pad.

Nicki froze, not knowing what to do. With her elbow, she knocked a pencil off her desk. When she leaned over to retrieve it, she caught a glimpse of Gavin. But instead of looking at her, Gavin had a puzzled look on his face as he stared at Mrs. Crain.

Nicki exhaled, put the pencil in her finger, and began to doodle some art in the margins. When she felt the hot gaze of Mrs. Crain leave her desk, she looked up.

Mrs. Crain held the journal of Father Jean Guerin.

Grandma Lily had almost died retrieving it, and in turn, Gavin almost died saving Lily. They'd brought the journal and Bic lighter to her great-uncle Migisi, only to be belittled and bitterly dismissed.

Now, Mrs. Crain held it.

When her teacher looked up, Nicki crossed her arms and stared with malice. Mrs. Crain set it down on her desk, then cleared her throat. "Mr. Hensely, you may leave early."

John Hensley blinked then quickly snatched up his work and bolted toward the door.

With the notebook in hand, Mrs. Crain walked over to her instructor's chair at her podium and sat down. "So, help me God, we are going to get to the bottom of all of this garbage."

Nicki turned around to check Gavin's reaction, yet it was Biff Forsberg who cleared his throat to speak. "I'm sorry. It was all my fault. I … I … thought your brother Cameron was the one responsible," Biff muttered, his eyes glassy with restricted tears.

"What?" Nicki spun in her chair to face the red-haired boy.

"I told some of the sophomore boys what I thought—about the fire, about the accident at the park, and about Isaac dying on the same route that Cameron took to the park each day. I swear I didn't have anything to do with—"

"You!" Gavin exploded from his chair, pushing desks out of the way as he rushed through two rows to grab ahold of Biff by the shirt and then throw him to the floor. "Give me their names or I'll beat it out of you!"

Just as fast as Gavin burst from his chair, Jimmy Nielson sprang from his own, coming up from behind the larger junior to wrap an arm around his neck.

"Let him go," Jimmy commanded, only to have Gavin shake Forsberg harder. Then Jimmy squeezed, and Gavin let go only to focus his aggression on the smaller boy.

Gavin rose, pulling the seventh grader off his feet to dangle on his back like a cape. He grabbed at the younger boy, but Jimmy refused to let go, his feet knocking against desks.

Nicki jumped to her feet, rushing closer to the fight, unexpectedly in defense of Gavin.

"Let him go!" she shouted, standing in front of Gavin but looking at Jimmy's face as he held on from behind. "Jimmy Nielson, let him go!"

Stunned, Mrs. Crain hadn't moved as chaos erupted around her classroom.

Gavin put out his hands in surrender, Biff squirmed backwards, and Jimmy released his chokehold, sliding off the junior and onto his feet. Nicki stepped in and wrapped her arms around Gavin in an unexpected show of affection that even surprised her. *Why have I been so cruel to him when he's only shown me love and kindness?* She felt safe for the first time in weeks.

"I know your brother wasn't the one who killed Isaac and Rory," Biff said.

"You think so?" Nicki snapped. "What makes you so certain it wasn't him? Isn't he half Indian and retarded? Isn't that what you little shits whisper whenever he goes by? 'Look, it's Can Man.'"

"He said he was sorry," Jimmy shouted, taking a step closer to his friend.

"Oh, he's sorry. Well, I guess that makes everything better, except for the fact that my brother has a blind eye now. Is sorry going to fix that?"

"No," Biff said with alligator tears sliding across his freckled cheeks.

"Who beat him up?" Gavin asked from behind Nicki.

"I don't know who beat him up; I wasn't there."

"Then who did you tell?"

"Everybody. Anybody. Chris tried to tell me I was wrong, but I wouldn't listen to him, and I got your brother beat up for no good reason."

"Look," Gavin said, stepping around Nicki, "she thinks I was either part of it or I was covering for the guys who did it. So, fess up kid. Who did you tell?"

"Carey Jensen. Dale Nase. The Berg brothers. The Morrison brothers. Andy Lane. Dan Heimdall. They all heard me say it."

"They have snowmobiles, don't they?" Nicki confirmed, looking at Gavin.

Gavin nodded.

"I'm sorry," Biff said and then turned to Jimmy. "I'm sorry I didn't listen to you either. I really thought it was him."

"Turned out it wasn't him, was it?" Jimmy asked bitterly. "And because of you, Chris almost got killed."

"Enough," Mrs. Crain snapped. "In these dark hours, we cannot afford to be a house divided. We must be strong and hold together or else evil will sweep us away."

What is she talking about?

"Now, sit down so we can talk," Mrs. Crain commanded, and they obeyed, pushing the desks back into a semblance of order so they could sit in a semicircle around her. "I have read this cover to cover, and I want you to know that you can trust me and that I'm your ally in this fight."

"How did you get that?" Nicki asked, glancing at Gavin, who showed equal confusion at the sight of the journal.

Mrs. Crain opened the notebook and flipped a few pages until she stopped and began to read, "*"Adam Thunder Face once told me of the Isanyathi, a Dakota word that translates as Guardians of the Frontier. Since Lily's blood is half Dakota, it seems a good word to describe all of those she gathered at the island: Bjorn Forsberg, Albert Fisher, Farrell Luning, Kermit Crain, Martin Nielson, Fawn Chevreuil, Migisi, and myself. The nine of us have become the new Guardians of the Frontier, sworn to protect those we love from the evil that slumbers in Lake Manitou.*"*

The boys were wide-eyed, but Nicki still fumed. "You didn't answer my question, Mrs. Crain. How did you get that?"

"It was given to my husband, Wally Crain, son of Kermit Crain, whom your grandmother trusted with her secrets. Sitting in front of me is the granddaughter of Jean and Lily Guerin, the grandson of Bjorn Forsberg, and the grandson of Martin Nielson. I think we're meant to be here together in this place, don't you?"

"How did your husband get the journal?" Nicki persisted.

"Migisi Asibikaashi gave it to him. The two of you were right to bring it to him after the fire. He was there six decades ago when evil last attacked our home. He knew that the only way to stand against it is to stay together. That's why I have to say something today. I know all four of you have been affected by this darkness that has descended upon our community, but we need to get past this."

Jimmy looked as if a hundred-pound weight had been lifted from his shoulders. "So, you believe, in the … you know?"

"Jimmy, I honestly don't know what to believe," Mrs. Crain answered and turned to Nicki and Gavin. "How much of this have you read?"

"Most of it," Gavin answered.

"All of it," Nicki replied. "But it's just nonsense, isn't it? There really isn't a monster lurking in the water or creatures in the woods. Someone tried to burn down my grandmother's house, just like someone tried to grab Biff when he was doing chores. How is any of the stuff in that notebook going to help us?"

"I have dreams about them," Jimmy said without reservation. "I see them sometimes even when I'm awake … and I can hear *him* when I sleep."

Biff stared opened mouth at his friend before he shifted closer and put a hand on Jimmy's shoulder.

Gavin asked, "What's he talking about?"

Mrs. Crain ignored Gavin, her gaze on Jimmy. "I've seen them, too. I believe you, Jimmy. During the New Year's Eve Blizzard, they crept up from Lake Manitou and stood around my old willow tree. I don't know if anyone else will believe this, but I believe you." She paused and looked up at the clock on the wall. "Now, we have thirty-four minutes before we're expected to rejoin the real world, so I want to have each of you tell the group what you know."

"I think I should start," Nicki said. "All of you are here because of a connection to me." She began by sharing the eccentricities of Grandma Lily, including her anxieties right before the fire.

Gavin jumped in, explaining how he had been given the journal after he rescued her grandmother from her burning house, which appeared to be caused by arson.

"And you found the lighter right outside her back window?" Mrs. Crain asked.

Nicki nodded. "Everyone was so worried about my dad and grandmother that nobody went back to the house until afterward. I guess they assumed she was just an old lady who left something on the stove. No one thought she'd be the target of murder."

"I've seen the lighter," Mrs. Crain explained, "and Wally also saw a suspicious man driving on the Nimrod road, smoking."

"What did he look like?" Nicki pressed.

"He drove a blue car and smoked a cigar. He wore a woolen hunting cap—"

It's him! "And a tweed jacket," Nicki interrupted. "I saw him! He drove a bright red car for this man who wore a white suit, who was looking for Grandma Lily. I've never seen her that mad. I didn't even know what was going on. My dad came to the door with a shotgun, but they told me it was some sort of door-to-door salesman. I remember seeing the other fellow leaning against the car puffing away at his cigar. Who is he?"

"I don't know, but I'd almost guarantee he is behind this aw-fulness. Father Guerin's journal describes servants of the Wintermaker."

"The Tak-Pei," Jimmy added.

"No, not the Tak-Pei, men. Whoever lit the fire knew Lily had the ability to stop them."

"What about Isaac and Rory?" Jimmy asked. "How could they be a threat to anyone?"

Mrs. Crain explained the history of Lake Manitou, beginning with the story of the twelve Dakota children sacrificed at Bleeding Rock, and then the more recent deaths between 1897 and 1898. "Before the Wintermaker can fully wake, his servants must be fed. I believe these evil acts add fuel to the growing fire."

Is this really happening? Why am I more frightened now than before I said anything? Nicki couldn't look anyone in the eye.

"What do we do?" Gavin asked.

"We begin by sticking together instead of tearing each other apart," Mrs. Crain answered. "This secret needs to stay with us, is that understood? As Brian knows, our enemy is out there somewhere, which is why we must be especially careful. Back in 1898, the final attack came in the summer, which gives us only a few months to make a plan. Until then, we need to watch out for each other; protect each other."

Biff raised his hand.

"Yes Brian?" Mrs. Crain called on him as if in class.

"Can I say something?"

Nicki realized he hadn't said anything since his confession.

"Go ahead, Biff."

"As I was trying to say earlier, I know it wasn't your brother Cameron," Biff began looking at her but stopped and turned to Jimmy. "I need to tell her about it."

Jimmy's mouth opened and a strange terror came over his eyes. *What's he holding back? What do they know?*

"Boys, we can't have any secrets here," Mrs. Crain insisted.

Jimmy closed his mouth and swallowed hard. "On Labor Day weekend, when we were camping at the State Park, Rory, Biff, and

I snuck out of camp on a canoe and paddled across the lake so we could sneak into the quarry."

"Why on earth would you do that?" Mrs. Crain asked.

Biff answered softly, "Because of what Wally told us, and what Rory told us. Rory said there was something really valuable in the quarry, so we wanted to sneak in and see what it was."

"What was it?" Gavin asked the same question Nicki was wondering.

"A tunnel," Jimmy answered vaguely. "At the bottom of the quarry. It led under Lake Manitou."

Biff took over the story. "Rory and I were caught, but no one found Jimmy. Now Rory is dead, and I almost got Chris killed. The killer knew I'd been there too."

"Someone from Haggard Quarry tried to kill you?"

Biff nodded. "Only someone who knows my dad goes fishing every year up to Leech Lake would have tried to abduct me because he would've known I'd have to do chores by myself."

"Why didn't you say something?" Mrs. Crain asked.

Biff looked at Jimmy. "Because I promised Jimmy not to talk about what happened that night. Plus, no one is going to believe me."

"Why not?"

"Because the guy who attacked me didn't match with the guy, I thought it might be," Biff answered, clenching his jaw in anger while tears welled in his eyes. "I don't want to make another mistake and get someone hurt."

"But you have a suspect?" Mrs. Crain asked.

Biff nodded. "But I'm not going to say it until I can prove it."

Nicki sighed. *Grandma Lily was right—the man in the white suit is behind all of this: Charani Bessant.*

Scars

Split Rock, MN
March 3, 1962

CHRIS LUNING STOOD at his second-floor window looking down at the truck that pulled in front of the house. Wally Crain handed his father something that looked like a newspaper along with a manila folder holding sheets of paper. The two stood out in the early March sun, which melted the snow drifts and caused the snow from the roof of his house to come trickling down over the ever-growing icicles.

His father abruptly handed the folder back to Wally, who took his father by the shoulder. For a moment, it seemed as if they were about to fight. Wally refused to back down, pressing the folder, but his father shook his head and held the newspaper up to Wally's face before turning back to the house.

Chris stepped away from the window and heard Wally's truck as it drove away. He looked down at the scar on his arm from the pitchfork Biff had thrown.

"Betsy!" his father shouted when he stepped inside the house.

Chris began a slow descent to the kitchen, unsure if he wanted to find out what his father had just learned. When he came around the corner, he saw his mother weeping with his father standing beside her.

"What's going on?" Chris asked.

His mother quickly wiped away her tears and rushed across the kitchen to wrap her arms around him. "Oh, it's wonderful news. They found the man who attacked you. He's dead and isn't going to cause you any more harm."

"What do you mean he's dead?"

His father held the same newspaper that Wally had given him. "We didn't want to upset you last night, but it looks like this is the weirdo responsible." He extended the newspaper to Chris and pointed at a black and white picture with the name Logan Troost printed underneath.

"This is … him?"

"Sure is. There's still no explanation for why he was doing it, but the state investigators did enough digging yesterday to announce that Troost was the guy who attacked you and most likely killed the others. I'd pour you a drink, Chris, if you weren't so young."

When his mother released him, Chris took hold of the newspaper, only to say, "Huh." Something just didn't feel right. He glanced down at the newspaper.

"You shouldn't read that. It might upset you."

"I'm okay, Mom. I just didn't expect him to be so … normal."

"Logan Troost was anything but normal," his father said. "I'm just glad this whole ordeal is over."

Chris skimmed through the details of the attacker. "Why would he drive all the way up from St. Louis?"

"Can't figure crazy."

"I'm going to call Chuck and Helen," his mother said in reference to Chris's older brother and sister-in-law in Georgia. "I need to let them know about this."

His father reached into his jacket and pulled out a pistol, which Chris had never seen. "I'm going to return this to Steve Knutson."

"Are … are they sure this is the right guy?" Chris asked as his father took a few steps towards the door.

"Of course they're sure. Your mom and I heard about this from Sheriff Betzing yesterday, but we waited to tell you until they had more information. It's the guy."

Chris sat down at the kitchen table while his parents went into motion. The newspaper was the *Daily Star* out of Minneapolis, which meant the column was being read state-wide. It made him sick to his stomach that so many people knew what had happened.

It also made him feel guilty that Rory and Isaac had died yet he had lived.

The article said Troost was found hanging from the Blue Knife River bridge, and investigators had found his car parked at Turtle Island State Park, which they believed he had used as a temporary base over the past few months, coming and going between Missouri and Minnesota, where Troost had been born, in nearby Brainerd.

There was chloroform in the trunk of the car, and he had to take a moment to breathe, remembering the man's hand clamping the wet rag against his face.

The paper intimated the attacks were sexual in nature due to Troost's prior incidents in Chicago, St. Louis, and Kansas City.

The coroner also confirmed that the pitchfork thrown by Biff Forsberg had indeed wounded Troost, whose wounds were found still bandaged. The "smoker" theory was also confirmed as Troost had on him a half-smoked pack of Camels and a plastic Bic lighter.

Chris jumped when his mother came to stand beside him.

"It's almost surreal, isn't it?" she asked. "How are you feeling?"

"Kinda weird."

"I'm sorry that you have to relive the whole experience."

In truth, Chris didn't feel too much trauma. The incident had lasted just a few seconds, and the chloroform had muddied most of his memories, including the color of the man's eyes.

His father appeared. "Sheriff Betzing wants to speak to you again. Would it be okay if he stops by later this afternoon?"

"Yeah, I suppose." Chris couldn't wait to talk to Jimmy and Biff about this. "Does this mean curfews are going to be lifted?"

His mother laughed. "I suppose it does."

CHRIS WATCHED TV the rest of the morning, and when a knock came on the door, he raced over, thinking it would be Sheriff Betzing.

It wasn't.

A familiar face stood at the door.

"Grandpa!" Chris said enthusiastically.

"Hello, Chris." Grandpa Albert opened his arms and the two wrapped each other in a prolonged embrace. "You and I have had a rough winter."

When the embrace ended, he saw tears in Grandpa Albert's eyes before he cleared his throat. "Is your father home?"

For a brief moment, Chris felt goose bumps running up and down his spine. He shook his head and stepped back. "I … I … thought you had pneumonia."

Grandpa Albert laughed. "I did, but the nurses got me back on my feet. It seems the Lord isn't through with me yet."

Chris noticed the manila folder Grandpa Albert carried. It appeared to be the same folder Wally Crain had tried to give his father. Up close, Chris could see it was labeled Hiawatha County Sheriff's Department.

"Did you hear they caught the guy who tried to take me?"

"I read the story, yes. In fact, I came here to talk to your father about it."

"Is something wrong?" Chris asked. *Does he know something else?*

"No, no," Grandpa Albert bluffed, badly. "When I read the news in the paper, I felt a certain … responsibility … to see how you were doing. I had a brush with death too."

"When you drove out onto the ice?"

"No. When I was a boy your age, I was playing by the edge of Split Rock Creek. The whole time I played, I was never more than a shout away from my father and others at the mill, yet … everyone assumed I lost my footing and slipped into the water … everyone except your grandfather Farrell. He seemed to know the truth before I did. Since the day he saved me, I asked myself why God spared me a certain death. Your grandfather broke both his legs rescuing me, and I always felt guilty about how it crippled him." Grandpa Albert glanced down at the folder. "I bet you ask yourself why God spared you?"

Chris nodded.

Grandpa Albert leaned in closer. "God saved you for a reason, Chris. Remember that. It might be for something minor or major, but regardless, you live a charmed life now."

Chris nodded again.

Grandpa Albert straightened back up but kept his voice low. "This man they found—is he the man who tried to grab you outside of the Forsberg barn?"

"Yeah," Chris said. "I mean, I can't be certain because the guy wore a mask, but it sure seems like the right fellow."

"Can you give your father this folder? It's important that he reads it," Grandpa Albert said almost bitterly and handed it over. "I wish I could stay longer, but after being stuck in the hospital, I have many errands to run and not enough time. I hope you understand."

After Grandpa Albert left, Chris stood there for a few minutes, holding the unsealed manila folder, before he sat down at the kitchen table with the folder in front of him. Finally, he opened it up. Inside, he found copies of police records and forms, with blue ink underlining and circling certain passages.

In the coroner's report, he found phrases like "inconsistent" in describing the wounds that had been made by the pitchfork. He also found a small paragraph detailing the chemical residue found inside the man's mouth that again seemed "inconsistent" with suicide.

Does this mean Troost was a pasty?

Why would the adults agree to a lie?

Does my mom know?

By the time his mother returned from the store, Chris understood why both Wally Crain and Grandpa Albert had been given the report by Sheriff Betzing, who arrived along with his father a little after noon.

The sheriff asked the same questions that Chris had been asked a dozen times, which Chris answered honestly, but then the interview took a strange twist when the sheriff asked to see his wound.

"Go ahead, Chris," his father said when the sheriff asked for him to take off his flannel shirt so he could see the wound.

The sheriff first inspected his arm. "Any infections or problems healing?"

"It swelled the first week," Chris answered.

"We cleaned it regularly with hydrogen peroxide and rubbing alcohol, along with some ointment the doctors gave us," his mother said.

"Well, it certainly healed nicely," the sheriff added and then reached into his bag to pull out a Polaroid camera to photograph the wound. Then he took out a tape measure.

"What's this all about?" his father asked. "You got the guy."

"Of course," the sheriff declared, distracted. "The big mystery is solved, but in any investigation, the little details still need to be understood." He measured the distance from the floor to the wound.

He doesn't think Logan Troost is the right guy.

The sheriff covered his suspicions. "The state detectives are confident in their work, but I like to understand the forensic science. I'm fortunate that I don't have cases like this happen often in Hiawatha County. Obviously, the perp did not have a doting mother like you Mrs. Luning tending to his wounds, which explains the difference. I just wanted to collect a little more data—for science."

After the sheriff left, Chris got the folder, bringing it to his father in the living room. "Grandpa Albert brought this over while you were gone."

His father snatched it away.

He believes the story about Logan Troost. Chris frowned. "What is it?"

"A restless mind. How can two people look at the same evidence and see totally different things? Some people will see only what they want to see, even when confronted with reality."

Chris understood those two people to be Wally Crain and his grandfather. *I can trust them.*

FOR MUCH OF the afternoon, Chris stayed in his room, reliving it all and studying the scar on his arm left by Biff's pitchfork. When another knock came on the door, he let his parents deal with the guest, until he heard his mother call his name.

When he came running down the stairs, he saw Jimmy and Biff standing at the doorway. Behind them stood Jimmy's older sister Alexandra and his mother Bonnie.

"Hey, we just wanted to stop by and see how you were doing," Jimmy said.

"We read about the guy in the newspaper," Biff added.

"It's just nice to be able to breathe again," his mother said to her guests.

"We were all in town, and the boys wanted to stop and see their friend," Mrs. Nielson said.

This is kinda weird. It looks like they patched things up. That's good.

"Well, come inside and have some cookies," his mother offered.

"I need to get Biff home, and we've got a trunk full of groceries to attend to," Mrs. Nielson replied, smiling apologetically.

"Oh, I understand. Thanks for stopping by."

"Take care, my man," Biff said, shaking Chris's hand.

"Yeah," Jimmy stepped forward next, repeating the gesture, but as he did, Chris felt a piece of paper between their palms. "We'll talk more on Monday."

Chris caught the paper with his thumb and then quickly tucked it into his pocket.

It wasn't until he reached the stairs that he pulled the note out.

Meeting at the MacPherson hunting stand. 2 P.M. Sunday. Be there!

CHAPTER FORTY-SEVEN

The Isanti Lodge

Old Copper Road
March 4, 1962

NICKI GUERIN TUCKED the wrapped object into her bag as Cameron watched, his hands clasped together nervously. She zipped it shut and set the whole bag on her bed. The yellow papers sat spread out on her comforter.

"And then I sing the song?"

Cameron reached into his pocket for a piece of folded cotton and handed it to her. She unfolded it a bit to see words written in his hand with permanent marker.

"I transferred the song to cloth because paper can get wet and ruined," he said. "You could put that through the wash and still be able to read it."

"That's a good idea, Cameron." Nicki opened it wider. "I still don't understand what any of this says or means though."

"It's okay. It is written pha … phonon … it is written how you're supposed to say it."

"What's supposed to happen when I sing it?"

"It will protect them from what is coming."

"Grandma Lily *still* thinks it is coming?"

Cameron looked down and began to sway nervously.

"Are you sure you don't want to come with?"

He shook his head.

He's scared of kids now. I don't blame him for not wanting to come with me. I don't know if I even want to do this. "I'm doing this because you're my brother and I want you to stop fretting, okay? After this, we'll let Grandma deal with all this hocus pocus stuff, okay?"

Cameron nodded.

"Okay, then, go downstairs and start talking to Mom and Dad about something so that they won't see me sneak away and start asking questions."

"What should I talk about?"

"Start talking about *Bonanza*. Pretend you're excited about tonight's episode and then start talking about some of your other favorite episodes. You're good about rambling, Cameron. I'll be home before supper, so don't worry about me."

Cameron left her bedroom and walked downstairs. Nicki could hear muffled voices from the living room as their plan went into action, and then she picked up her bag and slowly walked down the stairs. She snatched her winter coat from the hook and softly opened the front door.

The air was almost humid, and monstrous flakes fell from the March sky, purifying the terrain that had become stained as the accumulated filth of winter began to melt. Despite being so late in the season, the piles of plowed snow were still high, and it felt as if she walked down a tunnel as she left her driveway.

Even on Old Copper Road, the plowed snow had filled the ditches, leaving a knee-high wall instead of a descending ditch. Because there was no shoulder, she watched for any passing cars.

Not wanting to draw any attention to herself, her pace quickened as she passed by the MacPherson house, and halfway to the Forsberg farm, she spotted the little piece of cloth tied to the tree.

As she neared, she saw footprints in the fresh snowfall.

The others had already arrived.

Traversing the ditch proved quite difficult even if the distance was only twenty yards. She tried to follow the previous tracks, but her feet frequently broke through the snowpack, causing her to lose her balance. Eventually, she reached the woods, and with her hands passing from trunk to trunk, she managed to move better.

A few yards into the woods, she saw another piece of cloth, along with footprints that led away from the road. Three more small pieces of cloth led her up a hill and back down to the Crow Wing River, where she saw a tree stand built for deer hunting.

When she reached the tree, she could hear voices and saw the footprints of possibly three others.

"Hello?" she called out.

"We're up here, Nic."

The hinged door in the floor opened up.

The old gray deer stand looked much like a tree house. Four skinny birch trees had been used as posts for the structure, which stood ten feet above the floor of the woods. It was built of old barn planks, with hinged windows, which were closed on all four sides. At some point in time, it had been painted green, but only a tint of green remained on the gray wood. Two-by-four steps had been nailed into the thickest of the birch trees. Nicki climbed up into the stand.

"Hey," Jimmy Nielson with her grandfather's journal on his lap said from a spot beside the trap door.

"Hey," Nicki replied and then noticed Biff Forsberg sitting opposite him in the corner.

Gavin sat against the same wall. It was surreal seeing him here, for only a few months earlier, she and Gavin had gotten to second base when she brought him a thermos full of hot soup while he was deer hunting. She looked at him now and could only say, "Hey."

"Glad you could make it," Gavin greeted.

"I'm surprised you're not too cool to be seen with us," Nicki snapped.

"We promised Mrs. Crain we'd be nice to each other," Jimmy reminded. "We all know how serious this is."

I need to stop taking it out on Gavin. She nodded and gave Gavin an apologetic shrug. "Where's Christopher?" Nicki asked as she climbed into the deer stand and took her spot.

"Running late as usual," Biff answered.

"Someone should have brought him here," Nicki said. She looked at Gavin. "You should go pick him up."

"We've already talked about this, Nic. We need to be discreet," Gavin answered.

"Because of the Order of Eos? Do you think it's real?"

"I do," Biff said. "I've met with them back in Nova Scotia. I think they're grooming me to join it. Everybody's connected. The folks out here act like regular people, but it gets really weird the farther up the family tree you get. Half the people out here are related in one way or another or came out here because of the Sinclair family."

"Why would that matter?" Nicki asked, trying to catch up.

"Triton Corporation put up the Nicollet Dam and tried to move the Chippewa off the reservation," Biff explained. "Ultimately, they failed to get rid of the reservation, but only because of what happened in the Battle of Sugar Point. If there is a human face behind the mask, I'll bet it is connected to the Sinclairs."

"Mrs. Crain is right that we need to be careful," Gavin added. "After a hundred years, it will be hard to tell friend from foe around here. Especially after folks accepted the story about Logan Troost."

"Everybody believes it," Nicki muttered. "The only people that don't are meeting in a deer stand."

"If Logan Troost is not the guy who tried to kill us," Biff insisted, "then he is the tenth death at the shores of Lake Manitou since the fire. If we don't figure out the killer soon, it isn't going to matter—the Wintermaker will have his twelve."

"Did you finish the list from 1898?" Jimmy asked Gavin.

"I did," he said, taking a glance down at his own notebook. "Azero Gunn, a visiting businessman from New York, died in his bathtub in 1897, but he seems to be the first who died suspiciously. After that, it was the murder of Lily's grandfather Nanakonan and her mother Winnie, who died at the hands of Adam Thunder Face, who also killed Jonas Penny when they tried to take him at Carousel Island."

"And that matched up with the four roller coaster deaths last summer," Jimmy said, looking at his contemporary list.

"A boy by the name of Franklin Auerbach drowned near your house later that summer, and then Stefan Van Slyke died in an explosion at the original Dutch Boy Creamery," Gavin continued. "From there things are not as public, but I think I've got it figured out. Jimmy said that his grandpa Sig was an only child, and that Martin and Dolly Nielson had several miscarriages and infant deaths before Sig was born."

Jimmy nodded in affirmation.

"So that brings the death total to eight heading into the spring of 1898," Gavin continued. "Apparently, it really hit the fan during the days surrounding the Battle of Sugar Point up at Leech Lake, and down here, there was some sort of attack at the Jesuit School resulting in the deaths of a Gordon Graham and half a dozen rabble-rousers who'd come down to either enlist help or burn the school. That easily got the number to a dozen before Lily … did her thing."

Suddenly, all three boys were looking at Nicki. *It's my turn now.*

"Did you bring it?" Gavin asked.

Nicki hesitated a moment before nodding. "I still think we shouldn't dabble in things we don't understand. None of us know what any of this means." She held out the folded cloth with the phonetic words written upon it.

"Can I see it?" Gavin asked, and Nicki handed it to him.

"It's a song of protection," she said. "It will make us official members of the Isanti Lodge."

"What language is that?" Jimmy asked, moving closer to Gavin.

"Chippewa, most likely," Biff answered.

"Or Sioux," Gavin noted. "Wasn't your great-grandmother Mdewakanton Dakota?"

"I don't think it's either language." Nicki sighed. "I think its some ancient, forgotten language."

"If it's only a song of protection, I don't think God would mind you singing it, especially with it being a Sunday and every-thing," Jimmy offered.

"I think God would want us to trust in Him with prayer," Nicki retorted.

"We're not dealing with stuff from the Bible," Biff said sternly.

"What if we are?" Jimmy countered. "What if these Tak-Pei, as the journal called them, are some sort of demon? Remember the passage where Father Guerin compared the Manitou to the horned beast from *Daniel* and the seven-headed dragon in *Revelation*? My dad told me the story about a man trapped on his roof during a flood, and a guy in a canoe, a boat, and even a helicopter offer to rescue him, only to—"

"I've heard this one," Biff interrupted.

Jimmy glared at him. "The guy ends up dying, and when he gets to Heaven, he asked God why he didn't save him, and God said to they guy—"

"'I sent you a canoe, boat, and helicopter, what more do you want from me?' Wally Crain told us that story when we went ca-noeing in the Boundary Waters," Biff finished, receiving a smack from Jimmy.

Jimmy huffed. "My point is, Nicki, what if God gave us this song so we could use it?"

"Grandma Lily also gave us this," Nicki said, pulling the wrapped object out of her bag. Unfolding it carefully, she revealed the handmade dreamcatcher, shaped like a teardrop with a single branch of a willow tree.

"Cool," Jimmy said with wide eyes.

Biff frowned. "Does it do anything?"

"Possibly," Nicki hedged. "Grandma Lily used to have these all over her house. My mom said it was probably the reason the fire spread so fast."

"Or the kerosene," Biff muttered, earning another smack from Jimmy, which brought a smile from Nicki.

What's taking Christopher so long? He should be here, too. "If it works, one of the spirits trapped here at Lake Manitou will get caught in the web, and then we'll have answers. It seems that kids have an important part to play in the prophecy."

"Like Wishwee," Jimmy said, holding the journal tightly.

"Or the Legend of the Fisher Cat," Biff added. "The one where the Wintermaker has trapped all the Summerbirds to keep it forever winter. I bet Summerbirds represent kids."

"What about the boy with the strange eyes from the Seventh Fire?" Gavin asked.

Nicki was stunned at how the boys had transformed their interest from football to legends and myths. "What happened to the three of you?"

"Didn't you read it?" Gavin asked.

"Yes, and it sounded like a crazy person wrote it, and now the three of you sound the same. Grandma Lily sent the dreamcatcher to us because she thought that one of the spirits trapped here at Lake Manitou might be able to speak with us and share its knowledge."

"What if it is an evil spirit?" Jimmy asked.

"That's why I think it is a stupid plan," Nicki replied.

"Okay, then let's do this." Gavin shifted and pointed to a spot on the wall. "We hang it up, but none of us will go into the deer stand unless there is somebody else with. Okay?" At their nods, he continued, "Now tell me about this song."

Am I crossing a line? Am I a hero, or am I about to be damned? Nicki took the cloth back and set it across her lap. "The Tak-Pei are servants of the Wintermaker, our Horned Serpent from the tales, and while each of them has powers, they have their limits. They are bound to the Wintermaker and cannot stray far from water. With each death, they grow stronger, and collectively, their magic also grows. While only a Fire Handler like Grandma Lily can face the Wintermaker, this song will repel any of the Tak-Pei from harming us."

"Like a shield," Biff added.

"Right, like a shield," Nicki said. "These are only the syllables, and I don't even know if I will sing it right."

"You're Lily's granddaughter," Gavin said. "I don't know who else would be qualified to sing it."

Grandma Lily had the Isanti Lodge. I have—where is Christopher?

Nicki opened her mouth and sang the first syllable. Biff's freckled face cracked a grin and Gavin nodded in encouragement while Jimmy sat wide-eyed.

She glanced at the remaining phrases and closed her eyes. She could hear her syllables echoing against the cold wooden boards of the deer stand, and as they bounced back to her, it no longer sounded like her voice. In fact, it felt as if the sound came through the elements and molecules of the air, as if her voice opened cracks into a world that no longer existed yet came seeping through from the past to the present.

"Hey, what's going on up there?" Christopher Luning called out from below.

His voice took her from a distant place surrounded by water and immediately plunged her back to the present. Even so, her flesh tingled.

Jimmy opened the trap door while Nicki finished singing the last line of the song. Upon seeing her, Christopher blushed, as he'd done several times recently. She could barely keep a straight face as the dimple-cheeked boy popped his head through the hole like an alarmed gopher.

"Hello, Nicole," Christopher said after clearing his throat nervously.

"Hello, Christopher."

"Oh, brother," Biff muttered.

"What was with the singing?" Christopher asked as he finished his climb.

"It was a song of protection, I think," Nicki answered.

"Good, does it protect against serial killers?" Christopher asked.

"Why do you say that?" Gavin asked.

"Because I think Biff and Wally are right. I talked to Grandpa Albert since he was one of the original members of the Isanti Lodge—to tell him what we think—and he agreed that Logan Troost was probably the tenth victim and not the actual killer. He said back in 1898, it was more than just supernatural deaths. There were two secret societies, one was the Wijigan Clan, and the other involved some pretty connected political figures. According to everything Grandpa learned about these guys—"

"You're listening to the same guy who drove into the lake? He's half-senile, Chris," Biff joked.

"Grandpa Albert knows more about this stuff than any of us, and he didn't just drive into the lake, he was attacked by Tak-Pei."

Evil hides under the guise of accidents. It's picking us off one at a time.

"How does your grandpa know anything about Logan Troost?" Gavin asked to break up the budding argument.

"He's the richest guy in Split Rock, and he helped put both Sheriff Betzing and Police Chief Plant in office. I guess they owe him favors because my grandpa had official reports on his desk."

"Why do the *official* reports say it was Logan Troost?" Gavin pressed.

"Grandpa says the real killer probably has connections, which is why Sheriff Betzing is going along with it instead of raising a stink. Plus, Betzing isn't an *official* member of the Isanti Lodge like my grandpa."

Biff huffed. "We can sing all the songs we like to protect us from things that go bump in the night, but what's going to happen when this guy comes back to finish me off?"

The only reason Grandma Lily sent me this spell is that we are all in danger.

"Why don't you tell us who you think it is, Biff?" Gavin asked.

Biff shook his head. "What if this guy isn't acting alone? Don't you remember what Wally said about his dad witnessing a secret society ritual? If I'm wrong, then I ruined the reputation of an innocent man. If I'm right, then I *really* become a target. I don't know what to do."

"We're all in this together, just like Mrs. Crain said. She made us all promise," Nicki said.

"Fine," Biff relented. "I did tell someone. I told Wally."

I've done my part, now we need the adults to do theirs.

In Deep

St. John, MN
March 16, 1962

IN THE SPAN of two days, winter gave way to spring. The frigid temperatures in early March had been uncannily unnatural, which kept Wally Crain and Ulman Oil scrambling to keep up. In a typical year, winter relented to spring by mid-March, allowing school activities like baseball, golf, and track to get an early start on partially melted fields, but this year, 1962, left most of Hiawatha County still blanketed in a foot of condensed snow.

According to the radio, a final snowstorm was predicted, which could leave snow all the way into June. However, when the storm arrived it was only drizzling, and Wally thought they were in the clear. The cold drizzle turned to ice for much of the morning, forcing him to be cautious on slick highways, but by the time he returned to St. John to refuel, the ice turned to large raindrops.

"Strange weather," seemed to be the sentiment shared by anyone he greeted, and by the afternoon of the first day, the air became almost humid, and a strange fog formed on the ground.

By the morning of the second day, the world turned to a slushy hell as a warm front from the Southwest brought sudden temperatures in the sixties coupled with a steady downpour. Although most of the gravel roads were still frozen a few inches below the surface, Wally had to be careful not to get stuck in the pools of standing water, for the two inches of rain turned into six inches of water when the winter drifts began to melt.

Delivering oil gave him an opportunity to patrol the lake—for villains and natural disasters. He first checked out the Saw Mill and Split Rock Creek, where Steve Knutson kept the spillway free of ice. Next, he checked the Doc Jenkins Bridge, which was built without pylons, making it a low risk to create an ice dam. Finally, he checked Kanaranzi Creek.

Luckily, the rising water on the lake flowed through the culverts while the ice piled up back at the mill, but if the wind shifted, the ice pack could easily slide onto the road.

And plugging these culverts would leave Split Rock in a world of shit.

From the culverts of Buffalo Slough, Wally could see almost five miles of the gray lake, all the way to Turtle Island State Park, where the flow of the Blue Knife River had cut the sheet of ice in half, sending miles of windblown chunks into the shore. If the wind could shift slightly, the damage would be taken by the cliffs of Bleeding Rock or the shores of Carousel Island.

I'd better check the farms along the southern shore.

The oak trees hid his view of Lake Manitou until he reached the Nielson farm, where Old Copper Road turned sharply west to become Wadena Road. From the hill, he could see Turtle Island free of ice and significantly smaller than normal due to high water.

By the time he finished his route around the lake, his tank was nearly empty, forcing him to return to base to refuel before finishing the Saturday route.

As he was filling both his main tank and truck tank, Spencer Ulman, the younger son of the owner, came out with another pink slip. "Could you swing by Haggard Quarry?"

Wally felt a knife twist in his gut.

"Haggard? I didn't expect them to open for a few more weeks."

"Apparently their pumps are running twenty-four-seven trying to keep up with all this rain. Red Dobie said to make it a priority."

Red's back in town? "Sure, I'll take it. I'll head there first thing."

Especially after what Biff Forsberg told him, Wally felt a tingle of apprehension when he sat down in his seat and glanced over at the glove box, where his pistol and castration knife waited.

Could the boy be right?

Did my father only imagine a Horned Serpent?

Are men the real monsters?

Driving into Haggard Quarry, Wally understood the need for fuel. After a fall of heavy rains and a winter of heavy snows, the quarry had filled with water, leaving much of the equipment ankle deep, with drifts and piles of snow yet to melt. Even though most of the equipment and machines were dormant, a loud generator fueled a pump that drained the water out the back, western side of the quarry.

Wally drove toward the fuel shed. Parked beside it, a shiny 1958 Chevy Bel Air sat in inch deep water.

By the time Wally had situated the truck beside the fuel tanks, Red stood at the window of the shed waiting for him. Again, Wally glanced at the glove box before slipping out of his truck.

When he stepped inside the warm shed, Wally offered congeniality, "Good afternoon, Red. Quite the weather we've been having lately. I bet you wish you were back in Arizona."

"This weather is for shit," Red greeted as he handed Wally the clipboard.

"Is that your blue and white Bel-Air?"

"Yeah, my old truck gave up the ghost after being parked at the airport all winter. Picked it up at Luther Automotive in the Cities."

"It's a beauty." Wally purposefully dropped the pen, and with a nudge, sent it rolling under the counter. "Sorry, got another pen?"

While Red went to a drawer, Wally scanned through the delivery log, determining that the large piles of snow along the western corner had been an effort to keep the quarry open through the winter, and that since December, Best Oil Company out of Brainerd had been making deliveries.

Red handed him a new pen.

"I hardly recognized ya. You shaved your beard," Wally observed, seeing that only an inch of light red beard grew where several inches had previously draped onto his chest.

"Even though it's winter down there, it gets hot in Arizona."

A small kerosene heater kept the entryway warm, and another lit the small office off to the side. Wally saw a cot folded against the wall. Even though it wasn't glamorous, it was possible for a man like Red to live in the fuel shed office indefinitely.

"You're back quite a bit earlier than normal."

"Had a house fire. I used the insurance money to pick up the car. I don't think I'm going back to Arizona next winter. I've been back for a week or so now, but I still feel out of sorts. I lost half my goddamn stuff in the fire, and when I got back home, I found my house had been broken into."

"Someone broke into your house?" Wally could still picture the Plymouth speeding away. *Do I tell Red about my theory?*

"Sure did. It really pisses me off, too. I have no idea when it happened, but some son of a bitch went to the effort of plowing out my driveway at some point during the winter. Do you have any idea who'd do that?"

Perhaps Biff jumped to conclusions. "I don't, but … come to think of it, I was out on a fuel run near Nimrod—I think it was around November—and I saw a car that seemed to be casing your place. It looked as if he were about to turn into your driveway, but when he saw me, he let off his brakes, and took off."

"No shit?"

"I got a pretty good look at the guy while I was parked at the stop sign at the Nimrod road. The guy had a funny old hat and was smoking a cigar. It happened after the Stewart boy had been killed, so I paid close attention and reported it. The guy drove a 1950 Plymouth, dark blue. They put out an A.P.B."

"You don't say," Red said calmly but his eyes flickered with anger.

Wally wanted Red to keep talking, hoping to confirm Biff's theory somehow. "So, you were still in Arizona when this Troost fellow hung himself from the Blue Knife Bridge?"

Red nodded. "About then, yeah. I get the newspaper sent to Mesa, so I followed what was going on up here, but to be honest, I had a lot of insurance papers to deal with and didn't give it too much mind."

Neither man said nor did anything until Red broke the awkward silence. "So, a blue Plymouth, huh?"

"For a while, I thought the guy might have been a suspect, but as it turns out, he had nothing to do with any of the foul play. He might've been your guy, though. How bad was the break-in?"

"I didn't leave anything valuable, so it was mostly just rummaging through my stuff." Red let out an awkward laugh. "You know, Wally, when you get to my age, life is supposed to get easier. This has been the worst fucking winter of my life."

Do I have the balls to ask it? "This spring isn't shaping up to be a winner, either," Wally countered, handing the clipboard back. He went for it: "Is there a reason Haggard's been buying oil from Brainerd?"

Red frowned. "Yeah, I saw that too. A fellow leaves for a few months and shit falls apart. They've, uh … been quarrying that granite seam while I've been away. We've got our contract with you guys for the main season, so I guess they went with Brainerd just to keep the accounts separate. Now that things are firing up again, we're going back to Ulman. Nothing to worry about, Wally."

Keeping it off the books. Jimmy might be right about his tunnel.

"Well, if it keeps raining like this, you're going to need to buy another pump to keep up. Don't get yourself trapped down here."

"Don't worry about me. Those pumps can keep up with any rains. Do you remember that storm three years ago that dumped eight-inches? If they can keep up with that, they can keep up with this."

Even if Red belongs to Eos, he's just a foot soldier. Haggard is putting him in danger working in conditions like this. "I don't know. It's getting awfully sporty out there. Lake Manitou is up a couple of feet. It's close to cresting."

"Well, the edge of the quarry is ten feet above flood stage, and before it would flood this quarry, it would go right over Split Rock Creek and into the Crow Wing River. I'll be safe."

"Okay, take care, Red. See you soon."

Wally got back into his truck and looked over at the glove box. Even though he couldn't prove it, his gut told him the Forsberg kid might be right about Red Dobie.

Was he the man in the ski mask—or a red herring?

Summerbirds

Split Rock High School
March 19, 1962

JIMMY NIELSON STOPPED when he saw the massive snowflakes draped in front of the school windows. After a weekend of heavy rain, winter returned before lunch. Normally, it would have been a beautiful scene, with fluffy snow falling through the air just a degree below freezing, but winter had gone on far too long, and Jimmy wanted green leaves and grass to return.

"Think we'll get out early?" Biff asked, behind him.

"I hope not," Jimmy said. "We need to get tutored today after school, remember?"

Jimmy glanced over at the high school kids to see Nicki Guerin laughing as if there weren't a care in the world. He loved and hated her. *How can she carry on like that when she knows what's really out there?*

Chris walked up with a tray full of food and sat down next to them. "I don't think we're ever going to get to play baseball this spring."

Forget baseball. "If we do get out early, we need to meet. You guys could come to my house," Jimmy offered. "I think we need to make a visit to Mizheekay Island anyway. I've been reading all about islands in Chippewa mythology, and from what Father Guerin wrote, I think they have some special meaning. My sister could drive us.”

“Will Alexandra be able to get me home in time for chores? I don’t want to get stuck at your house or my dad will get all pissy.”

“And maybe you can get her to stay a while after school so we can meet with Mrs. Crain?” Chris suggested.

Jimmy looked over at the senior table where his sister sat with her friends, laughing. “If we get out of school early, she won’t want to stay. Mrs. Crain won’t want to stay either, not with it snowing so hard. She has to drive all the way over to Sterling Junction. But I’ll see if Alexandra will let you guys come with.”

During the span of lunch, two inches of white fluff coated the cars in the parking lot, and when the bell rang to send students back to class, Principal Carlson was nowhere to be seen. Sure enough, just as students were sitting down for attendance, the intercom ping brought a hush.

“May I have your attention,” Principal Carlson began. “I just received word from the Hiawatha County Sheriff’s department that due to high water levels, the Crow Wing Bridge south of town has been closed. As a result, all traffic should take Highway 34 east or west of town. Again, Highway 19 has been closed south of town due to high water. We will be dismissing school at 12:30. There will be no extra-curricular activities. Once again, we will be dismissing school at 12:30.”

JIMMY COULD NOT focus as the clock slowly ticked away the last few minutes. When the bell finally rang, he bolted to the senior hallway to find Alexandra.

“Can Chris and Biff come with us?”

“You can pick one.”

“Oh, come on.”

“One,” Alexandra insisted.

"Fine," Jimmy muttered and hustled down to the seventh-grade lockers, only to find Biff walking toward him.

"So?" Biff asked.

"Yeah, she'll give you a ride. Where's Chris?"

"His mom left a message that he's supposed to go help at the lumber yard. They need help with sandbagging."

That decides things. "Really? It's that bad?"

"Apparently."

Jimmy and Biff walked down to the commons and waited for Alexandra to come down the stairs. She all but ignored them, walking a step faster so both had to trail her by a few steps.

Once inside the car, she acknowledged them as they sat in the backseat. "Do you think they closed the Doc Jenkins Bridge?"

"I doubt it," Biff answered. "It's a trestle bridge, so it won't plug like the ones south of town."

Biff was right, but it was a realization shared by most of the other locals, who ignored the lengthy detour north of town to take the shortcut on Old Copper Road. Market Street traffic had backed up three blocks due to the road closed signs, and even when Alexandra turned toward home, they were stuck behind Bus 12, which chose the same shortcut in order to reach the farms south of town.

The water passing below the Doc Jenkins Bridge was so violent that a heavy mist rose from the channel like rain, forcing Alexandra to turn on her windshield wipers. As they climbed the hill, the bus kicked up muddy splatter that further dirtied the view.

"For Pete's sake," Alexandra huffed.

"Don't drive so close to it," Jimmy scolded.

"Pull over in my driveway," Biff added. "I'll clean it off with some snow."

Alexandra listened and pulled over. Biff exited from the rear passenger door and grabbed a fistful of snow, slapping it onto the windshield, and with help from the wipers, quickly cleared some mud. He slapped on another handful of snow, and between swipes from the wiper, he used his coat sleeve to wipe off the heaviest of the mud.

As Jimmy sat uselessly in the backseat, he saw Mrs. Crain and her daughters drive past them. He gave a little wave, realizing that she also had to take the shortcut in order to reach her home in Sterling Junction.

When Alexandra pulled back onto the road, they were the fourth of five cars in the convoy. Even from the backseat, Jimmy could see a maroon car, the bus, and Mrs. Crain descending the hill toward Kanaranzi Creek. A pair of headlights appeared on the opposite side of the hill.

"Holy shit," Biff muttered as they passed the Guerin Farm.

Lake Manitou had swallowed half of Louis Guerin's southern field. Instead of a field of reeds and a ten-foot sliver of water, a quarter mile of floodwater pressed against Old Copper Road, which now acted like a dike against the rising water.

"Should we turn around, Jimmy?" Alexandra questioned.

"They're not stopping," Biff observed as the green car continued toward the culverts and the lowest point of the road.

Jimmy was so focused on the passage of the green car that he didn't see the nightmare unfolding until it was almost too late.

"Oh no, no, no, no NOOO!!!!" Alexandra ended with a scream.

Jimmy had to lean toward Biff to catch sight of School Bus 12 turning onto its side as the soft shoulder of Old Copper Road crumbled into the lake. The nose of the bus hit the water, sending a wave that violently recoiled. A moment later, the bus rolled like an overturned turtle, its dark underside showing the exposed wheels.

In shock, Alexandra stopped just as Biff darted out the door. When Jimmy opened his door, he was almost hit by the car approaching them.

They are all going to drown.

Jimmy ran down the hill. Despite the volume of his own pounding heart and lungs, Jimmy could hear screaming: screaming from Mrs. Crain as she stood outside her car along the ditch, screaming from her daughters inside of the car, and screaming from the children inside the half-submerged bus.

And other voices too.

He heard some voices encouraging him to jump in the water to go save the children; other voices warned him of certain death if he jumped into the water.

As he reached the spot where the shoulder collapsed, he paused for a moment, saw the rear exit door of the bus a good ten yards from shore—and noticed it was moving in the current.

Biff, however, did not stop, and although Jimmy arrived at the water's edge a few heartbeats before him, Biff leapt without hesitation into the icy waters. A moment later, he popped up out of the water halfway to the bus.

Jimmy had no choice.

Biff was his blood brother.

The jump from the top of the ditch took Jimmy completely under water. As a young boy, he and his sisters would play in the shallow waters between the shore property of his farmstead and Mizheekay Island. Even though they were several years older, Jimmy could always hold his breath longer. Today after jumping into the frigid water, he began to wonder if he'd taken his final breath.

The voices in his mind came into sharper focus as the chaos grew stronger. Some told him he was about to die while others called for him to keep fighting to reach the bus.

His feet found the bottom of the slough and propelled him back to the surface, where the rear of the bus loomed in front of him. The current had pulled him toward the undercarriage, which provided him with a metal ladder to climb. Finally, pulling himself completely out of the water, he saw Biff at the exit door.

Because of the downward angle of how the bus entered the water, the butt of the bus was the highest point out of the water with the nose almost fully submerged.

"Help me with the door," Biff shouted, working against gravity and friction as he held on with one hand and tried to open the door with the other.

Jimmy grabbed hold of the corner of the bus with his left hand and trying not to slide right into the lake again, clutched at the door with numb fingertips. Together, he and Biff threw the door open, and the shrieks and cries of children filled the air.

"Don't worry!" Jimmy shouted. "We'll get you out of here."

He held onto the edge of the open doorway and grabbed one child after another and handed them to Biff, who stayed outside the bus.

Unfortunately, water was filling the overturned bus faster than they could evacuate it.

"Hurry up, Jimmy!" Biff urged. "The bus is starting to move."

The seats were on the ceiling and the ceiling had formed a metallic slide that prevented the smallest children from easily reaching him. The seams in the roof were the only friction the children could cling to—so Jimmy let go of the doorway. His body was so cold it'd become numb. Holding onto the upside-down seats, Jimmy descended knee deep in the water, letting the smaller children use him as a bridge of sorts.

Toward the nose of the bus, he could see the body of the bus driver, whose back emerged from the water. Two blonde haired girls were shoulder deep in the water, having twice lost their footing.

One by one, he passed the remaining children up to Biff. Through the window, he could see a man standing chest deep in the water, creating a chain that took the children from Biff and handed them to Mrs. Crain, who stood knee deep in water along the incline of the ditch.

"Get out of there!" a bearded man with a funny hat called from outside of the bus.

"There are still two more kids!" Jimmy shouted back, and with the encouragement of the voices in his mind, he let go of the seat he held. He slid down the bus roof into the darkening water, and emerged from with one girl in the crook of his left arm and the other draped over his back like a wet cape.

"Don't worry, girls," Jimmy explained. "I gotcha."

The bus rolled slightly. The tops of the seats emerged from the brown water. With his free hand, Jimmy pulled himself and both girls out of the depths and towards the door.

Jimmy looked in horror as the road was now thirty feet away. On the shore, the man had pulled Biff safely onto the bank.

"We're going to have to jump in," Jimmy explained looking at them. "Hold on as tight as you can."

Both girls were terrified yet nodded.

Jimmy's chest ached from the cold and his skin stung. He could feel an even sharper pain in his fingers. Still, Jimmy held the one little girl's hand tight enough that the waters wouldn't pull her away. As all three of them tossed in the current, Jimmy felt something unnatural begin —the spirits of the dead had come up from the depths.

Even in the darkness of the water, he could sense them, and the harder they pulled on the little girl whose hand he held, the deeper they dragged him into the water. He felt their freezing fingers clawing at his grip.

No. Please.

She slipped—they had her.

She was gone.

With the other girl clinging onto his neck and back, he found his last shred of reserve and propelled himself to the shore.

When Nancy Crain's hands reached for him—they burned. She pulled the little girl off him, and with his hands and feet firmly placed on the side of the ditch, he took a deep breath without weight around his throat.

He had a chance.

He turned, and though he could not see the other girl break the surface, he could see the current heading toward the three culverts.

Taking a deep breath, he filled his lungs, only to feel a man's hands reach under his armpits to hoist him out of the water.

"No, I can get her!"

The voices were silent in his mind.

Two souls had been claimed but countless others were standing with Mrs. Crain and Biff on the gravel road.

Still, Jimmy struggled.

"She's gone," the man holding him said. "You did all you could do."

The man was right. When Jimmy was lowered on the gravel bed of Old Copper Road, his muscles turned to mush, and he fell onto his side like a rag doll. The bearded man with the funny hat lifted Jimmy back up and put his arm around him as they both shivered.

With his face pressed against the wet tweed of the man's jacket, Jimmy watched as the bus rolled toward the culverts that led to Buffalo Slough.

Fight in the Dog

Split Rock, MN
March 19, 1962

CHRIS LUNING CALCULATED how fast the floodwaters were rising. Each time he tossed a new sandbag on the earthen dike, he would look across the Crow Wing River for the dead oak tree whose trunk served as a marker for him. When he'd arrived home from school, the water reached the bottom of a crooked branch, yet within an hour it was six inches up the bank from where it had been.

"Getting tired?" Billie Morrisette, the man who asked it, was turning to retrieve another sandbag as Chris looked at him.

On my honor, I will do my best. Chris shook his head.

Two-dozen men from the lumberyard had built a formidable dike in the span of a day. One wall of sandbags protected the bank nearest the mill; the second wall grew to protect the house. Luckily, the growth of the sandbag wall outpaced the rise of the river.

For now.

But a scout will help people at all times.

A truck came flying over the railroad tracks so fast that the front wheels went airborne until it came skidding to a stop on the gravel.

"Steve Knutson!" the man in the truck bellowed.

A man near Chris straightened his back after dropping the bag and waved his arm. "Here!"

The man in the truck sprinted toward him as Mr. Knutson jogged to cut down the distance. "There's been a bus accident involving your daughters. You've got to come quick."

The two men took off running, leaving Chris stunned. In just a matter of seconds, the truck took off, speeding away across the railroad tracks.

His father, who'd been organizing the men filling the sandbags, jogged over to him.

"What was that about?"

"The man in the truck said there had been a bus accident involving his daughters," Chris meekly explained.

"He lives in town," another man said, coming to join them. "Up on Seventh Avenue."

"Steve married a Tveit," another chimed in, "the red-haired gal who works at the bank. Her folks live south of town."

Soon, all the men had gathered around. From what Chris gleaned, Steve Knutson was the foreman at the sawmill and equal to his father in the hierarchy of Fisher Lumber. His two daughters, Molly and Danika, had taken the bus because of the early dismissal to stay with their maternal grandparents, who lived six miles south of Split Rock.

When the screen door of the house slammed, all the men paused as his mother came out with her overcoat hastily thrown over her shoulders. "There's been an accident with a school bus. It went off the road and fell into the waters of Buffalo Slough."

Nothing else needed to be said. The men immediately bolted for their vehicles, and the lumberyard filled with the roar of vehicles speeding away. Chris found himself alone with his mother, who put a hand on his shoulder as they walked back toward the house.

The telephone rang, and she jogged for the door.

By the time Chris slipped off his muddy boots, she was mid-conversation with whoever called. She pressed the caller for details about the accident, but all Chris heard were a series of "oh my" and "oh dear" before she stared directly at him with wide eyes.

"What hospital?" After the answer was given, she whispered, "Hypothermia."

His mother looked away, and the one-sided conversation continued on until Chris moved to regain his mother's attention. "What's happened?

"One moment," his mother told the caller, cupping her hand over the bottom of the receiver. "Jimmy and Biff were on the bus and helped pull most of the kids to safety, but they've both gone into shock because of the cold. They're being taken to the hospital in Brainerd."

It's happening. Nicki was right. Our war has begun. Chris shook his head, refusing to believe what he heard. "They didn't take a bus. They were with Alexandra in a car."

"What?"

"Biff went home with Jimmy and his sister. They weren't on a bus."

She turned back to the phone, and for a few minutes, she and the caller talked.

"What did she say?" Chris asked, impatient.

"She was pretty certain about the names being Jimmy Nielson and Biff Forsberg. Mrs. Crain saw the accident and helped bring the rescued children back to the MacPherson farm, where Ida tried to keep them warm. After they called 911, Ida called her brother-in-law Donnie, who brought Jimmy and Biff directly to the hospital because they were the worst off." His mother paused. "I need to call Edna to make sure she knows."

The hospital means they are alive. But what about Nicki? And Gavin? And Mrs. Crain?

Ten minutes passed without any news of his friends as his mother went from call to call trying to glean information. Overwhelmed and frustrated, Chris slipped on his boots and walked outside.

Sandbags remained where they had been dropped, yet the river still roared. The big snowflakes had turned into drizzle. When he reached the dike, he could see that the water neared the upper crook of the oak tree, rising another few inches since he'd left.

They were losing the fight.

Chris began to walk, following the flow of the Crow Wing River past his property and into the eastern woods. The recent rains had erased his worn trail in the snow, and now a muddy trail emerged.

He followed the path for a quarter mile, and when he reached the monstrous oak tree, the rope swing was no longer tucked into the board nailed onto the trunk of the tree. Instead, the thick barn rope dragged in the current of the flooded river. The wooden plank and knot that had served as a foothold had been devoured.

He looked to the other bank, where the deer stand stood near the shore, and moving between the birch trees, he saw gray figures.

Counting didn't matter, for he knew exactly how many he saw—twelve Tak-Pei. Some stood snarling at him while others slinked through the shadows, heading north.

Chris reached down and picked up a rotting branch four inches thick and two feet long. He hurled it across the river, where it struck the trunk of a birch tree before shattering into pieces.

Now all the Tak-Pei were leaving and gave him little attention. Only one stopped and lingered for a moment as its beady eyes stared back at Chris, who reached for another object to throw. He peeled a stone from the cold ground, but by the time he prepared to toss it, the twelfth monster followed the rest of the pack heading north.

What if something happened to Biff and Jimmy?

Did kids die in the bus accident?

Seeing the Tak-Pei on the opposite shore made some sense. The flowing waters of the Crow Wing River, which led to the Mississippi and then the Gulf and the ocean, served as an eastern barrier.

Why were they at the deer stand?

If the journal was right, the Tak-Pei served only one purpose and master—the evil spirit known simply as the Wintermaker.

Yet the Tak-Pei had initially gathered at the deer stand, and more likely than not, had used their foul magic to keep him from crossing.

Why did they try to stop me from getting to it? He suddenly knew the answer. *The dreamcatcher!*

Chris ran. His feet slipped from time to time, and once he completely wiped out, falling onto his side, but he ran until his lungs ached. When he burst out of the wooded river valley, he did not follow the road back to the lumberyard or his house.

I need an ally.

Instead, he ran toward Grandpa Albert's house.

By the time he passed the old, haunted house and Lyons Park, he knew he was close, and when he found the two brick pillars at the end of the long driveway, he paused for a moment before pounding on the door. When it opened, Grandpa Albert stood fully dressed in his winter jacket.

Grandpa Albert's eyes were wide at first, and he recoiled somewhat in fear, but then he cleared his throat and said, "I guess the moment has arrived. I'm glad I won't have to do this alone."

Do what alone? "I saw them on the other side of the river, heading north," Chris said. "They saw me from across the river and couldn't do anything."

Grandpa Albert nodded. His brow still had yellow bruises from his accident at the boat landing "I think I know where they are heading."

They headed toward the garage. Halfway there, Grandpa Albert stopped, winded from the walk. "They might be responsible for this foul weather, using it to divide us. We need to gather as many of the others as we can."

Chris nodded as they started walking. "Jimmy Nielson and Biff Forsberg just went to the hospital with hypothermia."

"Yes, I heard it on the police scanner," his grandfather said as he opened the door to the garage. "The accident has taken all of them away from us in our hour of need, including Wally. I know I must act, but I don't know what I should do."

"I do," Chris said firmly, and his grandfather pivoted around to size him up. "We need to go the deer stand."

His grandfather listened without judgment as Chris told him his theory, and within minutes, the two of them were in a line of cars on Market Street approaching South Street. When they got closer, Chris could see a police car with flashing lights as well as wooden barriers blocking off access to Old Copper Road. One by one, the police officer waved off onlookers—except for Grandpa Albert, who was surprisingly let through the barricade.

Chris peered out the passenger window for a glimpse of the angry waters of the Crow Wing River. "Do you really think the Tak-Pei are responsible for the weather?"

"Yes. When I was a boy, they summoned powerful storms to achieve their goals, and once again, they have used the weather to claim the last victims. The man who tried to kill you will soon learn this and know that his time to act has come. God saw fit to spare your life to serve a purpose. I just hope we will understand why."

At the top of the hill, Chris studied the Forsberg farm, but as expected, it was silent and empty. Glen, Edna, and young Julia had likely by now reached Brainerd to be with Biff.

The road was muddy and rutted, a sign that numerous emergency vehicles had driven there the past few hours. The clock on his grandfather's car read 4:53, but it seemed a lifetime ago that he, Biff, and Jimmy were sitting in the commons watching the big snowflakes fall.

Nearing the MacPherson farm, the first flashing lights materialized. A Hiawatha County Sheriff's deputy car parked at the end of the driveway and as they approached, the deputy stepped out to intercept them. While the deputy walked up to his grandfather's window, Chris could see a dozen more flashing lights a mile further down the road.

"I have important information for Sheriff Betzing," Grandpa Albert said, and from a pocket inside of his coat, he removed a small piece of paper.

"He's down at the accident site," the deputy responded, not reaching for the note. "Park by the house and I'll tell him you're waiting."

His grandfather rolled up his window and turned onto the MacPherson driveway, but he stopped after a few yards. "It'll be dark in a few hours, and there is no way I can climb a tree anyway. I will find the MacPherson boy and let him know what is happening. Do you have the pendant I gave your father?"

"What pendant?"

"The Heart of the Oak. He was supposed to give it to you."

Chris's heart fluttered. He only put it on at night and took it off in the morning. It was still on his end table. "No."

"Ah, it is only a piece of wood … When I was a boy, I was a runty little thing—not strong and athletic like you. My father told me, 'It's not the size of the dog in the fight; it's the size of the fight in the dog.' As soon as I step out of the car, I'll be noticed. But you—can you do this part on your own?"

"I'm not afraid of the Tak-Pei," Chris boasted, hoping his bravado would give him the courage he needed. "The deer stand is only five minutes away. A few pieces of cloth are tied to trees marking it. If I take too long and you need to, come find me. Plus, Gavin knows the way."

"Let's hope we don't have to find you."

I'll show everybody that I can be a hero. "I'll be back in a jiffy," Chris said and exited the car. He flanked the deputy's car widely enough not to be seen and darted across Old Copper Road and into the wooded ditch.

The three R's of personal safety are recognize, respond, and report.

He looked around for the gray creatures but saw nothing and felt nothing, and before he knew it, his hands were reaching for the boards leading up to the deer stand.

Chris didn't recognize any obvious danger.

He turned the thick latch and ducked as the trap door swung down. As he climbed into the cold yet dry shelter, he left the trap door open so enough light could fill the little room.

There, in the corner, he saw the dreamcatcher Nicki Guerin had hung in the corner the last time they'd all been together. Chris also found the prayer cloths and opened the folded fabric.

Is this what drew the Tak-Pei?

Chris looked over the strange syllables handwritten by Lily Guerin and cleared his throat. Instead of vocalizing the phrases, he carefully put them in his pocket.

Then he heard a strange clicking noise.

He flinched but didn't know where or how to hide. *I should report to Grandpa Albert.*

The second time he heard the strange rattling noise, he stood, peering out the window. Three ebony ravens sat in the tree.

They are talking to each other.

"What do you want?" Chris asked.

One raven turned and flew southwest over Old Copper Road. A second raven flew right at him before veering onto a northern path across the Crow Wing River toward Bleeding Rock.

The third raven stayed put. It let out a loud, guttural yawn, followed by a hoarse command, "Look."

Look at what? I'm looking right at you.

"Look!" the raven repeated.

The dreamcatcher.

Chris lifted the loom of feather and sinew. Nicki had expected a vision to appear immediately when they first looked into it—a spirit from Lake Manitou. Yet they had waited with no results and had left it to check back again later.

Everyone has forgotten except me.

As Chris lifted it up, his eyes looked through the tiny windows within the loom—nothing. Then he took the dreamcatcher to the window and pointed it in the direction of the raven, which had vanished. But holding the dreamcatcher in front of his face, the woods around the Crow Wing River began to change. The trees changed.

A face didn't appear—at first.

CHAPTER FIFTY-ONE

The Halls of Hades

Lake Manitou
March 19, 1962

WALLY CRAIN TOOK his boat out of gear, allowing the current to freely spin him. He sank down in his seat as grief sat upon his shoulders.

Thank God I wasn't the one to find her.

The nose of his fishing boat hit the soft edge of the ditch, lurching him forward before spinning him like a leaf on the surface of the water. Men on the road were pointing to the slough south of the road.

Having served in war, Wally had seen the faces of friends killed by the Japanese, but finding the corpse of a little girl would've been too much to take.

"Ken!" Wally shouted out as Ken Uselman crossed the gravel road in front of him. "Grab my anchor rope." Wally tossed the rope, and it stretched from the boat to the gravel road.

The fire chief picked up the rope, crossed the post of a highway sign, and pulled Wally's aluminum fishing boat onto the slope of the ditch. With the remaining rope, Wally harnessed it and carefully walked to the nose to jump ashore.

Thirty men, dressed in the civilian clothes they were wearing when the emergency call went out, watched as a duck boat fought the current exiting from the culverts. A moment later, David MacPherson carried the lifeless body of Danika Knutson to shore.

A wail came from her father, interrupted only by the frenzied efficiency of the local emergency workers. Yes, the girl looked dead, but miracles had happened before with drowning victims in frigid waters.

Yet Wally held no hope for the girl. A few minutes in the water was one thing. The girl had been lost for a few hours.

When the ambulance doors closed, Wally saw Sheriff Don Betzing and Fire Chief Ken Uselman standing away from the culverts and focusing on the rising waters of Lake Manitou. A crew of deputies sent the do-gooders back to their cars.

Dean Hoemberg was one of them. He split off from the MacPherson brothers, who were consoling David. He stopped next to Wally, whose hands were on hips as he looked out at the half-sunken school bus. "Woulda been a lot more dead if not for your boys."

My boys.

Wally had only fathered daughters, and at the suggestion of his wife, he'd found his paternal release through his scouts. From his wife's first frantic retelling to Dean Hoemberg, Biff Forsberg and Jimmy Nielson were credited for saving countless school children on the bus.

The kids were ready. Where were you?

An hour earlier, after Nancy returned home with the girls, Wally had hitched his boat to the truck and had driven right to Chippewa Beach, where he launched it without a dock and raced to the far end of the lake to help search for Danika Knutson.

Now, two more souls joined the others.

"You get the lowdown on what happened yet?" Wally asked.

Dean repeated what his wife had already told him about the first ten minutes after the accident. "Donnie got your boys to the hospital before hypothermia killed them."

Waiting for an ambulance might've taken the lives of both boys.

"The Nielson boy is doing better. He's pulled out of the shock. Donnie wasn't sure if the kid was going to make it."

That boy is our future. We need all of them to fill the Isanti Lodge. "How about Biff?"

"The Forsberg boy was a bit blue but talked the whole way to Brainerd. He helped keep the Nielson boy conscious."

"And the rest of the children are going to make it?"

"Molly Knutson seems like she's going to pull through even though she was in that lake for quite a while."

"Damn weather."

"I talked to Ray Kirkpatrick," Dean began, looking at the angry lake, "and the good news is that the Nicollet Dam is holding strong. Apparently, they've got a couple feet left before it flows over all four gates."

"Who do you suppose is tending the spillway gates at the Old Mill?" Wally asked.

"Oh geez," Dean said, scratching his head. "Steve Knutson is, um … isn't he?"

"Marlin Luning's sure to think of that."

Dean took a step away toward his car, parked up the hill nearer the MacPherson farm. "Sheriff Betzing tried to convince Louis Guerin to evacuate, but he insisted his farmstead was built on a hill."

"What hill?" Wally mocked. The water had already crested over the driveway, making the rest of the farm an island that rose just a few feet above the level of the lake.

"The county needs to issue some sort of flood warning system for fools like Guerin. This weather is getting scary. Even if it stopped raining right now, there's enough water coming down the Blue Knife to put all those lake homes in jeopardy, not to mention Split Rock itself."

"Are the Guerins in trouble?" Wally asked, looking back to his boat.

"Naw. He might end up killing his livestock, but his family will be safe waiting out the flood upstairs."

"He could bring the animals upstairs," Wally joked.

"Or haul the sheep up into the hay loft," Dean countered.

"I saw he has his big duck boat out and ready," Wally said, pointing to the exposed beginning of the driveway. "If the water keeps rising, he'll be able to use it to reach Old Copper Road."

But I better fill this back up with gas. I might need to come back and rescue the Guerins if things go sour. "Can you give me a shove?"

HALF AN HOUR later, Wally's boat was back on the trailer and he was heading home. Luckily, the roads to Sterling Junction were well-built with steep ditches and a hard-packed gravel base. Even at that, the rain, snow, and run off turned it into a slippery mess.

When he pulled into his home, Nancy stood at the front door.

Wally left the truck running and the lights on so that he could avoid getting drawn into a long conversation. Nancy would want details, and he didn't want to have to talk about the Knutson girl until he was done for the night.

As he approached, he called out to her through the glass. "I need some cash to go get gas for the boat."

Nancy didn't move from the door window.

"I need you to look at this first," Nancy said, handing him a stack of papers—one of her manuscripts.

He accepted it but took a moment to study his wife. She and his daughters had witnessed a traumatic accident, and while the girls were nowhere to be seen, Nancy didn't seem to be coping. "How are you doing?"

"I got the girls to bed early, but when I was in the shower, I suddenly remembered this. Look at it."

Wally glanced down. For a decade his wife had been hammering away on manuscripts that attempted to modernize mythology. He spotted the names Orpheus and Eurydice. "What am I looking for?"

"You don't remember, do you?"

Wally reread the page:

And Eurydice danced with the naiads, casting away her fears for her own life. For she knew the only way to escape the Halls of Hades was to learn the secrets of the water nymphs that protected their dark master. She needed them to love her. So, she drank from their cup and danced along the edge of the water, committing each note and verse to memory.

"I will teach the song to my love, Orpheus," Eurydice told herself. "All of this, I do for him."

She gave herself to the naiads, the spirits of the water.

When Apollo's serpent learned of her duplicity—

"Why are you showing this to me?"

"The naiads are water spirits, Wally. The Tak-Pei. Apollo's serpent? The Horned Serpent. I dreamt all of this under our willow tree. Remember how I spoke about my love story? The one between Orpheus and Eurydice. They're both singers."

"I don't—"

"Nicole and Gavin! She dies and descends into the depths, and he follows her. Something is happening, Wally. Here. At Lake Manitou. My dreams and reality are crashing together."

Does she mean this? Is she just hysterical? "Honey, you had a rough day."

"No! No, don't do that. Don't act like I'm imagining things. This is the flood of souls I wrote about, isn't it?"

He could read an instruction manual and follow directions, but his wife could look at a poem and find a dozen meanings. Wally looked down at the stacks of papers. He'd read all five manuscripts and told her each one was wonderful, whether he understood them or not. "What do you want me to do?"

"I can't stop thinking about Nicole. Is she in danger?"

Wally nodded. "I better run into St. John and fill up the boat with gas. Can you fix me some supper to go? I'll grab it on the way back."

Just then, the phone rang, stealing their attention.

"I'll be right back, honey," Wally said, handing her the manuscript and turning back to the truck.

He'd taken no more than a few steps when Nancy called out, "Earl, Brian Forsberg is on the phone and needs to speak to you."

Wet Tweed

Brainerd, MN
March 19, 1962

THE DEAD GIRL was wheeled into the emergency room. Separated by only a white curtain, Biff could see them valiantly, and violently, try to bring life to the body of Danika Knutson. His brain finally felt like it was working again, and although his body was wrapped in electric blankets, his head and eyes could still move.

Molly Knutson, the surviving sister, had tubes sticking out of her blankets and a mask over her face. Her parents stood in the opening of the privacy curtain.

Jimmy Nielson slept on the third table. He was also wrapped in rewarming blankets, and after the doctors warmed his blood with a machine, his shivering stopped, and the heart monitor began to count his sleep. Ed, Bonnie, and Alexandra all sat by his side.

The chairs beside Biff were now empty. His little sister Julia could not control her crying, and his mother insisted on taking her into the waiting room so the doctors could focus on him. His father, when he received confirmation that Biff was stable, exited toward the waiting room doors. None of them had returned yet.

What did they do with my clothes?

Inside of his cocoon, Biff was completely naked. The nurses had used scissors to cut off his clothes in front of everyone and had even squeezed warm water on his groin before wrapping him like a mummy.

The curtain opened and the doctors stepped away from Danika, her yellow raincoat and galoshes in a pile on the floor. Warm tears filled Biff's eyes, and he looked up at the ceiling.

His breathing became panicked, which brought one of the nurses rushing over. Under the blankets, Biff found his fists clenched in rage.

"Can I get you anything, Brian?"

He shook his head.

In Donnie MacPherson's truck, he'd seen the effects of hypothermia on Jimmy: lack of coordination, slurred speech, and confusion all took hold of his body.

Has my brain warmed up enough to think clearly?

Had he known how much it would hurt, he might not have jumped in the water to get to the sinking bus. Every cell in his body ached. Because of this, Biff practiced like he was studying for a test. He started from the gravel road, replaying every detail that had happened.

The maroon car.

The bus.

Mrs. Crain.

Alexandra.

The green Renault in the other lane.

Its headlights had been on as it came up Old Copper Road toward them. The bus moved from the center of the road, where its tires found the soft ground eroding by the floodwaters.

By the time Alexandra stopped, allowing Biff to climb out, the green Renault had stopped also.

And by the time Biff had retrieved the first student, a human chain had formed—the fellow in the maroon car stood beside Alexandra on the road, waiting and watching. Mrs. Crain stood knee deep in water at the edge of the ditch, helping the children onto the road. The other fella stood waist deep in water, catching and transferring the kids.

While…

Is it all coincidence?

It wasn't a red Thunderbird this time.

Nor was it a Plymouth.

Yet the man wore the same derby hat and tweed jacket Biff had seen nine months earlier. On the same road.

Is my brain playing tricks on me?

No.

Mr. Derby Hat was a man of action. He'd seen the bus slide into the water and stopped. He, too, jumped from his car and ran down to take action while Alexandra and Mr. Maroon Car just watched. Then he cast aside danger to wade into the water. He didn't think. He acted.

Yet when Jimmy was pulled back out of the water, Mr. Derby Hat took only a moment to catch his breath before slipping away to the green Renault.

Where was it? I know I looked.

In Mr. Stevens' Science 7 class, he learned the human brain, taking in data from open eyes, processed countless images of information per second. Even a few hours later, Biff's brain threw away most of what he'd seen to remember the trauma of the overturned bus and the cold needles in his flesh. He couldn't even remember what Mr. Maroon Car looked like.

Biff took a deep breath and returned to the moments before the trauma. The green Renault came down the hill, putting its brakes on near the culverts … then it slowly accelerated toward the convoy.

It passed Alexandra's car.

Biff looked at it.

Mr. Derby Hat sat in the front seat, but it wasn't the white-suited Indian, Charani Bessant, sitting in the backseat. No, that was another memory. This time, it was…

Miss Olavintytär.

His loins tightened the first time he'd seen her sitting at the fire in Nova Scotia, and thinking of her again, his balls felt cold.

Saara.

Mr. Derby Hat, ever the loyal servant, quickly returned to her and they drove off before the emergency vehicles—and the law—arrived, vanishing like fog upon the surface of the lake. The green Renault drove off toward town while everyone else waited.

Why would they be coming to town?

Biff pushed his heated blankets aside, and despite being naked, he risked the nurses to stretch his cables to the adjacent wall. With a glance, he punched the button for the outside line.

"Hello?" Mrs. Crain answered.

"Hi, this is Biff Forsberg. Is Wally home?"

"Why … yes… um … one second."

He could hear her call out for her husband, and a few seconds later, Wally answered, "What is it, Biff?"

"He's driving a green Renault and was heading toward Split Rock."

An Old Promise

Old Copper Road
March 19, 1962

SEVERAL VEHICLES DROVE up the hill toward the MacPherson farm including an ambulance and a truck driven by Steve Knutson.

They found the second girl, Albert Fischer realized as the ambulance drove past the farm. The accident scene shifted into motion as emergency workers down by the culverts and up at the farm also realized the tragedy reached a conclusion. In the somber chaos, Christopher emerged from the woods, looked both ways before crossing the gravel road, and continuing up the driveway to where Albert waited.

The sound of an engine caught Albert's attention, and when he turned, he spotted Wally Crain's boat heading across the lake.

Chris had to step into the ditch as several vehicles from the culverts drove up to the big yard.

Ken Uselman and Dean Hoemberg helped escort David Mac-Pherson into the house. Sheriff Betzing, seeing Albert watching with the others, walked over to explain what had just happened. As Albert listened, he added Danika Knutson to the list of deaths.

Chris stood beside him, a solemn expression on his face. Albert put his arm around the boy.

Sheriff Betzing ended his update with a gentle, "Now go home."

I'll call Wally in an hour—once he gets home. Albert guided Chris to the passenger door before walking around the front of the vehicles. Everywhere, car engines were starting and departing the MacPherson farm. At the end of the driveway, barricades were being set up to prevent anyone from accessing the crime scene on either side of Old Copper Road.

"Grandpa," Chris said as soon as Albert sat down in the driver's seat. Chris opened his jacket to show the willow dreamcatcher tucked away.

"Yes, yes, you have it," Albert said, feeling like the forgetful old man he'd become. From the boy's expression, Albert knew there was more. "What did you see?"

"I'm not sure," Chris said, squeezing his lips together tightly. "I first saw ravens and then … it was looking in a kaleidoscope. It's all gone now. I think the magic wore off, but for a bit, it was like looking into the past and future at the same time."

"And … what did you see?"

"Somebody was looking for me."

Thoughts of the Wintermaker filled Albert's mind. Years earlier, Lily told Albert about the dangers of the monster that lived in the water, how it was searching for a young victim to become the Omodai. Instead of taking him, Joseph Little Toad abducted Migisi, offering him as a living sacrifice to the dark god. *Is that what happened to the Knutson girl?*

The moment of panic subsided, followed by protectiveness. "Tell me very clearly about this person."

"It was a girl, I think. She said her name was Robin."

Robin!

"What's wrong, Grandpa? Do you know her?"

The loop was closed. I've done my part.

"Grandpa?"

"Yes, I know the name." Albert had waited a lifetime to close the loop of the past and future. A young Lily went under the willow tree in front of the convent, where an old man in a metal chair waited. Months earlier, Albert sat upon his metal folding chair as the apparition of Lily visited him from the past. *Closed.*

Or was it?

"There was a young man wearing a black hat," Albert began. "He must be from the future because…"

Levi MacPherson.

He claimed to be Lily's great-grandchild.

He said something about me being dead.

"Because what, Grandpa?" Chris asked, bringing him back to his unfinished point. "Did he say something about the flood?"

"Yes, in fact, he mentioned Robin. It was strange, so very strange. He said the Wintermaker was trying to attack the past."

"That's what Robin told me, too."

Albert felt a chill run through his body. "What did she say?"

"She said evil people had been sent to hurt me and my friends. She said a flood would kill them if I didn't do something to help. Robin said she needed me to be a hero."

"Think!" Albert's fear prompted him to snap, but he quickly softened. "What did she need you to do to save them?"

"She told me to just follow the raven."

"Follow it where?"

"She told me you already knew where to go."

The sawmill.

"Grandpa?"

But what do I need to do?

"Is Nicki Guerin going to be safe?" Chris asked.

The Guerins. Of course. Lily is an old woman, but Nicole Guerin and Gavin MacPherson need to—Levi!

"Yes, Chris. We're going to make sure she's safe."

Biff and Jimmy weren't the targets. The Knutson girls were the targets of the Tak-Pei. With Steve Knutson in Brainerd, and Marlin trying to save the house and factory, no one was minding the old sawmill. "Stay here for another minute. I need to let the others know what we need to do."

Sheriff Betzing had already left, but Ken Uselman gathered his men to help secure the roads.

The weather was getting worse, and night would soon be upon them. The front door was ajar, for a dozen people were still inside the makeshift triage unit. At the center of the chaos, David MacPherson shivered under his blankets.

Gavin MacPherson made eye contact, and Albert motioned for him to come over. From what Wally and Nancy Crain told him, the boy knew much of what was going on.

I have to trust him.

"Can I have a word with you?" Albert asked and stepped out onto the front porch.

"What is it, Mr. Fisher?"

"It's been quite a day, hasn't it?"

"Sure has."

"I'm not sure it's over. If anything, I think it's just beginning."

"Ya think?"

"You know my grandson, Christopher. He … saw something … something that led him to the deer stand across the road. Do you know what I mean?"

Gavin nodded.

He knows.

"Did the dreamcatcher…?"

Albert nodded. "Chris and I are going to drive over to the old sawmill—to keep an eye on things. I need you to make me a promise."

"Sure. What?"

Albert looked down the hill to the Guerin farm, an island in the growing floodwaters. "Keep an eye on the Guerin family for me. Keep Nicole safe."

"I will. As soon as we get everything sorted out inside, I was going to call her and make sure things are okay."

"That's a good plan. If you kids need anything, call Wally Crain."

"I'll do that. Be safe, Mr. Fisher."

"I'm a soul of caution," Albert joked, and turned to Chris waiting in the car.

We'll save the children together, Lily.

The Designs of Jeremie Bordeaux

Old Copper Road
March 19, 1962

BY SOME ACCOUNTS, the Bordeaux Farm was the first permanent structure built on the shores of Lake Manitou. Although the territory did not open to settlement until the 1850s, former fur trader Jeremie Bordeaux had already built a house, barn, and drying shed along the banks of Kanaranzi Creek when the lots went up for sale. Margerie Campbell, daughter of a Dakota translator, was gifted the land by Henry Sibley, and when she went to claim it years later, she ended up falling in love with the wily French squatter. Together, they raised almost a dozen children in the same home that watched all five of the Guerin siblings grow up.

Now, a flood threatened to wash away all the history.

After setting down a box, Nicki took a moment to catch her breath. *Did I do this?* She sensed something unnatural about the weather. *I never should have sung those words.*

Before all the chaos, Gavin had called and tried to tell her something about Christopher Luning, but the message was now all jumbled in her mind.

Christopher saw something, and it's probably all my fault.

The sweet boy she'd once babysat had gone to the lodge alone and returned with a dire message. The storm then interrupted what Nicki began.

She walked through her sister's bedroom and peered out the window. Her father was finishing tying a rope to a post near the corner of the barn. As he walked to the house, his boots sent up splashes from the wet ground, but then the water reached his ankles, and by the time he reached the center of the yard where the driveway had once been, it reached his calves. Nicki lost sight of him due to the angle of her bedroom window.

By the time she ran downstairs, he was already cursing as her mother complained about the mess he was making on the entryway floor.

"Where is Cameron?" Nicki asked.

"He's back in the barn trying to get those stupid animals up on the platform," he said before chuckling to himself. "They sure don't like standing on those planks."

"Are the animals going to be safe?" Nicki asked as her mother returned with some old towels to sop up the water her father brought inside.

"Sure, they will be safe. The barn is built on a rise, and the foundation brings it up another two feet, so they are almost three feet above the low spot out there on the driveway. If the water keeps rising, it will flow right around the house and the barn and right to Buffalo Slough. That's why I tied a rope. There might be some current later, and the rope will help us get to the animals."

"At least your father had enough sense to build the barn on a rise," Nicki's mother said with a tinge of sarcasm.

Her father rolled his eyes. "He didn't build the barn. He bought it from Jeremie Bordeaux. I'm beginning to see why he got the farmstead so cheap."

Lily wanted to be close to the lake so she could watch over it. Now, in our hour of need, she's way up at Leech Lake.

While her mother tended to her father's wet clothes and brought some hot soup to warm him, Nicki grabbed another box. Even though her father was confident about the water flowing around the house, her mother insisted on bringing the family relics upstairs so they could be safe.

She carried a box full of letters, bills, and records from her father's desk, but a moment before she would have set it down, the bottom of the box opened up, dumping the contents on her feet.

Oh, for Pete's sake.

She refolded the four flaps of the box and began scooping up the paper into some semblance of order. One letter caught her eye.

Dated 1924 from Eagle Butte, South Dakota, the letter was yellowed and ripped and addressed to her mother—Miss Hannah Mortenson. The sender of the letter was Fawn White Elk.

Dear Ms. Mortenson,

Be warned! I do not write you out of bigotry or disapproval of your youthful betrothal to my cousin's only son, Louis. I write to warn you about the consequences of marrying into a cursed family.

My family bears a terrible curse, which you, as a third-generation resident of Hiawatha County, might already understand. But the terrible past is the least of my concerns. I write to warn you of the future. Flee from Lake Manitou while you can. I know you plan to marry young Louis because you are pregnant, but if you give birth to this child, you are dooming the child to a life of misery and perhaps worse. Take your unborn child and run. Run!

If you love this child, do not allow it to become part of Lily Guerin's evil plans. Do not believe her lies. I could not reason with her, nor could I convince a son to turn against his own mother, but you—you still have a choice. Do not marry him, and for the love of God, do not allow your child to grow up near Lake Manitou.

Leave while you can!

Fawn

Nicki looked to the doorway, folded up the letter, and then slipped it into the front pocket of her shirt.

1924? That would have been Michelle. Learning her eldest sibling was born out of wedlock did not rattle her nearly as much as Fawn's dire warning to run from a marriage. *If Mother had listened, I never would have been born. I wonder why she kept this?*

A few minutes later, Cameron came in, stomping and sloshing just as her father had, much to her mother's consternation. With his help, they quickly moved the rest of the valuables upstairs and then caught their breath at the couch.

The four of them sat together in the living room, with both the television and the radio on. While the radio provided local updates and coverage, the television showed a grander view of how the strange weather had prompted flooding across the state. One report showed a man with a bow and arrow shooting sticks of dynamite into distant ice dams. Bridges, it seemed, turned into dams when the thick ice broke apart on the swollen rivers and collected against pylons.

Nicki, meanwhile, thought about Fawn's letter and her own ragged group of friends. While Jimmy and Biff avoided death today, they were taken away from Hiawatha County. The flood threatened both her home and also the home of Chris Luning.

"Will the water back up and flood us?" Cameron asked.

"It's already over the road south of town," her father said. "So, it can't get any worse for us."

"What about Kanaranzi Creek? Will the culverts plug?" Nicki asked.

"Most of the ice is already off the lake, so we should be fine. At worst, it has only three more feet before it goes right over Old Copper Road."

"Should we move our furniture upstairs?" her mother asked.

"It should be fine," her father declared.

They went on watching the storm as if it weren't merely feet outside of their door.

It had been hours since she had last heard from Gavin, so when the phone rang, she jumped from the couch and ran into the kitchen.

"Hello?" she answered, but it wasn't Gavin on the other end.

"Could I speak to Cameron?" a man asked.

Who is this? "Cameron. It's for you," Nicki called, holding the phone out to him.

"Who could that be?" Cameron wondered.

When her brother answered, Nicki lingered nearby, listening in.

The owners of Carousel Park had heard about the flooding and called the park caretaker to inquire about it. With plans on reopening in the spring, they suddenly grew nervous about their property and baited her brother into babysitting it with the promise of a hundred dollar bonus.

"Absolutely, sir," Cameron said. "I'll call back once I check on the park."

When Cameron hung up, she wanted to snatch the receiver to call Gavin, but not with her father at home. In the fall months, her father had been lukewarm about the relationship, but after Cameron's beating, he all but forced her into ending it. He saw the MacPhersons as symptomatic of the violence and hatred felt toward Indians in the community.

"Those damn people," her father muttered after hearing Cameron's explanation of the phone call.

"I don't mind checking. It's a hundred bucks, Dad."

"What if I need you here?"

"I can come back if it gets really bad, and they can keep their money," Cameron insisted.

Nicki saw an opening and took it. "I should go with him in case he gets stuck. He shouldn't go alone."

"You've got school tomorrow," her mother began, but with the weather reports on the television, there was an easy counter.

"Everyone is going to help sandbag tomorrow. All the schools near Brainerd are already closing. Cameron and I can play cards," Nicki said, and for impact, she quickly opened the junk drawer and pulled out a deck.

Her father nodded and turned back towards the television.

It hadn't been the struggle she expected, and in seconds, she was dressed and walking out the door with her brother. They climbed into his car; its back tires parked in the growing swathe of water dividing the yard.

"Listen, Cameron, I need to speak to Gavin. It's really important. When we get to the end of the driveway, let me out so I can go get him."

"I can drive you there."

"No, I don't want anyone seeing the headlights. If I can, I'll have him drive me back home or drive me down to Carousel, okay? I really need you to cover for me. It's important."

Suddenly, Cameron grew somber. "Is it about the Wintermaker?"

"I think so. The words Nokomis gave you, I … I just need to get to Gavin so I can figure stuff out."

"Okay." He started his car and backed deeper into the puddle before driving forward. She could see the second hill her father spoke of, and the driveway rose out of the water, but on the other side of the hill, the water covered the driveway where it turned toward Old Copper Road.

"How can you tell where the driveway is?" Nicki asked, suddenly panicked.

"I can see the fence posts on both sides of the ditch," Cameron explained as the car entered the larger puddle that had been two fields the previous summer. "I just need to keep it centered between the posts."

"We should go back and get the boat."

Cameron stopped and opened his door. "See, it is only a few inches deep."

"If you go off the driveway, it will be a few feet deep."

"Roll down your windows."

"Why?"

"In case I drive off the driveway we'll be able to get out." Cameron let off the brake and lightly stepped on the accelerator, creating a wake as the four tires cut through the water.

"Oh shit," Nicki said as her feet suddenly got cold. "We're sinking."

Water came roiling up from under the passenger seat floor mat.

"It's rusted through the floor," Cameron explained. "We're fine. We're heading back up the hill now.

Cameron was right, and the bulge of water that had come from the floor mat slowly drained away.

"You really need a new car, Cameron."

At the top of the driveway, he stopped. "Are you sure you don't want me to drive you there? It's raining hard."

"No. I'm fine." *Maybe we should stay together to be safe.* "Wait, can you even get to Carousel Park from here? They've closed the road where the bus went into the slough."

Cameron shrugged. "I guess I'll have to go back into town and drive all the way around Lake Manitou."

When they reached the MacPherson driveway, Nicki hesitated. "Can you wait here for a minute? If I can't get Gavin's attention, I'll stay with you then, okay? Turn off your lights and wait here for one song, okay?"

"I'll wait for two songs."

"Thank you, Cameron," she said and kissed him on the cheek.

Out in the rain, Nicki jogged up the driveway and stood outside peering into the well-lit, big lavender house. As her family did, the MacPherson family gathered around the television in the living room to listen to the news.

Before long Gavin rose from one of the green recliners and walked into the kitchen, giving Nicki her chance. She picked up a pebble from the driveway and walked up to the kitchen window, and as Gavin walked to the refrigerator, she tossed it against the glass, creating a loud plinking noise.

Luckily, he noticed it, and like a confused puppy, tilted his head toward the sound. When she stepped into the light coming from the window, he jumped and took a step back before leaning toward the window.

Nicki held her finger to her lips and pointed to the rear door of the mudroom. Gavin nodded and Nicki ran around to the rear of the house and waited outside the back door.

Gavin slowly opened the door and stepped out to stand with her under the awning. "What are you doing?"

"You need to finish what you were telling me about Chris Luning."

Gavin closed the door, joining her in the cold. "He went back to the deer stand without us. He said he saw not only Tak-Pei in the woods, but also someone in the dreamcatcher."

"He saw someone?"

Gavin nodded. "There was a spirit waiting for him."

"Who?"

"He didn't say or else he didn't know. The spirit warned that evil men were coming to destroy our world, and the Tak-Pei were going to rise up to fight them to defend their master. He really seemed shaken up. He told me that we needed to get Lily."

I agree. We need Grandma Lily. "When were you going to tell me this?"

"I just did. It's been chaos. I didn't have a chance yet."

"This is life and death, Gavin. Jimmy and Biff are in the hospital, and Lake Manitou is literally rising from the grave. We need to go get my grandmother."

"What? Now?"

"Do you have any other suggestions?"

"I can't go now. It's almost time for bed."

"Evil men are coming to destroy our world, Gavin. We either act or we let people die. It's better to ask forgiveness than ask permission. We need to go now. I just know it."

For a moment, Nicki thought she would lose Gavin to reason and routine when he opened the door and stepped back inside. But he reached for keys and his jacket, gently closing the door a second time as he rejoined her. "Let's go get Lily."

The High Road

Split Rock, MN
March 19, 1962

CHRIS LUNING HAD never felt so alive, and his grin couldn't be contained as he watched his hunched-over grandfather stealthily slip out from behind a tree and join him at the rear wall of the lumberyard.

His grandfather breathed heavily, but his smile could also be seen in the darkness.

The plan was working.

Earlier, after leaving the MacPherson farm, Chris and his grandfather crossed the Crow Wing River at the Doc Jenkins Bridge, drove up Market Street, and ran into a literal roadblock.

"All the bridges in the county are closed," the sheriff's department deputy told him. "I can't let anybody past until we get somebody to check out a sinkhole that formed."

By the time they turned around to the Doc Jenkins Bridge, it was also closed, effectively dividing the town in half. Grandpa Albert sped up the hill to get on the phone to complain, but no sooner had he made a few calls than he had an idea.

"Call your mother," he told Chris. "Let her know you're staying here tonight."

"But—"

"So she doesn't worry. I'll tell Grandma Eunice I'm bringing you home and that I might stay overnight to help tend to the men sandbagging."

Night soon arrived, allowing Grandpa Albert to park just off Market Street, and like two Green Berets, they snuck the rest of the way.

Chris could see the lights on his house and a small army of men helping to keep the factory and house safe from the roaring Crow Wing River just a few yards away.

Robin's words motivated him—*Evil people are trying to break the loop.*

Even if Nicki didn't know it, Chris was going to save her.

"The coast is clear," Grandpa Albert said. "Follow me."

Together, the two of them entered the dark lumber mill.

The interior of the sawmill was scarier than any ghost, apparition, or monster he'd faced yet. Shadows and sharp teeth surrounded them, but Grandpa Albert kept a fast enough pace that Chris couldn't stew for long. Up, up, up they went until they reached a doorway that almost touched the ceiling.

"What is this?" Chris asked.

"You'll see," Grandpa Albert said, fiddling with the locks and knob. When the door opened, it opened to an even darker hole. "Climb up and over and kick it open with your feet."

A small space of about two feet existed between the roof and wooden wall in front of Chris. "What's in there?"

"Nothing. They boarded it up to keep raccoons and birds out. Just lay down on your back and kick."

Chris trusted him, feeling thick old wood boards around him. Once on his back, his feet felt thinner boards, and with three stomps, the left side opened up to the outdoors.

The flume.

Chris kicked the board clear and crawled out of the warehouse and into the open sky. The flume once carried lumber from the saw mill all the way to the processing plant, but with access to train and truck, shipments of wood just arrived directly at the plant, rendering the flume well-built but quite useless.

"We'll be able to follow it all the way to the sawmill," Grandpa Albert declared once he found his way. "It's our own private bridge."

"Will it hold us?"

"It was built to hold hundreds of pounds per square foot," Grandpa Albert boasted. "But hold onto the edges just in case. Keep your head down until we cross the river."

As they passed, Chris could hear the men finishing the wall of sandbags. The men, who came in shifts, knew their jobs depended on saving the lumber mill.

"What's going to happen at the sawmill?" Chris asked once they crossed over the river and onto the western bank.

"Your father has inadvertently put the Guerin family in danger," Grandpa Albert explained. "To prevent his lumber mill from being swept away, he's closed the dam up at Split Rock."

"Why would he do that?"

"He doesn't know what's coming," Grandpa Albert said, pausing for a moment to catch his breath. He held onto both sides of the flume. "If something plugs the culverts, Lake Manitou will swallow up the Guerin farm—or worse."

"What's worse than that?"

"Steve Knutson should be watching the sawmill, but he's at the hospital in Brainerd. If the culverts plug, it won't just stop at destroying the Guerin farm. The dam on Split Rock is older than I am, and with enough pressure, it could collapse, sending a wall of water right into downtown Split Rock."

Dang. Nicki will be doubly impressed with me now if I save her and the whole town. "Are you going to be able to make it the whole way?"

"It's less than a mile. If I can't walk a mile, I don't—no sense talking about it. Let's get going."

While not as grandiose as pulling children from a bus, the mission to open the gates at the sawmill still meant he'd be a hero at the end of the day.

As they continued their covert trek, Chris couldn't help but wonder: *How did these evil people know about the weather? How could a person, even a sinister villain, know the culvert would plug?*

The Low Road

Haggard Quarry
March 19, 1962

WALLY CRAIN SLOWED his truck and trailered boat as he approached Haggard Quarry. He'd left the boat hitched to his truck in case of another needed rescue, but he never expected a phone call from Biff Forsberg—from the hospital.

Wally wanted to say *I told you so* to the others; he knew that the Blue Plymouth had indeed been a predator.

Although Biff had seen Mr. Derby Hat driving toward Split Rock a few hours earlier, Wally knew Old Copper Road was now closed, which meant he'd drive around the lake to St. John.

But first—I need to confront Red Dobie. Glancing to the passenger window, he could see the shore of Lake Manitou still a foot from the road. Ewan had been right about security of the quarry: long before a drop came over the road, the entirety of the Guerin farm would be filled and flooded as Kanaranzi Creek drained into the Crow Wing River.

The '72 Colt sat ready at his side.

Thank God I didn't act on what the kid said a few days earlier.

A few days ago, he'd tucked all three weapons—the Colt, the Barlow, and the castration knife—into his Orion fleece trucker jacket with intentions of acting on young Biff's theory that Red Dobie was the predator. Had the storm not arrived, he would have made the trip to either the supply shed or Red's home up by Nimrod.

Red is certain to be at the quarry.

A car approached from St. John, and Wally, listening again to the voice of reason, took his foot off the brake. Sure, Red was as thick as thieves with the Sinclair Clan and the mysterious Order of Eos, but could he be a killer? Granted, none of them were cartoon villains; they took orders and did what needed to be done. But for Red to one day crack and start murdering kids? And old ladies? And become a rollercoaster saboteur?

It's all the work of Mr. Derby Hat, and Red's going to give me a name.

All these thoughts filled Wally's head as a car approached, and through the temporary blindness of the headlights, he stiffened.

Ewan Haggard?

It made sense for the quarry's owner to show up in a crisis.

Wally imagined what the scene would have looked like if he'd drawn the pistol on Red only to have Haggard show up a few seconds later. The brake lights and turn signal confirmed that Ewan was going to babysit his business through the foul weather.

I'm not an assassin, Wally decided, and switched his foot from the brake to the gas pedal. *I'm just a deliveryman in need of some gas.*

He stopped at the gas station in St. John. While he filled up his truck, and afterwards the boat gas tank, he practiced what he'd say to Albert Fisher when he arrived in Split Rock.

Mr. Derby Hat had first been spotted by the boys on Old Copper Road last summer. Then he'd been spotted by the Guerin family that same day.

Between the Larson and Stewart killings, Wally had seen Mr. Derby Hat driving the Plymouth toward Nimrod ... where Red lived.

Is Red being set up?

Earlier today, Mr. Derby Hat had been driving toward Split Rock on Old Copper Road when the bus accident happened.

Standing at the counter of the gas station, paying for a Hostess Apple Pie and his fuel, Wally had to deliberately remember which pocket held his wallet and which pockets were holding the weapons.

What the hell am I doing? You're a goddamn truck driver, not a hero.

He returned to his truck and hesitated. *Just go home to your family. That's how you can be helpful.* Finally, he pulled out and began driving back south.

A pair of headlights crawled out of the quarry and for a brief moment, looked out toward the lake. Then, the car turned south, becoming a small red dot.

A moment later, another pair of headlights crawled out of the quarry and turned toward Wally.

A Bel Air—*Red's car.*

It had only been a glimpse between blinks, but Wally felt certain of that detail. He stopped accelerating but kept his foot off the brake. Ahead of him, the first vehicle picked up speed and vanished into the darkness. The road south led to Highway 10, which could lead any traveler out of Hiawatha County in a hurry.

The Bel Air headed north to St. John.

So much for confronting Red.

At the corner, Wally slowed to a crawl in case Red was watching him through his rear-view mirror.

Deeming it safe, he turned into the quarry and continued on.

When he came down to the bottom of the quarry, Wally gasped, seeing a sunken lake. The recent storms, both the snow and the rain, flooded the base, but he could see from the tires of the machines that the standing water was only a few inches deep. Having driven it a hundred times, he knew the path to the fueling station was on higher ground than other parts of the quarry.

His headlights caught Ewan Haggard's truck parked and running in front of the supply office. A second car, a 1959 Edsel, driven by Craig Healey, was parked without its lights near the pump station, which still operated.

The lights in the office were on…

…and a body rested on the deck in front of the open door.

Wally stopped his truck, reaching for the Colt on the seat beside him. He opened the door, and with his gun drawn, stepped out into the night.

Remembering what Biff had told him about security, he ignored the lights of the office for a moment, grabbed his big flashlight from his dashboard, and shined it on the far western wall where the purported security team camped at a discreet location.

Wally turned back to the shed, approaching the body cautiously. It had a knee up and an arm propped against a railing post.

Blood dripped off the edge of the deck. A lot of blood.

Wally's focus turned to the interior of the shed, but nothing moved. With a moment to focus, he confirmed the body against the rail was indeed Craig Healey, a man who should have been checking the operation of the pumps. Instead, half of his face was missing, and three bullet holes oozed blood from his chest.

Stop. Drive back up to the main office and call the cops.

Duty, not reason, pushed him forward.

At the doorway, Wally heard a gurgling sound. It continued for several seconds before a man's groan followed.

Blood streaked the hallway leading to the back of the shed, and the secret door described by the boys was left wide open to reveal the man-made tunnel leading toward the lake.

Leave. Run. This is too much for you.

Wally stepped into the light of the office.

If that was Red leaving, he'd be to the police station by now. Help should be coming.

Taking another step, he saw a phone, exposed wires showing, tossed against the far wall.

The gurgling noise continued.

Wally leaned down and took a sidestep to peer around the counter—there was a man, sitting.

After a moment of hesitation, Wally moved around the counter to see Ewan Haggard struggling to breath. He had a gunshot wound to his chest.

Weary eyes locked on Wally, Ewan's head bobbed in recognition, a slight smile first and then a grimace from his bloodstained mouth. "Fucking thieves," he muttered. "Fucking traitors."

Wally turned his attention to the backroom, taking quiet steps before deciding no one else was with them. He paused at the open secret door, stunned to see it exactly as described.

What were they doing here?

Wally walked boldly back to Ewan, careful not to slip on the man's blood. He crouched near his lifetime acquaintance. During World War Two, he'd seen plenty of dying men. Ewan was moments from death. "Who shot you, Haggard?"

"It was Dobie. Fucking traitor. Aleister Sinclair is…" Ewan grimaced. Two more bullet wounds could be seen in his belly. The wound in his chest explained the gurgling noise. At the extreme lower part of his lung, the collected blood simply sputtered out of the wound, allowing him to still breathe from his other lung without drowning on his own blood.

"You need to stop him, Wally."

"Stop who?"

"Red. He's insane. He's trying to wake … ah, gah … they, the fuckers, they … the dam. He's going to flood the quarry."

Wally stood, the hairs on the back of his neck standing on end.

"Brian's in danger," Ewan continued. "Red killed the Stewart boy. Sinclair doesn't want any witnesses. They took …"

"Brian is safe," Wally said, knowing the boy was with Nielson in the hospital in Brainerd.

"It's not time," Ewan muttered. "It's not time."

Wally walked around Ewan, reached under his arms, and tried to drag him toward the door. Doing so brought a violent reaction from Ewan and immediately Wally stopped, moving him back into a sitting position.

"Red is going to blow the dam."

"What?" Wally leaned in closer.

"Death magic. He's going to kill a bunch of folks."

"The dam?"

Ewan nodded. "It's not time. I don't know why. Stop him. Let me die in my quarry."

Wally stepped back, blood on his hands. Soon he was running.

Once in the truck, he set the pistol beside him, and when he turned the key, he felt blood sticking to his skin. *If cops showed up right now, I'd be arrested for this.*

He turned his rig around, careful to be respectful of the dead security guard. His truck climbed out of the quarry, and when it reached civilization, Wally saw a flash of light in the distance.

He stopped immediately, stepping out of the truck just in time to hear the rumble of thunder.

But it hadn't been lightning. And the rumble wasn't the sound of thunder.

His headlights illuminated the dozens of cabins and houses along the shore of the river.

CHAPTER FIFTY-SEVEN

River of Souls

Leech Lake, MN
March 20, 1962

T HE WINTERMAKER SPLIT into two parts. In her dream, Lily Guerin saw a faint shadow drift away from Haggard Quarry to the south. The shadow passed by Sterling Junction, turned east at Verndale, then continued out of Hiawatha County to the airport in Brainerd.

The corporeal form of the Wintermaker, however, headed north. He departed Haggard Quarry, reached St. John, and headed east—toward the reservation. She knew why the Wintermaker hated her people more than any other on earth, and the community of 148 souls was fixed in his gaze. Her heart pounded but the Wintermaker did not approach the community or school; instead he turned toward—Migisi.

In her lucid state, she could not warn him, so she hardened her heart for whatever unfolded.

Yet instead of continuing toward her brother, the Wintermaker headed for the Nicollet Dam, built on the second lot north of Lake Manitou.

Focus, Lily told her sleeping consciousness. *Look past the cloud of sleep.*

To do so, meant endangering herself. But for a better view, Lily revealed her location.

It worked.

The mask of the Wintermaker was pulled away to reveal a man with a red beard and a red stocking cap. He drove his car to the edge of the dam, where two vehicles were already parked.

The car's headlights pointed toward the dam with the windshield wipers on high. The servant of the Wintermaker honked the horn several times before sliding into the passenger seat.

A moment later, a solitary worker came out of the square blockhouse on the other side of the dam, jogging over the deck and climbing up and across the metal scaffolding above the old log chute. As the worker came down the metal steps, the Wintermaker's servant stepped out from the passenger door.

"Hey, Red," the man shouted over the roar of the water passing through the chute behind him. "What's going on?"

"I wanted to make sure you boys were doing okay. My old man used to manage this dam, but he never had a storm like this one."

"We've been working parallel shifts to make sure we don't have any issues with debris or blockage."

"You must've drawn the shortest straw, huh Kirkpatrick?" Red asked.

"Exactly," Kirkpatrick said, shaking Red's outstretched hand. "I'll show you what we're dealing with."

Kirkpatrick led him up and over the metal bridge that spanned the old log chute and onto the deck of the bridge. On the north side of the bridge, heavy metallic cables and orange buoys were stretched across the reservoir to snag trees and other debris that floated down the river. A few trees already caught on the line as well as a tree wedged in one of the timber gates.

"We've got to clear that gate tomorrow, but our five tainter gates are wide open just to keep up," Kirkpatrick said as they crossed the deck.

"What sort of water flow are you estimating?"

"Jake calculated nearly 40,000 cubic feet per second. It dropped off earlier this evening. Pretty wild if you ask me."

Red glanced over the spillway to the south side of the riverbed nearly eighty feet below. Far off in the distance, the highway bridge spanned the valley.

"Will she hold?" Red asked as they neared the blockhouse.

"Well, this old gal has been well maintained through the years," Kirkpatrick boasted as he opened the heavy metal door.

Red reached into his pocket for his pistol as a heavyset man set down a magazine.

Lily wanted to cry out, but her gift proved to be a curse as she was unable to stop the distant murder from happening.

"Look who's come to lend a hand." Kirkpatrick introduced Red as the man at the desk stretched out his hand only to be shot squarely in the chest.

The hot tip of the pistol singed hair as Red held it to Kirkpatrick's head. "We need to talk about these gates."

After that, Red was able to work without interruption. He no longer heard the whimpers and pleas from Kirkpatrick, nor did he hear the roar of the water through the gates and spillways.

He climbed up the steps from the inner workings of the concrete dam where he'd left Kirkpatrick's body. Trailing behind him, the detonation wire climbed up the stairs and through the control room where the other dam worker's body lay.

Why am I allowed to see this, Lily wondered, *if I am powerless to stop it from happening?*

The clock on the wall read three a.m. as he kicked open the door, trailing wire behind. He managed to cross the log chute bridge and go back down to the car with plenty left on the spool. He rigged it to the detonator and exhaled, watching as the water rose.

Everything was set.

Careful not to disturb the wire, Red jogged back over the deck. When he reached the water level control room, the water was already breaching the shoulder of the dam.

He pushed the alarm, filling the valley with its grating pulse. By the time he reached the cars, the roar of the water began again, more violently than it had before.

Red depressed the plunger, and the force of the explosion shook the ground as a wall of water crumbled the dam.

Half of the parking lot fell into the roaring void, taking the cars with it.

Red stood for a moment to admire his work before jogging north.

Lily, still asleep in her nursing home bed, could only watch from a distance. Instead of following the retreating servant, she followed the wall of water as it rumbled through the Blue Knife River cavern.

When it reached Lake Manitou, the wall dropped into the depths of the lake for just a few seconds before an even larger wave rose.

"You broke the agreement," a voice in the dark abyss said.

The real Wintermaker had seen her.

"A life for a life," the Wintermaker said. "You swore an oath."

"You are the one who broke the pact," Lily snapped. "You broke it the day Jean died."

"I fulfilled my part, and I gave him back to you. Now, I learn you lied to me. You withheld what was promised."

"How could I? The time has not yet come."

"Do you think you could trick me? Do you think my servants would not keep watch over me? I know what you will do, so I have sent them to make sure you will deliver your end of the bargain. You threaten to tear apart the web? Then I counter—I will tear apart your world. Look what waits for you..."

Beyond the depths of Lake Manitou, Lily scanned the darkness.

Far to the south, she saw Cameron, alone, surrounded by the Tak-Pei. He ran, terrified, until they trapped him at the shore, forcing him into the scaffolding of the broken roller coaster.

Farther up the shore, Lily saw floodwaters engulfing the house Jean had built. Louis and Hannah fought the flood as the house shifted on its foundations.

At Bleeding Rock, Lily heard a familiar song. The man in the tweed jacket and derby hat stood near a small fire, where a young woman with vibrant red hair sang a song that had been protected by the Wijigan Clan for generations.

Impossible.

Lily's spirit came snapping back into her body. The pain of her age and physical ailments throbbed, and her consciousness swirled to take control of her senses.

She felt a hand on her shoulder.

And heard a voice.

"Grandma Lily, wake up," the girl said. "Nokomis."

Lily turned to see Nicole and Gavin standing at her bedside.

"Nokomis, we need your help."

Lily looked over to the clock. *It's not time yet. There is still a chance to stop it.*

Cast Thy Nets

Haggard Quarry
March 20, 1962

WALLY CRAIN REMEMBERED the terror of the Japanese patrol boat that illuminated the U.S.S. South Dakota in a shower of light. The Japanese fleet had returned to Guadalcanal like a swarm of hornets defending their nests, and after a few immediate hits on enemy ships, the Task Force quickly became surrounded, including the U.S.S. South Dakota.

The shower of light had allowed three Japanese ships to locate and open fire on the South Dakota, whose engine room had lost power. Twenty-six shells hit the battleship in the engagement and would have undoubtedly sunk it if they had not kept firing back. When the shelling finally stopped, the ship stood alone as the battle drifted away from them.

Twenty years later, Wally still dreaded the thought of drowning in the dark.

The distant siren brought him to the present.

Caught by his headlights, he saw the shore absorb the initial blow, a wave of water several feet high that came from the north, bounced against the western shore, and continued south. Standing above the shore on the road, he heard the distant roar of the Blue Knife River amplified by the crashing waves not driven by any wind.

Wally ran to his boat, unstrapped the rear and security chain, took hold of the guide rope, and returned to the truck cab. He headed toward St. John, hammering his horn with the flat of his fist as he neared the cabins along the northwestern shore.

All around the lake, lights were turning on, but the water was rising faster than folks could evacuate their homes. By the time he reached St. John, the Blue Knife River had discharged enough water to swallow a side road. He turned the rig around and drove into the water until it reached the base of his door. The boat lifted from the trailer, and with a tug, he brought it up beside the cab of his truck, allowing him to hop in.

His awkward flop nearly flipped the fishing boat, but soon he had the motor running and was zipping across the lake.

Halfway across the body of water, his fears were confirmed: the Nicollet Dam had burst. Even over his motor, he could hear the sustained flow of water rushing into the lake. In his mind, he tried to make sense of the disaster.

What has Red done?

By the time he returned to the shore, he heard cries of help coming from the lakeside neighborhood, water had climbed halfway up the sides of houses.

At the closest house he saw a man standing on top of his porch railing with his hands on the edge of the roof, where a woman and two boys were sitting. As Wally pulled up beside him, the waves on Lake Manitou tossed his boat.

"Set the children in first," Wally said, doing his best to balance the boat. Once the children were in, he had them move to the other side so that the woman could enter without tipping it. Finally, the husband joined them, and Wally turned the full boat toward St. John.

Instead of finding a park, Wally saw the road leading to it and chose it as a boat landing. There were dozens of people heading toward the water and more sirens filled the air. His boat slid to a stop on the pavement of the flooded road, and strangers helped unload his cargo.

"Find me some sort of light," Wally shouted as his terrified passengers climbed out. The same strangers on the shore gave him a shove so that he could return to help others.

Even though night blanketed everything, the western shore came alive as the St. John community woke to the disaster that had befallen it. Soon the lights of vehicles flooded the shoreline, allowing Wally to easily pinpoint those in greatest need.

He pulled up to the closest house, this time seeing folks in a small second floor window. The water had risen ten feet, preventing a land rescue. He slammed into the side of the house and tried to cling to the siding so that the elderly man and his wife could lower their feet from the window.

"We heard a siren," the man said while holding onto his wife's hands as she descended to Wally, "but we didn't know what it meant. A minute later, waves slammed our front door open."

"The siren you heard was from the Nicollet Dam," Wally explained as he guided the woman to the rear of the boat. "The high water must've busted it wide open." The old man turned around and lowered his feet out the window.

He didn't have time to inflict his wrath on Red Dobie.

It was too late.

"Help! Over here."

Wally heard splashing and could see another elderly fellow pulling his wife on a tractor tire toward Wally.

"Stay there, I'll come to you."

He engaged his motor and pushed twenty yards to the next cabin. He could hear men on the highway behind the houses trying to reach the homes, but a fence, hedges, and several trees created a barrier. With the help of his two passengers, Wally balanced his boat as he pulled up to the wife and rolled her over the side of his boat. With the two elderly ladies balancing the craft, he and his elderly guest both reached out their arms and pulled the other man up and into the boat.

"Where did all of this water come from?" the baffled male asked.

"The Nicollet Dam burst," Wally answered, turning the boat around.

"Goddamn negligence. They should have torn that out years ago," the first man bitterly complained.

"Let's get you folks to safety before we plan any lawsuits," Wally muttered as he throttled the engines as fast as he dared.

As he neared St. John, he looked down the length of the seven-mile lake and wondered what sort of devastation had been caused elsewhere.

The place he'd dropped off the first load had risen another foot, but dozens of people waited to help. Once again, he slid onto the road and several good Samaritans rushed up to him. Two lit lanterns and an industrial flashlight were handed to Wally this time and four life jackets were thrown into the boat.

He heard another boat out on the lake, which must not have been put into storage for the winter. If it hadn't been for the bus accident, his boat would not have been ready either.

Up and down the shore, he could see household items and other oddities floating in the lake that had suddenly burst its banks, so he kept the engine controlled as he returned to the flooded homes.

This time as he neared the stretch of twenty cabins, he heard screams and shouts, but not from the confused residents. Instead, the hollering came from the road.

"Get out of there! Get out of there!" someone shouted, but Wally still could not see the problem. He heard others shouting too, but a strange roar kept him from understanding what they said.

With the flashlight, he turned the beam from house to house until he spotted a woman sitting upon a block boathouse and her husband standing on something, knee deep in water. Wally glided up beside the man who flung himself into the boat, rocking it precariously.

"Get out of there!" somebody shouted.

As Wally nosed the boat toward the boathouse, he noticed something very strange: current passing around the corner.

"The quarry breached! Get out of there!" a voice shouted.

Wally had to throttle his boat fully, and the husband was almost pulled into the water as he grabbed onto the light pole along the side of the boathouse while the nose of the boat ricocheted away. For the love of his wife, he held tight, pulling the boat back to the building. She slid off the flat roof quickly, and as soon as she did, Wally throttled the boat again, lifting the nose of the boat.

Several of the houses began to move from their foundations and follow the current toward the quarry. Wally headed directly for the road again, and when he arrived, he saw a crowd that had doubled in size. The water had dropped two feet since his last trip, a perplexing sign.

"Rope! Somebody get me a rope!" Wally had to wait at most a few moments before someone came running up, tossing him a coil of thirty feet of barn rope.

"The quarry has breached!" someone shouted, but Wally turned around for another go.

Death magic, Ewan had said. The more souls he saved, the weaker the death magic would be for the servants of the Wintermaker.

With several cars on both sides of the severed highway, Wally could see the glorious power of nature. Illuminated by headlights of the two dozen cars pointed at it, a cloud of mist arose out of the quarry.

The entire Blue Knife watershed shifted course as 40,000 cubic feet of water flowed through a cut along the western edge. What began as a slight trickle over the road and into the quarry quickly undercut the road, and as the river rose, the slight flow of water ripped out the pavement and road foundation, soon forming a brand new "split rock" as the water ate through the false bank created decades earlier.

A heavyset woman in a white nightgown came waddling through the doorway of her house, knee deep in water.

"Stay where you are!" Wally shouted to her and tossed one of the life jackets, which she hastily put on. "I need a rope to help me anchor or I'll drift away.

Year of tying knots helped him not only secure the boat during the rescue, but he also quickly fashioned a rope ladder to help the heavy woman gain a foothold while he hauled her into the boat for a final rescue.

Now closer to the quarry, he saw an opening in the trees and gunned the engine again with all its might. He went shooting right up onto the highway to the applause of the two dozen folks that stood on it.

This time, Wally leaned back and collapsed in his chair. Bystanders helped the woman from the boat, and Wally closed his eyes as the roar of the created Haggard Waterfall continued.

Then he heard someone calling his name.

"Wally, are you okay?"

It was Gavin MacPherson.

Wally nodded, and then noticed that Nicki Guerin stood behind Gavin. And beside Gavin's car, Lily Guerin stood.

Thank God. Lily will know what to do next.

The Sacrifice of the Fisher Cat

Mizheekay Band of Ojibwe Reservation
March 20, 1962

NICKI GUERIN GRIPPED the edge of her seat. "We're going to get stuck," she muttered as Gavin turned off the main road (which was terrible) and onto a side road (which was worse).

Along the side of the road, old drifts of snow still remained, accounting for the puddles that all but filled the side road. As Gavin's car moved, Nicki could see waves of water and a deep rut of mud being formed by his front tire, yet somehow they didn't get stuck.

In the backseat, Grandma Lily sat motionless, her jaw fixed, and her eyes focused on a distant place and time.

Could Fawn be right?

Is Grandma Lily a villain?

Even before they finished Chris Luning's story, Lily was prepared to leave. The more they tried to explain the situation, the angrier her grandmother had become.

"Meddling. Arrogance. All of this fear and death was caused by a small ripple the day that man showed up in his shiny red car looking for me."

"What man?" Gavin had asked.

"The stranger from last summer?" Nicki clarified, receiving a slight nod from her grandmother. "What did he do?"

"He was the pebble that disturbed the still waters—an unexpected enemy. Now we will see the waves he has made."

She grew silent after that, and the car ride from Leech Lake seemed to take forever after Grandma Lily had instructed Gavin, "Take me to my brother."

Migisi was outside his shack, wearing a black hat, a snapping turtle shell on his left arm, and a hatchet in his right hand. Considering all their driving, Nicki knew it had to be at least midnight, yet there the old man stood waiting as Gavin's headlights illuminated the end of the road.

"My brother looks ready for a fight," Grandma Lily said with disdain.

But who's he prepared to fight?

"Stay in the car."

Nicki shot a glance at Gavin as her grandmother opened the rear door, and the cab light came on, blinding them.

"Should we go with?" Gavin asked, motioning towards the door Grandma Lily had left open.

"I have no idea," Nicki admitted. "Let's give them a few minutes. They haven't talked in years. Shut the door so we can see."

The two elderly siblings stood toe to toe as a small fire burned behind them. Gavin's headlights illuminated the sweat lodge near the Blue Knife River. Suddenly, without any explanation, Grandma Lily walked off toward the river by herself.

"What is she doing?" Gavin asked.

"Who knows?"

"Should we follow her?"

"Somehow I have a feeling the answer is no."

Migisi turned in the direction of the car, took a step toward them, but then turned around and returned to the deck, where he pulled a heavy blanket over his lap.

And that was how it remained for quite a while, with the only change coming when Nicki reached out her hand to take hold of Gavin's.

"I shouldn't have made Cameron lie for me," Nicki finally said, thinking of her brother alone at the park.

"Do you want to leave?"

"I don't know. This is so surreal."

"Hey, it's okay. I'll take the heat for this if we get in trouble. I've made it pretty easy on my folks so far, and if we need to, we can show them Lily, right?"

"I don't know if it's better if they think we're fooling around or being completely crazy."

"I guess we're about to find out."

Nicki laughed through her fear. "We should go talk to Migisi— you know, to find out what my grandma is doing. She's been gone a long time."

Gavin turned off the engine and the lights, leaving only the red glow of the small fire to illuminate the area. Nicki wrapped her arm around Gavin's and walked with him to the little shack.

"Are the lambs curious why the farmer is sharpening his ax?" Migisi asked so morbidly that Nicki stopped walking, only to be tugged forward by Gavin.

"Where did Lily go?" Gavin asked.

"More likely than not to go make matters worse than they are. Come, stand with me for a while."

Gavin led her up onto the deck. "So, what's happening?"

Migisi looked at him carefully and then at her. "Love will not be strong enough to defeat the evil that slumbers. Tell me, lovebirds, would you be willing to die so that the other might live?"

Fawn wrote to try to save Michelle, but my older sisters are all safe, far away from home. Am I in danger? Nicki felt the terrible silence that followed the question, but before she could even think about an answer, Gavin answered, "Yes."

"Hmmph," Migisi muttered. "Because of my sister, I avoided love. I never married. I never sired any little lambs because I did not want to see my love used against my duty. Lily once had to make a choice between duty and love. Do you know what she chose?"

Fifty years after his death, Grandpa Jean still haunted Grandma Lily. Nicki knew the pain without knowing all the details. *What am I thinking? Grandma Lily is a hero.* "She chose love."

"She did. Lily also had to make a choice between love and family. Did she tell you that story?"

Nicki shook her head.

"If you had to pick between Gavin and your unborn children and your unborn grandchildren and unborn great-grandchild that came to you across the river of time—or your brother Cameron … who would you pick?"

How do you make a choice like that? "I …" Nicki hesitated, and Gavin looked away from her. She tightened her grip on his arm.

"Lily did not choose her little brother," Migisi said, "and to hurt her, I withheld having a family lest I add more lambs to the slaughtering pen." He shook his head.

"Where did Lily go? That is what you want to know? I've been contending with the Tak-Pei and the Jiibay each night while she hid up at Leech Lake, and now, with her ego bruised, she is about to go to war again. It is not a coincidence that she has already armed herself with a prized lamb and heir."

"Me?" Nicki asked. "What do you mean?" The letter felt even heavier in her pocket.

Migisi shook his turtle shell shield strapped to his arm. "I've learned much since I was a boy, but your grandmother was chosen by Manabozho to be a Wabeno, a powerful sorceress. She is going to collect her weapons for battle. She is gathering her shield right now, but you are her sword. If she thinks she is losing the battle, she'll use you as a weapon."

Nicki had grown up with sweet Grandma Lily, and only knew Migisi from a sprinkling of brief encounters. She didn't want to believe him. "A weapon? What do you mean?"

He pointed to the stars. "Do you see the Fisher Cat?"

Nicki looked for the Big Dipper.

"Long ago, the Fisher Cat battled the Wintermaker and prevailed because it was willing to sacrifice everything that it loved. Love is selfish. To win, you will need to sacrifice. My sister was not strong enough, and her false victory came at a great cost. What has she told you about it, little lamb?"

"A lot of people died."

Migisi cackled. "Prophecy is like a flowing river. If you were to place a small log into the headwaters and then run down to the delta of the river, the log would eventually float all the way down, fulfilling its destiny. If you try to stop the log from reaching the delta, the flowing waters will build and build and build behind your obstruction until they burst forth, bringing chaos and destruction down the river valley, yet the log will still arrive. My sister built a dam to save me."

"You seem ungrateful about it."

"Or guilty. She thought she could have both true love and family. Now I am a worthless old man, withering away, waiting for death to arrive. I learned long ago that I cannot stop the flow of the river, a lesson your grandmother has yet to learn. If you listen closely, you can hear her song upon the wind."

Nicki heard it, and it echoed in her bones. She grabbed Gavin tighter. Even though she could hear her grandmother's voice, she heard layers of other voices joining to act as a chorus. Normal sound bounced off objects to create echoes; the song seemed to pass through objects, causing them to resonate like a tuning fork. "What is that?"

"Magic from the dawn. I think she'd best explain that to you herself," Migisi said. "If she refused to teach me the secrets of the Wijigan, then I should not presume she'd teach them to her granddaughter."

The damp and the darkness made Nicki begin to shake, and she found herself holding onto the cross pendant her mother had given her. Even with Gavin's arm now around her, she couldn't stop shivering.

Gavin finally said, "Let's go wait in the car."

Migisi cast a look of disdain and shrugged.

Back in the car, Nicki still couldn't stop shaking, and in her mind, she correlated the song with the coldness she felt. Gavin turned up the heater, but the warm air did little.

"I'm scared, Gavin. It feels as if—"

An alarm began to blare in the distance and Gavin rolled down his window. Nicki did the same, pinpointing the sound to the south.

What has Grandma Lily done?

An explosion ripped the air as energy passed through it.

"What in the world was that?" Gavin asked and stepped back out into the night.

Nicki, choosing the shelter of the car, did not join him. She didn't want to know.

Gavin rushed to the edge of the reservoir while Migisi picked up his hatchet and shield, arming himself on the deck. In the distance, carrying an object in her cupped hands, Grandma Lily appeared.

Migisi headed toward her.

Gavin kept peering downstream, and when he saw the two sib-lings, he ran up to them, pointing back to the river.

Finally, the trio broke up, with Migisi stomping toward the sound of the explosion and Gavin and Grandma Lily walking back toward the car. Gavin stayed at her side and helped her slide into the back seat.

Nicki smelled something burning and saw that the cloth-wrapped object in Lily's hands had wisps of smoke coming from it.

"I think the dam collapsed," Gavin said once he jumped back into the driver seat. "I could see the water dropping along the shore."

"And it's all heading towards Lake Manitou," Nicki whispered. "Oh no, what about Mom and Dad? What about Cameron? He's all alone at the park."

"If the Wintermaker has broken his oath, they will go after your brother," Grandma Lily said, her voice hoarse. "I have put him in grave danger."

"How?" Nicki asked, Migisi's distrust seeping in. "What did you do, Grandma?"

"While I have been away, the Tak-Pei have grown strong, em-boldened, no doubt, by the Men of the Dawn. I have taught your brother verses from the Song of the Manitou, and now the Tak-Pei will force him to reveal the magic he has learned. We must stop them."

"That's a plan," Gavin admitted. "But we can't get to Cameron from the east, so we'll need to drive around Lake Manitou to the west, if we still can."

As Gavin backed up, his lights reached the edge of the woods, where Migisi crept into the trees.

"What is he doing?" Nicki asked.

"Hunting herrings," Grandma Lily scoffed. "He thinks I am wrong about the battle tonight. He doesn't understand the danger. I can sense an intrusion, and if I were to guess, someone is trying to break the loop."

"Is the Wintermaker really real? Or just some evil force like the Tak-Pei?"

"Right now, he sleeps. When I was your age, he almost took human form again, but I forced him back into the depths. As long as I have life in me, I will not let him rise again."

The car reached the highway and turned south.

The object her grandmother cradled in her lap appeared to have a good deal of weight, and although wrapped in musty old fabric, looked to be about the size of a football.

"What is that you have with you?" Nicki asked, but her grandmother tsked.

"I have nothing. You see nothing. Is that clear?"

"But—"

"Is that *clear?* The Tak-Pei will kill your brother to find what I hold in my hands. Men have killed to find this. Put this out of your mind, Nicole."

"Okay," she said and turned around.

Nevertheless, the object began to fester in her thoughts. She remembered a tale found in Father Guerin's journal about a Sioux warrior named Wishwee who had battled a terrible shape-shifting monster known as No Soul. To defeat the monster, the warrior had used a magical egg.

Is this the same object? Nicki felt a cold evil emanating from it.

Gavin was turning west toward St. John, but as they reached the ridge of the river valley, he stepped hard on his brakes.

"Holy cow. Would you look at that!"

Nicki had already seen it. For a moment, she thought she saw a tidal wave of water reaching over the highway, but it was only mist from the violent release of water upstream.

"What should I do?"

"We can drive around to the north. We could take the Sebeka road and then come back down south."

"No," Grandma Lily insisted. "Just drive through it."

"I can't even see if the bridge is still there."

"It will be," her grandmother said. "It must be. We will close the loop tonight and tie it tightly."

Gavin kept driving. His headlights pierced the rain cloud that rose out of the river valley. He turned his windshield wipers on high and entered the thick mist.

Through the accumulating moisture on her passenger window, Nicki could see the turbid water roiling through the valley toward the lake. "It's gone. The dam is totally gone."

Their passage through the water ended when another pair of headlights met them on the other side of the bridge. A man stood beside his car, his driver's door open; Gavin rolled down his window.

"What in the world is happening?" the man asked.

"I think the dam burst," Gavin answered. "I heard sirens right before an explosion."

Just then, red lights and sirens came over the top of the western valley as emergency vehicles from St. John rushed to investigate.

Gavin drove on, passing them on their descent.

A few minutes later, the trio arrived at St. John where dozens of vehicles and people rushed to the lake, creating a traffic jam.

Fortunately, there was no order in the chaos, allowing Gavin to pass through town and then sneak out onto Quarry Road.

Just like at the Blue Knife River, another storm cloud seemed to be sitting in the middle of the road ahead of them. Three or four cars made a roadblock of sorts, and Gavin pulled up behind them.

"Holy crud, would you look at that!"

The pavement, erosion rock, and shore had all been washed away as water that flowed over the road tore a channel from the flooded lake and into the quarry, creating a roaring waterfall that emptied into the belly of a giant hole in the ground. Half a dozen people stood gawking.

"How will we reach Cameron now?" Nicki asked. *I should have stayed with him.*

"We could turn around and drive west toward Wadena, cut down and around."

"We wait," Grandma Lily said. "The spirits of the future will come to our aid. They know I am their ally."

Gavin gripped the steering wheel before releasing a breath. "Okay, we'll wait."

He stepped out of the car, and Nicki joined him. Together, they walked closer to the chasm, now almost twenty feet across. Even since they'd arrived, the water level in the quarry had risen dramatically. On occasion, debris from the lake approached and, in a span of two seconds, was sucked into the chasm and over the edge of the quarry.

Distant shouts drew Nicki's attention away from the spectacle and toward the shoreline. A dozen men waded through the waters near a submerged housing development. Past it, Nicki saw a boat in the waters cut through a break and come shooting toward where they stood, skidding to a stop onto the pavement.

The bystanders, including herself, applauded. Gavin and others rushed over to help the stunned woman step out of the nose of the boat. The man driving leaned back in obvious shock and exhaustion.

"Wally, are you okay?" Gavin asked, and only then did Nicki recognize who drove the boat—it was Wally Crain.

Wally opened his eyes and looked around, a bit dazed. He looked at Gavin, and at her, but then his gaze drifted behind her. Nicki turned to see Grandma Lily out of the car and walking toward them. In her hands, she had the heavy object with the scorched fabric draped over it.

"They have my grandson," she said to Wally.

"Climb in, I'll get you there," Wally answered.

Nicki and Gavin helped Grandma Lily climb into the boat. She sat down beside Wally in the passenger swivel chair.

"You're a part of this, too," Wally said to them. "Push us off the road and climb in."

Nicki climbed in first, and with a shove, Gavin pushed them back into the water.

Terror gripped Nicki for a moment as the current pulled them toward the chasm, but Wally's boat engine growled, propelling them through the gap and into the lake.

Without even being told, Wally aimed the nose of the boat toward the southeastern corner of Lake Manitou.

We're coming, Cameron.

The Cloud Champion

Old Copper Road
March 20, 1962

ED NIELSON ROSE from his bed wearing his insulated long johns and walked through the formal dining room, turning to the steep stairs that led to the children's rooms. As he ascended the stairs, he had to remind himself that Rachel and Faye had grown up and moved away. He also had to remind himself that Jimmy was still at the hospital in Brainerd recovering from hypothermia and soaking up all the attention given to him from the nurses.

He stood at Alexandra's doorway for a minute, gently took hold of the handle, and slowly turned it. Through the crack, he could see her sleeping soundly and safely in her bed.

Relieved, Ed closed the door and walked to the end of the narrow hallway.

His fingers held onto the knob for several seconds before he twisted it and threw the door wide open.

The figure on the bed turned to face him.

"I think I'm dead," the figure said, and then blood poured out of the corner of his mouth and onto his chest.

Ed stood frozen.

The figure sitting on Jimmy's bed looked to be around sixteen. Unlike Jimmy's blonde mop, the intruder's sandy hair was shaved down to his scalp. The boy reached up and wiggled his jaw, which his fingers moved as if the bones had turned to jello.

"I'm looking for my father," the figure said, seeing Ed still standing in the doorway. "Have you seen him?"

Ed pushed his fear down and found his voice. "I think you must be lost. This isn't your house. Why are you here?"

The figure stopped playing with his broken jaw. "I was with my sister and my grandmother," he answered and then looked around. "This isn't her mobile home."

"I think it's time for you to go home now."

"Time? Yeah," the young man said and stood. "I think this is the wrong time. I need to go find my dad."

Instead of heading toward Ed at the doorway, the figure stepped right through the wall and vanished.

Ed had to steady himself in the doorway for a minute before he moved to the window. Peering out, he saw no sign of the figure nor did the boy leave a bloodstain on Jimmy's bed when he turned back around.

In the distance the faint sound of a siren began from St. John.

Ed quickly descended the narrow stairs. He passed into the kitchen and onto the front porch, which faced the lake. He stood in the doorway when a boom tore the night air.

For a few moments, his heartbeat was the loudest sound, then a grinding rumble grew.

Sweet Jesus, is that what I think it is?

Ed didn't go back for his jeans and flannel shirt, but instead slipped right into a pair of overalls and snow boots he'd left by the door.

The phone rang, and Bonnie appeared, answering it. As she listened, he knew—the Nicollet Dam had given way. He put his blue and white DeKalb Seeds cap onto his head and stepped back outside.

Sirens from both St. John and Split Rock began as he rushed to his truck.

A hundred yards from Ed's driveway, the paved Wadena Road met Old Copper Road, which he followed into the thick oak grove. For almost a mile, the old road descended from the bluff until he had to slam on his brakes—water crossed over the gravel road.

He pulled up to the edge of the water, seeing the Larson mailbox on the right side of the road and the distant sign marking the entrance to Carousel Park.

To reach Split Rock, he'd have to either go through the water or go all the way around. Before he could make up his mind, he heard shouting.

Ed stepped out of his truck and heard sloshing in the water coming from the Larson farm: Neil Larson, walking in chest deep water, pulled his wife in an eight-foot orange sailboat without a sail.

"Thank God, thank God, you found us," Mrs. Larson called out as Neil labored at the corner of the driveway and Old Copper Road.

In the distance, a cow swam toward them until it found footing on the flooded road.

"I got 'em," Ed said, wading out and taking the rope so that Neil could focus on walking up the hill to the waiting truck.

As both men pushed through the water covering the road, Mrs. Larson said, "I hear somebody calling for help."

Ed stopped. Sure enough, a male voice called out from the direction of Carousel Park. "Climb into my truck and get warm."

The shock of the current events left him breathing so heavily that he had to swallow and close his mouth for silence.

Then he heard it.

A man's voice—through the water and trees.

Ed called to Neil, "If you don't mind me borrowing your dinghy, I'm going to go see who's out there."

Ed went to the back of the truck and grabbed a shovel and returned to the dinghy just as another bewildered cow stepped onto
the road.

Bending down, he loosened the bolt that held the mast of the
boat in place, and once loose, he tossed it into the water-filled
ditch. With his shovel in hand, Ed used it to push off of the gravel
and into the water, and with the flat edge of the shovel, paddled
over the flooded road.

Three pigs, water up to their snouts, kicked with all their might
as he passed.

The current pulled Ed toward the Guerin farm, the source of
the livestock. In the distance, he saw trucks on the road and commotion. Even from a quarter of a mile away, he recognized the
trucks of the MacPherson brothers, and at the edge of the water,
he saw the figures of Mr. and Mrs. Guerin climbing out of a duck
boat.

Their entire farm had flooded.

"Cameron!" Mrs. Guerin shouted to the darkness. "Cameron!"

The MacPhersons joined the chorus of calls, all directed toward
Ed and the park. The culvert had plugged, preventing the Mac-
Phersons from continuing.

"Help!" a voice called out through the trees.

Ed put his shovel into the water and turned the dinghy against
the current and back toward Carousel Park.

It took sustained, violent paddling to gain ground, and once he
had to stop to hold onto a tree branch just to catch his breath.

Above him, a raven took wing, flying toward the commotion
coming from deeper in the park, nearer the lake.

The large wooden billboard welcoming guests to Carousel Park
was half covered by the floodwaters as he passed. The cries for

help fell silent, and for a while, all Ed could hear was the sound of his shovel slicing through the water.

The entire park was submerged, water crawling halfway up most buildings. Ed felt as if he was walking through an open graveyard.

"Hello?" he called out, seeing a parked car in the lot. "Is somebody there?"

An explosion of chaos answered him, but it came from afar.

This is what Lily warned me about.

A blend of a woman's screaming, a man's defiant yells, panicked cries for help, and a strange melodic chant came together with sounds of a boat motor and strange whooshing noises.

Oh God, I know those voices.

Ed pushed on, paddling past the main part of the park until he finally had a view of the lake and Carousel Island. The images he saw baffled him more than the boy with the broken jaw.

A young man dangled from the roller coaster tracks that passed over the water. His apparent goal was a man high in a tree, its branches swaying wildly from side to side. A few yards away, a young woman wrapped her arms around another tree as she sat in its lowest crook.

Beyond that, at the dance hall, a very soaked Wally Crain stood beside Lily Guerin, still dry. In her hands, she held a lantern that illuminated where they both stood upon the stage, just inches from being swallowed by the water. Between the roller coaster and the stage, an overturned boat spun in the current of the water, still tied to a tree.

"Hey, you folks look like you need help!" Ed shouted in their direction.

All heads, as well as two dozen red eyes, turned towards him.

"What the hell?"

The young man who dangled from the roller coaster tracks quickly pulled his legs back up to the tracks as the whole structure lurched. It lurched because two gray creatures let go and came rushing at Ed.

"Son of a bitch!"

The lantern that Lily held burst into flames that almost consumed Wally, who took a few steps away from her. Yet Lily stood in its fire, unharmed as fingers of flame reached into the air in front of her.

"I warned you what would happen," Lily shouted, the flames swirling over her head like a fiery tornado.

Now the rest of the red eyes were fixed on her. The gray creatures moved in unison gathering together for a moment, before plunging into the water—only to rise as a column of water that equaled the thickness and length of the roller coaster track.

Like a cobra, it raised and postured, but Lily's flames snapped at it, casting it back to the lake.

"You should not have broken the oath," Lily shouted. "Now your master will pay the price."

The gray creatures lashed out individually, and flame and water crashed, with some of the creatures being violently thrown through the roof of the hall, tearing it to pieces.

Ed saw two gray creatures running over the surface as if the lake was still frozen over. They were charging at him.

"Shit, shit, shit." It wasn't until the closest one was almost on him that he pulled the shovel from the water and swung. Even though it was not a solid blow, his swing sent the creature flying past him.

Just as the second creature reached the boat, Ed cocked the shovel back again, prompting the gray beast to dive low, striking the nose of the boat. The strong force flung him forward. To keep from flying off, Ed let go of the shovel for a second to cling to a rear cleat. While he managed to stay on the boat, the shovel slid past his feet and into the water.

The gray creature climbed up onto the nose of the boat. Its long fingers grabbed ahold of his legs, ripping the unlaced boots from his feet.

Once, when Ed had been doing chores, he had come around the corner to face a buck possum, which hissed and snarled and charged right at him. Halfway through that terrifying moment, Ed had raised his voice and yelled, "Get!"

It had sent the possum scurrying away.

Now, the horror of facing the oily creatures stole his voice. The tutelage of Grandpa Martin and Lily Guerin evaporated as a monster latched onto his leg at the calf. The second Tak-Pei snuck up from behind, wrapping its long fingers around his hand, prying his finger loose from the cleat.

Together they tried to pull him into the frigid waters of Lake Manitou.

Come Hell or High Water

Split Rock, MN
March 20, 1962

ALBERT FISHER KNEW something was wrong, but he ignored it. With hands on the edge of the flume, he put one foot in front of the other and kept moving.

I believe in Lily.

I believe in the future.

I know what needs to be done.

"Do you hear that?" Chris stopped, whispering. "I hear something."

There was nothing around them except the treetops along the slope of Bleeding Rock. Even so, he took a break to catch his breath.

Chris stared off into the woods.

"Do you have the dreamcatcher?" Albert asked.

"No, I left it back in the car. Why?"

"You might be hearing something that's not happening now. It could be echoes from the past or whispers from the future."

"This sounded like a woman singing," Chris explained.

"We need to get to the sawmill," Albert said. "Keep moving."

They'd gone no more than another ten yards when Albert caught the sight of a fire through the trees. He reached forward, taking Chris by the shoulder.

Thirty yards ahead, on the top of the bluff, a small fire burned on the flat stone of Bleeding Rock. A woman's voice found its way through the trees.

"Stay low and keep moving," Albert said.

"Who are they?"

Trouble.

At the thirty-yard mark, the flume cut behind Bleeding Rock. Several pines and the rim of the flume shielded them from view, but the details of the scene became quite clear.

The singer was wrapped in blankets, including one over her head, yet long strands of red hair came down over her shoulders and chest. She was beautiful and young.

Albert gasped when he saw the body of a young boy, naked and pale upon the rocks. His blood shimmered in the grooves.

Chris ducked down so quickly that he knocked the side of the flume. Albert lowered himself, too.

"It's the man in the red Thunderbird," Chris said. "The driver—not the guy in the white suit."

The singing stopped.

"What is it?" the man in the derby hat asked.

"Spies," the woman said. "It's one of Odin's spies."

"Should I shoot it?"

"No," the woman answered. "We don't want to be found until the ritual is complete. We need to finish the song. Throw a rock at it."

It?

A moment later, Albert understood when an angry raven quorked after a rock bounced off a tree and rattled to the ground. *Odin's spies—the ravens.*

"Keep moving, Chris," Albert whispered. "Quietly."

Chris listened, and soon the two passed away from the camp-fire. In his mind, he compared the dead boy to all those he knew. He didn't recognize the boy, but that didn't take away from the horror of what they'd discovered. He peeked back, and in the slivers of light, he saw the man pacing the perimeter of the fire with a pistol in hand.

That's not my fight, Albert decided and continued ahead.

Even if he'd had two six-shooters on his hip, it was almost impossible to get down from the flume. The most he could do was to throw twigs at the two villains.

A few minutes later, a second strange sound filled the air. A siren.

"Hurry Chris, I don't think we have much time left."

The distance between the ground and chute almost became level, providing an opportunity to exit. A bit farther, Bleeding Rock dropped down to the flat parking lot of the boat landing.

Chris turned and asked, "Should we get out here?"

"No, the flume leads right to the top floor of the sawmill.

In the distance, a strange rumble filled the air.

"What is that?" Chris asked.

Death is coming.

A siren from the Split Rock water tower filled the air.

"Grandpa, I'm kinda scared."

"Me too, Chris. Me too."

In the distance, the three-story sawmill waited. Beneath them, Bleeding Rock dropped down to the flat parking lot of the boat landing. Albert saw a brand new green Renault Dauphine parked in the deep shadow below the bluff. He turned back to the distant fire, but no light could be seen.

If monsters were waiting in ambush, he honestly couldn't think of a more horrifying place to confront them. An old building with faded red paint, filled with gigantic blades capable of ripping the largest trees into pieces, waited just a hundred yards ahead of him.

A nightmare from my childhood.

With Steve Knutson, the sawmill manager, at the hospital with his surviving daughter, the task fell to them to save both the Guerins and the town.

Albert led his grandson through the old nightmare, passing from the top floor, to the second floor, and finally to the ground floor.

Albert turned on the lights—

It can't be this easy.

"We need to open the pond gates. If the water rises any higher, it will let the Tak-Pei reach the Guerin family."

Chris nodded.

"If we don't open the gates, the pressure will build until it bursts and sweeps away half of Split Rock," Albert assessed. He didn't fear for himself, but he did fear for Chris and the others. "I'm glad I have your help. I probably couldn't do it by myself. Let's go, Chris."

They walked around to the front of the sawmill, which faced Lake Manitou.

The logging dam had been built of cement seventy years earlier. The bedrock that descended from the Bleeding Rock outcrop met the water's edge, where blasting had created a foothold. In this foothold, a fifteen-foot wall rose from the edge of the water, with two tiered footings on both sides of the creek holding back metal gates. When all the metal gates were dropped into place, the water level on the lake could rise up to ten feet from its natural level. In the 1890s, the dam created a large lagoon in front of the mill, where logs could be wrangled right up to the saw.

To protect his house and lumberyard, his son-in-law had lowered nine of the ten metal gates into position, shifting the outlet to distant Kanaranzi Creek. Even with the final uppermost gate open, if the pressure wasn't released, the flood would rip out the entire dam, and a ten-foot wall of water would destroy Split Rock.

Hang on, everybody. Help has arrived.

"So how does this work?" Chris asked as they walked up the arms of the dam towards its gates.

"There are pins on this side that need to be inserted, and then the wheel winch on the other side lifts them out of the water." Albert clutched his left arm as sudden pain gripped him, and he leaned back against the metal rails to catch his breath.

"Are you okay?" Chris asked.

We're doing this, come hell or highwater. He nodded.

"Why don't you just insert the pins and tell me when to start cranking?" Chris offered.

Albert patted him on the shoulder. "Go wait on the other side. I'll try not to fall into the water again."

He watched Chris walk across the platform; Albert glanced to the rising waters of the lake and then to the angry water of Split Rock. He turned back to see Chris found the large metal wheel.

"Wait until I've inserted the pin!" Albert called, standing on a metal platform along the creek side of the dam. "Now give me some slack."

Chris reversed the wheel and Albert pushed the pin through.

"Okay, now crank it slowly. It's only twelve inches, but there are millions of gallons of water behind these gates. Are you ready?"

"Ready as ever." Chris turned the wheel, and for a moment, the water grew silent as the metal gate rose to block the water that passed over it, but as it lifted, the water simply went under the gate, spraying out like a fireman's hose twenty yards towards the creek. The pressure was so unexpected that Albert had to take a few steps backwards.

"Keep cranking, slowly!"

Chris gave it another crank, and the volume grew exponentially louder. Albert tried to picture all the flooded houses along the lake, especially the Guerin house. Each inch the thick metal gate was lifted would cause the lake to drop an inch proportionally.

Though the volume of the creek was now deafening, the ninth gate joined the tenth gate high above the span of the dam.

Chris walked across the dam, motioning for Albert.

This time, the lake itself folded into a twenty-foot V as water pulled the surface of the lake toward them.

"It's so loud!" Chris said, laughing a bit.

To be young again, Albert envied. "I'll use my flashlight to signal when to begin!" Albert shouted over the roar. "We've got three more feet to go to save folks. It's going to get a lot louder. Are you ready?"

Albert knew that dropping five feet from the lake and adding it to the river would easily top the sandbag dike back at the lumberyard and house, but the water would funnel through Split Rock like nature intended—instead of all 10 feet bursting through at once. "Will you be safe where you're standing?"

"Don't worry about me. I'll be fine."

Chris went over to the other side of the dam and manned the wheel again. Once the pin was inserted, Albert flickered the flashlight and then repeated the process, adding the third metal gate above the dam.

With two feet opened, the water formed a torrent that shot out around fifteen yards before dropping into the channel, whose rock walls could barely contain it. It splashed and frothed out of its bed and two feet of lake water rushed into the small gap.

Chris returned back across the metal bridge, putting his hands on the posts of the safety chains as he passed. "I don't think it's safe to open the other two … We should wait."

Why do my teeth suddenly hurt? Am I clenching my jaw? The pain in his left arm grew worse. "If we wait any longer, it will be too late," Albert said, putting his hand to his chest.

"Are you okay?"

Albert wiped at his face, but the spots he saw were not water spray. Then a cramp began in his chest that felt like a growing fire spreading. He rubbed at the spot as if he could make it go away.

Not now. I'm not done yet.

He flickered the button on the flashlight at Chris. "One more, and then I'll take a break." The chains rattled, and Albert slammed the pin into place. *Ah, it must just be a muscle cramp. I feel better.*

But his fingers grew numb, and instead of signaling Chris, the flashlight fell from his grasp and onto the ground, illuminating the loading area and parking lot.

"Chris—"

Two gray figures fell from the sky, sliding to a dusty stop. At first, they seemed confused, looking around at their new surroundings, they faced the lake—growling defensively—then they turned around, noticing both him and Chris.

They found us, Albert realized. He remembered advice Lily had given him decades earlier—the Tak-Pei could not cross the threshold of the river. "Stay on the other side of the dam. Go, Chris!"

Albert took a step up to stand between the sawmill and the creatures, only to fall forward onto his face.

No strength. No weapon.

…This is not how I wanted to die.

The Tak-Pei advanced, but whatever their plans, it didn't really matter to Albert, who chuckled at their attempts to intimidate him.

It's time.

CHAPTER SIXTY-TWO

Omodai

Old Copper Road
March 20, 1962

LILY GUERIN UNDERSTOOD her mistake the moment she placed her bare hands upon the stone and sang the first syllable.

Time froze.

The magic trapped within the large white egg poured over them. Her intention had been to use it as a weapon—to once again defeat the evil Tak-Pei woken by death magic. Instead, the magic opened doors to the future and past, threatening to drive Lily insane.

Focus on saving the children.

Without the children, there is no future.

Beside her, brave Wally Crain stood upon the old stage on Carousel Island. With his fishing boat, he'd ferried them to the island to rescue Cameron. Although she and Wally were upon the solid foundation of the old bandstand, the floodwaters were only inches from sweeping them away.

If I die, the loop would be broken.

This is what the Wintermaker wants.

The Wintermaker had betrayed her and now openly attacked her and her family.

Her grandson Cameron was stuck in a tree, the branches swaying from his weight. Nicole tried to steady the boat at the base of the tree. Dangling from the broken roller coaster tracks, young Gavin MacPherson, future father to the Omodai, risked his life to reach his future brother-in-law.

Kill any of those three and the prophecy shatters.

The Tak-Pei must know this.

Out on the open water, two of the dozen Tak-Pei found valiant Eddie Nielson, who floated on a small raft towards them.

Behind her, somewhere on Bleeding Rock, Lily sensed the greatest danger. A song filled the air, confusing the magic within the Philosopher's Stone, which now unleashed, listened for instruction.

I'll show them who controls the Stone.

I'll destroy them all for threatening my family and friends.

When Lily was a young woman, she'd placed her hands upon the stone and sang the words from the Dawn. Her entire focus had been on Jean, along with Migisi, and this tunnel vision blinded her from what else she could see.

Now, an old woman of seventy-nine, she looked past the present.

In the past, she could see not only her sixteen-year-old self but also Wiyipisiw, her ancestor that brought the evil stone to an evil place. She saw him as an older man, then as a younger man as he first discovered Lake Manitou.

Far beyond that, she saw a woman mourning the death of a beloved father, singing the same words passed down to her.

But the future is what distracted her.

She could see the intersection of past, present, and future, the place where the loop closed.

Levi—the boy in the snakeskin boots was here.

He had visited her on the fateful day at the cave—the day she took hold of the Philosopher's Stone. Now, he sat upon the ruins of the bandstand, watching from the future.

"You weren't kidding about the island," Levi said, a crooked grin on his face. "You're, um…"

"Lily," she finished.

"Well, yeah, but I was going to say that you're younger. You're old, but you're not like, brittle-old. Folks in the Isanti Lodge told me all about what happened on this island, but I had to see for myself. That must be the Water Drum. What are you doing with it?"

"Defending my grandchildren. The Wintermaker broke his promise, and now he will pay the price. I'll rip him from his tomb and cast him into the River of Souls, where he can face his forestalled judgment."

"Yeah, about that…" Levi slid his hands in his pockets. "That's what the gal under the willow said you would do."

Lily thought of the two women from her visions. One was a young girl, blonde and innocent. The other was wounded, a woman with a shattered visage. "She sent you?"

He's the one. He's the one who'll defeat the Wintermaker.

Levi spoke through the window in time created by the loop of willow. "She's trying to help us from the future. She told me you were in trouble. She said that if you attack the Tak-Pei and rip the Wintermaker from his tomb, you will effectively break the loop and shatter the prophecy yourself—no Eighth Fire, no Second Coming, none of it. Poof, gone in an act of revenge."

"The Wintermaker must be stopped," Lily argued. Looking at the young man's face, she felt as if she was once again debating with her beloved Jean.

"Yeah, but not by you. Do you see the other witch, there on Bleeding Rock? She's trying to change the past. She's connected to someone from the future, who's trying to stop the Eighth Fire from happening. That gal back at the willow also sent Albert to deal with it. You, however, hold the key to the future in your hands."

"What am I supposed to do?"

Levi hesitated. "The Wintermaker did not betray you."

"But he did. They killed Jean, and I could heal his body, but could not pull his soul out of the depths. The Wintermaker offered to—"

"Oh, don't hesitate now, Lily. You almost said it. The Wintermaker offered to return the soul of Jean Guerin in exchange for…?"

He knows my dark secret. "The Omodai," Lily confessed. As a young woman, it seemed a fair trade for the man she loved. Now she understood her "deal with the devil" meant giving the Wintermaker one of her descendants. *But only as bait for a trap. Jean, Fawn, Migisi, and the others would destroy the Wintermaker as soon as the foul serpent rose from his hole.*

"And that means—"

Lily wanted to scream in frustration. "I had no other choice. I was stuck in a loop. I'd seen the future, and in that future, I had children and grandchildren and—"

"Great-grandchildren," Levi said, gesturing to himself.

It wasn't supposed to end like this. "If Jean died, none of it could happen, so there was no other choice. I had to make the promise. I had to sacrifice the future in exchange for the present. The Wintermaker returned Jean to me, but for my sins, I only had him for a short time. I needed more time."

"And that is why your brother Migisi never had children, and your cousin Fawn fled to the Rockies with her family. For the prophecies to come true, you had to make a deal with the Wintermaker. Is that it?"

Deal? No. It was never meant to be like that. The Omodai—a vessel. I only needed to provide him with a host so he could rise up from his slumber.

Bait! Bait for my trap! "For the Wintermaker to be defeated, he must rise from his tomb. Is there another way?"

"Apparently yes. Lily … listen to me carefully. You've been tricked. Someone else is using the tree. If you continue with this plan, you'll become the villain in this story."

"I was going to save my family."

"How?" Levi mocked with a laugh. "By using the Philosopher's Stone to uproot the Wintermaker from his tomb? You're about to nuke the whole thing."

"He lied to me."

"No. The Wintermaker knows if he is to rise and claim his victory over death, that he'll need the stars to align, which means he'll need the Omodai, the Song of the Manitou, and your Water Drum, along with the magic found in the Serpent Star. Your plan is *his* plan."

"But his servants," Lily protested, thinking of Charani Bessant, the witch up on the hill, and the faceless killer who'd preyed upon Lake Manitou since starting her house on fire.

"They are his servants. They are here to stop *you*."

"Stop me from doing what?"

"I get it. I understand the choice you made. You chose Jean over your brother, your family. Yet now you hold the Philosopher's Stone to do what? Destroy the world in order to get revenge for losing your husband? The Wintermaker doesn't want oblivion, which is what you were about to give the world. For better or worse, the prophecy must happen, which is why that gal from the future sent me to stop you from breaking it today."

Can I trust myself?

Lily looked down at the Philosopher's Stone. She knew now how to fully unleash it. *But it's not time for Iyash to battle the Horned Serpent. We haven't even reached the time of the Seven Fires. What am I doing?* "What should I do?"

"Stay the course. In the future, you and I are allies. My little brother and I help you close the final loop. I'll go along with this plan of yours if you promise to trust the path you're on. The world is not coming to an end in 1962. Do you see the Serpent Star in the stars above? No. Do not attack the Wintermaker today. Put the Tak-Pei to rest. Let the others do their part. You can't save all the Summerbirds. I wait for you in the future, and you'll close the last loop, and then I'll do the rest."

He knows he is the Omodai.

He trusts me.

When she hesitated, Levi gestured to the chaos around them. "Now put an end to this madness."

Levi faded as Lily focused on the present, looking down to the powerful weapon she held in her hands. She could feel the malice and hatred within it as if stone wanted her to destroy the world.

How do I let the Wintermaker get away with so many deaths?

I deserve my revenge, don't I?

Or am I the villain?

She looked around the trap she'd stepped into.

With the power of the Philosopher's Stone, she could toss aside the two Tak-Pei attacking her precious Eddie. She could tear the limbs off the witch up on Bleeding Rock. She could rip into the foundations of Lake Manitou and pull the Wintermaker from his tomb.

No, I will not be the villain, nor will I be the hero. I'll trust Levi and the others to finish the fight for me.

I must trust what God had planned for me.

She put away her thoughts of vengeance and followed another path into the future—a path where she did what Levi suggested.

But the cost…

An hour into the future, the crisis would be over. And by tomorrow, the flood waters and the evil magic surrounding Lake Manitou would be washed away.

But I cannot save all the Summerbirds.

Lily took a final look at her loved ones, knowing the heartbreak she'd feel tomorrow.

The frozen moment in time released.

Lily rejected her villainous act of vengeance and commanded the tornado of fire and water back over the island. Within the chaos, ten Tak-Pei swirled.

Sleep, she told the enraged Tak-Pei. *Sleep.*

Water sprayed her face, but soon, the swirl only held flame, and within the flame, the black spirits of the Tak-Pei. The fire met the concrete and instead of the Philosopher's Stone transforming lead into gold, she transformed fire, water, spirit, and concrete into a temporary prison for ten of the Tak-Pei.

And now my heart must pay the price for my great blunder.

Beside her, Wally Crain fell into the water, but quickly found his way back to her side. The trap would not claim his life.

Chaos surrounded her, overwhelming her senses, but in the distance, she heard a voice shouting, "Get!"

Her eyes turned to her favorite student, Eddie Nielson, out on the lake facing the last two Tak-Pei.

"GET!" Eddie shouted. "Get off of me!"

Out of the corner of her eye, two dark creatures were tossed into the air above Lake Manitou, their confused, beady red eyes growing smaller and smaller.

Eddie survived the attack.

Nearer, she heard the whimpers of Cameron, the stern instructions of Nicole, and the calming affirmations of Gavin, but she kept her focus on sealing the Tak-Pei in the concrete. For good measure, she pressed down on one end of the concrete, which shifted the entire slab.

It will buy us the time we need.

Now out of the floodwaters, Lily sat down on the high end of the slab. As Wally climbed back up to her side, Lily cradled the white egg on her lap.

Her selfish heart swelled when she saw Cameron being lowered into the fishing boat along with Nicole and Gavin, who turned the boat to go collect Eddie from the overturned raft.

"Is it over?" Wally asked from beside her.

"No," she said, adding silently, *a terrible price must still be paid.* Her eyes looked away from Bleeding Rock and the sawmill, for she already knew who would live and who would die.

The waters receded, but the pain in her heart grew.

"You saved me, Nokomis," Cameron declared as the nose of the fishing boat ground onto the sloping concrete.

But I could not save all my Summerbirds.

"We need to get everybody warmed up or hypothermia will set in," Gavin said, taking charge. "There's a landing beneath the Forsberg house." He pointed to the lights of the farmhouse.

No one's home. Lily felt a different kind of chill creeping into her body. *But this is the terrible path I must take.*

As she climbed into the fishing boat, she put all of her trust in the hands of Glen Forsberg, Albert Fisher, and his grandson Chris.

The Grandfathers Paradox

Fisher Sawmill
March 20, 1962

THE TWO TAK-PEI approached Grandpa Albert, who began to chuckle in agony. Part of Chris wanted to rush forward to attack; the other part wanted to run into the woods on the other side of Split Rock Creek.

Face difficult situations even when you feel afraid.

He could not run away but rushing to his grandfather was also stupid. *A scout must stay mentally awake. Think!*

The sound of metal echoed in his memory. Grandpa Albert slammed the last pin into place.

The Tak-Pei want the gates to fail!

Chris rushed across the platform to the big wheel. His tired arms found new life as the metal gate lifted from its closed position and the torrent of water was released.

In doing so, he drew the attention of the Tak-Pei.

They rushed to the edge of the water but appeared afraid to cross some unseen barrier. As the gate reached the midpoint of its ascent, the spray of water doubled, and the creatures backed away.

They're afraid of the rushing water.

Chris remembered a story from the Bible about a horde of demons being afraid of getting cast into Lake Galilee by Jesus. *If the Tak-Pei are demons, they don't want to ever leave Lake Manitou.*

To his amazement, the gate began to appear above the surface of the water. Inch by inch, Chris became the hero who not only saved Nicki Guerin but also the people of Split Rock. With five gates lifted, and five gates still in place, the surge of floodwater would find two places of release without ripping out the safeguards.

I've done it, Grandpa! I've done it.

As the gate fully lifted out of the water, the spray settled into the roaring waters of the creek, giving him a clear view across the lot.

At the edge of the creek, two Tak-Pei lifted something and threw it at Chris.

The dark headlights should have been the first clue. The second clue should have been the fact that it was the green Renault. Last, just moments before it was too late, Chris saw that the car had no driver.

…What?

Leaping away, Chris threw himself to safety as the nose of the car hit the wheel, crushing it. The current grabbed the tail of the car, pulling it down the creek where it smashed, rolled, and twisted on its journey to the Crow Wing River.

Chest on the dirt, Chris looked up to see a black figure inches in front of his face.

He flinched, expecting death.

Instead, the black eyes of a raven looked back at him.

Robin!

The bird took flight, but instead of fleeing to the woods, it flew to the top of the sawmill and perched upon the edge of the roof.

I'm supposed to follow it.

An angry Tak-Pei tossed a metal signpost at Chris like a javelin, missing him by just a few inches. Chris crawled to his feet and ran for the doors of the three-story sawmill.

No sooner had he stepped into the sawmill than the opposite door was ripped right off its hinges.

What am I supposed to do? Fight them?

"Up!" the raven called out. "Up, up"

Chris obeyed and clamored up the first set of stairs to the second floor. *Of course, I can sneak away in the log flume.*

The path was blocked.

But it wasn't the Tak-Pei standing there.

A man stood at the window, looking down at the creek.

But the creek didn't belong to the present. Back at the deer stand, the dreamcatcher had shown him an alternate reality, which reminded Chris of a kaleidoscope. Now, the world around him became wrapped in magic, and Chris heard the cause.

A song, the voice of the red-haired woman surrounding them, filled the air. *They're trying to change the past.*

Outside the window, Split Rock Creek flowed within its banks, with dozens of boulders visible. A boy in a blue jacket played near the edge of the shore.

The boy stood abruptly but not because he saw Chris peering down at the window. The boy in the blue jacket stood because Grandpa Albert was crawling across the parking lot toward him.

He's still alive.

Suddenly, the sawmill shook.

In the present, the Tak-Pei took hold of the corner of the building, threatening to push it off its foundations.

A dark image appeared in the window. The raven landed in the window. "Protect," it commanded.

I don't have a weapon! Who am I supposed to protect?

Time slowed.

The boy in the blue jacket took a step backwards; he was afraid of the old man crawling toward him.

"Protect!" the raven screamed.

Chris flinched, and so did the figure standing by him. Chris studied him. *I know him from old pictures hanging on walls.*

The strangely cut beard, the wild eyes—*Farrell Luning.*

Am I supposed to protect him?

Chris reached into his pocket to retrieve Nicki's two pieces of cloth, with Lily's strange words written upon them. *Of course, I am. Only a jerk would protect himself. I need to protect the loop. I need to protect my grandfathers.*

"Kaw ree," Chris began, and then repeated. "Kaw ree, tsip-pore, raam."

The building stopped shaking.

The distant singing also stopped.

Chris continued, singing syllable after syllable until the entire spelling had been read.

Then the past unfroze.

The boy in the blue jacket fell into the creek.

Grandpa Farrell clutched at his heart, where the oak pendant hung from around his neck. In one fluid motion, he lifted his legs over the windowsill and dropped into the waters.

The raven flew off, leaving Chris alone, peering down at a moment that had already happened decades earlier.

Farrell Luning should have died.

Young Albert should have died.

But in the roaring creek, they found each other. Farrell Luning dragged the boy to the shore.

The window to the past closed as the magic dissipated.

Grandpa!

Chris saw Grandpa Albert was inches away from the edge of Split Rock Creek, resting on his side.

But then the entire building shook…

…and Chris was falling through the window.

Before hitting the cold water, Chris found several small consolations in the manner of his death. The Tak-Pei had killed him, yes, but not before he'd helped open the dam to save others. Jimmy and Biff had saved a dozen, but he'd saved many more. He hoped Nicki Guerin would be impressed by his heroism.

The next small consolation came when he realized he'd fallen into the waters of the creek rather than the lake; he would not be stuck in Lake Manitou for all eternity like the others.

As his body entered the raging waters, he thought of how he'd defended the loop by protecting his two grandfathers as they, too, fell into Split Rock Creek. He hoped Robin would be pleased by this.

Chris felt a rock crush his ribs, but the force of the blow lifted his body upwards, and for a brief moment, his hands grasped hold of the top of the rock.

He fought to hold on, but soon, his entire body grew numb, and then his fingers slid free.

"Take my hand," Grandpa Albert called out.

Chris took the outstretched hand.

He pulled his grandfather tight in an embrace, only to realize that they were both in the current of the river.

But it was neither Split Rock Creek nor the Crow Wing River.

It was something else entirely.

"I'm glad you're with me, Grandpa."

"So am I, Christopher. So am I."

Walpurgis

Old Copper Road
March 19, 1962

GLEN FORSBERG SAT alone at the dining room table. Although a few hours late, the cows had now been milked, allowing him a few moments to process it all. He clasped his fingers together, set his elbows on the table, and rested his forehead against his knuckles.

His knuckles still hurt.

He lifted his head. The skin over the middle knuckle had ripped and was pulled over in a crust of blood. He hadn't noticed it while milking the cows, but now, it throbbed. He'd punched his own vehicle rather than punch the sheriff deputy who told him access to Old Copper Road was closed.

"I need to take care of my cows!" Glen had shouted, hitting the metal in frustration. Ultimately, they let him pass.

On the wall, he saw pictures of his family. He almost lost Brian earlier in the day, and he'd already lost his oldest son Paul to meaningless arguments and petty issues. His wife and daughter did their best to either obey or avoid him.

Am I gruff or just a miserable human being?

The answer came from a picture of his father, Bjorn.

"You can't just sit on the fence," Bjorn had said to him years ago. "Yes, you can devote yourself to farming, but you also need to devote yourself to your family. The Forsberg family has a proud heritage, which means respecting the past as much as respecting the future. You have a choice to make. What will it be?"

Glen had rejected his father. Sure, he followed in his father's footsteps as a dairy farmer, but he rejected the rest. To make matters worse, he purposely courted and married Edna Haggard. Bjorn had driven him from his duty to the Isanti Lodge, and Glen had driven away Paul to the Far East simply by being a hard man.

Despite all of his efforts to lead a simple life, evil found its way to his doorstep. *And today I almost lost Brian.*

For the first time since he was a child, Glen wept.

Once the first tear came, he bawled and, after a few brief moments of weakness, he stuffed it all away and walked into the kitchen to find something to eat.

At seven o'clock, he waited by the clock and phone, but Edna didn't call.

Something's wrong.

Are the phone lines down?

He checked and didn't find a dial tone.

And here I sit all alone.

An hour passed.

Two hours passed.

Glen stood up from the kitchen and paced around his house. He wasn't ready to sleep, and he didn't want to hear the radio or watch the television. Instead, he put on his coat and went outside.

After passing through the interior of the barn, he stepped out to the back pasture, where the cows had begun to bed down for the night. He watched his herd, one by one. He didn't draw any attention to himself, lest he confuse them by his unexpected appearance.

He wasn't the only one watching the cattle go to sleep.

A raven fluttered down from the trees to take a position atop the rear of the barn.

Glen gave it little thought as he tried to understand the world. A child predator had come all the way up from St. Louis and singled out his son, cutting a hole in the ice, acquiring chloroform, and then dragging a sled all the way to where he stood.

It doesn't make any sense.

If Brian had been alone, he might've been the third victim.

Next, he tried to imagine what had happened with the bus today. Brian had gone from a bully of low character to a hero, risking his life to save the children trapped in the bus.

I wish I could take credit, but I just sent him off to Haggard and ignored the problem.

Albert Fisher tried to warn him of impending doom, but Glen had ignored him. Albert reminded him too much of his father Bjorn who had also talked like a fanatic about a war of good and evil.

And here I sit—on the fence.

The raven left its perch, passing back to the trees, and just then, a siren called out in the distance.

It's coming from the lake?

He started walking since his farmstead was built on the downslope of the granite bluff that separated the lake and the river.

That's a siren all right, but it's not coming from St. John. It seems to—

Something like a cannon shook the air.

All the hair on his arm and neck stood on end, and he felt a chill that wasn't from the weather.

Protect, a voice in his mind called out.

Glen bolted back to the house, and in the mudroom, he found his Winchester twelve-gauge shotgun and loaded six shells.

He knew all the mumbo-jumbo about Bleeding Rock, and after the past few months, he wasn't taking any chances. He stepped out the door—a guardian.

Back on the granite spine, he looked to the south. The lights were on in the MacPherson house, and further down the hill, he saw lanterns on Old Copper Road near the scene of the bus accident.

Did the investigators arrive already?

The sound of a freight train rumbling down the tracks turned his attention toward the north, and looking out across Lake Manitou, he thought for a moment he saw the legendary Horned Serpent, only to realize it was a rise of flood water entering the lake from the Blue Knife River.

The Nicollet Dam.

His breathing grew shallow, and his heart started racing, Glen took a few more steps north, imagining how a few more feet would cause Lake Manitou to spill its banks at several locations, including Split Rock Creek. If the dammed lagoon at the Old Sawmill failed, it could flood the town.

Is anyone there?

He started to run.

His trek took him toward the place where Isaac Larson died; the boy's death was first believed to be an accident and later attributed to Logan Troost.

He stopped abruptly when he saw a fire burning atop Bleeding Rock.

First, he saw the child. Having seen Brian, and all the other children, dealing with the effects of hypothermia, his mind went to a strange place: *Did they miss one?* But the child had not come from the bus nor did he drown. Blood filled the channels in the rock.

Next, Glen saw the red-haired woman, wrapped in a blanket, sitting in front of the fire. She sang strange syllables to the darkness, and even though Glen didn't understand the language, he could feel she was evil.

Then a figure moved.

A gunshot filled the air and simultaneously, the bark on the nearby tree burst from the trunk, striking Glen.

He stepped behind the tree as another bullet ripped into the woods.

"Hey!" Glen shouted out. "What do you think you're doing?"

No explanation was given.

Shit!

Glen flipped off the safety and slipped the barrel of the shotgun past the tree. He fired blindly before stepping out. Pumping a new shell into the chamber, he fired again, and again.

The man in the tweed jacket and derby hat grunted but did not go down, so Glen fired again—and again. The last two shots hit the man's left arm and gut, but the pistol remained in his hand.

Glen pumped the last shell into the chamber.

The pistol rose—but not in Glen's direction. It leveled at the young woman and fired into her forehead.

Without thinking, Glen blasted the man in the tweed jacket squarely in his chest, just below the collarbone.

Son of a bitch. What the hell just happened?

Something crashed closer to him—from the Old Sawmill.

Even though the shotgun was empty, he carried it with him as he ran. He arrived to see the entire mill lurch off its foundation, and someone fall from the window.

Glen ran, scrambling down the hill, across the empty parking lot and toward Split Rock Creek.

At the edge of the creek, Glen found the body of Albert Fisher.

The Jaws of Defeat

Old Copper Road
March 30, 1962

BIFF FORSBERG HATED funerals, but he kept his mouth shut and meekly got in the car for the fourth funeral of the week. His little sister Julia had to be physically prodded to the backseat by his mother, who practically lifted her by the arm on the way from the front door to the car. His father Glen came from the edge of the feedlot, and without a word, slid into the driver's seat, started the engine, and backed out.

So that's how it's going to be with him?

His father had always been a bit of a mystery, but now, Biff no longer saw him as a father but a figure to be feared.

He dared not say a word about his discovery and sat in silence as they drove north.

At the Doc Jenkins Bridge, Biff glanced south, able to see the path of destruction caused by the flood where it mangled the lumber mill but left the Luning house still standing.

Biff had no more tears.

Chris Luning's body had been found a day after he died, and even though Biff read all about his buddy's heroism in the newspaper, it still didn't make sense how he'd fallen into the waters of

Split Rock Creek moments after saving the town from another dam failure.

As the car drove up Market Street, Biff decided he would have gladly exchanged all of downtown and the dozens of old lousy houses just to have his friend back.

The washed-out section of road on the north end of town had been repaired, allowing the Forsberg car to pass right by the place where Chris had been killed. If the stories were to be believed, something struck the front of the sawmill, knocked the building off its foundation, and tossed Chris into the waters. Biff dreamed a dozen ways his friend had died—some filled with monsters and terror and others with just a tragic slip of a shoe. Chris had been the fourth funeral.

I never got to tell Chris I was sorry.

Mount Olivet Cemetery, built on a hill that overlooked Lake Manitou, was just a mile from Split Rock. Filled with hundreds of gravestones, it had once been a place of wonder for Biff. Now, he knew the stories of its nine newest additions to the cemetery.

The first funeral had been for Danika Knutson, who along with the bus driver Allan Wittrock, had been the first victims of the flood. The flood had also claimed the lives of Colin Kirkpatrick, Duncan Samuelson, and Red Dobie, the men who'd been killed when the Nicollet Dam collapsed. None of their bodies had been recovered.

The second funeral had been for Uncle Ewan, who along with Craig Healey been killed trying to protect the quarry when the floodwaters cut through the road to create a new bay on Lake Manitou.

Albert Fisher, who'd been buried the day before, died of a heart attack, although some said it was a broken heart. He'd been found dead at the wreckage of the old sawmill where he and Chris had managed to avert a crisis by removing enough floodgates to save the community.

How do I trust any of these people ever again?

A cast of familiar faces gathered for the fourth funeral. The Nielson family, including a shaken Jimmy, already waited at the gravesite. Two other families stood united by the tragedy—the Guerins and MacPhersons. Neither Nicole nor Gavin seemed too keen to even acknowledge that they'd once gathered in the Isanti Lodge, nor did they try to speak to Biff. When Wally Crain arrived with his wife and daughters, they had an unexpected guest—Lily Guerin, who came with a bundle of flowers.

Biff could only clench his jaw in anger. He'd been left with so many questions that at times, he felt like he was going to pass out, so he just focused on his breathing.

The guests of honor all arrived together.

Chris's older brother Chuck solemnly stood with his wife Helen and son Karson, who despite a darker skin tone, looked just like Chris had when they were in elementary school. Marlin Luning and his wife Betsy emerged from the cars next, helping the grieving widow, Eunice Fisher, to the grave of her husband.

Biff kept his clenched hands in his front pockets while the funeral service began.

You're all a bunch of liars.

The heroes and villains all wore masks to hide themselves from the Hiawatha County community, and none more so than Biff's own parents. Edna Haggard-Forsberg mourned the tragic death of her brother. Glen Forsberg, wearing the mask of a dairy farmer, would shrug off the fourth funeral just as he'd done with the three others, and then go back to his routine.

Biff found himself studying his father the most.

He now knew the villains in the story. Only Morgan Marquette had not lost any skin in the game, with Sean Stewart losing his son and Uncle Ewan losing his life. Biff had been there when Charani Bessant and William Olcott were invited to the quarry for a private tour. He'd also been there when he helped Molly Knutson and Jimmy Nielson out of the water and into the tweed arms of Mr. Derby Hat.

Men, not monsters, brought death and mayhem to Hiawatha County.

As Albert Fisher's coffin was lowered into the ground, Jimmy wept with the others, but Biff could only focus on his father's hand upon his shoulder.

In that moment, he looked up and his father nodded.

He knows I know.

Glen had been waiting in the barn when Edna brought Biff back from the hospital and to the changed world of Lake Manitou. Under doctor's orders, Biff had been sent to his bed, but by midafternoon, he received the news that they'd found Chris, dead. Edna went to her kitchen, and Biff bolted to the woods.

At Bleeding Rock, he'd found traces of blood.

Standing at the cliff, he could see the devastation the Nicollet Dam had done to the lake—the overturned bus, the flooded quarry, the ruined cabins, the final nail in the coffin to Carousel Park, the displacement of the Guerin house and barn, and to the north, the crushed sawmill.

Returning from his sojourn at Bleeding Rock, he looked down at the compost pile. A winter's worth of straw and cow manure piled up between the woods and the back door of the barn. The MacPhersons would soon show up with a wagon to scatter the prized fertilizer upon their many fields, yet instead of a tight, high pile, it'd been spread wide.

The soil found along the slopes of Bleeding Rock did not allow for anything to be buried as deep as they were burying Albert Fisher at Mount Olivet, which is why Biff had found the bodies.

The garden shovel, not the barn shovel, had been left leaning against one of the trees—proof of his father's involvement.

Next to the manure pile, Biff found where dirt had been tossed as well as some dried blood. Shoveling shit was one thing, but digging into the rock and debris of Bleeding Rock was something that only a Forsberg understood.

Glen Forsberg had been exhausted when Biff returned from the hospital.

The three graves explained why.

After Uncle Ewan's funeral, and without the recovery of Red Dobie's body, Biff waited for the opportunity and then returned to the macabre scene.

The garden shovel had been returned to the garage, and the compost pile now covered the three graves—but only by a few inches.

By the third day, Biff had to know, but his father still wore his dairy farmer mask, forcing his son to find the answers himself.

So, Biff dug.

He didn't recognize the face of the boy—neither from Split Rock, St. John, or any local school.

But he knew the face of Mr. Derby Hat. He wore the tweed jacket, and with the blade of the shovel, Biff moved enough soil to be able to kneel down and check his pockets. His father had been hasty, leaving behind a custom-made zippo, with hood, striker, and fuel flask that slid out of its ornate sheath, which featured the Eye of Ra. He slid the lighter into his own pocket, replacing the soil.

The person in the third grave surprised him. He'd expected to find the body of Dobie. After all, the newspapers sold lies that he'd been claimed by the flood, one of the victims when the dam gave way. Some speculated that the boom following the sirens had been the three men trying to clear debris with dynamite when something went wrong. Experts, however, found evidence that the dam breached, and that the rumble had simply been the concrete giving way. Both theories took the lives of the two workers and Dobie.

Now, looking around the crowd at Albert Fisher's funeral, Biff wondered which side told the lie. Did Triton want to wash its hands of its rabid dog? Or was it the Isanti Lodge that dealt with Red Dobie?

The garden shovel had created a new mystery for Biff to solve. Instead of the bearded face of Red Dobie, Biff found himself looking at a thing of beauty—the face of Saara Olavintytär. Instead of seeing the glow of Nova Scotia firelight, her face was stained with soil, blood, and gore left from a shot to the forehead. Red Dobie and Saara had been sitting at the same fire with him, and Biff wondered if one of the kids in Nova Scotia was now decomposing in the anonymous grave beside Saara.

All these thoughts filled his head as the funeral service concluded with Lily Guerin setting flowers on Albert Fisher's grave.

Biff's father steered him back to the car.

The mysteries weren't getting solved today.

Until It Puckers

Old Copper Road
March 30, 1962

FOR THE FIRST time since she was a girl, Lily Guerin could see the boulders at the bottom of the Blue Knife River. Although the foundation of the Nicollet Dam remained farther downstream, the reservoir had emptied over the past few days, returning to what it had been decades earlier.

Her escort, Wally Crain, patiently waited at her side. Both had come from the funeral of Albert Fisher aware that the fight was not yet over. At least the immediate future was now set: in twenty-four years, at the age of one hundred and three, Lily would close a loop in time just as the power of the Serpent Star returned.

"Tonight will be the last night I spend near Lake Manitou," she told Wally.

Wally gazed down to the exposed riverbed and nodded. "I understand."

Do you? The only one who truly understood her plan stoked a cold fire in the distance. Her warriors in the Isanti Lodge had rallied. Two had made the ultimate sacrifice to keep the path to victory alive. A younger generation had joined the fight while older members like Eddie Nielson and Glen Forsberg found themselves guided by fate.

Decades earlier, her beloved cousin Fawn abandoned her when she learned about the price Lily had paid for the life of Jean Guerin.

Was a decade of love worth five decades of loneliness?

Lily had no other choice. The blood in her veins had the capacity to destroy the Wintermaker's plans, but like the legend of Iyash and the Horned Serpent, she needed to appear weak and desperate for the monster to expose itself to danger. In just a few short years, she would have her revenge against the monster of Lake Manitou.

Until then…

"I must say goodbye to my brother," Lily said.

"I'll go wait in the truck."

"No," she said softly. "Come back in the morning. There is much my brother and I must discuss."

Wally turned, and Lily began walking toward her brother.

Migisi was passing his sweat lodge. The coals had turned to ash in his fire pit, but the sun on the spring day provided its own warmth. He dropped a handful of dry kindling, and with some smaller sticks, pressed it into the coals. When smoke began to appear, he piled the sticks on top, and then set three smaller logs in a pyramid above the warming fire.

"I was beginning to think you'd forgotten about me," Migisi said.

"I had to attend another funeral."

"You do understand it won't be the last."

"It will be the last for a while."

"Do you really think so?" Migisi asked.

"I do. Our enemies are divided, and the damage done will force them to wait for the return of the Serpent Star. We must be ready."

"So, you're going to abandon me again? Do you still plan to run off to Leech Lake?"

Lily went to put a hand on her brother's shoulder, but he quickly moved to avoid it. "I'm not abandoning you. For better or worse, the choices in my life have set us on this path. It's not safe for me to linger here."

This time, Migisi did not argue. The past few days had brought the two of them together, and the more he understood the enemy, the more he understood the horrible choice she'd made so long ago.

At least he doesn't see me as an enemy.

But Migisi still viewed her as a necessary evil. "It will take a few moments for the fire to warm the stones. Come, sit with me on the porch and tell me again what I must do in the coming days."

Once situated on the porch, they prepared for war. The ranks of the Isanti Lodge needed to be restored. With the passing of both Albert and Chris, and the abject failure of Marlin Luning, the heirs would be Chuck Luning and his boy Karson. Convincing them to return from banishment in Georgia would be a tricky affair. With Wally Crain as leader and mentor, both Brian Forsberg and Jimmy Nielson would be groomed for the future. Both would be men in 1986 when the Serpent Star returned.

Migisi chuckled, interrupting Lily. "The silver lining in you moving to Leech Lake is that Leonard White Elk might be willing to visit more often."

"I wish I could've made Fawn understand."

Migisi scoffed. "She understood your choices. She just thought you were a monster for making them. I'll explain what happened to Leonard and try to convince him how much we need Benjamin to strengthen our ranks."

"I worry about Nicole," Lily finally admitted. Having seen the horrors on Carousel Island, Nicole reacted without any acknowledgement of the incident. While Cameron went into complete shock, Nicole pretended as if nothing had happened. "I worry she will turn the next generation against me. We might need to find a priest to guide us."

"You said that was my role."

"Yes, but you are a priest of Manabozho. There are several prophecies at work, and the Isanti Lodge will need the guidance of a priest with a Christian perspective. Nicole will need his counsel to understand her part in this."

Instead of arguing, Migisi nodded.

Well … that's a first.

FOR ALMOST AN hour, the two of them sat together on the porch, reflecting. The stones in the yard continued to heat. Migisi finally stood, went inside, and returned with food and drink.

"You'll need your strength," he told her.

Lily wondered if it was best to continue on an empty stomach, but Migisi had finally caught his herring and she would do what she had to.

As a boy, her brother would stand upon boulders in the channel of the Blue Knife River, waiting for river monsters to swim by. Although he was now in his seventies, he led an active, living-off-his-small-patch-of-land life. When Lily arrived a week ago with Nicole and Gavin to obtain the Philosopher's Stone, her brother already stood vigil as the warrior he never got to be. So it came as no surprise that he caught a mighty fish in his nets that night.

Lily drank as much of the soup as she could and then stood. Migisi took the signal and quickly finished, and together, they walked to the sweat lodge.

She found the dying man within. Unlike a traditional An-ishinaabe sweat lodge, which was constructed with ritualistic purpose, this lodge had a darker purpose. The fire pit at the center had almost grown cold. The head of their prisoner lifted.

"I remember your father," Lily said to him. She found her spot beside the fire, sitting on the ground beside the living head. "My beloved Jean told me all about his fears of the Order of Eos, but as a girl, I could only see the internal threats of my Wijigan blood. After all, Joseph Little Toad believed he was fulfilling his religious duty when he offered my brother as a host for the Wintermaker."

The old pain had cooled compared to the hatred she felt for the man who brought so much death back to Lake Manitou. But she calmed her rage along with her moral misgivings. *I need to understand my enemy.* "What did you call the Wintermaker again?"

A whimper preceded the two raspy syllables. "Surtr."

"Yes, a monster with many names. Your father Halvar understood the delicate nature of prophecy, and when he learned about the heretic Joseph Little Toad, he found common cause. He rode onto the campus of our new school, removed the mask he wore, and revealed to us what was happening. You see, he understood, even as a servant of the Wintermaker, that the prophecy would not be fulfilled until its proper time. Yet his own son almost destroyed everything because of jealousy and fear."

Migisi threw open the flap, and light beamed into the darkness and onto the face of Red Dobie, who was buried up to his chin in solid stone. Dobie groaned when he saw the heated stones.

Lily now understood better than any law officer what happened. She and Migisi understood more than the Grand Master of the Order of Eos, young Ross Delhut, could guess.

Levi, the unborn Omodai, assured her she was on a path to victory, which would undoubtedly happen with the return of the Serpent Star in 1986.

But who attacked us from the future?

Under slow torture for the past few days, Dobie gave them all the information they needed about their elusive enemy.

A civil war broke out within both the Order of Eos and Triton Corporation, between the elder Aleister Sinclair and the young Ross Delhut.

A generation earlier, the Sinclair family sent Halvar Dobie to Hiawatha County to not only manage the Nicollet Dam but to also spy on the actions of the American branch of Triton. The role of embedded spy passed to his son Red, who grew up with other Order of Eos members like Ewan Haggard, Morgan Marquette, and Sean Stewart.

Unlike the American businessmen, the Sinclairs were deeply religious men, secretly worshiping the old gods. After consultation with his Finnish witches, who could still sing the old songs, Aleister Sinclair sent Dobie on a mission: protecting the sleeping god beneath Lake Manitou.

So Red began by trying to murder Lily. In the dead of night, he doused her home with gasoline and lit the flames with his Bic lighter. By the time the flames were discovered, he'd safely jogged to anonymity.

With Lily out of the way, Dobie prepared for the coming of Saara Olavintytär. To do this, he needed to sacrifice lives so that death magic could awaken the spirits of the sleeping giants, as he called them. It began with sabotage at Carousel Island, which only gave Red four deaths. But it woke four dark spirits. After that, the spirits that Lily knew as the Tak-Pei began adding to the count.

The unexpected twist had been the Forsberg boy.

From meeting Charani Bessant to sneaking into the quarry with the Stewart boy, Forsberg became a security risk. Dobie abducted and killed the Stewart boy first yet failed to nab the Forsberg boy while his father was away from home. To deflect blame, Dobie found a patsy, sacrificing Logan Troost and letting him take the blame for three deaths.

But to Lily's surprise, Dobie's plan was not to resurrect the Wintermaker like Joseph Little Toad had attempted in 1898. No,

Red's plan was to provide enough death so that Saara Olavintytär could reach back through time to destroy the roots of Lily's story. To do this, Dobie needed more than just a dozen deaths—he needed a disaster.

On his vigil along the Blue Knife River, Migisi caught Dobie jogging back to his farm near Nimrod.

Now, Migisi sat down beside his prize and looked to his sister. "It's time to sing."

At this, Dobie let out a long groan.

"Does my singing bother you?" Lily asked. "For years, I thought the Men of the Dawn might just be an imagined enemy. I questioned my mind. I questioned my dreams. All I wanted to do was protect the children, and it turned out, you were the devoted servant of the Wintermaker. The blood of children is on your hands. Now we need to understand the rest."

Migisi leaned in. "In the days of old, prisoners were slowly roasted alive so that they could divulge the secrets of our enemies. Those who cooperated were given a quick, clean death, but those who withheld were kept alive for days, just like you. All of this torture we've put you through has troubled my tender-hearted sister. Tell us what we need, and I promise you, I'll give you a quick death tonight."

Dobie groaned again.

Although Lily could only see his head, she knew why he suffered. Using the power of the Philosopher's Stone, she'd manipulated the solid stone to swallow his body up to his chin. Under his feet, the Philosopher's Stone provided a flame that could hurt or heal upon her command.

"I don't need to hear any more tales about the Order of Eos," Lily began. "I've heard plenty about the plans of your masters. I need to hear about your enemy."

"My ... my enemy?" Dobie asked.

"You've been tricked," Lily said. "I need you to tell me everything you know about Charani Bessant and what you told him about the Wintermaker."

"Bessant is a nobody."

"Is he?" Lily asked. "What is the saying? Better the devil you know than the devil you don't. I know Men of the Dawn; I've lived beside them my whole life. Yet behind the Face of Death was the face of Charani Bessant."

"I've already explained this," Dobie whimpered. "Aleister Sinclair hired him and sent him off to Yale to act as a spy for young Ross Delhut. He orchestrated everything that happened here at Lake Manitou over the past year, but he was Sinclair's man."

"Like you," Migisi added.

Dobie nodded.

"Oh, I'm sure Aleister Sinclair is a proper villain we'll have to deal with in good time, but I don't understand what a scholar like Bessant gets out of all of this. If he was your ally, why wasn't he with the others at Bleeding Rock?"

"What?"

Lily saw a cold hate in her brother's eyes as he bent low to intimidate Dobie. "If successful, Sinclair's sorceress would have destroyed the town of Split Rock and, in doing so, sent enough magic back to 1898 to change the course of time. It was a bold plan."

Lily felt emboldened too. "They failed, and the flow of destiny continues toward the ultimate defeat of your god. I'll be there to laugh at him when his soul descends where it belongs in the abyss. But Charani Bessant was not with them."

Dobie's eyes could not hide his concern.

"Take me back to the quarry," Lily said. "Right after you shot Ewan Haggard and his security guard, what did Charani Bessant do?"

"My god is real," Dobie protested. "I hope you live long enough to see him rise, for he'll kill everyone you love before killing you and restoring the world to the way it once was."

Migisi's eyes widened.

Each of us assumes our faith is right, even my brother. "Time will tell."

"Why did you take him to the quarry?" Migisi pressed.

"To show him our god was real," Dobie insisted. "Where is the archeology to prove Christ ever walked the earth? Where is the archeology to prove Manabozho ever walked the earth? My god is real. We found him buried under Lake Manitou."

Lily felt her heart flutter. "Did you let Bessant take him?"

"Of course not. The quarry is hallowed ground to us, and what's under Lake Manitou even more so. He only wanted to visit the tomb. He only wanted proof."

"Did you accompany him the whole time?"

"No, but after he returned, he didn't have anything. I saw. Blowing the dam had two purposes. Sinclair didn't want to risk Delhut doing something stupid, so the destruction of the Nicollet Dam locked the door to our discovery."

Then why did Bessant flee at Sinclair's moment of victory?

According to what Wally learned, Bessant fled the country by private plane out of Brainerd.

Dobie moaned. *He won't last much longer.* "Answer this. How did Sinclair's witch know the Song of the Manitou?"

Dobie doubled-down, finding inner strength to stare back at her defiantly. "Like I said, our god is real. She learned the secrets the same way Odin learned them—the roots of Lærad betrayed you."

Of course, the old willow is at the heart of everything.

Lily nodded to Migisi, stood up, and left Red Dobie to her brother.

On the opposite shore of Lake Manitou, tucked into Jiibay Hollow, the old willow held the answers.

Dearly Departed

Upper Hay Lake, MN
July 5, 2029

T HE RAVEN WAITED in a basswood tree outside the cabin for Robin Berg. The adults had gotten wasted the previous night, and outside the sliding glass door, the signs of their debauchery could still be seen: alcohol, drugs, destruction, filth, and for a change, fireworks. Spent canisters, charred science experiments, and tiny shreds of paper littered the backyard that faced the lake. The party lasted most of the night, which meant nobody was waking up until at least noon.

Robin looked back into the suspended chaos of the cabin, and with her canvas *Attack on Titan* backpack over her shoulders, quietly closed the sliding glass door behind her.

The raven lifted from the tree and flew west.

She ignored the paradox that was Upper Hay Lake and took the side stairs off the deck. There, parked in the narrow space between garages, she found the ATV the boys had used the previous night. There was still two-thirds a tank of gas remaining, and according to her smartphone, she was only thirty miles away from her answers.

Oh, fuck it. What's the worst they can do to me?

She fired up the ATV, waited for just a moment, and then slowly drove away.

Her trip took her across Highway 371 (which she knew) and into Cass County (which was all wrong) along a series of paved county roads. The closer she got to Lake Manitou, the thicker the pine forest grew. At 110th Avenue, 60th Street turned into Wadena County Road 7 (which was all wrong).

Having visited Lake Manitou countless times in her dreams, she kept the ATV going, but when it turned south, her heart sank.

The town of Split Rock was gone.

The entire valley was gone.

What happened?

At the intersection of Highway 7 and Highway 9 where two small county roads also converged, Google Maps proudly declared the location to be Oylen, which Wikipedia claimed to be an unincorporated town that didn't even list a population despite the handful of buildings. Even a catastrophic flood, like the one during the spring of 1962, would have left twisted steel and broken foundations. Instead, the river flowed over stone and sand as it passed south to distant Crow Wing State Park.

Something far worse than a flood did this.

She parked the ATV on the shoulder and hopped off. Placing her hands on the railing of the bridge, she let her mind return to her dreams of Chris and Grandpa Albert. The mansion made from bricks from the old nunnery should have been along the eastern hill overlooking the river—gone. Both tributaries, Split Rock Creek on the north side of town and Kanaranzi Creek on the south side of town—nonexistent. As real as it was, with its sounds and smells, the Crow Wing River was also half-a-mile too far east.

They both died for nothing.

Robin felt as if Albert's death was sad but poetic. As a boy, he'd almost died in the roaring waters of Split Rock Creek, and decades later, it felt like closure to have him return to the same place—this time as a hero.

But poor Christopher...

Robin felt tears streaking down her cheeks, and even after wiping them away with the back of her hand, they still blurred her vision. She let go of the bridge railing and took a few steps west—toward where Split Rock Creek was supposed to be.

What did I learn?

The loop needed to be closed. The Wintermaker had found a way to communicate to his servants, speaking through one of the roots of the tree from the future to be heard in the past. He chose to attack in 1962 with the help of Red Dobie, first waking the Tak-Pei and then sending the witch. Their plan had been to use the Nicollet Dam to send a wall of water to give Saara Olavintytär enough death magic to stop Lily. When Albert's heart gave out, Chris gave his life to prevent the town from being swept away.

No! Weren't you paying attention?

Robin ripped her backpack off, unzipped it, and went to the back pages of her Dream Journal where she listed all the heroes and villains.

Uncle Ewan and Ross Delhut were villains listed under the heading: ORDER OF EOS. These were the bastards digging up the Wintermaker and searching for the Philosopher's Stone. These guys wanted to resurrect a buried god in order to return the world to some Nordic Midgard where they would rule as Jarls. Back in 1898, Eos tried to steal all of the Blue Knife River valley from Lily's family through violence and political maneuvering. Villains! Yet Rory Stewart died. Uncle Ewan died. Haggard Quarry was flooded. The Nicollet Dam was destroyed. Eos got its ass kicked.

By whom?

Team Red Thunderbird.

Biff noticed. Wally did too.

Red Dobie might've been born into Eos, but there was some civil war happening within the secret society involving Aleister Sinclair and Finnish witches. And Charani Bessant. In all the chaos of storms, floods, bus accidents, Tak-Pei, and Lily Guerin almost ripping the world apart to save her Summerbirds, Robin almost forgot about the non-Indian Indian Charani Bessant. *Where the fuck did he come from and where the fuck did he go?*

A raven "kraa" caught her ear. It sat on a dead oak tree on the western shore of the Crow Wing River, staring down at her. Ahead of her, County Road 9 was lined with thin birch trees and an ATV trail. Further up the gentle slope, birch trees transitioned to taller, darker pines.

Am I insane? Did I dream it all? It has to be real.

Robin stopped and turned around but not in defeat. Instead, she returned to her ATV. The gas tank neared half full, meaning she still had another 50 miles left before she stranded herself out in the sticks of Wadena County.

If I run out of gas, I'll just walk back to the cabin.

She throttled the engine and steered it up the hill—west.

A half-mile up the asphalt road, she came to an intersection with roads leading north and south. To the south, she saw the Crow Wing River bend back west—about where Fisher Lumber Mill should be located. To the north, on a road labeled Wilderness Drive, she saw a mile of straight open road, which she took.

Seven miles south of Nimrod, the terrain was entirely desolate. There were no houses or farms and even the once majestic forests had been turned to empty fields of grass and shrub with pockets of new growth woods.

Yet after a mile of nothing, Wilderness Drive bent to the northeast. The reason—a bend in the Crow Wing River. Robin could see it from the road, just a few feet below the surface of the county road.

A load of rock and gravel dumped from this road would plug the river, she realized, backing it up and sending it over its banks.

Time is like a river, Migisi had once said.

Could time be changed as easily as a river channel?

Robin again slipped off her old *Attack on Titan* backpack. In the old anime series, the characters lived in an inverted version of Earth, with Africa pointing north to Antarctica. *Is that what this is? Does Hiawatha County exist under my feet? Could I dig a hole to reach it? My shrink would love to find out how far down I'd have to dig before admitting the truth.*

Her pencil drawing of the town of Split Rock showed the Crow Wing River passing through town at a slight southwest angle before making a big bend near the Fisher Lumber Mill—*where they were sandbagging.* After passing by the Doc Jenkins Bridge, it curved back to its current channel near Bullard Bluff.

Wilderness Drive is Market Street, which means—

Robin spun the ATV around, throttling the engine without any care for gas mileage. At the intersection of County Road 9, she made a sharp turn west, picturing Lily Weber walking to town from the reservation.

A gravel road diverged from the highway, allowing Robin to turn to where Split Rock Creek should have been. Once again, thick brush grew where the old sawmill should have been, and as the ATV passed the only thing close to a roaring creek was a couple of swampy ponds and—

Robin gasped and squeezed the brakes.

In the midst of the unkept growth, a grassy patch no bigger than a front yard grew—and a white skull peaked through the soil.

It was too big to be a real skull, and as she approached, she realized the rock formation was also too irregular to be an oversized sculpture either.

The stone formation was natural, yet she slid off the ATV and approached it cautiously. As she walked around it, she could see that it was a massive rock, buried by the sediment of Wadena County. Finally, she found the confidence to climb up on it, taking off her backpack and sitting atop the stone.

With her eyes open, she remained in the wilderness of Wadena County, but when she closed them, she could see Hiawatha County. Tall green pines ringed the shores of the blue lake, and beneath where she sat, pieces of the boulder were strewn in the passage of Split Rock Creek.

Split Rock…

The rock she sat upon was whole, blocking any rainfall or precipitation from flowing to the nearby Crow Wing River. Instead, the water seeped slowly through the sediment and into the sandy aquifer below the surface. Robin opened her eyes to a world where everything had been destroyed—Lake Manitou, Hiawatha County, and every living member of Lily Guerin's family.

A few months back, the raven had brought her to the women in the willow, who told Robin that she was the one who could help defeat the Wintermaker—if she trusted them. But all the facts led her to believe that the Isanti Lodge had been the ones defeated.

How do I fix this?

Who did this to Hiawatha County?

Or am I just crazy?

Robin picked up her yellow backpack and climbed back on her ATV to head back to the cabin.

But I can risk a few more miles first.

Under County Road 9, she knew Lake Manitou existed, even if Split Rock and St. John were nowhere to be found. The Blue Knife River didn't flow south from Nimrod, but she stopped where the Nicollet Dam was supposed to be. There, instead of finding Turtle Island State Park, she found a little sign—West Lyons Cemetery.

She pulled off the road, driving along the edge of the cemetery where a few hundred gravestones stood. None of them held any of the names from her dreams. Frustrated, her eyes again filled with tears, and instead of mourning the deaths of Albert and Chris, she mourned for all of them, and if her dreams were right—for the unknowing world she lived in.

Pulling back onto the road, she continued south for home. She throttled her ATV, and it flew down the road as fast as a car.

She'd gone less than a mile—about the width of Lake Manitou—when she saw something on the road ahead.

The black raven stood in the middle of the highway, looking right at her. Robin squeezed the brakes and shut off the engine.

Its beady eyes studied her for a moment, tilting its head in curiosity. It shivered, fluffing its feathers, before croaking out a single syllable in English: *Trick*.

And then it flew off.

THE END

The Dreamcatcher Chronicles
will continue with Book Three:
THE TRICKSTER

ROBIN BERG'S DREAM JOURNAL
"WHO'S WHO IN HIAWATHA COUNTY"
1962 PEOPLE

<u>Those who Live on Old Copper Road (Starting at Split Rock)</u>

The Forsberg Family: #bearclan #guardians
    BIFF—the sulking hero. #gingershavenosoul!
    Glen—his father, a dairy farmer. Bjorn's son.
    Edna—a <u>Haggard</u>, his mother.
    Paul, his older brother. Serving in Vietnam? #idleavetoo
    Julia, his younger sister. #someonetoremember

The MacPherson Family: #sonoftheparson
    GAVIN—the hunky neighbor. #fredfromscoobydoo
    Duncan, a third-generation farmer.
    Ida, his wife.
    Donald, Dave, and Donnie—Gavin's uncles.

The Guerin Family: #skullclan #ravenclan
    LILY GUERIN—Tewapa Tew Asibikaashi. Old but not
    super old yet. Mixed heritage. Maternal line=Lakota.
    Paternal line=Anishinaabe. Married Jean Nicholas Guerin
    (d. 1910). #thefirehandler #thespider #heroandvillain
    Louis—her angry son. Kinda messed up.
    Hannah, his wife. (Mortensen). Granddaughter of Olaf
    Berg!
    Charlotte and Michelle, Lily's granddaughters.
    #idleavetoo
    Cameron, her only grandson.
    NICOLE, her youngest grandchild. #meangirl #omodai
    #ravenclan

Carousel Park: #askingforit #swampcastle
    Charles Tveit—owner. Eos connection?
    Fred Shoemaker—Carousel Park manager. #negligent
    Walter Zibas, Leona and Mary Brady, and Gladys Kruger
    #victims

The Larson Family: #houseinthewoods
ISAAC LARSON-Victim
Neil Larson, a third-generation farmer. Why does their farm seem familiar?

The Nielson Family: #martenclan #warrior #cloudchampions
JIMMY-Biff's Best Friend/Cousin. #poetwarrior
ED NIELSON, his father. Grandson of Martin Nielson. Son of Sig Nielson and Danielle Bordeaux. #teacherspet
Bonnie, his mom. Glen FORSBERG's sister!
Rachel and Faye, Jimmy's older sisters. #idleavetoo
Alexandra, his sister.

The Berg Family: #poorwhitetrash #sirnotappearinginthisfilm
Anton Berg, a farmer. First family to farm in Hiawatha County.
Emile, his son.

The Crain Family: #craneclan #leaders
WALLY CRAIN, an oil deliveryman. Son of Kermit Crain and Mabel Berg.
Nancy, his wife. An English teacher and writer.
Cindy, Margaret, Janet- his daughters.

The Order of Eos: #menofthedawn #badguys
THE DELHUT FAMILY: #American branch #Detroit
ROSS DELHUT-Newest head of the Order.
#northstarsteel #tritoncorp #michaelcorleone
Hiram Delhut (1870-1961). #vitocorleone
THE SINCLAIR FAMILY: the English branch of Eos.
Aleister Sinclair-old school. #barziniallalong
#musicmogul
Aamu Huuhtanen-a Finnish witch.
THE TERRONT FAMILY: the French branch of Eos. #rubber plantations
THE LOCAL GUYS: #tritoncorporation
Ewan Haggard, owner of Haggard Quarry and partner of Triton Corporation. Member of the Order of Eos.

Sean Stewart, a merchant and partner of Triton
Corporation. Relative of Ewan Haggard.
Meredith—his wife.
Rory—his son. #victim
Myles—his youngest son. #someonetoremember
Morgan Marquette—a mortician and partner of Triton.
RED DOBIE—Runs the quarry for Haggard. Son of Hal-
var Dobie, the guy who ran the Nicollet Dam back in
the day. Tomas Dobie? #redherring #oldschool

TEAM: WTF?: #enemyofmyenemy
CHARANI BESSANT—some religious expert? A spy? A
thief? What did he steal? #traitor
William Olcott, a hired gun.
Saara Olavintytär—another Finnish witch. Eos or WTF?
#howdoessheknowthesong?

Those Along the Blue Knife River:
MIGISI ASIBIKAASHI—a Mizheekay Reservation el-
der. Son of Big Squeak and Winnie Weber. Trained as a
Midewiwin. Not a Wabeno. Possible Jessikkid.
Norval Riel—superintendent of the Turtle Island Jesuit
School, possible agent of the Periphery and replace-
ment for Paul White Wolf.
Sakima Riel—Norval's son.
Sally Gray Sky—the school secretary.
Colin Kirkpatrick—an engineer at the Nicollet Dam.
Duncan Samuelson—an engineer at the Nicollet Dam.

Those who Live Near Split Rock:
The Fisher Family: #Fishclan #intellectuals
ALBERT FISHER—son of lumber baron, George Fisher.
#isantilodge
EUNICE, his wife.
Betsy—his only child. Married to Marlin Luning.

Ed Johnson–his groundskeeper.

The Luning Family: #Loonclan #leaders

CHRIS LUNING–an honest-to-goodness boy scout.

Marlin Luning–his father, the lumberyard manager, son of Farrell.

Chuck Luning–his older brother. A pilot in Georgia.

Helen Luning–his sister-in-law. Sister of Minnesota Viking Ellis Redding.

Karson Luning–his nephew.

The Knutson Family: #wrongplace #wrongtime

DANIKA KNUTSON–the dead girl. #victim

Molly–her twin sister.

Steve Knutson–her father. Sawmill manager.

Kate–her mom. A Tveit??

Everybody Else:

Donald Betzing–Sheriff of Hiawatha County.

Hal Plant, Police Chief of Split Rock.

Charlie Roy, deputy.

Ken Uselman, Chief of the Fire Department.

Rich Van Slyke–teacher and coach at SRHS.

Sophomore Creeps: Charlie Morrison and John Thaxton.

ROBIN BERG'S DREAM JOURNAL
"LEGENDS AND LORE"
#1962

Anishinaabe—Some say the word means "Beings Made out of Nothing" and others "the Original Man," so don't quote me on this. Also known as the Chippewa and Ojibwe. Their religion is known as the Midewiwin Way (Migisi) and they kinda have something like God (Gitche Manito), and even an earthly mediator similar to Jesus (Manabozho). Despite not having the stone tablets of the Ten Commandments, they have a moral code known as the Seven Grandfathers. Despite slight variations between regions (Ottawa, Potawatomi, etc.), their society is built upon a clan system, taught to them long ago.

A. Ah-ja-jawk (Crane)—the chieftains
B. Mahng (Loon)—the chieftains
C. Gi-Goon (Fish)—the intellectuals
D. Mu-kwa (Bear)—the police
E. Wa-bi-zha-shi (Marten)—the warriors
F. Be-nays (Bird)—Spiritual Leaders
G. Wa-wa-shesh-she (Deer)—Gentle People

Asibikaashi—the Chippewa word for spider.

Dream Catcher—a loop of willow with a sinew web created long ago by Grandmother Spider, a creation deity (Lily coincidence?) and decorated with beads and feathers. The most common tale about the Dream Catcher is that it keeps evil spirits away from sleeping children.

Fire Keeper—a position of social and religious importance, similar to the way a priest conducts various social and religious ceremonies (like Norval Riel).

Gii-igoshimo—a vision quest ceremony involving fasting.

Gitchi-Animikii—translates as Great Thunderbird (Migisi). A mythic creature that is the enemy of the water serpent known as the Horned Serpent. Literally, it seems to be some sort of eagle, but spiritually, it seems to be akin to a guardian angel protecting against the forces of evil.

Gitche Manito—The Great Spirit.

Hela—the Goddess of Death in Norse mythology, whose two-faces have the appearance of a young woman on one half, and the other is a rotting face of a corpse.

Horned Serpent—a prominent figure in many myths and legends. Literally, a water serpent, yet this figure seems to also represent the universal serpentine symbol for evil. Nidhogg is a Norse dragon that guards the world tree. Jormungandr is another Norse water serpent. At times, it is synonymous with a watery manitou. Its enemy is the Thunderbird.

Ironwood Log—a relic mentioned in the Seven Fires Prophecies. The Ironwood Log is the container for the sacred scrolls (most likely birch bark) that held the prophecies. Generations prior, the Ironwood Log was hidden. Prophecy believed this sacred container will one day be found, and its secrets revealed to the Anishinaabe and all mankind.

Iyash—a mythic hero in Anishinaabe folklore. These tales range from the Atlantic to the plains and feature a hero who stands against the evil Horned Serpent.

Jessakkid—a gift from the Great Spirit. Comparable to Seers, Exorcists, Necromancers, or Prophets.

Jiibay—Anishinaabe word for ghost. Typically, the dead travel the River of Souls (Milky Way) which is similar to the Greek Styx or Hebrew Sheol. But nothing's typical in Lake Manitou.

Land of the Midnight Sun—the final resting place in Chippewa Culture.

Lærad—An alternative name for the Norse world tree, also known as Yggdrasil. The roots of Lærad are found in three locations: Hvergelmir, the bubbling, boiling spring; Urðarbrunnr, the Well of Fates; and Mímisbrunnr, in the land of the Giants.

Manabozho—the Mediator. A physical embodiment of the Great Spirit, who came to earth in human form to teach the people. The name varies widely (Hiawatha, Glooscap, Nanabush) but the tales seem to indicate a shape-shifting ability.

Mide—a priest in the Midewiwin religion.

No Soul—a mythic figure in Sioux Culture about a shapeshifting, immortal monster that lives in a cave. The hero Wishwee is able to destroy the monster with a "white egg."

Nokomis—the Chippewa word for grandmother.

Noozhishenh—the Chippewa word for granddaughter.

Ojiig—the legendary hero (a marten/Fisher Cat) that frees the Summerbirds trapped by the evil Wintermaker. Now represented by the Big Dipper constellation.

Omodai—the Chippewa word for a container, like a bowl, cup, or vessel.

Pewabic—the Chippewa word for clay or vitriol.

Philosopher's Stone—the European term for an object sought after for thousands of years. Known commonly as the substance that can turn lead into gold, the scientific lore goes far beyond a simple alkahest that can transform matter into being the key or origin to all matter. The word vitriol, for example, is a Latin phrase used during the quest to find the original stone, which transforms anything it touches into ormus, a blue-green byproduct similar to copper.

Pillagers—a group of Chippewa living around central Minnesota and Leech Lake.

River of Souls—it is the way a soul travels to its final resting place. It is seen as the Milky Way, with the entrance to the Land of the Midnight Sun found at the Pleiades, which the Chippewa refer to as the Sweating Stones.

The Sacred Fire—a concept found in the Seven Fire Prophecy. It is the goal of the Chippewa (and humanity) to light this Sacred Fire following the fulfillment of the Seven Fire Prophecy. With the lighting of the Sacred Fire, humanity is doomed to destruction. The spiritual answers needed to light this Sacred Fire will be revealed in the era of the Seventh Fire.

The Sacred Shell—a concept found in the Seven Fire Prophecy. As a symbol, it is literally the megis shell (cowry shell) that guided the Anishinaabe along the Seven Stopping Places. The lore suggests that the Sacred Shell was lost during the early years of the migration, and although the Chippewa found their way to the Seventh Stopping Place without it, it will be key during the era of the Seventh Fire to understanding the truth behind the original prophecies.

The Serpent Star—a unique term used to describe Halley's Comet. Although the belief is not held by most Mide, it is believed by some that the arrival of the Serpent Star was a harbinger for the arrival of a new era. Thus, the arrival of Halley's Comet in 1682 began the Third Fire, 1758 began the 4th Fire, and 1835 began the Fifth Fire.

The Seven Fires—a sacred prophecy given to the Anishinaabe generations ago that prompted their departure from their brothers in Nova Scotia to their sacred lands in Minnesota. The exact language of this prophecy varies from region to region. This is the account told by the elders in Hiawatha County:

The First Fire: A warning to leave the east (1456-1532-1607?)
- Midewiwin Lodge established
- The Anishinaabe became a "new" people
- Follow the sacred Megis shell
- Seek a Turtle-Shaped Island
- Seek a Land Where Food Grows on the Water

The Second Fire: A Lost People (1607-1682?)
- The Sacred Shell was lost
- Camped by a Great Body of Water
- A Boy Will Show the Path

The Third Fire: Finding the Path (1682-1758?)
- The way is learned
- A Land to the West

The Fourth Fire: Two Prophets Warn (1758-1835?)
- Beware the Light-skinned race
- Face of Brotherhood
- Face of Death
- Bringing poison and pollution

The Fifth Fire: A Great Struggle (1835-1910?)
- All Native Peoples Struggle
- Abandoning the old teachings

The Sixth Fire: Deceived by a Promise (1910-1986?)
- Grandchildren will turn against the elders
- Light-skinned race will take the lands
- Near destruction of the Native people

<u>The Seventh Fire: Retracing the Steps (1986-2061)</u>
- A young prophet with a strange light in his eyes
- Elders will help them retrace their steps
- A New People will appear
- The Water Drum will sound its voice.
- The Sacred Fire will again be lit
- The Light-Skinned race will have a choice between:
  An Eighth Eternal Fire, or...
  Destruction of earth

<u>The Seven Stopping Places:</u>
1. Montreal Island
2. Niagara Falls
3. Lake St. Clair
4. Manitoulin Island
5. Sault Ste. Marie
6. Madeline Island
7. Lake Manitou?

Song of the Manitou—a verbal chant taught to the Wijigan Clan to be used with the Water Drum. It is rumored that the original text was kept in the Sacred Shell so that the Sacred Fire could be lit in the era of the Seventh Fire.

Summerbirds—from the tale of Ojiig and the Wintermaker. In the story, the Wintermaker collected the Summerbirds in snares, refusing to allow them free, and thus, preventing the seasons from ever changing. Because of this, the hero Fisher Cat went to the lands of the north, freed the Summerbirds, and was chased into the stars by the Wintermaker, who hunts him still.

Sweat Lodge Ceremony—When a child approached adulthood, they would enter a sweat lodge for a "vision quest." After four days of fasting, it is believed that the spirit of the individual travels from the lodge to the crescent moon and the star world. The lodge is built of willow and covers a pit where hot stones are collected. The four doors of the lodge are manned by representatives of the Cedar Man, Bird Man, Bear Man, and the Door Man. Outside a fire is kept to heat the stones, which the Fire Man oversees. The Conductor oversees the ceremony, often including an apprentice for the purposes of training.

The Tak-Pei—the Little Men of the Forest. Known by names all over  the world (Canotila, gnomes, fossegrim, Pukwudgies, memegwesi), the sinister spirits near Lake Manitou often appear in the shape of an oily porcupine.

Tewapa Tankiyan—Lake with the Crooked Lily Roots. The illustrious mapmaker Joseph Nicollet visited present day Lura Lake in Blue Earth County, where the mystical qualities of the lily root were harvested for use in vision quests. Coincidentally, the man who dubbed the Undine Region with the moniker "Blue Earth" also traveled north of the mouth of the Crow Wing River, where he also noted blue earth and lily pads near Lake Manitou.

Turtle Island—akin to the Promised Land of the Hebrews, in some tales, the turtle is symbolic for the whole of North America as well as an Ark symbol in flood tales. Yet for the Anishinaabe, Turtle Island is the distinctive island at the end of the Seven Fires quest. While other Chippewa communities believe the ultimate Turtle Island could be Spirit Island near Duluth, Madeline Island of the Apostle Islands, or even Turtle Mountain in North Dakota, the Chippewa in Hiawatha County believe it to be found in Lake Manitou.

Undine—the Water Spirit. The term in Alchemy has seeped over to popular culture in the form of the mermaid, water nymph, and siren. During his mapping of Minnesota, Joseph Nicollet labeled present day Blue Earth County (where he noted the copper vitriol) as the Undine Region.

Wabeno—the Fire Handler. Like the Jessikkid, little is known about this exotic priesthood of the Anishinaabe. The adherents of this secretive religious society are known as the "Dawn Society" and are considered servants of Manabozho, blessed with the ability to handle fire and perform other feats of magic.

Wanagiyata—the original Sioux word for Lake Manitou, which translates as Place of Souls.

Water Drum—found in the Seven Fires Prophecies. The concept of the Water Drum has been woven into Anishinaabe culture in the same way the symbol of the cross has found its way in Christian ceremony. Although commonly found, the typical Mide had a symbolic representation of the original Water Drum in the same way Catholic

Priest carry only a symbolic cross. The original Water Drum was part of creation, representing all that was spiritually and physically needed for life. In the tale of its creation, it was used to bring health and life back to a sick boy, who went on to teach the Mide-wiwin way to future generations.

Wijigan—The Skull Clan. For generations, this Anishinaabe clan was supported by the community, but following dark deeds at Madeline Island and Lake Manitou, the Chippewa purged this clan from their society.

Wintermaker—the mythical villain now represented by the constellation Orion. Possible connection to the Dakota tales of "Red Horn." When this constellation appears at the horizon, he brings winter and death with him. His enemy is the Fisher Cat. His goal was to prevent the changing of the seasons, which is why he used his magic to trap the Summerbirds.

ABOUT THE AUTHOR

Imagine the love child of Rambo and Ma Ingalls. That's Jason Lee Willis. Overly nurtured by his Vietnam War veteran father and Lutheran church secretary mother, he grew up in the fantasy realm of South Dakota before his exodus brought him to mysterious Minnesota for college.

His love of mythology and storytelling led him to a career as a high school English teacher, where he guided his students in writing poetry, short stories, and even screenplays. As a professional storyteller, he's done historical lectures, book talks, radio segments, podcasts, and a video channel on YouTube, The Minnesota Alchemist.

Willis currently lives in Minnesota, where he lives the life of a hobbit by gardening, writing, walking around barefoot, wearing vests, fishing, and going on adventures with his wife, Julie.